BBC

DOCTOR WHO

THE SANDS OF TIME

The Doctor Who *Monster Collection*

Prisoner of the Daleks
Trevor Baxendale

Touched by an Angel
Jonathan Morris

Illegal Alien
Mike Tucker and Robert Perry

Shakedown
Terrance Dicks

The Scales of Injustice
Gary Russell

Sting of the Zygons
Stephen Cole

Corpse Marker
Chris Boucher

The Sands of Time
Justin Richards

THE MONSTER COLLECTION EDITION

DOCTOR WHO

THE SANDS OF TIME

JUSTIN RICHARDS

BOOKS

1 3 5 7 9 10 8 6 4 2

First published in 1996 by Virgin Publishing Ltd
This edition published in 2014 by BBC Books, an imprint of Ebury Publishing
A Random House Group Company

Doctor Who is a BBC Wales production for BBC One.
Executive producers: Steven Moffat and Brian Minchin

The Random House Group Limited Reg. No. 954009
Addresses for companies within the Random House Group can be found at
www.randomhouse.co.uk

A CIP catalogue record for this book is available from the British Library.

ISBN 978 1 849 90767 5

Editorial director: Albert DePetrillo
Series consultant: Justin Richards
Project editor: Steve Tribe
Cover design: Two Associates © Woodlands Books Ltd, 2014
Production: Alex Goddard

Printed and bound in the U.S.A.

INTRODUCTION

The starting point for *The Sands of Time* was an image. Or rather, the notion of a sequence. I discovered that the Victorians occasionally held 'Mummy Parties' – where people were invited to an evening event with drinks and food, and the centrepiece was the unwrapping of a genuine Egyptian mummy – ostensibly for educational purposes, but really just for the sensationalism of it.

What if, I thought, the guests gather, and some prominent dignitary is late, but they go ahead anyway. And when the decaying mummy is unwrapped, inside the genuine, ancient wrappings is the missing guest. That idea obviously developed and evolved, but it gave me something to start from – how could this have happened? (In fact, I liked the mummy-unwrapping so much I used it again, in a rather more academic setting and with a very different pay-off in my later novel *The Parliament of Blood*.)

Since this is a *Doctor Who* story, the answer would have to involve time travel. I always start planning a book by deciding what it is *about* rather than what happens. I knew I wanted to write a book that was about time travel and its implications. It seemed to me back in 1995 that for a show that involved so much time travel, *Doctor Who* rarely explored the implications and complications of time travel. It's an imbalance which has since been corrected, of course – but back then we weren't nearly so timey-wimey.

It would also be about Egyptology, given that mummy-unwrapping scene. And if you're doing a *Doctor Who* story that involves the mysteries of ancient Egypt then you can't ignore the Fourth Doctor story *Pyramids of Mars*.

So it was that *The Sands of Time* began to take shape. The shape it took ended up as a large flow chart – over about a dozen A4 pages – since Peter Darvill-Evans and Rebecca Levene at Virgin Books needed to be convinced that all the temporal toing and froing actually worked and made sense. Peter was so impressed with the diagram that he had it hanging on the back of his office door for several months – probably so he could marvel at the insanity of the mind that had created it!

My outline is always like a short-story version of the novel, though for this novel it was actually not that short at about 8,000 words. Looking back through it, I saw a potential problem. There was no character, apart from the Doctor and Tegan, who went right through the whole of the book. Given the constraints on what you can do with the Doctor and an established past companion, that meant there was no one who could both act as a point-of-view character, a touchstone for the reader, and who could also grow and develop tangibly as a result of their experiences in the novel.

Fortunately, thanks to the flow-chart timeline, it was relatively easy to see how such a character could be added – and who it should be. So Atkins was promoted to proto-companion. My plan for him was that he should start out like the character of Mr Stevens in *The Remains of the Day*, but then his experiences soften and liberate him to the extent that I could perhaps give him the happy ending that Stevens is unable to achieve simply because of who he is.

Having got the story planned out, my next challenge was to decide how to tell it. To an extent, circumstances helped here. I knew that in the four months I had to write the book

I would be travelling a lot to the USA on business. Luckily, I had a (relatively early and primitive!) laptop computer for my work. So I needed to structure the story so that a large part of it was in the form of relatively short chapters or chunks which I could write as complete, discrete sections whenever I got some free time while travelling. I can still remember which piece I wrote in a coffee bar in Miami airport, which section was accompanied by weak, fizzy American beer and a plate of nachos in a Marriott hotel in Atlanta, which took form on an uncomfortable chair at the departure gate of Birmingham International…

Most of the short sequences between chapters were initially written like this. In narrative terms, many of them are not needed. But their inclusion gives the book not only an interesting structure but a scope and scale that would otherwise be lacking.

I think the resulting novel has stood up to the Tests of Time quite well. I have happy memories of writing it. There's not much that I'd change, I think, looking back on it now. There is a mistake, though – and one which perhaps eagle-eyed fans of *Downton* might spot. Lord Kenilworth's housekeeper doesn't feature much in the story, but she is called Miss Warne. At that time, the housekeeper would be addressed as 'Mrs' whether she was married or not. It's an easy one to correct, but actually I decided to leave it as it is. It's important to her story that we are aware that the lady is unmarried, and writers should never underestimate the importance of clarity.

Justin Richards
October 2013

As ever, this is for Alison and Julian.
Thanks for the Time.

Thanks also to Craig, Peter and Andy for
reading the first draft and being rude enough.
But not too much.

Ancient Egypt
c.5000 BC

The woman was still alive as unnatural thunder cracked across the sky. The lightning forked through the thrashing rain, stabbing at the desert sand. Rain splashed across the dunes, running down the bank towards the entrance of the tomb, washing over stone that had been parched for a thousand years.

She was hardly more than a girl, her eyes betraying her fear as she shivered in the warm rain. The priests stood either side of her, holding her arms out from her body. Their heads were lowered – perhaps in shame, perhaps in an effort to keep them dry.

She screamed as the spirit she hosted was split, ruptured and ripped from her mind. She collapsed to her knees, held up only by the grip of the priests. Damp sand gritted into the white cotton of her dress. The muscles in her neck tightened with the pain and her cries echoed through the night, blotting out the thunder. But she was still alive.

The gods watched from the ridge, silent and still, the rain running down their masked faces and splashing from their robes. Then Anubis and Horus stepped forward and made their considered way down towards the burial party. The lightning flashed across their ritual masks, picking out the reflective detail of the gold and deepening the dark holes of their eyes. The woman raised her head slightly as they stopped in front of her. Her left eyelid flickered while Anubis raised the lid from the canopic jar. Then her body spasmed again as

Horus touched her cheek, drew out the enclosed spirit, left her with only the instinct and intuition she had inherited.

She was still alive, but Rassul did nothing.

He watched as they dragged the girl's sagging body towards the tomb. He followed, taking his designated place as the last of the relics were carried after her. The ring of Bastet, borne on a velvet cushion; the snake statue of Netjerankh; the scarab bracelet; the figure of Anubis, god of the rituals of death. Rassul followed, holding the hourglass before him like the talisman it was. And at his back he could hear the Devourer of the Dead snapping in frustration as she was cheated of her victim.

The girl was still alive as they removed the dress. She could stand alone now, unmoving apart from her eyes. She was still alive as Anubis directed the priests to smear her naked body with bitumen.

She was still alive as they started to smother the bandages round her. And Rassul did nothing.

As the wrappings reached her face she screamed again, head back and mouth wide, as if to remind them she still had her tongue. A single word, screamed in terror, anger and accusation. A single word hurled at Rassul as he stood before her. And did nothing. The next twist of cloth cut off her voice, bit deep into her mouth and gagged her.

She was still alive as the bandages covered her forehead, leaving a thin slot through which Rassul could see her eyes widen. She was watching him, locked on to him. And he could see her pupils dilate, could almost feel her terror.

The opening of the mouth. Her scream had been like a pouring in of energy. His muscles tightened and his whole body tensed. A single word.

In that instant he knew what he must do, saw his destiny mapped out like a procession snaking across the desert.

He felt his life stretch out ahead of him, guided inexorably towards a new purpose.

Rassul placed the hourglass in the appointed position. He watched them lower the mummified body into the inner sarcophagus and drag the heavy lid across it. He watched the priests follow the gods from the tomb. He turned back as they reached the doorway, bowed in reverence, and made to join the procession.

Then he reached out, and turned the hourglass over. A tiny trickle of sand, a thin line of time, traced its way into the lower glass bowl. Rassul watched for a moment, then followed the last of the priests. He waited outside as they closed and sealed the doorway.

The gods were already gone. The priests waited no longer than was necessary to complete the final rituals. Like Rassul, they had heard the thumping on the inside of the sarcophagus. Like Rassul, they knew she was still alive.

Lord Kenilworth spluttered into his single malt, wiped a sodden handkerchief round his damp collar, and looked again across the room. He was sitting alone at a map-strewn table close to the window. He had been examining the maps for most of the afternoon, tracing out routes to possible sites and discarding them for lack of substantiating or corroborative evidence. Across the extensive hotel gardens outside, if he cared to look, he was afforded an excellent view of the pyramids. But for the moment, the presence of the man who had entered the bar puzzled him more than the ancient monuments he had spent a good deal of his forty-seven years studying.

'Good God, Atkins,' Kenilworth blurted, half rising as the man approached him. 'What the deuce?'

'I'm sorry, sir. I realise this is somewhat unexpected.' Atkins lowered his head slightly as he spoke. 'But a matter has arisen.'

'*Unexpected*? I should say so.' Kenilworth waved the tall man to a chair, and wiped his brow.

Atkins sat, assuming an upright posture which emphasised his near-immaculate attire. If Kenilworth noticed the mud and sand clinging to Atkins's shoes and the cuffs of his trousers, he did not mention it. He waited.

'So what is this matter that brings you all the way from London? What is it that causes you to neglect your duties – and my household, I should add – and come to Cairo in person rather than send a telegram?'

Atkins coughed politely. 'We are actually in Giza, sir.'

'I know where I am, thank you. And I rather think I may be permitted to stray a couple of miles from my residence. Especially since my butler seems to have wandered several thousand miles from his.' He gave a single curt nod to emphasise the point. Then he laughed, a short snort of mirth. 'You gave me quite a turn, though, I don't mind admitting.' Kenilworth set down his drink on one of the maps, rubbing his thumb against the cool surface of the glass for a moment.

A shadow fell across the table, and he was suddenly aware that another figure had joined them. The man was standing beside Kenilworth's chair, silhouetted against the window and framed between the shapes of the pyramids outside.

'Who the devil are you, sir?' Kenilworth asked, pulling the maps off the table and rolling them up. Out of the corner of his eye he noticed Atkins grab the whisky tumbler a moment before the map was pulled from under it.

'This gentleman, sir,' Atkins said quietly as he replaced the tumbler on the table, 'has a proposition which I believe you will find of interest.'

'Does he indeed?' Kenilworth peered into the setting sunlight. The man was tall, but Kenilworth could make out no features. There was just a shadowed oval where his face should be. 'Well then, sir, out with it. What proposition is it that causes you to hijack my man and bring him half across the globe?'

The man's voice was young, but at the same time it commanded respect. It was cultured, lacking any discernible accent beyond being English. 'You are looking for a tomb,' the man said. 'A blind pyramid south of Saqqara.'

Kenilworth's eyes narrowed. 'How do you know that?' He turned to his manservant. 'Atkins?' he asked accusingly.

Atkins shook his head, a barely perceptible gesture. 'I think you should listen to the gentleman, sir. I have good reason to suspect he can provide useful information.'

Kenilworth snorted again, and reached for his drink.

The stranger bent forward slightly. 'Mr Atkins is right, Lord Kenilworth.'

'Really? And what information, pray, can you provide me with?'

The man straightened up again. 'You must be prepared for some hardship, I'm afraid. There will be danger, death even, ahead of us. But if you're agreeable I can offer my services to your expedition.'

'And what exactly are you offering?'

The man turned away, towards the window, and looked out at the pyramids. The sun was edging down between them, its rays streaming across the hazy desert sands. He was silent for a moment, as if considering. Then he seemed to come to a decision and turned back to face Kenilworth.

'I can lead you to the tomb,' he said.

CRANLEIGH HALL, OXFORDSHIRE
1926

The orchestra occupied a large area of the terrace. One end of the lawn was taken up with the buffet and bar, the rest was free for the guests. Some of them stood and ate; some of them chatted idly amongst themselves; some of them danced in the small area of the terrace free of musicians; some of them watched the dancers as they skidded merrily through the Charleston.

Lord and Lady Cranleigh weaved their way endlessly and effortlessly through the guests. They smiled and exchanged small talk. They nodded and accepted good wishes and compliments. They agreed with any comments offered unless they related to religion or politics, in which case they went out of their way to be non-committal before moving hastily on.

'Beautiful, absolutely beautiful,' Smutty Thomas told them for the fourth time as he waved his most recent flute of champagne vaguely in the direction of the happy couple. 'Lovely church. Bishop's a good sort.' Champagne splashed onto the grass at Lady Cranleigh's feet. She smiled, pretending not to notice.

'Speeches – excellent. Superb,' Smutty Thomas concluded, nodding enthusiastically.

Lord Cranleigh laughed. 'We haven't had the speeches yet.'

Smutty Thomas frowned with some difficulty. 'Well,' he decided at length, 'they will be good.'

'Indeed they will,' a voice said from just behind Cranleigh.

It was at once breathless and controlled, as if the speaker had just run a hundred-yard dash but not broken a sweat. 'I shall especially enjoy the anecdote about the pig in Exeter College.'

Lord Cranleigh gaped. 'How could you possibly know—' he began, turning to face the man who had spoken. As soon as he saw who it was, his surprise turned to delight and understanding. 'Doctor,' he said with a beam, 'how good of you to come.'

'Not at all.' The Doctor smiled back and took Cranleigh's proffered hand. 'Congratulations. The wedding cake tastes lovely.'

'We haven't cut it yet,' said Lady Cranleigh.

But her husband just laughed again and waved an admonishing finger at the Doctor. 'I can never tell when you're joking, Doctor.'

'Are you here alone?' Lady Cranleigh asked. She had been looking past the Doctor, scanning the nearby guests for his companions.

'I'm rather afraid I am.' The Doctor's smile faded.

'May be just as well,' Cranleigh observed. 'I rather think Miss Nyssa's appearance here might cause some little confusion.' He turned to the swaying Smutty Thomas. 'You know she's the image of Ann,' he confided. 'Two peas in a pod. Quite uncanny.' But his friend seemed more concerned with keeping his champagne within the confines of the wavering glass than in Cranleigh's words.

Ann Cranleigh patted the Doctor's shoulder. 'It's nice to see you, anyway,' she said. 'But you must bring Nyssa and Tegan and Adric to visit us soon. You are always welcome here.'

'Indeed,' Cranleigh agreed with his wife. 'We owe you a lot, Doctor.'

'Thank you,' the Doctor said. He bit his lower lip as if

pondering something important. 'I know you're a little busy at the moment,' he said at last, 'but I was wondering if you could do me one small favour.'

'Anything I can do, Doctor,' Cranleigh said seriously. 'So long as it's not money,' he added with a wink.

The Doctor laughed. Then at once he was solemn again. 'No, it's not money. And actually, it's really your wife I must ask. Though I can give you a little while to think about it.'

'In that case,' Lady Cranleigh took the Doctor's arm, 'you can ask me as we dance.'

'Dance?' The Doctor was dismayed. He twisted round as she led him towards the terrace and shot Cranleigh a despairing glance.

Cranleigh raised his glass in response. 'See you later, Doctor,' he called, turning back in time to catch Smutty Thomas as he fell.

Aubrey Prior froze. The glass hovered for a moment in front of his open mouth, then he blinked suddenly and put it down. The light from the heavy chandelier reflected off the cut facets of the lead crystal and made the vintage port glow as if lit from within. It was one of the best of the many ports that Aubrey Prior had tasted.

'How long have you known? Are they sure? My God, how do you—' Aubrey shook his head. 'Sorry, I – Sorry.'

Cedric smiled sadly across the room. He was standing with his back to the fire, resting his arm along the mantelpiece. 'I've known for quite some time really,' he said. 'Though it took me a while to believe it.'

'But there must be something – some treatment or other. If it's a genetic instability or defect in the DNA—'

Cedric held up his hand to stop his nephew. 'In a few years I can believe that you and your colleagues will have tinkered around with our genes to the point where you can cure anything, Aubrey.' He stared distantly at the chandelier for a moment. 'But I don't have a few years. All I have is a few weeks.'

'Weeks?'

Cedric Prior nodded. 'Three at the most, apparently. Though God knows I feel better now than I have in ages.' He looked round the drawing room, slowly scanning the furniture and ornaments. To his nephew he looked as if he was seeing the room properly for the first time. Or the last. 'I was hoping that he would come during my lifetime, that I would find out at last what it's all about…' His voice tailed off and he shook his head slowly and sadly.

'He?' Aubrey stood up and went over to join his uncle at the fire. They were friends as well as relatives, and Aubrey had been looking forward to the evening for weeks. Probably for longer than his uncle had left to live. He put his glass down on the mantelpiece. Suddenly he didn't seem to want the drink.

Cedric Prior was still staring into space, his eyes glazed over. Aubrey waited a while, but his uncle seemed deep in thought. 'Would you like me to…' Aubrey gestured vaguely towards the door.

Cedric looked at him. 'What? Oh, no. No. Sorry I was…' He looked towards the door where Aubrey had pointed. 'Yes, yes. We must go. It's time you knew about your duties, knew about the task our family is charged with.'

Aubrey followed his uncle into the hall, wondering vaguely if his brain had been affected by the illness. He was becoming certain of it when Cedric Prior led him to the cupboard under the stairs and indicated that his nephew should follow him inside.

'In there? Really, Uncle, I do think—'

'Come along, I've waited all your life to show you this.' Cedric grabbed his hand and pulled him inside. Then he immediately stooped down and started to fumble with the floorboards.

Aubrey peered over Cedric's shoulder, and saw that he was levering up a brass ring set into the wood. As soon as his fingers could gain purchase on the ring, he pulled. And a section of the floor of the cupboard lifted up accompanied by a cloud of dust. 'A trapdoor.'

Cedric smiled and nodded. 'Down you go.' As his uncle stood aside, Aubrey could see a set of stone steps leading down into the cellarage beneath.

Aubrey had expected a dim area filled with cobwebs and dust. Instead he was greeted with a large stone-floored room, brightly lit and draped with deep red velvet curtains round the walls. On low tables and shelves around the room were various ornaments and statuettes. But Aubrey hardly noticed them.

On the far side of the room, was a dais. Two stone steps led up to the raised rectangular area. And standing on a stone table in the middle was a sarcophagus.

Without looking to see if his uncle was behind him, Aubrey walked slowly across the room towards the coffin. His feet rang on the stone floor, the sound deadened and absorbed by the heavy curtains. As he stepped up to it, he could see that the sarcophagus was dark with age. Once it had been covered with intricate, colourful hieroglyphics, three rows of tiny pictures around the outside of the human-shaped case. But now they had faded and blackened in the air so that only the outlines and shadows of them were visible as they caught the light.

Aubrey reached the top step, and looked into the coffin. He drew in his breath sharply as he saw the bandaged body. From the size and shape he assumed it was, or rather had been, female. He shook his head in disbelief. 'My God. How long have you had this here?'

Behind him, at the foot of the staircase, Cedric Prior laughed. 'I didn't put this here. I wasn't told who did.' He stepped forward, lowering his voice slightly. 'And I knew better than to ask.' He stepped slowly up to the sarcophagus and stared inside for a while. 'She is your responsibility now, Aubrey.'

'Mine?'

'Oh yes. As my sole heir you will get the house and all its contents. Including her.'

'But what? I mean…' Aubrey waved his hands over the bandaged form. 'What's it for? What do I have to do with her?'

'Probably nothing. She lies here like this, untouched and undisturbed until our family's duty is discharged.'

'And when is that?'

Cedric reached inside his jacket and pulled out an envelope. It was brittle and yellowed with age, and a fleck of paper flaked off and floated to the basement floor as he teased open the end. From inside he drew a piece of card. He handed it to his nephew.

'An invitation card?' In fact it was half a card. The faded gilt of the rounded edge ended in a jagged tear where the card had been torn across. Aubrey read the half sentences on the printed side, trying to fill in the missing words and phrases.

'Probably you will pass that on to your next of kin just as I do,' Cedric said quietly. 'But there is a chance, just a chance, that during your lifetime he will come.'

'Who will?'

'Whoever has the other half of that invitation card. He will come to claim the mummy, and you must release it to him.'

'And when that happens?'

Cedric Prior shrugged. He traced his finger along the edge of the ancient coffin and stared at the rotting bandages across the woman's face. 'I wish I knew,' he said quietly.

CHAPTER
ONE

The Doctor was deep in thought. Nyssa could tell as soon as she entered the console room. She had heard the melodious chime that meant they had landed while she was in the TARDIS corridor. Now she could see that the central column of the control console had come to a halt.

The Doctor was leaning over the console, staring across it through the misted transparency of the central column. A single line creased his apparently young brow as he gazed into the empty middle distance.

As Nyssa watched from the doorway, the Doctor shook his heard suddenly, sending his blond hair into a frenzy as he set off rapidly round the console. He was muttering under his breath, consulting instruments and frowning at read-outs.

Tegan's voice came from close to Nyssa's ear – her friend was standing right behind her. 'Have we landed?'

'Yes.' Nyssa stood aside to let Tegan into the room. 'But I'm not sure we're where the Doctor intended.'

'So what's new?' Tegan positioned herself so that the Doctor could not help but notice her as he started another circuit of the console.

'Ah. Tegan,' he said as he almost ran into her. 'Good. Yes. We've landed.' He plunged his hands deep into the pockets of his long cream-coloured jacket and peered over Tegan's shoulder at the console.

'We can see that, Doctor,' Nyssa said as she joined them by the console.

The Doctor pulled his hands from his pockets and tapped an absent-minded tattoo on the nearest control panel. 'Only,' he said quietly. Then he suddenly stopped tapping his fingers and peered closely at the controls on the panel.

'Only what, Doctor?'

For a moment he did not move. Then he straightened up, his face creasing into the frown of a late schoolboy with no excuse. 'We're not where we should be,' he said, as if totally surprised.

'We guessed that,' Tegan told him.

'Hmm?' the Doctor asked in a pained voice.

'Where are we, then?' Nyssa asked him before they could start arguing over the exact percentage of accurate landings the Doctor had recently accomplished.

The Doctor turned sharply towards Nyssa. 'I don't know,' he said as if the question had only just occurred to him.

'I'll try the scanner,' Nyssa offered.

It showed nothing.

'It's just black,' Tegan said, earning a scowl from the Doctor and a shrug from Nyssa.

'Perhaps it is just black outside. A void of some sort.'

'No, Nyssa. The scanner's playing up, that's all.' The Doctor closed the scanner screen and waved a hand dismissively at the control console. 'It'll sort itself out soon enough.'

'What will?'

'What? Oh, relative dimensional stabiliser failed. It's happened before, so the TARDIS will know how to fix it. Then we can be on our way.'

'As simple as that?' Tegan did not seem convinced.

'Er, well no, actually. Not quite.'

'Thought not.'

'We need to recalibrate. Won't take a moment.' The Doctor grinned. 'Once we have the data.'

Tegan looked from the Doctor to Nyssa. Since the Doctor did not seem about to elaborate, Nyssa explained. 'We need to know where we are, so we can work out how to get back on course.' She hoped she had understood the problem.

'Quite right, Nyssa. Where and when. Once we know that, we can have another go.'

'So we have to go outside.'

The Doctor nodded. 'Exciting isn't it?' He reached for the door control, and the main doors swung heavily open.

'Come on, you two.' The Doctor already had his Panama hat in hand. He stuck it on his head as he pushed past Nyssa and Tegan to get to the doors. 'Where's your sense of adventure?'

'Mine died a long and lingering death somewhere in Amsterdam,' Tegan said quietly to Nyssa. 'Where's yours?'

'I'm not sure I ever had one,' Nyssa replied. But she followed them out of the TARDIS anyway.

The room was large and unlit. The only illumination was the moonlight spilling in through the dusty windows. As she peered into the gloom, Tegan could make out dark shapes along the length of the room. A black river flowed round them, and as her eyes adjusted to the darkness she could see that it was a carpet. It traced a route through and around the shapes. The Doctor was already making his way down the room, peering at shadows. As she watched, he removed a pair of half-moon spectacles from his top pocket and put them on.

Tegan made to follow him, conscious of Nyssa beside her. Something caught at her hand, just for a second, then let go. Immediately, Tegan gasped in surprise and jumped back.

Beside her, Nyssa laughed. 'It's just a rope, Tegan.'

'I can see that.' And so she could – now. The rope stretched

17

along the side of the carpet, cordoning off the area outside it. To get to the carpeted path, they had to step over the rope. As they made their way after the Doctor, Tegan saw that the rope was strung between low posts along the way. She was beginning to understand where they were.

'They're caskets,' Nyssa said as they reached the first of the larger shadows. The central aisle of the room was a line of similar shapes. They were all open caskets about seven feet long and three feet wide. And each seemed to contain a body.

Nyssa was examining the nearest casket. 'The body is wrapped in some sort of protective covering,' she pointed out. 'I think it must be an advanced process derived from cryogenics. A way of preserving a body so that it can later be restored to life.'

This time Tegan laughed. She was glad that for once she knew more than Nyssa about something. 'Advanced process? I don't think so.'

'Oh, be charitable, Tegan.' Somehow the Doctor had popped up between them and was staring into the casket. 'The process is pretty advanced, considering. And the basic idea was exactly as Nyssa said. They thought the soul was reunited with the body after burial. So the body had to be preserved to endure the rigours of the afterlife.'

Tegan's eyes had adjusted enough to the dim light for her to be able to see Nyssa's smirk. 'Doctor, they're mummies,' she said. 'Whatever Nyssa thinks, we're in a museum. A museum full of sarcophaguses and ancient Egyptian stuff.'

'Sarcophagi,' the Doctor admonished. 'But you're right.'

They looked around again, able now to see rather more clearly. The sarcophagi formed a row down the centre of the room. Along the sides of the room, more caskets and sarcophagi stood upright. The TARDIS was almost at one end of a wall, just one more box in a large collection of strange-shaped caskets. Dotted about the room were low tables, each with one or more objects standing symmetrically upon it. The objects ranged from statuettes to urns, from glass cases of jewellery to fragments of papyrus.

'And this is not *just* a museum,' the Doctor continued. 'This is *the* museum – at least as far as Earth is concerned.' He slowly turned a complete circle, surveying the room with apparent pride. 'This is the Egyptian room of the British Museum.' He set off down the room again. 'All we need to know now, is the time,' he called back over his shoulder.

'It's night time,' Tegan called after him. 'And it's cold.' She was still wearing the camisole top and thin shorts she had taken to Amsterdam. They had been fine there, but she was conscious now that they were really little more than glorified underwear.

'Did they really think they would revive in an afterlife?' asked Nyssa. 'After this?' She gestured at the bandaged figure lying in the coffin in front of them.

'Guess so.' Tegan shivered. 'Made for some good films though – mummies lurching to life and staggering after their victims.' She made a clumsy lunge for Nyssa, who giggled and stepped out of the way.

'If he's going to be much longer, I'll have to get a coat.' Tegan watched as the Doctor moved slowly amongst the relics and jotted odd notes on a small pad that had appeared in his hand. 'Aren't you cold?' she asked Nyssa.

Nyssa shook her head. She was wearing brown corduroy trousers and what appeared to be a matching velvet tunic.

Tegan came to her decision. 'Right,' she said, 'I'll be back in a minute.' She nodded towards the distant figure of the Doctor. 'Don't let him wander off,' she told Nyssa. Then she headed back towards the TARDIS, pausing only to curse at the low loop of rope she tripped over on the way.

Nyssa smiled as she saw Tegan trip against the rope again. She returned her friend's embarrassed wave, and watched her enter the TARDIS. Turning her attention back to the bandaged body in the sarcophagus in front of her, Nyssa wondered about the rituals and beliefs of the culture that took such care of their dead. She tried to estimate the age of the corpse, and then of its coffin. But she soon gave up, blaming both the bad light and her lack of background information. She would examine a couple of the other artefacts, and then ask the Doctor. If she felt confident enough she might even hazard an estimate of the age of one of the relics.

The first piece that Nyssa looked at more closely was a bracelet which lay on one of the tables by the aisle. It was large and heavy, hinged to open outwards and close around the wrist or perhaps the lower arm. As she twisted it to catch the moonlight, Nyssa could see that it was gold, inlaid with a blue enamel which she did not recognise. On one half was a picture. It seemed to show a child perched on top of a clump of leaves. The figure held a staff with a looped top and wore a headress adorned with a rearing snake. The picture was framed by the twisted shapes of two other snakes, their tails meeting above the child's head. The background was faded and worn, but the reliefwork itself was well-preserved and delineated. If she looked closely enough, Nyssa could even see the line of the mouth where the figure held its finger to its lips, as if asking her to keep silent.

She carefully replaced the bracelet on the table, none the wiser. A larger object might yield more clues. Nyssa made her way to a sarcophagus standing upright against the wall.

The sarcophagus was larger than she had expected, a good two feet taller than Nyssa. It seemed to be made of wood, and was carved into roughly the shape of a person – presumably of its occupant. Nyssa guessed from the relative sizes of the casket she had already seen and of its occupant that there was plenty of space inside even when the casket was full. The real person would have been nowhere near as big as their coffin.

A stream of moonlight illuminated the side and top of the sarcophagus. This was partly why Nyssa had been drawn to it, and she could see that the face painted on the head section was of a woman. The rest of the body was adorned with small pictures of animals and birds. There were also several human figures, but with the heads of other creatures. A single pattern, a stylised eye, recurred across the ornate coffin. An eyebrow looped above it as if in surprise, and two lines fell away from it. One was perpendicular to the eye, the other slid off to the left at an angle, thinning out before ending in a solid circle as large as the pupil. In the glinting dusty moonlight they looked to Nyssa like tears across the front of the coffin lid.

It did not take Nyssa long to decide that she had no chance of deciphering the symbols and pictures without help. Instead, she turned her attention to the face of the dead woman. She had to stand on tiptoe and lean forward over the extended feet jutting out from the base of the casket. Half the face was in shadow, but she could see the rest of it quite clearly. She could see the wide staring eyes and high eyebrows, the painted cheekbone and soft line of the nose. She stared at the flaking lips, turning up slightly even as a dimpled line shadowed down from the corner of the mouth. She reached up and ran her hand over the flat paint of the curled dark hair that cascaded down from a central parting to hang unevenly over the artificial shoulders. And she felt a cold trickle of fear run its course from the nape of her neck down her spine.

Tegan was wearing the longest, heaviest cloak she could find in the TARDIS wardrobe. She had considered changing her clothes completely, but she was not at all sure she trusted the Doctor to hang around for the length of time it might take to find something suitable. So she was wrapped entirely in a black cloak of some thick worsted material, the heavy hood pulling at her shoulders as it hung loose about her neck.

Her first problem was negotiating the rope she remembered all too well was strung across her path. She had to hoist the cloak up and over with each leg. Once on the other side of the rope she congratulated herself on the operation, smoothed the cloak back down to her ankles, and looked round for the Doctor and Nyssa.

She could see neither.

But then, as her eyes adjusted again to the gloomy light, she made out a figure towards the far end of the room. As she watched, it straightened up, silhouetted for a moment against the lighter doorway in the end wall. It stuffed its hands into its trouser pockets and turned slowly one way, then back the other. Tegan smiled and set off towards the Doctor.

She was about halfway there when she caught sight of movement from the corner of her eye. Her immediate thought was that it was Nyssa examining some other artefact. But it was not a person, more of a momentary glow. She stopped and turned back towards the light source.

But there was nothing there. Just another sarcophagus standing by the wall. It was tall and wide, shaped like an upright figure just as all the others were. The arms were crossed over the chest, each holding a staff. The headress over and around the face was alternate lines of black and a lighter colour, but it was too dark for Tegan to make out any details. She watched it for a moment. The sarcophagus stood silent, still, and lonely.

Just as Tegan was about to move on, she became aware of

a faint humming sound. It was not unlike the background noise in the TARDIS console room. She looked round to see where it was coming from. Had the TARDIS door swung open behind her, perhaps caught and kept ajar by her cloak? But the door was not open; and the sound was coming from behind her. From the sarcophagus. From the sarcophagus which was now lit with an eerie inner light that seemed to emanate from the lighter strips of the headress and spill out down the rest of the body.

The strobing blue light mesmerised Tegan for a second. It held her attention and her mind. Then just as she broke free of the image and found her voice, the light cut out.

'Doctor,' she called across the room. Her voice echoed over the relics and skidded across the coffins.

In the distance, the Doctor's silhouette turned sharply in the direction of the noise and broke into a run. Lit for a moment in the doorway behind, another figure slipped silently and swiftly into the room.

The hand was large and rough and smelled of fish. Nyssa had enough time to notice each of these facts, and to let out the beginnings of a surprised shriek before the hand closed completely over her mouth. Her cry stopped as abruptly as her assailant grabbed her.

Across the room, Nyssa could see the dark figure of Tegan and the hurried outline of the Doctor as he arrived beside her and clasped her shoulders, asking her what was wrong. The tableau receded as Nyssa was pulled back through the room in the opposite direction. The man holding her grunted with the effort as he tried to prevent her from crying out or wrenching herself free.

Nyssa bit and wriggled and stamped, but nothing she did seemed to shake her attacker's resolve or his grip. She pulled

23

at the huge hand clamped to her mouth, but without success.

In the distance the Doctor glanced briefly towards them. Nyssa could imagine him peering into the blackness and wondering where she was and what her stifled cry had been. Her eyes widened in blind appeal and she struggled all the more violently.

But the Doctor turned back to Tegan, moved her aside and started to examine the sarcophagus behind her. In a last desperate effort, Nyssa twisted in the doorway, her foot lashing out at a nearby display table and her half-free hand catching at the doorframe as she was dragged from the room.

'Look at the workmanship,' the Doctor said again as he wiped imaginary dust from the figure's face. 'Definitely Osiran influence.' He waved a hand at the stylised line of the eyebrows by way of proof. 'Well, at least we know what drew the TARDIS off course.' He turned back to Tegan, only slightly daunted by the fact that she appeared not to be paying any attention to him and was instead looking round the room behind them. 'Probably caused the stabiliser failure too, come to that.' He jammed his hands back into his pockets and leant suddenly forwards. 'Tegan, if you don't want to know, then please don't ask,' he finished as if continuing the previous sentence.

As he had suspected, she did not register the change of subject or the criticism.

'Where's Nyssa?' she asked instead.

'Oh, I expect she's—'

The Doctor's expectations were cut short by the sound of a table crashing to the ground. The sound echoed round the room as the table spilled its contents across the floor. Something smashed in a minor explosion of plaster. Something else skidded and rolled across the ground, spinning to a stop at the edge of the carpet.

Tegan and the Doctor both turned towards the source of the noise, towards the far end of the room. And saw the silhouetted struggling as Nyssa was dragged through the doorway by a large dark figure.

'Hey!' Tegan shouted, tripping on the edge of her cloak as she tried to break into a run. As she stumbled, the Doctor leapt past her and vaulted a collection of relics which stood between himself and the door. Behind him he was aware of Tegan struggling with her cloak. In front of him he saw Nyssa finally disappear from view, the door slammed shut behind her.

The door was unlocked. But the room beyond was empty.

The Doctor paused for the briefest of split seconds. Then he was off again, racing across the small room, and crashing through the door at the end of it. He heard it bang into the wall in front of him and slam shut again behind him as he skidded down the stairs. He heard Tegan's muffled shouts as she followed. He caught the smallest glimpse of Nyssa's flailing trailing leg as it disappeared round a bend in the wide stone staircase ahead of him. But when he reached the landing below, there was no clue as to which way to go. The stairs continued on down, but three doorways gave out onto the floor he was now on. The Doctor paused for breath and to listen for any hint which way to go. But all he could hear was Tegan clattering down the stairs behind him.

'Which way did they go?' Tegan asked as she reached the landing, her cloak swirling behind her.

The Doctor adopted a pained expression. 'Do you really think I'd be hanging around here if I knew that?'

'Great. So what do we do now?'

'We think.'

'Think?'

'Yes, Tegan,*think*. It can be really quite useful – you should try it occasionally.'

Tegan snorted. 'And what good will thinking do Nyssa? We need to find her.'

'For example, why do you think they – whoever *they* are – have taken her? Hmm?'

'It doesn't matter why, Doctor. We've got to find her.'

The Doctor smiled and waved a finger at Tegan. 'But if we knew why, we might know where. As it is, we have to guess. And I would guess they're taking her somewhere else.'

'Brilliant,' Tegan said, sounding as though she actually meant something quite different.

'Tegan,' admonished the Doctor. 'Somewhere else would suggest they're taking her outside the building. Away from the museum.' He nodded, primarily for his own benefit. 'So we need to be outside. We need to find their means of transport.'

'Transport?'

'They're not going to drag Nyssa kicking and screaming through the streets of London, now are they. Would you?'

But the Doctor did not wait for an answer to this. Instead he started down the staircase again. 'Come along,' he called back over his shoulder as he jumped down another three steps.

The night air was cold and dry. What breath Nyssa was able to exhale between the fingers of the clammy hand covering her mouth was forced through as a warm humid mist which drifted and thinned into the foggy distance. Nyssa had all but given up struggling and was trying instead to slow her progress as much as possible. She had heard the clatter of pursuit and her hope now was that the Doctor could catch up with them.

As she was dragged backwards out of a side entrance to the large building, Nyssa had no way of knowing where she was headed, but she had a good view of where she had been. She spent little time in considering how much this was like travelling with the Doctor, and more dragging dragging her feet sluggishly through the thin sprinkling of snow which covered the frozen cobbles. Her heels bumped over the small rounded stones and her calves were jarred by the jolting.

Further back along the dark shadow of the building, another door was opened into the foggy night. It swung heavily outward and sprung back slightly as it reached the limit of its hinge. A moment later the Doctor bounded through the doorway, followed closely by Tegan. At the same instant, the man pulling Nyssa stopped.

Nyssa's immediate thought was that the man would release her and make a run for it. The Doctor and Tegan were now so close that they must catch him. The Doctor was waving and shouting; Tegan was struggling to keep her cloak from under her feet. The fog parted before them as they dashed forward.

But then Nyssa felt herself hoisted roughly up a couple of high steps and bundled through a small door. At the same time the hand was released from her face and the ground jolted beneath her. She was thrown back on to an upholstered bench seat. In front of her a pair of eyes gleamed darkly, and gaslight reflected for a second from the blade of a knife. Behind her, Nyssa could hear the Doctor's continued shouts above the accelerating rhythm of the horse's hooves and the crack of the coachman's whip.

The carriage was soon swallowed up by the foggy night. For a while the sounds of the horse's hooves on the snowy cobbles and the clatter of the wheels made their increasingly muffled way through the thick fog. Only when they were gone did the Doctor stop running. He drew in a deep breath, threw his rolled Panama hat down into the roadway and carefully stamped on it.

Tegan caught up with him in time to see him retrieve the hat, unroll it, dust it down on his coat and jam the cold, soggy result back on his head. Then he sat down in the snow, pulled his knees up to his chest, and stared into the night.

Tegan said nothing. She pulled her cloak closer round her and raised the deep hood, aware of the cold despite the enforced exercise.

'That street lamp.' The Doctor nodded towards the nearest one. 'Interesting, don't you think?'

'No.' Tegan crouched down beside him. 'Doctor, we lost Nyssa.'

'Yes, I know,' the Doctor said without a trace of sarcasm. Rather he seemed in a thoughtful mood. 'And we'd better find her.' He leapt to his feet and strode over to the lamp post. 'Given the lighting technology, the ambient sound and,' he waved an arm through the misty night, 'pollution, I should say we're round about late Victorian.'

Tegan could see no reason to disagree. 'Does that help?'

The Doctor thought for a moment. 'Probably not,' he admitted at last. 'But I like to get things straight in my mind. And we still need an exact date to reset the TARDIS navigation systems.' He walked round the lamp post, leaving a slushy trail in the snow. 'That Osiran lodestone must have picked up some residual vortex energy from the TARDIS time track. That would explain why we were drawn off course, and might have caused the stabiliser failure.' He stopped his circumnavigation and peered pensively at Tegan. 'Also why the sarcophagus appeared to glow. Probably leaking out the time differential to prevent a short.'

'Does *that* help?'

'Possibly. If the sarcophagus and Nyssa's kidnapping are connected. Though I don't see how they could be. Perhaps this gentleman can enlighten us.'

It took Tegan a second to realise what the Doctor had said. Then she looked round to see who he was talking about. She was still looking when she became aware of the sound of footsteps. Almost immediately, a figure pushed its way through the fog in front of them and stepped into the gaslight.

The man was tall, his figure fleshed out by the cloak he wore. A tall black hat exaggerated his height as he walked towards them. His face, as it caught what light there was, was thin. He looked to be in his late thirties. 'Ah, there you are,' he said in a deep, measured voice.

The Doctor and Tegan exchanged glances. 'You were expecting to find us here?' the Doctor asked.

'Indeed, sir.' The stranger switched on a smile. 'I have a communication.'

'For us?' Tegan pushed forward to see the man better. 'Something to do with Nyssa?'

The man frowned and seemed genuinely surprised. 'To do with what?'

Tegan shrugged and turned away.

The man continued: 'I'm sorry, Miss Jovanka, I did not understand the reference.'

Tegan stopped dead. 'You know who I am?' She turned slowly back. The Doctor too seemed surprised.

'Indeed.' There was an awkward pause. Then the man seemed to sense that perhaps he needed to elaborate. 'How could I forget you so soon?' he added helpfully.

'You've met before?' the Doctor gestured between the stranger and Tegan.

The stranger laughed, a surprised rather than an amused laugh. 'But of course,' he said. 'As you well know, Doctor.'

Tegan decided to try a different approach. 'How did you know we were here?'

The man shrugged. 'Lord Kenilworth said I would find you here. But if I had missed you, I assume you are still at the Savoy.'

'Absolutely.' The Doctor moved Tegan aside and reached out a hand. 'Spot on. Now, about this communication.'

'Of course, sir.' The man fumbled inside his cloak and drew out an envelope. He handed it to the Doctor. 'It's for tomorrow afternoon, as agreed. Now, if you will excuse me, I must be getting back. I still have various duties to discharge this evening.' He bowed slightly to them both, then turned and walked into the fog. In the distance, Big Ben began to chime midnight.

The Doctor examined the envelope. He showed it to Tegan. On the front it was addressed in a neat efficient hand to 'The Doctor'.

'Curiouser and curiouser,' he muttered as he opened it.

Tegan stood on tiptoes and looked over the Doctor's shoulder as he pulled out the card inside. He glared at her briefly, and she smiled back. Then he held the card so they could both see it in the light from the gas lamp above.

It was a plain white card, edged in gold. It was about five inches long by three inches high. Tegan read it twice.

LORD KENILWORTH

At home

Monday 10th November, 1896

Kenilworth House, Embankment

A Mummy from Eygpt to be unwrapped at half-past two

'Not that unusual, Tegan,' the Doctor said after a while. These events were not uncommon. The Victorians loved to marry ceremony with antiquity and some semblance of learning.'

'Maybe, Doctor,' Tegan said, 'but I'd say it's pretty weird to get invited at midnight by a complete stranger to a mummy-unwrapping party.'

The thin layer of snow cracked and collapsed under Tegan's feet. Her breath formed clouds in front of her face, and her feet ached. She felt as if they had been walking for days, though she suspected that it was probably only about an hour all told. She was barely paying attention to the Doctor's lecture on the history of Victorian London and glanced only occasionally at the features of interest he pointed out along their route.

He should get an umbrella and do the tour-guide job properly, she thought as he took her arm again and waved a learned hand at yet another bridge across the Thames. But for the most part she was thinking about Nyssa, and she suspected that behind his erudite manner the Doctor was as well.

Finally seeming to sense that he was making no progress in distracting Tegan, the Doctor had quietened. They made their way along the Embankment in silence broken only by the background hum of the city and the foghorns of the boats on the river. A gaslight haze lay over the nearby rooftops, fading into gloom and darkness in the distance.

'It smells,' Tegan said at last. She felt this was a fair comment on the Doctor's appreciation of Victorian architecture.

'Smelt a good deal more before they put the sewer in,' the Doctor said, immediately back into his undaunted spiel. 'All the sewage used to just go into the river. Now it gets carried ten miles east.'

'What happens to it there?'

The Doctor lowered his head and kicked at a swell of soft

31

snow. It exploded in a puff of white dust. 'It just goes into the river at Barking,' he muttered and quickly went on: 'Another marvellous feat of Victorian engineering.'

'A sewer?' Tegan was not convinced.

'Mmm,' came the enthusiastic reply.

'So where is it?'

'Ah, well. They roofed it over and called it the Victoria Embankment,' the Doctor smiled through the gloom. 'We're walking on it.' He broke into a grin. 'And we've arrived.'

Just ahead of them Tegan could see the tall shape of Cleopatra's needle cutting into the foggy sky. The bulky shape of a carved sphinx watched it diligently from beside them. Clawed hands of bronze gripped the edge of the stone plinth as the silent figure continued its vigil, poised to leap forward into the night.

But the Doctor was not interested. He had turned inwards and was pointing out a large rectangular building. The façade was lined with row upon row of large square windows, each row separated by a balcony. Just visible at the top of the building, flags hung limp from poles at each corner of the roof in the still night. Between the flags, lit from beneath and catching the vestiges of moonlight that struggled through the thick air, large capital letters proclaimed proudly: SAVOY HOTEL AND RESTAURANT.

'Shall we, Miss Jovanka?' the Doctor asked theatrically as he waved an operatic hand to indicate a paved path through the line of young trees.

Despite the lateness of the hour, the reception clerk was busily sorting through papers and allocating them to pigeon holes. The small square openings covered most of the wall behind the heavy mahogany desk, which itself occupied a fair extent of the far wall of the hotel lobby.

THE SANDS OF TIME

The clerk looked round as the door opened to let in the Doctor and Tegan. He was middle-aged with slicked back dark hair fashionably greased to his head. The Doctor approached the desk while Tegan waited at the back of the room. The clerk shot them a look of annoyance as Tegan glanced round the foyer. The area was large and ornate, as she had expected. The carpet was deep pile and deep red, and a huge staircase ascended from one corner of the reception area. Beyond it, a corridor led out of sight while a pair of double doors stood propped open to reveal the glory of the dining room. Several immaculate waiters were making their weary way round the tables positioning cutlery.

Tegan's sweeping gaze brought her attention back to the clerk, and she saw his expression transform into one of delight as the Doctor approached the desk. He seemed to exude pleasure as he hurried to check a couple of pigeon holes, and returned to the desk with a pair of heavy keys.

'No messages, sir,' he said before the Doctor could say a word. 'Not for you or for Miss Jovanka.' He smiled across at Tegan, who frowned beneath her hood. Then he seemed to catch sight of the Doctor's expression.

'I'm sorry, sir, were you expecting a communication?' He returned his attention to the pigeon holes. 'Let me just check again.'

The Doctor turned and shrugged. Tegan returned the gesture, unsure whether her cloak had masked the movement completely.

'No, sir. Nothing at all.'

'Well, never mind,' the Doctor reassured him. 'Not your fault.'

'Your keys.' The clerk handed them to the Doctor.

The Doctor took the keys and started towards the staircase. He stopped abruptly in mid-stride and turned back to the desk. 'There is one thing you could do for me.'

'Of course, sir. Anything.'

Tegan could see the edge of the Doctor's hesitant smile. 'Miss Jovanka and I have been discussing it and we can't seem to quite remember. Tell me, how long have we been staying here?'

The clerk's jaw dropped perceptibly.

'Er, exactly, that is,' the Doctor finished.

Still not convinced, the clerk reached under the desk and produced a heavy leather-bound book. He licked a suspicious index finger and riffled through the pages until he found what he was looking for. Finger marking his place, he peered at the Doctor slightly suspiciously. 'You signed the guest register at three-twenty-seven, sir.'

The Doctor's lips tightened and his eyes narrowed. Tegan could see he was wondering how to frame the next question. 'Three-twenty-seven,' he said at last. 'And that would be on, er…' His voice trailed off into the embarrassed corners of the room.

'Yesterday, sir,' the clerk said with the slightest hint of a reprimand.

The Doctor nodded half-heartedly. 'See, Tegan,' he said at length. 'I told you so.'

Tegan said nothing. She was tired; she was confused; she was cold; and she was worried about Nyssa. She stamped across the foyer and relieved the Doctor of one of the keys, then continued towards the staircase. As she turned across the half-landing and ascended out of sight of the foyer she could hear the clerk's muffled voice from below.

'I assume you remember the way to your room, sir.'

'Ah, er,' the Doctor's voice followed. 'I don't suppose you'd like to remind me of the general direction?' There was a pause and Tegan could only guess at the clerk's expression.

The Doctor's voice became clearer as he hurried up the stairs after her. 'No, well – just a joke,' he admitted unconvincingly. 'Ha ha.'

It was something of a relief eventually to find rooms 106 and 107. It was also just as well, Tegan reflected, that the keys had numbered brass tags attached.

The Doctor motioned for Tegan to keep quiet as he silently slid the key to room 106 into the lock and slowly turned it. The lock clicked quietly and the Doctor flung open the door.

The room appeared to be empty. The bed was turned down, and the curtains drawn. It appeared in every respect to be an ordinary, if somewhat plush, empty hotel room. The Doctor grunted his disappointment and grinned at Tegan. 'Let's try 107.'

The procedure was repeated with the adjoining room. Tegan stood well clear as the Doctor gave the door a hefty push to open it. He stared into the room for a moment, frowned, and then smiled at Tegan.

'That must be your room, I think.'

'Why?'

The Doctor yawned, stretched, looked down his nose at her and pushed past towards the open door to room 106. 'I'll see you in the morning,' he said as he stepped out of sight. 'I need to think over a few things. I'll call you for breakfast at eight.' His face suddenly reappeared in the doorway for a moment. 'Green's not really my colour,' he said. 'Goodnight.'

Tegan watched the door to 106 close and heard the key turn in the lock. She had no idea what was going on, but at least she could get a few hours sleep. Now at least she had a decent place for the night, and things could hardly get any more confusing.

Then she stepped into her room. Laid out on the bed was

a Victorian dress, trimmed at the neck and cuffs with delicate lace and pleated at the waist. It looked to be about the right size for Tegan. It was pale green.

The dining room was surprisingly quiet. There seemed to be more waiters than guests at breakfast. Tegan felt decidedly over-dressed until she entered the room. Then she transferred her social worries to her conspicuously short hair.

The Doctor on the other hand seemed to have made absolutely no concessions to the era or the establishment, and was acting as though he felt good about it. He was dressed as always in his cricketing gear and pale frock coat. He smiled affably at the staff and nodded politely to the guests. The only moment of uncertainty in his progress through the room as they followed a waiter to their table was when an old man who had seemed to be asleep mumbled, 'Hello, Doctor' as they passed. 'Don't have the kippers,' he added in a stage whisper as they were almost out of earshot.

The waiter led them to a table by the window. Snow was still covering the ground outside, but it was a bright crisp morning, the sun shining on the murky surface of the Thames just visible between the young trees lining the embankment. It reflected in rather more glory from the bronze hide of one of the sphinxes guarding Cleopatra's Needle.

'Ideal,' the Doctor told the waiter as he surveyed the scene. Then he yanked out a chair and sat down, legs immediately stretched out under the table.

'Thank you, sir.' The waiter smiled. 'You did seem quite comfortable here last night.' He pulled the opposite chair out for Tegan, pushing it gently into the backs of her knees to forcing her to sit suddenly and indecorously.

'You mean at dinner?' the Doctor hazarded.

'Indeed, sir.'

Tegan gave a short humourless laugh. She was getting used to everyone knowing where they had been and what they had done before they had even arrived. 'I suppose you can remember what we had to eat, too,' she muttered.

The waiter dropped a napkin into her lap. 'You had the cutlets, Miss Jovanka. You expressed some disappointment, as I recall.' He smiled at the Doctor as he pulled the napkin from the Doctor's glass and politely handed it to him. 'Whereas the Doctor was kind enough to compliment the chef on his oysters.' He stepped back a pace, perhaps to double-check the perfect alignment of the table against the window. 'Enjoy your breakfast, sir.' With a slight bow, the waiter turned on his heels. 'Madam,' his voice drifted back across his shoulder, as if as an afterthought.

Tegan watched him across the dining room. When the waiter was well out of earshot she leant across the table and grasped the Doctor's wrist. 'Doctor, what's going on?' She asked. 'And what are we going to do about Nyssa?'

The Doctor was already busily checking the breakfast arrangements. He opened the lid of the heavy silver teapot and peered inside for a moment, then he counted his way through the cutlery and checked the temperature of the toast in the rack. 'Well,' he said at last, 'as to what's going on, I haven't a clue.' He grinned. 'Interesting, isn't it?'

'And Nyssa?'

The Doctor stopped midway through pouring the milk. 'Yes,' he said seriously, 'well, as I said last night, I think our best course is to attend this mummy party this afternoon and see what clues we can pick up there.'

'And until then?'

'Oh, come on, Tegan, first things first.' He picked up the teapot. 'And the first thing I need is a cup of tea.'

*

Kenilworth House was a large, imposing stone-clad building several storeys high. It was set back slightly from the embankment, the rear of the house looking out over the river. The Doctor and Tegan followed a narrow footpath round to the front of the house and found themselves facing a large gateway. The heavy ironwork gates stood open, and a pair of carved jackals looked down at the Doctor and Tegan as they passed.

Tegan spared a hurried glance for the stone creatures as she and the Doctor started up the driveway. The skidding of carriage wheels on the gravel and the encouraging call of a driver to the horses drew her attention back to the house. The carriage was pulling away from the porch which jutted out over the front door, shielding it from the cold afternoon sun and shadowing the woodwork. The bay windows on the upper floors leant towards them as if watching as they approached. Tegan did not look back for fear that the jackals on the gateposts had turned to monitor their progress. Instead she followed in the Doctor's footsteps as he crunched nonchalantly up the drive, hat on head and hands in pockets.

The door was opened before the Doctor's hand reached the bell. It creaked inwards to reveal a tall thin man. It was the same man who had handed the Doctor the invitation the previous night.

For a second, nobody moved. The man stood framed in the doorway; the Doctor's hand hovered close to the bell pull. Tegan stood a step down from the Doctor, a chill running up her spine. Then the moment was broken like the tension on a lake when the first drop of a thunderstorm splashes into it.

'Who is it, Atkins?' a gruff voice called from inside the house.

The man in the doorway – Atkins – stepped back, opening the door fully and gesturing for the Doctor and Tegan to enter. 'The Doctor, sir,' Atkins said as the they entered the hallway, 'and Miss Jovanka.'

The next few minutes seemed almost like a dream when Tegan tried to recall them afterwards. She remembered being greeted by Lord Kenilworth in the hallway. She was not quite sure how they knew it was Lord Kenilworth, perhaps they did not find out until later. But whoever they thought he was, the large man in his forties was genuinely pleased to see them. He seemed to radiate equal amounts of pleasure, relief and excitement as he pumped the Doctor's hand and clapped Tegan on the shoulder.

'Thank heavens, Doctor,' he chuckled loudly. 'I know you said you'd probably be late, but you cut it a bit fine. We were quite worried, actually. Thought we might have to delay the big moment. Can't start without you, after all. Not after everything we've been through, eh?'

'Quite,' the Doctor muttered, as he allowed himself to be led to the drawing room. Tegan hurried after them, trying not to trip over the hem of her dress.

The drawing room was big and square. The dark walls were hung with portraits, the only subject Tegan recognised being Queen Victoria. A large fireplace dominated one wall, the burning logs sparking and crackling and throwing shadows of the people in front of it. And the room was full of people, or at least that was the impression Tegan got. Thinking back later, she decided there could only have been perhaps a dozen guests. But as they all stopped in mid-conversation and turned to watch her enter the room behind the Doctor and Kenilworth, they seemed like a multitude.

The small crowd parted for the approaching Doctor as if he were Moses. People stepped back respectfully, clearing a way through to the far corner of the room. To the area below Queen Victoria's stern vigil. To the sarcophagus.

'I think, Doctor, that we might as well start right away,' Kenilworth said as they approached the trestles on which the ornate mummy case rested. 'Professor Macready has kindly offered to assist.'

Macready was a small man with little round glasses and thin grey hair. He stood the other side of the sarcophagus, so his head seemed almost to rise out of it. He gave a nod and a smile as the Doctor and Tegan arrived at the coffin, as if they were old friends. Around its sides Tegan could see rows of intricate hieroglyphics, centuries old, blackened and beginning to fade. The coffin itself was shaped like a child's rough outline of a broad human form, arms pressed to the sides of the body, feet together.

The lid had been removed from the sarcophagus. Tegan stood at the foot of the case as she looked inside. Her head was whirling – she was not sure quite what was going on or why they were there. Some part of her mind was aware that the Doctor and Macready were shaking hands across the sarcophagus, across the mummified body lying inside. Another part of her brain was beginning to realise that the Doctor was intended to perform the unwrapping, to remove the bandages from the body that had lain undisturbed inside the coffin for millennia.

'How old, do you think?' the Doctor asked as he and Macready surveyed the bandaged form inside.

'Oh, I agree with you, Doctor.' Macready's voice was thin and reedy. His glasses caught the flickering firelight as he surveyed the ancient form. 'Four thousand years at least.' He drew a pale hand up the length of the body. 'The sarcophagus is, as you rightly surmised, of the Middle Kingdom. And the bandages themselves would seem to date from the same period.' He peered closely at one of the bulges wrapped close into the side of the body. 'Notice how the bandage is rotting over this arm, Doctor.' The Doctor and Tegan both craned forward to see.

'This side too,' the Doctor observed.

'Indeed.' Macready nodded slowly. The crowd was leaning forward too now. Too polite to press closer, but eager to hear and see the deliberations. 'You will also notice,' Macready continued, 'that the legs are not so closely bound as one might expect.' He poked a thin finger as the wrappings. They gave slightly at his touch.

'You think they were loosened after burial?' the Doctor asked slowly.

Again Macready nodded. 'Unusual, I know. But possible. One does hear rumours that this happened, though this would be the first case documented so thoroughly.'

'What?' Tegan asked. 'What are you saying? That someone loosened the bandages – someone tried to unwrap the mummy?'

The Doctor took a step towards Tegan. He seemed unsure whether to put his hand on her shoulder, and eventually settled for resting it on the lip of the coffin. 'Professor Macready is suggesting, and I think he is correct, that this poor unfortunate was bandaged up and then buried while still alive.'

'That's horrible.' Tegan wanted to turn away, but instead she leant closer and looked into the bandaged face. It seemed so calm now, just decaying stained cloth. She tried to imagine the figure writhing and twisting, tried to imagine the heavy lid of the sarcophagus thumping down and entombing the still struggling form. Tried to imagine the darkness and the terror. 'Four thousand years ago,' she murmured as the Doctor reached into the coffin.

With Macready's help, the Doctor managed to tease free a corner of bandage with a pair of tweezers that he had produced from somewhere. He held the edge of material for a moment, looking round the faces of the assembled crowd. Kenilworth nodded to him, and the Doctor tugged gently.

The bandage pulled free and began to unravel like an old sweater. As Tegan watched in horrified amazement, the cloth fell away from the mummy's head. She watched in fascination, ready to look quickly away when the full horror of the face was revealed. She could imagine it already, the smell of the rotting bandages evoking half-remembered images of mummified faces from forgotten textbooks and childhood museum trips. Four thousand years.

But as the flesh beneath the bandages glimpsed into view, it did not seem to have the pitted grey pallor of decay. Instead it looked smooth and white.

'Good grief,' Tegan heard Macready mutter as a mass of brown hair untangled from the wrappings. 'Is this why you wouldn't let us examine her until now?'

'Oh no,' the Doctor breathed, a tell-tale hand gripping the side of the sarcophagus.

Tegan said nothing. From the end of the coffin she could see clearly the whole of the mummy. She could see the four-thousand-year-old wrappings as they clung loosely to the bandaged form. She could see the tattered ends of the cloth pulled from the mummy's head. She could taste the stench of decomposition and decay rising from the corpse's ancient shroud and she could feel the weight in her stomach lifting and rising in her throat as she looked at the face of the mummy.

The face was perfectly preserved. The eyes were shut, the mouth closed. The hair was a tangled mess from the millennia it had spent woven into the bandages. And now that she could see the face, Tegan could recognise the shape of the rest of the body, outlined by the sarcophagus and by the rotting cloth. The figure in the coffin, dead for over four thousand years, was Nyssa.

The Legend of Osiris

When Osiris the king returned victorious from the campaign, his brother Seth feigned friendship. Together with Nephthys, his sister-wife, Seth invited Osiris to a great banquet to celebrate his safe return.

Isis, the wife and sister of Osiris, and the sister of Nephthys and Seth, begged her husband not to attend, fearing some treacherous intent. But Osiris was in good humour, magnanimous in victory. He spoke to Isis and together they agreed to go to the palace of Seth.

Seth had organised a great feast. There were grapes and figs, calves' heads, the forelegs of oxen and hearts of cows. There were geese and ducks. The wine flowed freely and all the royalty and dignitaries of Egypt were in attendance.

Osiris was the guest of honour, made welcome by his brother Seth. He was seated at the head of the table, as befitted his position. And his brother Seth and his sisters Isis and Nephthys made merry with him.

Then, when the feast was ended and the wine was almost gone, Seth had a great sarcophagus brought into the banqueting hall. It was traced in gold and inlaid with lapis lazuli. The casket was the best workmanship of the greatest craftsmen in all the Kingdoms of Egypt. And Osiris asked his brother for whom such a rich gift could be intended.

Seth let it be known that the sarcophagus was a prize – the greatest prize in history. And the prize would be won by the man who best fitted the sarcophagus, that it should bear him in glory into the afterlife.

So the nobility of Egypt each tried the casket for size, eager to win so great a gift from the brother of the king. But they were each by turns too short, or too tall, too fat or too thin. And it seemed that none of the guests could win so great a prize.

Then Nephthys urged her brother Osiris to try the casket himself. Osiris at first declined, his wife Isis fearing some entrapment. But Seth laughed at his brother's apprehension, and Osiris agreed to try the test.

So Osiris lowered himself into the casket, laughing with his brother Seth. It fitted Osiris as if it had been made for him. And so it had.

When Osiris was lying in the casket, Seth slammed shut the lid and, still laughing, he sealed it. Then he called his guards, and had the coffin hurled into the Nile.

As the coffin floated into the night, Seth's laughter mingled with the grief of Isis. And the tears of Isis dripped into the river and flowed after the entombed body of her brother and husband Osiris. And Nephthys saw her sister's grief, and she found it good.

(Translated by Tobias St John,
from the inscriptions of the tomb of An'anka)

CHAPTER
TWO

The water was clear, sunlight diffused through it like lemon juice. The liquid was warm and viscous. Tegan swam with increasing difficulty, her movements slowing as she struggled towards a surface that was not there. She had lost all sense of direction, and the light source had turned out to be the coral-covered expanse of the ocean floor. She twisted and turned, lost in the killing colour of the reef, her lungs bursting under the pressure, her eyes glazing. Then, as the strength slipped from her like the stream of bubbles rising from her mouth, she felt herself drifting, floating.

As she sat hunched on the edge of a heavy leather armchair in front of the fire, Tegan relived the swelling terror of an afternoon swimming on the reef. She clutched a glass of brandy she could not taste, staring at the flickering of a fire she did not see. She remembered the raw panic which welled up in her stomach and slowly permeated her whole being as she realised she had lost all sense of direction. She began to swallow water and to splutter her life away. She was barely aware of the Doctor and Kenilworth behind her as they examined the body of Nyssa, half heard their whispered discussions. But she knew she was sinking and that the surface was receding from her. This time she would not suddenly break free into the cool breeze of the Australian afternoon and gasp in retching lungfuls of air.

It had been difficult to cope with Adric's death. But even that had been so much easier. She had not actually seen him, had not actually looked into his dead face and seen the calm silent form which life had deserted. She had not begun to imagine the horror of his last desperate moments of existence, had not re-enacted them in her mind and relived them in her imagination. In a sense, Adric's death had been remote, reported, something written in a book or seen in a film. It was a death defined more by his subsequent absence than by the event itself.

But this was different. This was the mind-numbing loss of a friend brought home with unmitigated immediacy. When Adric had died, it had been a sudden shock. And Nyssa and Tegan had been able to help each other to cope with the loss, had been able to comfort each other in their grief, had shared emotions which the Doctor seemed unwilling or unable to risk.

Now Tegan was alone, drowning in her grief. She sat before the fire, unable to bring herself to look at the coffin or the body of her friend behind her. She clutched the lead crystal of the brandy tumbler, feeling the gut-wrenching emptiness of the loss which she had refused to imagine the whole time that Nyssa was missing. She wondered how long the Doctor had suspected the worst; wondered if he had somehow known; wondered why he seemed not to care.

Then the Doctor was there, kneeling beside her, folding his hands round hers as they clutched the warm glass. She could see for the first time the depths of emotion and the years of hurting in his eyes as he looked at her. She could see that he too felt the pain and the loss, even if he could not show it in the same way as she could. She knew that it would be best for him if he could give expression to his grief and voice to his pain and set it free.

'Oh Tegan,' the Doctor said. His voice was barely more than a whisper, flickering in time with the pale flames of the fire glinting off the cut facets of the glass she held so tightly in her fragile hands. As he held her, Tegan released her first painful sob. Her whole body convulsed with each heaving choke. She lowered her head till it rested on the Doctor's shoulder, and cried.

'Why?' she managed to gasp between her tears. 'Why Nyssa?'

He shook his head. 'I don't know, Tegan. I wish I did.' The Doctor turned and looked over Tegan's shoulder, back towards the sarcophagus still resting unmoved in the corner of the now deserted drawing room. 'It's strange,' he muttered. 'So long, and yet so perfectly preserved.' He shook his head slowly, still holding Tegan's hands around the glass. 'It's almost as if…' His voice tailed off, and he looked from the coffin to Tegan, then back again.

'I wonder,' the Doctor said, leaping to his feet. He looked back down at Tegan, brow creased in thought for a moment. Then his expression suddenly brightened. 'May I?' he reached down and took the glass from her hands. Tegan thought for a second he was about to help her to her feet. But instead, he drained the brandy in a single swallow, smacking his lips together appreciatively. Then he handed her back the empty glass and dashed across the room to where Kenilworth was still standing silently by the casket.

The Doctor reached inside the coffin. 'Will you time me, Lord Kenilworth?' he asked. 'I'm going to feel her neck for a pulse again.'

'If you wish, Doctor.' Kenilworth pulled a gold watch from his waistcoat pocket and flipped open the front cover. 'But there was nothing earlier.'

'Four thousand years is a very long time. An induced metabolic coma would explain the body's preservation, and it would have to be extremely deep to be sustained for that length of time.'

'You mean – she might not be dead?' Tegan put her empty glass down on the low mahogany table beside her chair and stood up. 'Nyssa's alive?' she asked.

The Doctor was staring into the casket. 'It's possible,' he said. 'We did feel for a pulse just now, but only for few seconds – perhaps thirty. In a coma this deep, there might be a pulse only every few minutes.' He paused, face creasing into a frown as if he was willing Nyssa's heart to beat. 'It is possible,' he repeated. 'Just possible.'

The bed was hard, made of some sort of rough wood. In fact it was more like a bench than a bed. The smell of fish was everywhere, which might have given Nyssa a clue that she was somewhere very close to Billingsgate. Except that she was unconscious. And she had never heard of Billingsgate.

She drifted into and out of awareness, her mind hovering between blackness and a misty haze. Sounds wafted through the gloom as she floated nearer to the surface of thought, mixing with the smell of fish, insinuating their way into Nyssa's mind. She heard rather than listened, absorbed the noises as she breathed in the smells.

'She was found at the appointed place. There at the appointed hour. She is the one.' The voice was refined, cultured but with a guttural accent which caught the vowels at the back of the throat.

But the voice which answered rasped as if it was forced through broken glass: 'You will send her back?'

'As it is written. As I remember it happening. I have seen her, and she is the one.'

A pause. Then the gravelled voice scraped again in the darkness: 'Then the time is near. After all the millennia, a mere century and then…'

The blackness drifted in again. The mists clouded Nyssa's thought and fogged her hearing. The sounds drifted away again into the distance. A few phrases, odd words found their way through the night.

'The journey … the alignment will be right tonight, the stars are set … power is building …'

'The watchers report the museum is clear … we must return at once …'

Dinner was a rather muted affair. Usually when Lord Kenilworth was recently returned from an expedition, he and his wife would talk animatedly about what had happened variously in Cairo and London over the past few months. The previous night had followed this pattern, broken only by anticipation of the unwrapping, and by Kenilworth's strange assumptions about what Atkins had been doing in his absence.

But tonight Atkins poured a little wine into his Lordship's glass, and listened to the silence. He had not attempted to understand why Lord Kenilworth supposed that he had accompanied him on his expedition. He must have known otherwise. And even if he did not, Lady Kenilworth was as insistent as Atkins was that Atkins had not stirred from London in the past four months. The conversation had been ended by Lady Kenilworth's suggestion that they talk about the impending unwrapping, and Kenilworth's half-heard mutterings that the Doctor had said there would be some confusion over events.

As Atkins removed the dinner plates and motioned for Beryl the maid to supply pudding bowls, he reflected that the previous night had been crystal clear by comparison. After the subdued silence of the soup and the quiet politeness of the entrée, conversation had risen to new levels. And confusion with it.

'Four thousand years, and you say she's just asleep?' Kenilworth shook his head and reached for his wine. 'Dashed queer business, if you ask me.'

'It's a metabolic coma,' the Doctor repeated patiently, hand palm-down over his wine glass as Atkins reached forward with the bottle.

Atkins moved on to Miss Jovanka. She watched glassy-eyed as he replenished her drink, and then all-but drained it in a single gulp. Atkins pretended not to notice, just as he feigned disinterest in the conversation. He had heard matters from the colour of the Queen's bedroom curtains to the future foreign policy of the Empire discussed in this room, and he took it all in his measured stride.

Tonight's conversation was more unsettling than others, though. Perhaps because of his involvement on the fringes of yesterday's related discussions, perhaps because of the evident distress of the Doctor and Miss Jovanka, perhaps because of the seemingly lifeless body lying in an ancient casket in the next room... Atkins felt that tonight he might permit himself to discuss some small aspects of the deliberations with Miss Warne when they went over the plans for the household for the following day.

'Dashed queer,' Kenilworth repeated. 'Don't you think, Atkins?' he added as the butler passed behind him.

'I'm sorry, sir? Oh, I really couldn't say.'

Kenilworth snorted. 'I must say, you've clammed back up since we returned. You know I value your views on these matters.'

This was news to Atkins, but he nodded politely and hazarded an opinion as he was asked. 'If the young lady is merely asleep, sir, then could we not wake her up?'

'Good thought, good thought.'

'Well, Doctor?' Miss Jovanka seemed to take her first

interest in the conversation. 'Can we help her?'

'Perhaps, Tegan. Perhaps.' The Doctor pushed his plate to one side, the food untouched. Atkins carefully removed it before the Doctor's elbow could sink into the spotted dick. 'It is possible, though rather tricky. I have to break into the coma in precisely the right way and that depends on how long Nyssa has been unconscious, where she was found, what condition the sarcophagus has been in, all manner of things. Even how she was transported here is important. Ideally the body should have been kept as level as possible.'

Kenilworth wiped his upper lip on a napkin. 'Well, of course it was,' he said through the double damask.

The Doctor stared at him. 'Could I ask why?'

Miss Jovanka, the Doctor and Lady Kenilworth waited for the reply. Atkins contrived to fill a glass close to his Lordship so as to hear properly.

Kenilworth eventually finished refolding his napkin. He seemed perplexed. 'The sarcophagus was kept level, even to the point of stringing it up in a hammock on the return voyage, because you insisted on it, Doctor.'

The Doctor gaped. 'I did?'

'Indeed. I'm not sure I follow what's going on here, Doctor. Your memory seems as fickle as Atkins's does. The other stuff you mentioned – location and condition of the body and all that – you know already.' He stood and motioned to Atkins. 'I think we'll take port in the drawing room.'

'But how?' Miss Jovanka called after Kenilworth as she got unsteadily to her feet. 'How does the Doctor know?'

Kenilworth turned in the doorway. 'Not you too, Tegan. He knows, as you do, because he was there when we found the tomb.'

The carriage clattered to a halt in the snowy night. Nyssa

had no way of knowing how long it was since she had last been here, but she recognised the impressive stone façade of the British Museum as she was dragged roughly from the carriage. She stumbled groggily down the damp wooden steps and slipped on the cobbled street. Her foot sank through the crisp crust of ice and skidded on the slush beneath. At once she was hauled to her feet.

'Gently, Yusuf, gently.'

Nyssa found herself looking into the tanned face of a short but broadly built man in an opera cape. It was a round face, made to appear rounder by the complete lack of hair. The face was broken into a grim smile which looked as though it was set in position. Nyssa got an impression of a depth of experience which belied the apparent age of the man. Then she saw that while his skin was smooth, it was also cobwebbed with hairline cracks, like an old oil painting of a young man. He continued to smile humourlessly at her, talking over her shoulder to the man holding her arms behind her back.

'The goddess did not choose this one so that you could bruise her fair skin.' He reached out a callused hand and ran a rough finger along Nyssa's cheek. She flinched, tried to back away. But the man behind her held her still. 'No, Yusuf, she has a better use for her than that.' He stared into her eyes for a while. Nyssa held his gaze for a moment, then looked away, sought refuge in the dirty white of the churned up snow at her feet.

'Does your father have other daughters?' The hand on Nyssa's cheek caressed her chin, gripping it suddenly and pulling it upwards so she was forced to look into the man's face again. It was not a rough gesture, rather it was almost gentle. 'It would be a shame if such beauty was unique.'

'My father's dead.' And for the first time Nyssa found she really believed that. He was not coming back; he had not just gone away; her father was dead. A short word that covered a condition that would last for ever. No funeral, no time for tears, just an emptiness so deep that it ached. 'Dead,' Nyssa repeated, and the word hung in the cold air with a blunt monosyllabic finality.

The man nodded slowly. 'I have heard it said that a father should not outlive his children,' he said quietly, so that only Nyssa heard him. Then his mouth twisted into a sudden smile and he snapped his fingers. The bald man was immediately handed a thick roll of cloth. The man gripped the hem of the cloth and let a long cloak unroll. He draped it over Nyssa's shoulders and pulled it tight around her. Then he stepped back to admire the result. 'There,' he said, 'that's better.'

'Who are you?' Nyssa was aware that her voice was shaking. She hoped the man thought it was from the cold rather than from fear. 'What do you want with me?'

'So many questions, so little patience.' The man started to turn away.

'Why have you brought me back here?'

The man paused, then swung back to face her. His face was still set in its half-smile. 'Oh Nyssa, Nyssa,' he shook his head.

She gasped. 'You know who I am?'

'Of course. I have always known. Or at least, it sometimes seems that way.' He gave a slight bow, barely more than an inclination of his bald head. 'I am Sadan Rassul, High Priest of Sutekh and Nephthys, as was my father before me. And I have been waiting for you.'

He turned away again, cape swirling in the breeze, and started to walk slowly towards the main doors of the museum. Yusuf pushed Nyssa after him, and she was aware of others following behind him. A single flake of snow landed on the smooth back of Rassul's head. It lingered for a second in the gaslight before melting slowly into a drop of water which ran down his hairless neck like a tear down a mourner's cheek.

As she stumbled her way after Rassul, Nyssa realised that the others were walking with the same measured tread as their leader. It reminded her for a moment of a ceremonial procession on Traken.

It reminded her of a funeral cortège.

The candles guttered and danced in the draught from the open door. The light flickered across the relics and played along the walls. It pooled on the floor, reflected off the high windows.

If she had not remembered the path they had taken to get back there, Nyssa might not have recognised the relic room. As she was guided in, it seemed to Nyssa that every available surface hosted a candelabra. Each of the candles kept its own tiny halo within reach, allowing it to toss and twist but never to break free of the fizzling wick. Shadows crept across the room, and then jumped back into the gloom as a flame edged towards them for a second before changing direction again. Trails of oily black smoke spiralled upwards towards the ceiling as if rising through murky water, desperate to reach the air.

The dark figures of her cloaked captors processed slowly through the room. A dark cat watched their progress with statue eyes; the dead faces painted on the sarcophagi followed their journey to the far end of the long room. Nyssa let herself be carried with the tide. She could smell the acrid candle fumes, could taste the caustic smoke in the back of her dry mouth. She tried not to cough and the effort brought tears to her eyes. Tears that she had been trying to keep inside.

As they neared the end of the room, Nyssa could smell something else. There was a perfumed, sweet, almost sticky smell. Incense and flowers, honey and myrrh. She looked round, trying to locate the source, and out of the corner of an eye caught sight of the flicker-lit blue of the TARDIS. She gasped, taking in a deep mouthful of the sticky sweetness. She almost laughed for joy, but the sound stuck in her throat as she was pushed forward, away from the hope of escape.

Her vision was blurring, hazing over as a firm hand on her shoulder drew Nyssa to a stop. She blinked back the smoky tears and saw that she was standing in front of the sarcophagus Tegan had been examining. A lifetime ago. The dark, impassive, carved face stared back at her. The arms were crossed over the chest, each hand holding a staff. Almost unconsciously Nyssa copied the gesture, bringing her cloak tighter about her. A phrase of Tegan's lingered in the back of her memory: 'Cross my heart.'

Beside the sarcophagus stood tall incense burners, one each side. Through the increasing muzziness of the sweet haze, Nyssa registered that the sticky smell was dripping from the smoking contents of the bowls of the burners. She swayed on her feet, feeling the weight of her body rock on the backs of her heels for a second.

Rassul stepped in front of Nyssa. He bowed low to the sarcophagus, then turned to face her. With a swift movement he shrugged off his cape. Beneath it his chest was bare, adorned only with a gold necklace which hung in heavy strands across his torso. Below it he wore what looked like an ornate skirt.

Nyssa swayed again, as if in the breeze, and noted with a light-headed giggle that he wore sandals on his feet. The leather twisted into an oval over his toes. The shape mirrored the curled end of the stave the sarcophagus figure held.

The other figures clustered round behind Nyssa, attention fixed on Rassul. When he spoke, his voice had taken on a deep, plangent tone that echoed round the room, glancing off caskets and cutting a path through the smoke and incense.

'The time is now.' He raised his arms above his head. 'We bring the chosen one to the gateway at the appointed time. It is as it was written; as I remember it to have been.' Rassul turned back to the sarcophagus, crossing his arms across his chest, imitating the carved figure. 'I make the sign of the eye, and send you a new receptacle. The chosen one.'

Somewhere deep within the sarcophagus a hum of energy was building. A blue light flickered with the candles across the face of the casket.

'From across the ages, we provide your continuing imprisonment, and your ultimate release. When Orion is aligned, when power is rife, then it is said that you will live again.'

The noise was rising like a major chord on a large organ. The blue light strobed into a swirling vortex of colour, and the front of the sarcophagus dissolved into a whirl of light bleeding into its dark outline.

'The waiting is almost over. I begin the final act.' Rassul's laugh echoed over the chord.

Nyssa felt herself propelled towards the vortex. She struggled for a moment, but then realised that nobody was holding her, nobody was pushing her. But in the second she looked behind, she saw a figure through the incense-mist, a figure standing behind Rassul's followers. Watching. The figure stepped back into the shadows as Nyssa turned away again. But she had caught a glimpse of him, had seen the shadow of his ruined face. The image that her retina retained, however, was not the pallid glow of the moonlight on the sunken, blackened features of his face. It was the snow clinging to his matted hair and his heavy cloak. The snow which seemed to have crystallised into a layer of ice, when it should have melted in the heat from his body.

Nyssa was being drawn closer, into the kaleidoscope of light. She clasped her hands tightly over her shoulders as the blackness closed around her and Rassul's laughter faded into the hazy distance.

'Cross my heart,' Tegan's voice murmured in Nyssa's ear as she fell from consciousness and into the casket. 'Cross my heart, and hope to die.'

'I'm sorry, Lord Kenilworth, but I'm going to have to ask you to trust me.' The Doctor clenched and unclenched his hands as he spoke.

But Kenilworth snorted at his exasperation. 'Well, wouldn't be the first time, would it?' He drew on his cigar and let out a breath of smoke. It drifted across the drawing room, thinning and dissolving somewhere above the mantelpiece. 'Reckon you deserve that, though, after everything.'

'Yes, well,' the Doctor scratched his head, half stood up from where he was seated on the sofa, then sat down again. 'I'd rather we didn't discuss that in any detail, if you don't mind.'

'Why not?' Tegan was standing on the far side of the room, arms folded, staring down into the coffin. She looked up, and the Doctor had to twist in the sofa to see her properly. 'What's happening here, Doctor?' She held his gaze for several seconds. 'I want to know.'

'Well, if we're to help Nyssa, there are some things I need to know. But I'm wary of knowing too much.'

'Not much fear of that so far.'

'Tegan,' the Doctor chided.

'So what do you want to know, eh?' Kenilworth was examining his port. He took a sip and nodded appreciatively.

The Doctor picked up his own glass, stared at it for a moment, then put it carefully back on the table beside him.

'I must ask you to bear with me, Kenilworth. I'm going to ask you about things which you will tell me I already know. But please answer my questions about where and when the mummy was found as best you can. And please don't add any extra information, I only want a direct answer.'

Kenilworth shrugged. 'Fire away, old man.'

The Doctor turned back to Tegan. 'And I'd be grateful if you could curb your natural inquisitiveness for a while, Tegan.'

She stared at him. 'Doctor, Nyssa is in a coffin here, dying.' Her voice had dropped an octave. 'I want to know why. And I want to know how to save her.'

'So do I, Tegan. Believe me, so do I.' The Doctor heaved himself out of the sofa and crossed to her. He hesitated a moment, hand raised, then he patted her gently on the shoulder. 'But there are wider implications. There's great danger in knowing too much. We will help Nyssa – I think we already have. But we can't risk damaging the web of time.'

'Please, Doctor,' Tegan whispered. 'She's all I have left.' The Doctor blinked. 'Apart from you.'

'I'm doing what I can, Tegan.' He shook his head. 'If good old Blinovitch could see me now, he'd be turning in his urn.' The Doctor gave a short laugh.

Then he stuffed his hands into his trouser pockets and coughed, staring at the floor. 'Sorry,' he muttered, and turned away.

A stream of bright sunlight made Nyssa blink. It brought tears to her eyes, and she rubbed at them as she sat up. She found herself sitting up inside a box. Or rather a casket – it looked like the same sarcophagus she had fallen into in the British Museum, but without the lid.

She looked round the room. A large glassless window allowed the sun to shine directly into the stone-floored room.

A gold jug and goblets stood on a low wooden table by the door, and heavy tapestries hung across the walls. Two chairs stood angled towards the casket, which was raised on a dais. In one of the chairs sat a man.

Nyssa's first thought was that it was Rassul. He wore a similar necklace and kilt, and he was completely bald. But he was older, much older. Wrinkles creased his brow and the flesh on his chest sagged over a full belly. Behind him stood a young woman, her dark hair cut into straight lengths to her shoulders. She wore a skirt similar to the man's kilt, and an ornate halter top which looked as though it was made of gold and studded with semi-precious stones. The stones glinted in the sunlight.

'Welcome,' said the man. 'I am Amosis, priest of the goddess.'

'Goddess?' The sunlight seemed less intense now that her eyes had adjusted and Nyssa glanced back towards the window. Outside she could see the pointed silhouettes of two huge pyramids outlined against the horizon, the sun shining between them, hardening their edges.

'And this is Sitamun, handmaiden to the goddess.' Amosis gestured to the woman. She smiled nervously and stepped forward so she was level with the priest's chair.

'What goddess? What's going on? What is this place?' Nyssa was suddenly incredibly tired. She felt herself slumping back into the casket.

'Why, you are the goddess,' Amosis said quietly. 'Or at least, you will be.'

Nyssa felt the cold base of the casket hard against her back.

'I welcome you as the chosen one of the gods. The new Nephthys.'

THE VALLEY OF THE KINGS
2000 BC

The air was hot and close, sweat dripping from the stone walls of the passageway. Massud beckoned, waving the smoking torch to illuminate the way. The others stumbled after him, elation at their success so far tempered by trepidation about what lay ahead.

They had been digging for days. Or rather, for nights. Long nights, hidden from the daily observations of the priest-guardians of the tomb on the far side of the valley. The tunnel was low and narrow, in contrast to the high vaulted ceiling of the wide, sloping passageway they had intersected. Their goal, their calling, their goddess was in sight. So they stumbled onwards, oblivious to the heat and the humidity, not caring about the stale air or the darkness. They feared only the goddess, and failure.

The heavy doors were sealed with a crimson rope. It was tied tightly around the huge handles, knotted and dipped in wax. The decay of the ages clung to the cord, and it exploded in a cloud of dust and frayed fragments as Massud cut through it with his knife. With a backward glance to his comrades – sufficient to gain their confidence and approval, but not enough to be infected by their anxiety and fear – he pushed against the heavy double doors. And with a creak of ancient protest, they swung slowly open.

The Eye of Horus watched unblinking, disapproving, from where it was inlaid in the passage floor. A faint glow suffused the air around the ornate pupil, a reflection perhaps of the torches above it as they clustered in the doorway. Then Massud stepped tentatively over the threshold. And the eye at his feet flashed brilliant red.

The wind ripped through the passage like a typhoon. Massud was the only one of them inside the doorway, and yet the hurricane that erupted from inside seemed to sweep past him. He staggered forwards in the eye of the gale, while his comrades were blown against the passage walls. He was oblivious to their fate as he battled his way onwards into the tomb.

Behind him, Massud's brother Ahmed crashed into one of the open doors. Blood streamed from his face as he collapsed back onto the floor and tumbled away. Thutmos the camel trader clawed at the cracks between the stone slabs on the floor, his fingers tearing and the skin rippling on his cheeks. He clung on for several seconds, then bounced down the corridor like a Shabti doll hurled from the tomb doorway.

Within the tomb, Massud struggled onwards. He was leaning into the wind, his loose clothing blown back against his body as he inched forwards. As he reached the sarcophagus, he lost his footing and crashed to the floor. His knee crunched on the flagstones and he screamed in pain. But he dragged himself onwards. So close now, so close.

In front of him he could see the relics placed on low shelves round the head of the casket. He could see the canopic jar, its stopper carved in the shape of the head of Anubis the jackal. The god's ceramic eyes watched his progress unblinking. Massud's hand reached out towards the jar, and the red glow from the passageway outside seemed to grow stronger even as the screams of his friends died away.

With a final effort, Massud hurled himself forward. His fingertips connected with the stopper, and the jar tottered for a long second. The wind dropped, as if holding its breath with Massud, while the jar rolled on its base and rocked back again. It teetered on the rim, then slipped from the low shelf into space.

The wind returned, stronger than ever. Massud was swept against the wall of the tomb, the back of his head smashing against the carved stone and splitting open like a rotten egg.

The last thing Massud saw before he died was the canopic jar rolling towards him across the floor of the tomb. It was still intact, but a dark crack ran the length of it. Perhaps it was enough, enough for him to pass through the Hall of the Two Truths and for the goddess to welcome him to the afterlife.

The jar rolled itself to a halt against Massud's face. The glazed eyes of Anubis stared into those of the grave-robber, and the wind died away. The jar rocked slightly in a growing, viscous pool of blood. And darkness returned.

Rassul woke suddenly. His head felt like it was splitting. And through the crack in his mind he could feel something forcing its way in. Was it guilt? Anger? He did not need to ask himself what he should feel guilt or anger about. And that acceptance of the truth was itself unusual.

He rose stiffly from his wooden bed and went to the window. He was alone of course. He had not shared his bed since his only wife had died in childbirth. So long ago now, so alone for so long. Outside, the pyramids stood stark against the night sky. A jackal called out somewhere in the distance, a long lonely wail.

As he turned to go back to bed, he saw a figure standing in the shadows by the door. He could not see who it was, but the servants all knew better than to disturb him without good cause.

Before Rassul could say anything, the figure spoke. Its voice was cracked like an old flute playing in the wind. 'The tomb was broken into tonight.'

'Robbed?' Rassul did not need to ask which tomb. Only one mattered – the tomb he lived to protect.

'No,' the figure said. 'The robbers did not complete their task.'

'The gods be thanked.'

'But they have started something. Something that must be finished.'

'What do you mean?' Rassul was worried now. For a second he saw the hourglass, sand dripping from the upper bowl as it sifted through the seconds of eternity. Why had none of the priests alerted him to the events if the robbers had been disturbed? 'Who are you and how do you know this?' he demanded.

The figure rattled a laugh. 'A jar was cracked. The priests are discovering it even now, binding it with hessian and praying for guidance. They will come to you soon for advice. You are the one chosen to watch over the tomb, the one granted the lonely years of vigil. They fear for their lives, and for the life of Egypt.'

'Cracked.' Rassul could taste the same fear, he knew how the priests would be feeling. 'But not broken?'

'No,' the voice sounded almost sad. 'But the crack is enough. The process begins. Your own feelings are proof enough of the power of the goddess.'

'My feelings?' Rassul stepped back a pace. The guilt and anger had made him shout, had confessed the truth of what the man said.

'Your feelings,' the voice repeated. 'And my presence.'

A sudden thought occurred to Rassul. 'Wait, how did they get past the test of the Shabti?'

The figure's laugh was a dry, rasping death rattle. 'We were told the answer before we entered the tomb.'

'You? Who by? Only one person knows the secret of the riddle.'

'Exactly. One who serves the goddess, and yet knows it not. One who will be her servant in the empty years ahead now that the chain of events is started, now that the inevitable is set on its course.'

The crack in Rassul's head seemed to split wide open. He could see clearly for the first time, knew his destiny. And he remembered meeting the man in the marketplace, recalled slipping him the papyrus on which he had scrawled the answer. Sadan Rassul, the only living man to know the secret of the riddle, but until now he had not known his own purpose.

The figure's croaking voice broke into his realisation. 'You know what you must do. You have always known. And now is the time.'

'A replacement vessel,' Rassul murmured. But he knew that they must find another form of container, the canopic jar could not be repaired or imitated. They would have to pray that the gods again provided the means to their ends.

'Yes,' the figure in the shadows hissed. 'You see, already the spirit of the goddess is within you. You will be a good servant to her in the long lonely ages ahead.' The figure reached out its hand towards Rassul. It was holding something, gesturing for him to take it.

'Me?' Rassul was aghast. 'But why me? Why not you?' Yet even as he questioned how he would come to serve the one he was sworn to keep in thrall, he knew that the shadowy figure spoke the truth. And he took the hourglass the figure was holding out to him, the sands spiralling down into the lower bowl. He had known already what he had to do, had known since the tomb was sealed and he had started the hourglass sands on their courses. It was the only way he would ever –

The figure broke into his thoughts again: 'I am not fit for the years that lie ahead, for the waiting and the planning.' The final words were almost a gasp as the figure collapsed: 'I am dead already.' It fell forwards into the room, making no attempt to save itself or break the fall. The body landed with a dull thud at Rassul's feet.

Outside he could hear the commotion as the messenger from the priests hammered on the door and demanded to be let in. He could hear the servants moving around downstairs, and the bolts being drawn.

And at his feet, sudden in a shaft of moonlight, he could see the dark mass of congealed blood. It caked the back of the head of what had once been a man. The skull was smashed inwards, split open like a rotten egg.

CHAPTER
THREE

The enamel of Tegan's teeth was hard against her knuckles. She and Kenilworth stood at the end of the sarcophagus. In front of them, Nyssa's bandaged body lay silent and still.

The Doctor had finished unwrapping Nyssa's head, and was leaning into the casket. His right hand was against her cheek, her hair spread dry and dusty over his fingers. With his other hand he was pinching the bridge of his nose, head back and eyes tight shut in concentration.

Suddenly the Doctor moved. He took a deep, rasping breath, opened his eyes, and stretched. Then he yawned, blinked, and smiled broadly at Tegan.

'That should do it,' he said with evident satisfaction.

'She's going to be OK?'

The Doctor nodded. 'Yes. A bit tired when she eventually wakes, but otherwise fine.' He laughed and made his way along the casket, clapping Tegan on the shoulder as soon as he was within reach. 'Ironic really, four thousand years asleep and she'll be tired.' He walked over to the fire and held out his hands to warm them.

Kenilworth and Tegan laughed with him.

'Well, that's that then, eh, Doctor? Glad it's finally over, I must say.'

'I'll stay with her till she wakes,' Tegan said quietly.

The Doctor turned back from the fire. 'Ah,' he said. 'Actually, there are a couple of things I should mention. I'm afraid it's not over. Not yet. And I don't think you'll want to wait here for Nyssa to wake up.'

'Doctor, I want to be with her when she comes round. She should see a friendly face.'

The Doctor drew a deep breath. 'I doubt it would actually be very friendly, Tegan.'

'What do you mean?'

The Doctor started a slow tour of the room. He picked up ornaments and ran his finger over dust-free surfaces, avoiding meeting Tegan's gaze as he spoke. 'Nyssa's been in a deep coma for a very, very long time. It's rather like a diver going down to the deepest depths. The body adjusts to the change in conditions. And the deeper you go, and the longer you stay there, the more slowly you have to return to the surface.'

'Pressure?' Kenilworth asked.

'Something like that, yes. Oxygen levels in the blood, pressure, whatever. In Nyssa's case, her metabolic rate has been so slow for so long that it would be fatal to wake her too quickly. We have to raise the levels slowly. Very slowly, in fact.'

'So it will be a while before she wakes up?'

The Doctor nodded.

'How long?'

'Well, er, longer than you'd want to wait here, I think, Tegan. I can't say exactly but I've aimed for a good round figure. Should be accurate within a minute or two.'

'Twenty-four hours?'

The Doctor sucked in his cheeks and examined the frame of a particularly interesting portrait.

'A week, more like,' Kenilworth suggested. 'As the Doctor says, it'll be a very slow process.'

'A week?' Tegan crossed to where the Doctor was now admiring the canvas. 'Doctor, do we really have to wait a whole week to see if Nyssa's all right?'

'Hmm?' He seemed to realise Tegan was talking to him only when she tugged at his sleeve. 'A week? Oh no. Nothing like.' He returned his attention to the picture. 'More like a century,' he muttered. 'Just look at the brushwork on that.'

Tegan had never liked brandy, but she seemed to be drinking a lot of it recently. She gulped down the glassful that Atkins brought her. She was sitting on an upright chair beside the sofa where Kenilworth and the Doctor were comparing notes on the quality of the port. Her hands were shaking and she was barely aware of their conversation.

'Doctor,' Kenilworth said at length, his tone becoming more serious, 'will it really take a hundred years for your friend to awaken?'

The Doctor nodded. He drained the last of his port and held the glass up so that the firelight was caught dancing in its facets. 'Could I ask you a favour?'

'Of course.'

'It's a big favour,' he warned.

Kenilworth shrugged. 'Doctor, I owe you my life several times over. Whatever it is, it's not a big favour for you to ask.'

'I don't want to know – no details, please.'

'And the favour?'

The Doctor stood and placed his empty glass on the mantel shelf. 'Look after our friend until she wakes.'

'I don't think I'll be here when she wakes, Doctor. I don't think any of us will.'

'Maybe not,' the Doctor said hesitantly, shooting Tegan a warning look. 'But perhaps you could make arrangements of some sort? She must be kept level, and undisturbed.'

Kenilworth thought for a while, sipping at his port. Eventually he nodded. 'There is a cellar we don't use. I'll have it cleared out and she can rest down there. We'll block off the access except for a trap door or something. I'll arrange for the responsibility for her safety to be passed on to someone I can trust when, well – when the time comes.'

'Thank you.' The Doctor smiled. 'Now, I'd better wrap Nyssa's head again. The bandages are impregnated with various chemicals which help preserve the tissue over the years. She'd never forgive me if she woke up with wrinkles.' He grinned as Tegan managed a half-smile.

When he had finished, the Doctor sat down beside Kenilworth again. 'There is just one other small thing,' he said, patting his pockets.

'Oh?'

The Doctor took a card from his pocket. It was the printed invitation to the unwrapping. He held it up so that both Kenilworth and Tegan had a good view of it. Then he ripped it in half, taking care to make the edge ragged and uneven. He handed one half to Kenilworth.

'A hundred years from now,' the Doctor said, 'someone will come for the body, will come to see Nyssa when she wakes.'

Tegan looked up from her empty brandy glass.

Kenilworth nodded. 'I understand,' he said. 'And to identify themselves…'

The Doctor nodded. 'They will bring the matching half of the invitation.'

Sitamun had been a handmaiden in the temple of Nephthys since she was a child. Her father had been a priest of the temple, and his father before him. Sitamun's elder brother was also a priest, and his son would doubtless follow the same calling. But Sitamun was blessed above them all, for she was handmaiden to the returned goddess herself. And whatever might be written or said about the goddess Nephthys, this incarnation seemed kind and gentle.

The scribe followed Sitamun into the temple chamber. Together they kissed the floor in front of the goddess.

'I wish you wouldn't do that,' the goddess said again. She leant forward on her throne and waved them away. The chair was wooden, with high arms and a low back. The seat and back of the chair were painted crimson, the rest was leafed in gold.

Sitamun smiled and bowed. She knew she was being tested. Not to show due honour would be to invite the legendary wrath of the goddess.

The goddess was in a quiet mood. She did not speak of the strange things she had mentioned when she first appeared to them, and she seemed less distracted and annoyed than previously. Perhaps she was coming to terms with her earthly manifestation.

Sitamun stood to the side while the scribe set up his wooden palette.

'Who is this?'

Sitamun bowed low. 'He is a junior draughtsman, my goddess.'

'And what is he doing?'

'He is here to make a drawing of you.'

The draughtsman smiled nervously and held up the red ochre, reed brush and plaster sketchpad. 'I am merely to capture the outline of the goddess,' he bowed.

'Why?'

'Why? I'm sorry, I do not understand.'

The goddess leant back heavily in her chair and sighed. 'Why?' she repeated. 'What for?'

'So that the senior draughtsman can correct it with his black ink, and the painters may paint it.'

The goddess said nothing for a while. The draughtsman began to draw his grid on the pad. Sitamun hoped that the answer had satisfied the goddess.

'Then what? What is the painting for?'

The goddess seemed to be making an effort to keep her voice low and calm. Concentrating on trying to understand the question and the mood of the goddess, Sitamun answered without thinking. As soon as she had started to speak, she remembered the warning of the high priest, reiterated by the priest Amosis. But it was too late, the words were out.

'For the lid of your sarcophagus, my goddess,' she said. 'For your funeral and burial tomorrow.'

Atkins was discussing the arrangements for the next day with Miss Warne when the bell rang. They had gone over the menus for the day, and had exchanged views on the performance and demeanour of the new scullery maid. Atkins enjoyed their talks at the end of each day, though of course he could never tell Miss Warne that. The very suggestion that he might derive some satisfaction other than purely professional from such discussions was out of the question, but he did not wish to burden Miss Warne with that possibility.

The flag showed that it was the bell pull in the drawing room. 'If you will excuse me, Miss Warne,' Atkins said as he rose, 'I shall just attend to his Lordship.'

'I should have thought he had already retired for the night,' Miss Warne said.

Atkins felt a little discomforted to sense her gaze on him as he crossed to the door. He turned back, ignoring the brief smile Miss Warne flashed him, and deliberately failed again to notice how perfectly her dark hair framed her oval face. If he were ever to compliment her, it would be on her professionalism or perhaps her choice of correct attire rather than any cosmetic appearance. But aware that perhaps his eyes had lingered too long on the pale skin and the dark eyes, he decided a mild rebuke was more in order. 'It is not for us to question the habits of his Lordship, or to try to predict his timetable,' Atkins said sternly. Then he turned and walked stiffly and quickly from the room. If he knew that Miss Warne was watching him as he traversed the corridor, his deliberate stride did not indicate it.

'Ah, Atkins,' Lord Kenilworth greeted his butler as he entered the drawing room. Kenilworth was standing in front of the dying fire, staring into the last embers as they glowed weakly in the grate.

'Sir?'

'Deuced annoying.' Kenilworth turned to face Atkins. 'The Doctor and Miss Tegan have just left. On their way back to the British Museum for whatever reason.'

'Indeed, sir.'

'Fact is, what with one thing and another, all those instructions and so forth…' Kenilworth's voice trailed off as he looked across the room at the open sarcophagus.

'Instructions, sir?'

'Hmm? Oh yes, lots of them. We'll sort it out in the morning, I think. Anyway, meantime I forgot to ask the Doctor whether we should replace the lid on the sarcophagus. He didn't say, but you never know.'

Atkins waited patiently for his master to elaborate. He had little idea what Lord Kenilworth was talking about, but it was not his place to ask. His Lordship always knew best.

'Well, anyway, the lid's at the British Museum in any case. Along with all the other relics we donated to poor old Russell Evans for his collection there. So, perhaps you could catch up with the Doctor, or even meet him there, and ask?'

'Of course, sir.' Atkins wondered if it was still snowing

outside. He would need a coat for sure, like last night.

'Sorry to send you out in this beastly cold again tonight. But, you know, might be important.'

'No problem at all, sir.' Perhaps Miss Warne would oblige by waiting up and organising some hot soup for when he returned. It had been most welcome the previous night. He really ought to have thanked her, he supposed. But at the time it seemed quite natural that she should provide some warm sustenance.

'Good man,' Kenilworth said.

Atkins took this as a dismissal, and saw himself out.

As she slowly ascended the staircase, in marked contrast to their race down it the previous night, Tegan reflected that at last they were doing something. That said, she was not entirely sure what it was. Partly this was because of the Doctor's inability to answer straight questions with a straight answer, and partly it was because her mind was still dulled by shock and the after-effects of the brandy. But for the first time since Nyssa had disappeared, Tegan felt the Doctor was displaying some sense of purpose and deliberation rather than rushing from one enigma to another.

Everything seemed to be going well. The Doctor was in a good mood, whistling his way through the light sprinkling of snow. The side door to the museum was, by some miracle, unlocked, and nobody challenged them as they made their way back up to the Egyptian Room.

But then they opened the door and went in.

The room glowed. Light flickered and spilled out onto the stairway as soon as the Doctor opened the door. They stepped hesitantly over the threshold and looked around.

Every spare surface seemed to have a candle set upon it. Most had burned a good way down, some had burned themselves out into pools of congealed smouldering wax. The air hung with the smoke and the smell.

'Someone's been busy,' the Doctor commented quietly as he made his way further into the room.

Tegan followed. 'I'll say. What's going on?'

The Doctor shrugged. 'Wish I knew.' He grinned at her through the smoky air. 'Perhaps one of the mummies has a birthday and they thought they'd celebrate.'

'Yeah,' said Tegan, 'sure. They'll be doing the "Monster Mash" next.'

The Doctor rocked back on his heels and exhaled loudly. 'I hope not,' he said. Then he spun round and headed off down the room. 'Still, it'll have to keep,' he called back as he went.

Tegan started to speak, then changed her mind. She shook her head and set off after him. 'Looks like a cheap remake of *Tales from the Crypt*,' she muttered, scowling at a sarcophagus lid standing upright against the wall as she passed.

Then she stopped, in mid stride, turned and went back. She peered through the smoke-haze at the face on the sarcophagus lid. Then she shook her head again, blinked several times, and went closer. 'Look at this, Doctor,' she called.

'Tegan, Tegan – what is it now?' the Doctor asked as he spun round and headed back towards her.

'Look, Doctor. Look at the face.'

'It's just a sarcophagus,' the Doctor said, not bothering to look. 'They painted representations of the, what shall we say – owners.' He followed Tegan's gaze and peered at the face painted on the lid. 'Some of the paintings were actually quite good,' he said slowly. Then he went closer and looked again. Finally he reached out and flicked a grubby handkerchief over the cracked paintwork. 'Actually, it reminds me of someone,' he said, puzzled. 'If only I could remember who.'

He stared again at the female face, framed by curled brown hair. 'Unusual for her not to be wearing a straight wig.'

'Doctor,' said Tegan quietly, 'it's Nyssa.'

The Doctor spun round instantly. 'Where?' he demanded looking round the room.

'There,' Tegan pointed. 'The painting.'

The Doctor looked again. 'Do you know,' he said after a while, 'I think you're right. This must be the lid of Kenilworth's sarcophagus. I wonder how it got here.'

'You should know,' a deep voice said, 'Doctor.' It came from somewhere behind Tegan.

'I'm sorry?' The Doctor and Tegan both turned to see who had spoken. As if on cue, figures stepped out of the shadows all round the room.

They were cloaked and hooded, each holding a candle. The guttering flames threw sharp shadows across their faces, making them look to Tegan like characters escaped from a Munch painting.

'Sorry,' said the Doctor as he and Tegan backed away, 'we didn't mean to interrupt. Please just carry on with whatever you were doing.'

'We'll see ourselves out,' Tegan suggested.

But the leading figure shook his head beneath his hood. 'Oh no,' he said in his deep, accented voice. 'I think now that you are here, we can find some role for you to play in our humble proceedings. Don't you?'

He waved an arm, and dark figures leapt forward from either side, grabbing the Doctor and Tegan and dragging them into the centre of the room. Tegan struggled, kicking and trying to pull her arms free. But she was hampered by her own cloak and the restrictions of her Victorian dress. She could do little to prevent herself from being dragged across the room.

'At least they're taking us towards the TARDIS,' she hissed to the Doctor.

'I'm not sure that helps, actually,' the Doctor replied through gritted teeth. 'Careful with that elbow,' he warned one of his captors as he was wrenched away.

The shout came from the doorway, loud and clear, commanding and confident. 'Stop that, do you hear?' Another figure, tall and thin, stepped into the candlelight. 'These people are colleagues and friends of Lord Kenilworth, and you will answer to him if they are mistreated.'

'Indeed?' asked the leader of the cloaked figures.

'Yes, sir. Indeed.'

The leader laughed. 'The admirable Atkins. I think perhaps you had better join our revels.'

Before he had time to react, two more silhouettes stepped from the shadows by the door and dragged him over to join the Doctor and Tegan.

'Good plan,' Tegan said.

Atkins seemed a little flustered. 'What the devil – what do these people want with us, Doctor?'

'I'm not sure yet. But I'm afraid Tegan is right, you would have been better advised to make a run for it.'

By now the Doctor, Tegan and Atkins had been dragged to the far end of the room. They were facing the sarcophagus which Tegan had seen glow the previous night. Behind them the TARDIS stood stark, and unobtainable.

'How kind of you all to join us,' the leader of the assailants said. 'I feel I know you so well, that perhaps I should introduce myself.'

'Yes,' Tegan told him, 'perhaps you should.'

'I am Sadan Rassul, servant and high priest.'

'Really?' asked the Doctor. 'Of whom?'

'Of the one true goddess. Despised and rejected by her

brother and her nephew, but her time is coming. Soon,' Rassul whispered, 'very soon now.'

'Well, I've nothing booked for the next few years,' the Doctor hazarded. 'I'm happy to wait around for an audience. How about you two?' he asked Tegan and Atkins.

'I fear Miss Warne will have some broth waiting,' Atkins said seriously. 'And of course his Lordship will wish to know that I conveyed his message to you.'

'Silence,' Rassul hissed. 'Your time is over.' He stepped closer to them and threw back the hood of his cloak. Beneath it he was completely bald, the candlelight reflecting off the top of his head almost like a halo. The skin of his face was smooth, but Tegan could see faint hairline cracks just visible below the surface, as if his head were made of porcelain and the cracks ran under the glaze. 'You know,' Rassul said, 'how Osiris was tricked by Seth and placed inside a casket which fitted him exactly?'

'No,' said Tegan.

'Yes,' said the Doctor, 'I do recall something of the sort.'
Atkins nodded.

Rassul ignored them all anyway. 'The casket was sealed and thrown into the river.' He paused and looked at his captives closely. 'A fitting fate for those who seek to deny the goddess her freedom, her life.'

'And what makes you think we'd do a thing like that, eh?'

'Don't be facetious, Doctor,' Rassul snapped angrily. 'I was there. I saw all that you did. But it will come to nothing now. The process is started, the goddess will live again.'

'You do take your religion very seriously, don't you?'

Rassul's answer was quiet, almost whispered. 'You don't know how seriously, Doctor. You just don't know.' He shook his head, almost sadly. Then he straightened up and snapped his fingers like a whip cracking.

Immediately Rassul's followers started herding their prisoners across the room. As they retreated, Tegan looked behind her and saw that they were being driven towards a group of several large sarcophagi leant against the wall. She felt a sudden tightness against the back of her legs, and with a crash the rope barrier fell over behind them.

Before long, their backs were pressed against a hard, cold wooden surface. In front of them, Rassul raised his arms high above his head. 'As the legend said,' he cried out, 'they shall be sealed forever in a fitting coffin and cast into the flowing depths.' He turned towards the darkest shadows in the corner of the room, as if to get some confirmation or assurance. And it seemed to Tegan that an even darker shape within the shadows nodded its approval.

Tegan could see the Doctor reaching out behind himself to try to keep his balance, felt the lid of the sarcophagus behind her move aside, and saw Atkins tumble backwards into the darkness. With a cry, she followed, the Doctor a moment after her. She could hear Rassul's laughter echo round the room outside as the door slammed shut on them.

The snow had stopped falling, but the fog was heavy. The torches held by Rassul's followers glowed eerily in the thick night as they made their way along the deserted streets.

It took eight of them to carry the heavy sarcophagus, holding it on their shoulders like pallbearers. They made their cumbersome way down towards the river, their path lit by the two lines of cloaked figures ahead of them. Rassul and another, darker figure followed behind.

When it reached the bridge, the procession slowed and halted. The bearers turned so that they held the sarcophagus out, over the parapet.

'So be it,' said Rassul, his voice all but lost in the fog. And the men carrying the casket let it drop into the river below.

Rassul and the other figure leant out over the edge. As they watched, the casket resurfaced, water sliding off its lid. Then it sank back into the river, almost disappearing from sight as it was swept downstream. It turned slowly as it was washed away, out of the torchlight.

'It is done,' breathed Rassul, although he did not sound as if it was a relief.

'I have just one more journey to make,' the figure beside him croaked huskily. It turned and, in the flickering torchlight, Rassul could see inside the hood the figure wore. 'But for you, it continues.'

Rassul nodded. 'But the end is approaching,' he said, unable to look away from the ruined remains of the figure's hooded face, trying not to inhale the stench of rotting flesh. 'Soon the goddess will live again.'

In the kitchen of Kenilworth House, Susan Warne stirred a pot of vegetable broth and wondered where Henry Atkins had got to. Perhaps this evening he would thank her for her efforts. She knew that almost certainly he would not. But there was just a possibility that he might value her kindness, might show her some appreciation.

The Legend of Horus

The sarcophagus bore the body of Osiris down the great river, the Nile. It travelled for many days, until it washed up on the shores of the river at Byblos. The sarcophagus stuck fast in a hollow tree by the flowing water. And there it remained while Seth ruled the kingdoms of Egypt in his brother's place.

But Isis searched along the Nile for her husband's body. After many days she found the casket, and she brought it back to Egypt and concealed it in the marshes.

Disguised as a kite, Isis visited the hidden body of her brother-husband. Each day she tried to breathe new life into the bones of Osiris. She spoke the words of power, the spells she learned from Thoth. And Osiris stirred in death and began to reawaken. As he slowly recovered and gained strength, Osiris remained hidden in the marshes of Egypt. After a while Isis conceived, and was with child by her husband.

But Seth discovered his brother was again alive, and ordered that Osiris be found. And when his soldiers had found where Osiris was hidden, Seth had his brother torn to pieces, and he scattered his brother's remains into the River Nile.

Isis wept again for her husband. And again she searched along the river for him. She spent many days and months until she had recovered all the pieces of her brother's body. Then she placed them together, reforming his once noble form. And she bound it together with strips of linen – the first mummy.

So Osiris became an Ankh, travelling down to the underworld to become King of the Dead. Meanwhile on Earth, Isis gave birth to the son of Osiris. And she called him Horus – the falcon who sees all.

Until he came of age, Isis trained Horus in the arts of war and taught him the wisdom of his father. When the day came that Horus ascended to adulthood, he went to his uncle Seth, and he challenged him for the throne of Osiris. The gods watched the conflict that followed, and they helped Horus to avenge his father.

Seth and his sister-wife Nephthys were defeated and imprisoned. And the gods declared Horus the rightful king of all Egypt.

(Translated by Tobias St John, from the inscriptions of the tomb of An'anka)

CHAPTER
FOUR

The desert air was hot and dry. As the sand dunes gave way to the greener banks of the Nile, the air was a little more humid, but the breeze soon drove away what moisture there was. The reeds waved in the wind and shimmered in the heat haze as the river ran quietly on. A single tree stood on one bank, towering over the reeds, split and blackened and dying. It was still, even as the reeds around it waved and swayed quietly.

Then the calm of the riverbank was broken. A noise like thunder rose from the river, swelling and vibrating. The sound ground its way heavily into a grating rhythm louder than the cry of a hippopotamus. It grew louder with each discordant strain until it crescendoed with a thump of achievement.

The tree quivered and shook as a heavy object washed up against it, jamming hard in the mud. In a moment it was quiet again. Just the river, the breeze, the reeds and the tree. And the solid blue box of the TARDIS stuck fast in the muddy bank of the ancient River Nile.

Atkins was beginning to lose his cool. And not before time, thought Tegan. He seemed to have taken being accosted by cloaked and hooded figures and bundled into a large sarcophagus almost in his stride. But Tegan had been pleased to see that he took slightly longer to adjust to the fact that the sarcophagus was in fact a dimensionally transcendental TARDIS in which the Doctor and Tegan were quite relieved to find themselves. Even so, he seemed remarkably unperturbed, considering.

'An interesting phenomenon, Doctor,' he had commented. 'I'm sure his Lordship would be most intrigued to examine it. He has an interest in such things, as I am sure you are aware.'

After that he seemed perfectly happy to stand straight and still, with his hands firmly clasped behind his back. He watched the image on the scanner together with Tegan and the Doctor, but apart from verifying that the pictures being relayed showed that the TARDIS was being carried from the British Museum, over a bridge and then dropped into the Thames, he displayed very little interest in the technology behind the display of the images or the stability of the floor considering the movement of the exterior.

'It's merely a window, is it not?' he replied when Tegan asked him why he was not surprised.

She saw the Doctor stifle a grin. She hung her cloak on the hat stand and thought about this. Perhaps Atkins was right. From her twentieth-century perspective, everything had to be a technological marvel. From Atkins's point of view, it was a new version of an established and unremarkable concept. The difference was in what he assumed, and in his attitude of disinterest.

'Actually, it's very sad,' the Doctor murmured to Tegan as she stomped off to join him at the console.

'What is?'

The Doctor nodded towards where Atkins stood watching them with apparent disinterest. 'No sense of wonder,' the Doctor said quietly. 'He's lost the fascination and awe, thrown out the child when he became an adult. Sad.'

Tegan looked at Atkins again. He did not look particularly sad, or as if he had any notion that he was missing out on anything. Particularly wonder.

'Boring, more like,' Tegan said as they landed.

Without bothering to check the scanner, the Doctor pushed the red lever which opened the door, and ushered Tegan and Atkins out into the heat.

And that was when Atkins began to lose his cool.

Tegan too had felt the heat immediately. Leaving the TARDIS was like walking into a spongy wall. But while the sudden change had seemed to disorient Atkins and leave him even more perplexed that the interior of the TARDIS, to Tegan it was like coming home to Brisbane in high summer.

The Doctor stood, hands in pockets, hat on head, and surveyed the scenery. Atkins stood, mouth open without saying anything. Tegan called out that she was off to change into something cooler as she hurried back into the TARDIS, her long skirts sweeping a trail of damp mud after her.

By the time she re-emerged, back in her rather lighter and cooler chemise and culottes, Atkins and the Doctor were engaged in conversation. Atkins was pointing into the hazy distance while the Doctor stared at his feet, which were shuffling in the sand. Tegan climbed up the muddy riverbank to join them.

'Doctor,' Atkins was saying, 'I am quite prepared to accept your word for it that this is indeed Egypt.'

'Thank you.'

'I have been to the country with his Lordship on several expeditions and recognise the general climate and landscape.' Atkins gestured round, nodding to Tegan as he noticed she had rejoined them. His nod stopped short as he noticed her attire. But he recovered himself almost immediately and returned to his point. 'However, I cannot accept that those are the great pyramids.'

'Why not?' Tegan asked as she shielded her eyes from the

bright sun and stared in the direction Atkins had indicated. 'At least they don't look too far away.'

Atkins and the Doctor both stared at her.

'Er,' Tegan began, feeling that she ought to say something. 'They are quite big, though.'

'Bigger than you think,' the Doctor said. 'Several days' walk, at least.'

'You're kidding.'

The Doctor shook his head. 'Remember the first time you saw a wide-bodied airliner?'

She nodded. Atkins looked blankly from the Doctor to Tegan.

'Was it as big as you had imagined?' the Doctor asked.

Tegan laughed. 'Much bigger. Huge. I thought it might be as big as a small house, but it was bigger than a street.'

'Well,' the Doctor pointed to the largest of the pyramids on the horizon. 'Inside that one, you could fit nearly nine hundred of those, and leave room to walk round and look at them.'

Tegan thought about this. 'Big, then.'

'Huge,' the Doctor agreed.

Atkins coughed politely and broke the ensuing silence. 'I would contend, however, that the suggestion that those are the great pyramids of Giza is not sustained. While their configuration and size is, I shall admit, the same, Miss Jovanka—'

'Tegan,' she cut in.

'Miss Tegan,' Atkins corrected himself without hesitation, 'you will see at once that their constitution is entirely different. You will observe, for example, that they are rather lighter in colour, almost shining as they reflect the sunlight. The tops too are of quite a different appearance.'

As Tegan's view cleared and her eyes adjusted to the heat-haze, she could see what Atkins meant. The pyramids were on the horizon, the sun seemingly right above them. And they gleamed in the reflected light. Tegan had never been to Egypt before, though she had seen numerous photographs and films of the pyramids. The structures she knew were of sand-coloured stone, ragged at the edges and blunted slightly at the tops. These buildings were subtly different.

They were gleaming white, clean as porcelain. And their perfectly outlined shapes were topped with gold. The pyramids Tegan knew were magnificent; these were magnificent too, but they were also splendid.

Beside her, the Doctor sighed. 'Those are, I'm afraid, the pyramids you know, Mr Atkins.' He gazed at them for a moment, shaking his head in obvious admiration. 'Inexplicable splendour of Ionian white and gold,' he muttered. Then he turned back to Atkins. 'There is just one small thing I should explain, though.'

'Don't tell us, Doctor,' Tegan said. 'This is ancient Egypt, right?'

The Doctor nodded.

'Terrific.'

'*Ancient* Egypt?' Atkins asked. 'I am not familiar with the place, I'm afraid.'

'It's not a place,' Tegan told him. 'It's a time.'

Atkins gaped again. He was getting rather good at it, Tegan thought.

'No,' he said at last. 'You cannot seriously expect me to believe that I have been transported back thousands of years in time. That is simply incredible.'

'Oh, really?' the Doctor smiled. 'More incredible than being transported thousands of miles? You seemed to accept that with equanimity.'

Atkins considered. And while he did, Tegan edged closer

to the Doctor. 'I thought you said we couldn't prevent what happened to Nyssa,' she said quietly. 'So why are we here?'

'I don't think we can,' the Doctor replied. 'Time is already set in its course, crystallised upon a particular web-way. But we have to try.'

'That's not what you said when we wanted to go back and save Adric.' There was a note of accusation in her voice. Atkins had been about to say something, but he seemed to sense the tension, and kept his peace.

The Doctor did not answer at once. He looked down at the TARDIS, and then back towards the distant pyramids. Finally he turned to face Tegan, and looked her directly in the eye. 'When Adric died, I knew we couldn't save him. Just as I know we can't stop what happened to Nyssa. Everything I have learned about how Time works, about my – our – relationship with it tells me that's the case.' He turned away, looking back at the TARDIS, lying wedged against a dead tree while the River Nile washed round its base.

'So?'

'So.' The Doctor turned back to Tegan. He smiled a sad half-smile and placed a hand on her shoulder. 'What if I'm wrong?'

They stood in silence for a while. Then the Doctor set off across the sand towards the pyramids. 'Come along, we've a long walk ahead of us.'

Atkins shrugged and followed. Tegan waited a moment before she too started walking.

'It is time.' Amosis stood in the doorway.

Sitamun looked up as he spoke. She had been washing Nyssa's feet; now she dried them quickly with a rough cloth, and cleared away the bowl and water.

'Already?' Nyssa asked. The last day had been a waking

nightmare. She had tried to leave the temple, but each time been escorted back by priests with short swords. She had assumed she had some time – perhaps years even – before whatever ritual fate awaited her was enacted. But she had no doubt from Amosis' tone and his words what he meant.

'The high priest will escort you to the procession,' Amosis said. 'Everything will be according to the *Spells for Coming Forth by Day*.'

'Really? At least it sounds nice.' Nyssa tried to sound defiant and sarcastic. She tried to sound like Tegan. But her words seemed to herself more like those of a child.

Her last attempts at defiance ended when Amosis said: 'It is also known as the *Book of the Dead*.'

In the following silence, Sitamun bowed to Nyssa. 'I shall watch the ceremony, though I may not attend it. And I shall pray to Anubis for your *ba*, your soul,' she said. Nyssa could see that the handmaiden's eyes were moist, but even so she was surprised when Sitamun leant suddenly forward and kissed her on the cheek. 'May you heart weigh heavy, Nyssa,' she said. Then she turned and ran from the room.

Nyssa stared after her. Sitamun had never called her by her real name before.

As she watched the doorway, a figure appeared from outside, paused silhouetted on the threshold, then stepped into the room. He was short, like all the Egyptians Nyssa had met, but quite broadly built. His head was shaved and he wore a ceremonial chain of office round his neck, hanging over his bare chest.

'You?' Nyssa gasped.

The newcomer looked surprised. 'My goddess? We have not met before. I am the high priest of Nephthys.'

'Rassul,' Nyssa said quietly, 'I know. We may not have met before,' she told him, 'but we shall. We shall.'

'I doubt it,' Rassul said. 'Today is a day for celebration. Today is the day of your funeral.'

Nyssa thought for a word or phrase he might remember in the years ahead. She struggled to remember some detail that might hit home or make an impression. That might hurt. 'I have heard it said that a father should not outlive his children,' she said quietly.

It certainly had an effect. Rassul swayed on his heels, the shock flaring in his eyes. 'I would not pray for your father,' he said at last, 'but for his daughter.'

The face was enormous, jutting up from the sand as if dropped from above into the desert. They could see it from miles away, slowly looming larger as they approached.

'That, I do recognise,' Atkins said as they got close enough to begin to make out the details of the features – the line of the cheek and the fractured nose.

'The Great Sphinx,' the Doctor agreed.

'But it's buried.' Tegan could recognise the face too now, but without the huge lion's body to support it, the nature of the statue was completely changed.

They walked round it once. 'People have been digging it out ever since it was built,' the Doctor said. 'Whenever that was.'

'You mean you don't know?' Tegan teased.

'Well, not exactly. Always meant to pop back and see. But the trouble with being a Time Lord is that you never seem to have the time.' He grinned and motioned for them to continue towards the still distant pyramids. As Tegan approached, he put an arm round her shoulder. 'The Egyptians call the Great Sphinx *Abu el Hob*,' he told her.

'The Father of Terror,' Atkins said quietly as he joined them.

'Yes,' the Doctor seemed surprised. 'A rather literal translation, but accurate nonetheless.'

The wrappings were tight and smelled of resin. Nyssa struggled, trying to tear her limbs from the priests who held them pressed against her body. But as the embalmers continued their work, seemingly oblivious to Nyssa's shouts and struggles, she felt her power of movement more and more restricted. Sitamun had not returned, and Nyssa felt alone, helpless, and terrified. Rassul stood watching as the embalmers completed their work.

Only Nyssa's head was now free of the linen wrappings. Amosis was behind her, and she twisted to see what he was doing. He seemed to be mixing powders in a small bowl. As she strained to watch, he dripped some liquid from a small earthenware bottle on to the powder. Immediately it started to bubble and smoke. Amosis held the bowl away from him, taking care not to inhale the fumes, and turned to Rassul.

Rassul took the smoking bowl. He too avoided breathing in the smoke which was now drifting across the room. Nyssa could smell the pungent aroma; it was like the ceremonial incense burned on Traken at religious ceremonies. As Rassul brought the bowl closer, she tried to pull away. But her entire body was held firm within the wrappings.

'The start of eternity,' Rassul said quietly as he held the bowl one-handed under Nyssa's chin. 'Drink deep of the fumes of oblivion and know what it is to join Osiris in his netherworld of darkness.'

Nyssa tried to keep her head upright, to pull her face away from the smoke rising from the bowl. But with his free hand, Rassul grabbed her hair and forced her to look down into the fumes.

'No, the Doctor will stop you.' Nyssa hoped she sounded

confident, but she doubted the Doctor would find her now. 'He always stops people like you.' She struggled for a moment, shaking her head and trying to pull away. But already she could feel consciousness slipping from her.

'No, please—'

Nyssa's eyes closed, the smoke stinging under her eyelids.

'Tell me about the Doctor.' Rassul's voice floated through the mist, quiet and reasonable.

The smoke was her world, and she felt herself drifting into a deep sleep. The sounds and smells of the room around her, including her own voice as she obeyed Rassul's command, floated into the distance. Her last thought as she lost consciousness, her last thought for millennia, was that wherever she was going, she might find her father.

From his expeditions with Lord Kenilworth, and from general interest, Atkins knew a little of the history and geography of Egypt. When Kenilworth had first started his excursions, obsessed with the notion of making new and exciting discoveries, Atkins had been the only other member of the party. While he was not one to show overt appreciation or emotion, some of his employer's enthusiasm and passion had rubbed off. Atkins had passed many of the lonely evenings in Cairo hotels, while Kenilworth tried vainly to drum up financial support, reading through some of his employer's textbooks and reference works on the subject. If Kenilworth had noticed his manservant's increased interest and erudition, he had been polite enough not to mention it. But he had taken more and more time and trouble to include Atkins in the running of the expeditions. Lady Kenilworth seemed content to leave them to their play, her interest in travel and things Egyptian being limited to her desire to be near her husband.

When he had, sadly, been forced to suggest that Atkins look after Lady Kenilworth and the London house while he was away on his latest expedition, Atkins had secretly been devastated. But Lady Kenilworth was recovering from a fever and unable to travel, so she needed the support of her butler as well as her housekeeper. Atkins was sure it was for reassurance and because of her ladyship's illness rather than any slight on the abilities of the supremely capable Miss Warne.

Atkins was pleased he had been able to offer some small assistance to the Doctor by translating *Abu el Hob*. He had felt the same suppressed tremor of delight at the Doctor's appreciation and surprise as when he had first been able to offer informed advice to Kenilworth. So it was in a lighter mood, all problematic thoughts of travelling through the ages and across the continents put aside, that he followed the Doctor and the strange Miss Tegan.

He walked proud, bold and upright, and wondered if perhaps he could remove his jacket. After some deliberation he decided that it would probably be permissible, provided, of course, he did not loosen his necktie or collar. He carried his jacket over his arm, and wondered whether the Doctor, in his white sweater and long frock coat was not beginning to feel the heat.

'Do you know where we're going?' Miss Tegan asked the Doctor.

The Doctor nodded. 'Of course. I took the precaution of ascertaining from Lord Kenilworth where the tomb was.'

'And where is it?'

The Doctor stopped, and Atkins caught them up as he pointed to a small pyramid. It stood alone, smaller and closer than the main pyramids, nestled in a hollow as if it had been dug out of the desert. Unlike the other pyramids, which gleamed and shone in the bright sunlight, this pyramid was jet black. It seemed almost to absorb the light rather than to reflect it. As Atkins looked, he fancied he could just make out small figures gathered at the base of the pyramid. Some sort of welcoming party for an ant-tiny procession which was making its way slowly across the desert sands towards the structure.

'I rather fancy that it's over there,' the Doctor said.

There were eighteen oxen, each steaming hot breath through its flared nostrils and kicking up dust from the sandy floor. The sledge they dragged through the dunes bore a single inlaid casket. Behind the dust-cloud followed the priests and then the mourners.

The shrieking and ululation wailed itself to a halt as the oxen drew up outside the black pyramid. They stamped and blew as the priests surrounded the sledge. The priests lifted the heavy casket and carried it ceremonially to the high doorway into the pyramid. The step up from the sand to the floor level formed a natural dais. The coffin was first lowered to the floor, then raised upright on the threshold so that the stylised female figure looked out over the assembled crowd.

As at most funerals, almost all of the mourners were hired professionals. They tore their hair, smote their chests and shrieked as if the coffin contained Osiris himself. There was only one person present who could be termed a friend. Standing alone, crying quietly at the back of the mourners, was the handmaiden Sitamun. Alone until she was joined by the Doctor, Tegan and Atkins.

She watched them walk out of the desert and stand at the back of the crowd. Their clothes and their conversation were strange – just as the goddess's had been strange when she first joined Sitamun and Amosis in the anteroom of the temple.

Sitamun edged closer and listened, though she understood little of what the newcomers were saying.

'I'm afraid it looks as though we may be too late,' Atkins pointed to the sarcophagus standing upright in the pyramid entrance. 'That is the casket in which your friend was incarcerated, is it not?'

The Doctor nodded grimly. 'Looks like Blinovitch was right after all,' he said quietly. 'Still, it was worth a shot.'

'A few hours, that's all.' Tegan wiped a tear from her cheek. 'A few sodding hours earlier and we could have stopped them.'

'No, Tegan, no.' The Doctor patted her shoulder. 'It had already happened when we decided to come here. The web of time has crystallised at this node; it might as well be set in stone.'

'So what do we do?'

'Well, we'll just have to try something else. We still have a couple of options, and we're no worse off now than we were before we came.'

Tegan was not convinced. 'It's just, you know – being so close and yet…' She searched for a way to express her frustration, anger and grief. She gave up. 'Oh, rabbits,' she said.

'I am afraid I follow very little of this,' Atkins confessed as they watched the priests fuss round the coffin fifty yards away. 'But I'm not sure how rabbits will help. Unless you are planning some new feat of temporal prestidigitation?'

'I'm afraid not,' the Doctor confessed.

'Why don't we just go back to yesterday and try again to save your friend?'

'Blooming Blinovitch,' Tegan told him.

The Doctor tried to explain more. 'The link between the time zones – between us and the here and now, if you like –

has already been established. Probably by the very fact that Nyssa was brought here. So from now on time moves on at the same relative rate. We spend a day hunting for Nyssa, and a day passes in this time. It's as if the two times, yours and Nyssa's, are joined together by a steel rod, so you can't move one without adjusting the other by the exact same amount.'

'And why is that?'

This threw the Doctor for a second. 'Why? Er, well according to Blinovitch it's something to do with temporal dynamics and their relationship to the real world envelope. But I think it's really because otherwise things would just be too easy.'

Atkins considered. 'So we really are too late.'

The Doctor did not answer immediately. He stuck his hands in his pockets and looked down at the sand at his feet. Then he raised his head and looked Atkins in the eye. 'That depends on what for.'

They held each other's gaze for a long moment. Then the Doctor flashed a sudden smile, turning abruptly to the young woman who had moved so she was standing next to Atkins. 'How do you do,' he said, his teeth gleaming white in the sun, 'I'm the Doctor. How can we help?'

The woman hesitated, looking from the Doctor to each of his companions in turn. Eventually she asked: 'You are friends of the goddess?'

They looked at her blankly.

'Of Nyssa?'

The most senior priests removed the lid of the casket, leaving the base and the mummy inside standing in the pyramid doorway. The mummy itself was not completely wrapped. The head was still free of bandages, lolled to one side as if in sleep, dark hair falling in loose curls about the linen shoulders.

At the back of the crowd of mourners, Tegan turned away, her hands to her mouth.

'Oh God,' she gasped. 'Doctor, I can see her face.'

High Priest Rassul, in full regalia, approached the mummy. He held up the ceremonial adze, the loose sleeves of his gold cloak falling like wings to his sides as he held it aloft. Then he turned in a swirl of golden motion and pressed the adze to the mouth of the mummy, parting the girl's lips so that the adze grazed her clenched teeth as she seemed to kiss the blade. As he held the adze in position, Rassul chanted the ancient words of power, the standard litany to restore sight, speech, and hearing to the dead.

Except that the woman was not dead, and would not have her senses restored. Her *ba*, her soul, would remain forever locked with the *ka*, the vital force of the body, within the mummified body. And together with them...

Next Rassul weighed the heart. He chanted the words of the incantation for the mummified woman: 'Oh heart of my being, do not witness against me. Do not betray me before my judges.' It was not her real heart, for that still beat, although more and more slowly, within the woman's breast. Instead a golden replica of a human heart was placed on one side of the scales. The Anubis-priest dropped the feather that symbolised Maat on the other side. And as the scales fell in favour of the heart, the feather lifted away. The priest dressed as Anubis hissed his appreciation, and carried the scales from the pyramid doorway.

Then Rassul took the canopic jar. He carried it carefully, reverently, to the coffin. He held it high above his head so all could see, and then he turned and held it out to the mummified goddess. Rassul's body blocked the crowd's view, so they did not see him tear the stopper from the jar;

did not see him thrust the open end towards the face of the goddess; did not see the goddess's hair blown back as if by a breeze. And they did not see Nyssa's eyes snap open, or the hint of a smile that traced across her mouth before the eyes closed again for millennia.

'The weighing of the heart,' the Doctor said, 'is the ancient Egyptian way of sorting out the wheat from the chaff, or the sheep from the goats.'

'It is to test innocence and purity,' Sitamun said. She did not understand what the Doctor had meant and felt she should explain.

'Huh,' Tegan almost laughed. 'Nyssa should have no trouble there.'

'But I don't recognise that last ceremony,' the Doctor went on, ignoring Tegan's comment. 'Do you know what it was?' he asked the handmaiden.

'It was the return of the spirit,' she said simply.

'Why?' Tegan said. 'Where's it gone?'

'I do not know.'

'Well, what does the ceremony usually mean? What does it enact?'

Sitamun shook her head. 'I have never seen it before,' she confessed quietly.

'You mean this is your first funeral?'

Sitamun looked at Tegan, puzzled. Then her face fell and she almost burst into tears. Tegan's words seemed to her, a temple handmaiden responsible for the souls of the dead and their departure, an accusation of negligence of her most holy duties. It was Atkins who held her hands and spoke kindly to her.

'I am in service too,' he said. 'We are not asking you to betray a trust or to dishonour your employers in any way. But the Doctor and Miss Tegan are desperate to help their friend – our friend. And to do that, we need your help.'

'It is not that,' Sitamun told him when she had recovered her composure a little. 'I wish you well. Nyssa was a friend of mine also.' She turned to address Tegan directly. 'I have attended many funerals, as is my station, but the ceremony of the return of the spirit is never performed.' She looked round at her new friends. 'It is a ceremony written solely for this occasion,' she said.

The others exchanged glances.

'And what is it? What is the ceremony about? You must know something.'

'I know only that it concerns the jar, Doctor.'

'Jar? What jar?' The Doctor grabbed Sitamun, her dark skin whitening under the grip of his fingers.

'Doctor,' Atkins murmured, and gently removed the Doctor's hands from Sitamun's bare shoulders. 'Any small detail may help us,' he told her.

Sitamun decided to start from the beginning and tell them everything. Even what she was sure they must already know. 'Your friend, Nyssa,' she said, 'was sent to us by the gods. She appeared to us in the temple at the appointed place and hour as the perfect sacrifice to appease Horus.'

'Appease him for what?'

'Many years ago, many hundreds of years ago, grave robbers entered the sacred tomb of the goddess Nephthys.'

'Who's Nephthys?' Tegan asked.

'Sister of Osiris,' Atkins told her.

'And more importantly,' the Doctor said, 'the wife and sister of Seth.'

'So why the big fuss? What did they steal?'

'Nothing,' Sitamun said. 'They all died in the tomb. It was the will of the gods.'

'But?' prompted the Doctor.

'But, a canopic jar was cracked.'

'So what was in this jar?' Tegan asked. 'Raspberry jam?'

'I do not know.'

'And why the importance for this ceremony?'

'I do not know. I say only what I have heard. But the jar was cracked many centuries ago, and recently it has started to crumble. The priests were worried, whispering in the temple corridors and meeting after dark.' Sitamun considered, remembered some of the looks she had seen on the faces of the priests as they left the meetings. 'The priests were scared,' she said.

'And then Nyssa turned up, and everything was suddenly all right again?'

Sitamun nodded. 'Yes, Doctor. And now she will be entombed in the black pyramid with the mummy of the goddess Nephthys and the sacred relics of power.'

Behind them the priests replaced the lid heavily on the casket, and lifted it onto their shoulders.

'Entombed for all eternity.'

They carried it slowly into the black pyramid. As they crossed the threshold the stygean darkness swallowed them up.

They watched as the priests re-emerged and the stone door was slotted into the opening. Then the priests bowed, and the rested oxen were led away. The mourners lined up to be paid, and started to drift back towards the huge pyramids on the distant horizon.

The Doctor shook Sitamun's bemused hand. 'You've been very helpful,' he said. 'Thank you. And thank you for being kind to Nyssa too. I think she must have needed a friend.' He turned to Tegan and Atkins. 'Come along you two, we've got things to do.'

'Like what?'

'Like get back to 1896 and make sure Lord Kenilworth finds the mummy and gets it safely back to London. Otherwise, no matter what Blinovitch might think, we'll never have found out what happened to Nyssa, and she really will rest in there for all eternity.'

Sitamun stood alone for an hour. She looked at the pyramid where her friend was buried while the three strangers walked back into the sandy wastes of the empty wilderness.

LONDON
1975

The gleaming whiteness of the scientist's newly laundered lab coat contrasted with the stained bandages wrapping the mummy. The scientist smiled – white teeth, white coat, in a white room standing by a white-faced bank of equipment.

His assistant stood ready beside the stainless-steel trolley, ready to wheel the mummy into the scanner. His lab coat contrasted with his dark skin.

'How does it work?'

The scientist turned to the control panel, tapped a dial and adjusted a knob. 'It X-rays the subject from all angles to create a three-dimensional composite image of the body. It will show the outline of the body within the bandages, and any jewellery folded inside.' He inspected a few more readings, then nodded to the assistant. 'Right, let's get started.'

The assistant gently rolled the trolley along its track into the circular opening of the huge metal tunnel of the scanner. 'How appropriate that it should be a cat that releases the secrets of the goddess,' he said quietly, shutting the heavy lead door behind the trolley.

'Releases?' The scientist was beside him, checking the seals on the door. 'And what cat is that?' he asked. Not really interested, most of his mind on the task ahead.

The assistant gestured at the machine. 'C.A.T.' he spelled out.

'Ah. Computerised Axial Tomography.' The scientist made a final minute adjustment, and threw the main switch. 'Well, let's see what secrets our friend is keeping, shall we?'

The monitor screen glowed into life, throwing negative images onto the glass as the scanner recorded the details of the mummy from every angle. Somewhere outside an owl hooted in the night, and a train whistled in the darkness.

The images blurred across the scientist's retina. The points of light against the dark looked more like the night sky than the innards of the mummy. He was vaguely aware of his new assistant standing beside him. The assistant was muttering something that the scientist could not catch or understand. Words in his native Egyptian tongue. Phrases that sounded full of strength and power. The volume built with the steadily increasing hum of the CAT scanner.

The scientist continued to watch the pictures of black and white intensity blasted across his retina. He watched the woman taken to the tomb; he watched the mummy placed in the casket; he watched the tomb sealed. He felt the energy and understanding building inside his mind.

And beside him, Sadan Rassul continued to intone the words from the scroll of Thoth, and called on the power of his goddess.

CHAPTER
FIVE

Atkins was not at all sure how to approach Lord Kenilworth. He spent most of the time in the TARDIS on its journey back to 1896 pondering the problem. The Doctor had made it clear what it was he was proposing and that he thought Atkins should perform the introductions. But Atkins felt that it might be seen as a little presumptuous for him to suggest to his master where he should direct his latest expedition.

So as they entered the lobby of the Mena House Oberoi hotel in Giza, Atkins decided his best recourse was to repair to the bar to get his spirits up. Or rather, down.

'What a splendid idea,' the Doctor said, pointing across the room. 'How did you know he'd be here?'

Atkins said nothing. Now that he could see Lord Kenilworth, maps and papers spread out on the table in front of him, Atkins realised that the bar was indeed the most likely place for him to be.

'Well, go on, then,' the Doctor hissed in Atkins's ear. He elbowed him into the room, and gestured for Tegan to stay near the doorway. 'Let us handle this,' he said quietly to her. Tegan's grunt of annoyance melded with Kenilworth's snort of surprise as Atkins crossed the room towards him.

Atkins kept his expression as blank as he could as he crossed the room. Kenilworth wiped a handkerchief across his face and stood up, as if not quite able to believe what he was seeing. 'Good God, Atkins – what the deuce?' he gruffed as Atkins came within range.

'I'm sorry, sir. I realise this is somewhat unexpected.' Atkins bowed his head so as not to meet his employer's eye. 'But a matter has arisen.'

'Unexpected? I should say so.' Kenilworth waved him to a chair by the table.

Atkins sat, his legs suddenly feeling less secure as he took his weight off them.

'So what is this matter that brings you all the way from London?' Kenilworth leant across the maps and documents at Atkins. 'What is it that causes you to neglect your duties – and my household, I should add – and come to Cairo in person rather than send a telegram?'

Atkins coughed politely. 'We are actually in Giza, sir,' he said, wondering how best to explain the situation.

'I know where I am, thank you.' Kenilworth sat back in his chair. He picked up his whisky tumbler, and made to take a sip. Then he changed his mind and held it up to the light instead. 'And I rather think I may be permitted to stray a couple of miles from my residence. Especially since my butler seems to have wandered several thousand miles from his.' He nodded abruptly, then laughed. 'You gave me quite a turn, though, I don't mind admitting,' Kenilworth confessed in a stage whisper. He replaced his drink on the table.

Atkins glanced round for the Doctor. For a moment he felt panic welling up in the pit of his stomach. The Doctor was gone. Then he realised that the Doctor had followed him over to the table and was standing beside Kenilworth's chair.

Kenilworth seemed to notice the Doctor at the same instant. 'Who the devil are you, sir?' he asked, quickly gathering up his papers and maps.

Atkins snatched the whisky from the top of a map just before the paper it rested on was pulled away. He carefully set it down again on the bare table top. 'This gentleman, sir,' he told Kenilworth, 'has a proposition which I believe you will find of interest.'

'Does he indeed?' Kenilworth craned back to get a good view of the Doctor's face. 'Well, sir, out with it.' He shielded his eyes from the setting sun and continued to stare at the Doctor standing over him. 'What proposition is it that causes you to hijack my man and bring him half across the globe?'

The Doctor blinked, exchanged a look with Atkins, and stuffed his hands into his trouser pockets. 'You are looking for a tomb,' he said eventually. 'A blind pyramid south of Saqqara.'

Kenilworth flinched visibly. 'How do you know that?' He turned to cast an accusing stare at Atkins.

Atkins began to shake his head in denial, then changed his mind. There was no point in prevaricating. 'I think you should listen to the gentleman, sir. I have good reason to suspect he can provide useful information.'

Kenilworth reached for his drink. His expression suggested he was not convinced.

'Mr Atkins is right, Lord Kenilworth,' the Doctor said quietly.

'Really? And what information, pray, can you provide me with?'

'You must be prepared for some hardship, I'm afraid.' The Doctor had been leaning forward towards Kenilworth. Now he straightened up. 'There will be danger, death even, ahead of us. But if you're agreeable I can offer my services to your expedition.'

'And what exactly are you offering?'

The Doctor turned and looked out of the window towards the pyramids. He seemed to be considering his next words, and Atkins realised that this was the point where he had to decide if he was going through with his plan, when he had to decide that this really was the best course of action.

At last the Doctor answered Kenilworth. 'I can lead you to the tomb,' he said quietly.

By the time Tegan was formally introduced to Lord Kenilworth, he was the bluff, avuncular man she had already met. He had taken to the Doctor as soon as they started to examine the maps and trace possible routes for the expedition. He found himself sucked into the Doctor's obvious enthusiasm, and impressed by his intelligence and insight.

Before long, an outline plan had evolved and Kenilworth was busily giving instructions to Atkins to relay to the Egyptian bearers concerning provisions and scheduling. Tegan dithered on the edge of the discussions. She had glanced at the maps and the pencil marks showing possible routes and stopping points. But since she already knew where they were going and what they would find, she had found it hard to maintain an interest.

She sat alone at a table in the corner of the room and watched the sun edge its way below the silhouettes of the pyramids. Outlined sharply against the light, they seemed unchanged from the pristine, gleaming structures she had seen the day before. Or three thousand years previously, depending on your point of view, she reflected. Now, if she could make out details, she would see that they were pitted and scarred. The earliest man-made stone structures in the world were showing their age.

By the time the discussions broke up, Tegan was feeling tired, bored, and old. Atkins was charged with assembling the members of the expedition for a meeting at eleven the next morning, and Kenilworth debated whether to have one last nightcap for so long that the barman brought him a whisky to keep him company while he made his mind up.

The Doctor crouched down beside Tegan and pressed a hotel room key into her palm. 'Get some sleep. Tomorrow will be a long day.'

'It seems like it's a long life,' she told him.

The Doctor smiled broadly. 'You're telling me,' he said.

The huge metal blade swung in a slow arc above Tegan's head. But the intense midday heat was hardly alleviated by the large ceiling fan. She sat at the back of the bar with the Doctor, wishing she had insisted on bringing clothes more designed for the climate than for the period.

Kenilworth was standing at the front of the room, one foot resting on the brass rail round the base of the bar. Everyone else sat round tables nearby, listening intently as he went over the outline arrangements for the expedition.

Tegan looked round her new colleagues and tried to remember their names as Kenilworth recapped on the details of the previous evening's discussions.

Nearest to the bar was the ever-attendant Atkins. He sat almost to attention, back rigid and straight, paying close attention to every syllable.

At the next table sat Russell Evans and his daughter Margaret. Evans was a pale, thin, greying man in his sixties, every bit as doddery as Tegan had imagined a Victorian representative of the British Museum would be. His daughter was of an uncertain age, probably in her early thirties. She was dressed in dowdy tweed despite the heat, her hair tied in a tight bun from which auburn strands struggled to escape. Her features, Tegan decided, would have been attractive had they not been so severe.

Behind Margaret was Nicholas Simons, Evans' assistant. He was young and enthusiastic, taking copious notes of everything Kenilworth said, scribbling them in a small leather-bound pocketbook. Between sentences he chewed nervously on the end of his stubby pencil, and tried to ignore the glances Margaret Evans threw his way. Tegan wondered whether he realised what was going on, or whether he was simply unnerved by anyone looking his way. She spent a few minutes trying to catch his eye and was eventually rewarded with his fleeting expression of panic and renewed scribbling. Margaret Evans glared at Tegan, who smiled innocently in reply before turning her attention to the next table.

Here sat a figure whom Tegan had at once recognised from Kenilworth's unwrapping party, although he did not know her or the Doctor. It was James Macready, an old friend of Kenilworth's who had apparently accompanied him on several previous expeditions. He was probably about Kenilworth's age, approaching fifty. In contrast to his friend he was a small man with little round glasses and thin grey hair. He nodded almost continuously and stoked away at a pipe which he never quite got round to smoking. Occasionally it approached his mouth, only to be waved in an approving gesture as Macready nodded again.

Opposite Macready was the head of the Egyptian bearers, Menet Nebka. His men would carry the bags, coax the camels, set up camp, and do the actual excavation. It had struck Tegan that really they could have mounted the entire expedition without their British employers. But since they were entirely motivated by the money, there would hardly have been any point. On an expedition grounded in uncertainties, their wage was the only constant.

Kenilworth laughed loudly at some joke of his own, and was rewarded by a few nods and smiles from the assembled group as they made their way from the room. Tegan grinned her approval, wondering what she had missed while she had been looking round. She would ask the Doctor later, except that she suspected he had been paying as little attention as she had. She followed them out into the heat of the desert sun.

The journey took three days. For Atkins it was three days of relief from the confusion and excitement of his trip with the Doctor and Tegan. It was also rather more stimulating to be planning the details of the expedition with Kenilworth and Macready than arranging the domestic arrangements at Kenilworth House with Miss Warne. Though he was surprised to find that he rather missed the housekeeper's company.

The Doctor, for all his expertise and pre-knowledge, took a back seat. He seemed content to be carried along and organised by the others, making only occasional comments and suggestions now that he had shown Kenilworth the point on the map for which they were aiming.

Tegan was even less interested in the arrangements than her companion. But Atkins was not surprised at her frequent comments concerning the length of the journey, the heat, and the rate of progress. She complained almost as much as Nebka's bearers.

Atkins leant forward in his saddle to examine the map which Kenilworth was holding. His Lordship steadied his camel, and drew a finger along the path of the route still to be traversed.

'Another day,' Kenilworth said. 'We'll camp here,' he pointed to a small blank area in the middle of the large blank area of the featureless paper that purported to be a map of the area.

Atkins and Macready both nodded agreement, and Atkins pulled his camel round and set off back down the line of camels. He passed the word as he went: 'Another two hours, then we'll set up camp. We should reach the excavation site by noon tomorrow.'

'Thank goodness for that,' Tegan replied, struggling to prevent her camel from sitting down and giving up on the spot. She pulled violently on the harness, and it bucked, almost throwing her off. Then it turned its head slowly round and spat at her.

'They will be at the pyramid by midday tomorrow.'

Sadan Rassul lowered his binoculars, taking care not to catch the light of the sun on the lenses as he did so. The two Egyptians behind him showed no sign of having heard him, but since the words were mainly for his own benefit, he was not worried. He crawled back from the edge of the sand dune, stood up and started down the slope towards where they had left the camels.

The two Egyptians turned to follow their master. If they smiled, it was because they knew their real work would soon begin.

The Doctor and Tegan had adjacent tents at the back of the camp. Tegan was less than impressed with her accommodation. It did keep out the sun but not the heat. And at night, it let in the freezing cold. There was barely room for one person inside, yet frequently either Macready or Evans insisted on visiting to see how she was coping with the adverse conditions. If she was lucky, she saw the Doctor once a day. But most of the time he spent alone in his own tent, apparently asleep. Tegan suspected he was actually thinking and calculating options and possibilities. Unless he really was asleep, of course.

Simons never came near Tegan, which she assumed was partly out of a nervous sense of self-preservation, and partly as Margaret Evans rarely let him out of her sight. Atkins was always too busy, though he greeted her with characteristic politeness and a stoic lack of emotion on the rare times she ventured into the burning sunlight to see how the boring process of carrying sand from one place to another in wicker baskets was going. On these occasions, Lord Kenilworth always made time and took trouble to include her in discussions and to enthuse about how well things were going. The only way Tegan could see that progress was judged was by the relative sizes of the pile of sand and the hole in the desert floor at the base of the high sand dune.

It was on one of those rare occasions when the Doctor was with Tegan, listening as ever to her complaints about the weather and the level of local entertainment, when Atkins arrived. He stood politely in the entrance to the little tent and waited for the end of the conversation.

'Hello, Atkins,' the Doctor smiled.

Tegan glared.

'Good afternoon to you both,' Atkins replied. 'His Lordship wonders if you would be good enough to join him at the excavations.'

'Who? The Doctor?'

'He asked me to convey his compliments to you both, Miss Tegan. He thought you would be interested too.'

'I've seen enough sand to last a lifetime, thank you.'

The Doctor cleared his throat. 'I don't think it's sand that Lord Kenilworth is interested in showing us,' he said. 'Is it, Atkins?'

'Indeed not, Doctor.'

'What then?'

'Nebka's men have uncovered the entrance to the pyramid.'

The short tunnel into the desert floor made the dune seem

even higher. A wall of sand towered over the Doctor, Tegan and Atkins as they approached the excavations. The entrance mouth was wide, narrowing as it burrowed beneath the sandy hillside.

It looked as if the opening disappeared into total darkness. But as Tegan approached, the sun angled into the hole in the sand, and she could see that in fact the hole ended abruptly at a wall. And the wall was completely black.

Tegan shook her head and laughed. In her mind's eye she saw the Doctor, four days earlier, looking round to get his bearings, then drawing a large X in the sandy desert floor with his index finger and saying, 'Dig there.'

The topography of the surrounding area had altered considerably. But Tegan could see now for the first time, with the huge pyramids of Giza outlined on the distant horizon, that they were back at the point they had visited thousands of years in the past. With a precision that anyone unfamiliar with the Doctor's casual expertise would have found difficult to believe, the excavations led directly to a buried black marble door. The door that led into the pyramid where Nyssa was entombed.

'You were right, Doctor,' Kenilworth said loudly as he greeted them. 'Incredible. I'd love to know where you get your information.'

The Doctor smiled. 'Years of research,' he said. 'Many years.'

Before Kenilworth could comment, there was a cry from the tunnel. It was followed quickly by another shout and before long a loud chorus of voices was jabbering away in Egyptian.

'What is it now?' Kenilworth asked angrily. 'They've done nothing but complain ever since we got here.'

Atkins set off to investigate. While he was gone, Macready

joined them and he and Kenilworth complimented the Doctor again on his wisdom and expertise. By the time Atkins returned, Tegan was sick of hearing how clever the Doctor was. She was firmly of the opinion that the last thing one should do with an appreciation of the Doctor's undoubted brilliance was to tell him about it. And the Doctor's smug and insincere denial of his own genius was the most annoying aspect of the whole experience.

'Well, what is it?' Macready asked when Atkins returned.

'A religious problem, sir. It seems that they have uncovered some hieroglyphs around the entrance that are rather worrying to their somewhat superstitious outlook.'

'Really?' the Doctor said. 'What hieroglyphs are those, I wonder?'

'It seems to concern several variations on the symbol which represents the Eye of Horus, Doctor.'

'Indeed,' Kenilworth seemed resigned to the problem. 'Very well, then. I suppose we shall have to take the usual action.'

'What's that?' Tegan asked.

'First we agree to reduce their onerous duties,' Atkins replied.

'Not really a problem, since we shall want to open and examine the pyramid ourselves,' Kenilworth pointed out.

'And then,' Atkins continued, 'we offer them more money.'

Despite the offer of increased wages, and Kenilworth's insistence that once the main door was open they could retire to their tents, the Egyptians refused to do any more work. The Doctor paid little attention to the negotiations, and Tegan kept him company as he examined the doorway.

The excavation was a huge pit in the desert, at the base of a sandy mound. On the side of the pit below the mound, the wall of sand was interrupted by the shining black marble of the pyramid side.

It sloped back into the sand above, revealing little more than the high doorway. The stone was still smooth and polished, which the Doctor suggested indicated either that the pyramid had been buried for much of its long life, or that it was constructed of incredibly durable material. Or both.

Around the doorway, hieroglyphics were carved into the black stone. As Tegan shifted position, the sun caught them and darkened the blackness in the cuts that formed their shapes. They were difficult to make out – darkness in the blackness – but the symbol the Doctor had pointed out as the Eye of Horus was repeated several times.

'It's sprung,' the Doctor said thoughtfully after a while. He stood back and framed the doorway between artist's hands, peering through the window between his thumbs and index fingers. 'There must be more to it that that,' he said after a while.

'Why?'

'What?' he seemed to have forgotten Tegan was with him. 'Oh, too straightforward. That's why.' He pushed experimentally at a point on the door about a third of the way up its nine-foot-high edge. 'If it were that simple,' he said as he exerted more pressure and gritted his teeth, 'you could just do this.' He stepped away and waved a hand at the door to show the futility of his actions.

And with a rumble of stonework, age, and weight, the heavy door opened slowly outwards. The Doctor's smile froze on his face. 'I don't like that,' he muttered.

The light from the oil lamps glistened on the stone walls and danced across the flagstones of the floor. They crowded into the narrow passageway, looking along the long corridor as it sloped upwards into the pyramid with a mixture of awe and apprehension. Tegan could feel the tension in the air, a tightness that might precede a thunderstorm.

Kenilworth led the way, the Doctor close behind with Tegan. Atkins and Macready were close on their heels, with Russell Evans and his daughter beside them. Simons brought up the rear, glancing up now and then from his pocketbook as he scribbled frantically.

'First dynasty?' Macready suggested, and Evans nodded his agreement. Simons flicked over another page.

'I think that is where we are heading,' Kenilworth said eventually. He raised his lamp above his head, and pointed towards the end of the long corridor.

Tegan could just make out another doorway. It was filled with a pair of huge double doors, the handles tied with frayed and rotting cord. She took a step towards the doors, and gasped out loud.

Kenilworth's lamp cast its light sideways as well as forwards. As Tegan moved, she saw that the light was illuminating what had been a dark patch of wall beside her. Now she could see that it was an alcove. And in the alcove stood a woman. At once Kenilworth and the Doctor were at Tegan's side. She gave a sigh of relief and shook her head in disbelief at her own nervousness. The woman was a statue, her twin looking across the corridor at them from an identical alcove on the other side.

'Remarkable,' breathed Kenilworth, stepping aside to let Evans and Macready take a closer look. The Doctor frowned in the lamplight, and Margaret Evans shuffled closer to Simons.

The statues were life-size. The woman they depicted was strikingly beautiful. She was tall and slim, her dark hair folded up onto her head in a cloth headress. Her features were

119

aquiline, and her eyes large and cat-like with huge pupils. She was dressed in a simple robe which reached to her knees. If it had once been white, it was now discoloured with age and dust.

'Shabti,' Atkins said quietly to Tegan.

The Doctor nodded, and seeing Tegan's puzzlement said: 'Shabti figures were put in the tomb to serve the dead. The Egyptians assumed that there would still be work to be done in the afterlife, so they provided servants to do the washing up.'

'Indeed,' Atkins agreed. 'Not all were life-size. Some were just small dolls.'

'But,' the Doctor said, leaning close so Tegan could see his significantly raised eyebrow, 'they were usually in the image of the person buried in the tomb.'

Tegan looked back at the figure in the alcove. Evans, Macready and Kenilworth were examining a detail of the carved fingers. Evans traced a finger over the woman's ornate ring and pointed to a bracelet carved onto her wrist.

'She doesn't look like Nyssa,' Tegan said.

'Not even close,' the Doctor agreed.

'Perhaps a stylised representation?' Atkins suggested.

The Doctor shook his head. 'No. Too tall. The features are completely different, and the, er…' He struggled for a suitable phrase, carving a female figure in the air with his hands.

Tegan let him flounder for a while before coming to his assistance.

'The bust's too big,' she said. 'But why all the interest, anyway?' she continued before Atkins could react. 'They're just wooden statues.'

Whatever scathing response about the figures' preservation, workmanship and archaeological importance the Doctor was about to deliver was curtailed. He and Atkins stood gaping at Tegan. Before she had time to ask what the problem was, the Shabti figures stepped out of their alcoves and into the corridor in front of her.

Everyone started talking at once. Margaret Evans screamed and clung to Simons, which seemed to surprise him even more than the Shabti. The others drew back along the corridor, with the exception of the Doctor.

'Fascinating,' he said. 'You know, I doubt there's any real danger.'

Then the door at the entrance of the pyramid slammed shut. Everyone fell silent, exchanging frightened and puzzled glances in the flickering torchlight.

The voice was melodic, almost musical. It resonated within the corridor, seeming to be born out of the air itself. 'Intruders, you face the twin guardians of Horus.'

Tegan looked round. The voice seemed to be coming from above, from the corridor ceiling, or an upper floor of the pyramid, but she could not be certain.

'The corridor is now sealed, and has become a Decatron crucible. The answer you will give the guardians controls your fate – instant freedom, or instant death. Where is the next point in the configuration? This is the riddle of the Osirans.'

The sound echoed off the stone walls for a split second after the words were finished. There was silence for a while.

'Doctor?' Kenilworth said eventually. 'What does it mean?'

'It means we're in trouble. The corridor is in effect an airlock, and they can pump out the air, or unseal the entrance, depending on our answer to the riddle.'

'But what riddle?' Macready asked.

The Doctor smiled. 'Let's ask, shall we?' He strode up to the two Shabti figures and inspected them closely. 'Now then, I assume you two have a question for us.'

In response, the two female statues raised their arms in unison. As they did so, the ceiling of the corridor glowed into life, small squares pulsing into brilliance on the illuminated background. A curved line cut across the roof, the squares of light arranged along the right side of it.

'Just as I thought,' the Doctor said with a nod. 'Thank you.' He turned back to the others. 'Now all we have to do is work out the next point in the configuration.'

'But what's it a configuration of?' Tegan turned her head sideways to try to make sense of the image.

'Well, if we knew that there'd be no riddle.'

Kenilworth craned his neck to see. 'It does look vaguely familiar.'

Macready and Evans both nodded.

'I've seen it somewhere before too,' the Doctor admitted. 'Wish I could remember where.'

At the back of the group, Simons began to copy down the image into his notebook. Tegan could see him framing it up and checking he had the proportions approximately correct. The snake-like ribbon curled down the left side, and several squares were arranged to the right. The three most central were almost aligned. But the top one was offset slightly to the left. Three squares were apparently randomly arranged to the left of the central cluster, two to the right.

Simons stared at what he had drawn, then back at the high ceiling. 'It's a map,' he blurted out in surprise.

Tegan was not convinced, but Atkins was nodding thoughtfully beside her.

'Good grief,' Kenilworth said. 'And we all know what of.'

'Do we?'

'The thick line curling down the left is the River Nile,' Atkins explained. 'The squares are the major pyramids.'

'Of course,' Evans was standing on tiptoe to get as close as possible. 'This is fascinating. Look Margaret.' He waved his hand at the roof, nearly losing his balance. 'This shows the main pyramid complex at Giza, plus the pyramids at Abu Ruwash and Zawyat-al-Aryan.'

Margaret seemed less impressed. 'So what is the next point?'

Macready addressed them all. 'That, I think is a problem. These points mark the positions of the greatest pyramids, the first-rate ones, if you will. Each of them is marked.'

'So we need to show where there's another first-rate pyramid,' Tegan suggested.

Macready shook his head. 'As I said, Miss Tegan. *Each* of them is marked. There are no other points in the configuration.'

'Unless,' Kenilworth said, 'there is one we don't know about.'

'Yes, that's possible isn't it? Why not this pyramid?'

The Doctor coughed. 'This pyramid is minuscule by comparison to those. And he's right, Tegan – there are no more pyramids of that scale to be found.'

'Great. Terrific.'

'So,' the Doctor said, 'I suggest we turn our attention to this.' And he turned to indicate an illuminated section of wall behind them.

The hieroglyphs meant nothing to Tegan, but the more learned members of the party swarmed over them. After ten minutes the noise had subsided and everyone was back to staring glumly at the wall.

'Can't they read it?' Tegan asked the Doctor quietly.

'Oh yes. That's the easy bit. It's a series of eight numbers, starting at seventy and finishing at twenty-three hundred. The values in between seem to be random. At least, they don't conform to any pattern or sequence I can think of.' He leant forward. 'And I can think of lots,' he added.

Tegan grunted. 'Well we should thank our lucky stars you're here, then.' She looked back at the glowing ceiling and the silent figures standing motionless below, arms raised as if in adulation. 'Who are these Osirans, anyway?'

'Hmm? Oh a super-powerful race from the dawn of time. They come from Phaester Osiris, which is—' The Doctor broke off. 'Of course, I should have realised.' He clapped Tegan on the shoulder so hard it hurt. 'You're brilliant.'

'I am?' She was not convinced.

But the Doctor was already gathering everyone round. 'Right, I think I've got it, with a little help from Tegan. It is a map, and the figures are distances. But it isn't a map of Egypt.'

'Not of Egypt?' Macready was surprised. 'Doctor, you can see for yourself how accurate the positioning of the pyramids is.'

'Exactly. But this is a map of the geography from which the pyramids' positions are copied. Look, see how the line of points in the middle is slightly skewed, with the topmost point slightly left of true.'

Kenilworth was shaking his head. 'It's baffled scholars since Napoleon's time that the later pyramid is smaller and is not on the line of the other two, Doctor.'

'Precisely. Why would any Pharaoh build a pyramid smaller than his predecessors if he didn't have to? And why not continue the line so incredibly accurate between the first two?'

'All right,' said Tegan, 'why?'

'Because the pyramids themselves are a map.' The Doctor pointed up at the ceiling. 'That isn't the Nile,' he said, 'it's the Milky Way.'

'What?'

'And the points are the stars in the constellation of Orion. Rigel, Mintaka, Betelgeuse...' The Doctor reeled off the names as he pointed them out. 'The numbers are the distance of each from Earth in light years, or more importantly the distance a thought can travel in a year, which is pretty much the same thing. Rigel, for example, is nine hundred light years away. And the three points almost aligned are what you know as Orion's Belt.'

'Then where is the next point? What star is missing?'

'Like the pyramids, I'm afraid, they are all there.' The Doctor thought for a while. 'Orion was important to the Osirans, and hence to the ancient Egyptians. The Osirans taught them all they knew, after all.'

Evans and Macready were exchanging looks which suggested they thought the Doctor was insane.

'Go on, Doctor,' Tegan encouraged, glaring at Macready.

'Well, it's something to do with a power configuration. Looping stellar activity through a focus generator and aiming at a collection dome. Or rather pyramid, knowing the Osirans. I'd say the final point in the sequence is Phaester Osiris itself.'

The Doctor drew an extendible pointer from his top jacket pocket. Tegan wondered if he was about to continue his lecture with slides as he pulled it to its full extent. But instead he pointed it at the corridor ceiling.

A point of light flared into existence as the rod touched the stonework. The final point in the sequence.

'Of course,' Kenilworth said. 'The great Sphinx.'

But before anyone could comment, the twin Shabti figures lowered their arms and stepped aside. The ceiling dimmed, and the glowing section of wall faded back into the stonework. Far behind them, the main door clicked open and remained ajar, a thin line of daylight forcing its way into the passage.

'These Osirans–' Kenilworth started.

'Time for that later, Kenilworth,' Macready pointed to the far end of the corridor. 'The tomb!'

They made their way warily along the rest of the corridor, scanning the walls for other alcoves or figures. But they reached the double doors without further incident. Macready had a pocket knife open, reaching for the red cord which bound the door handles. Simons was head down again, scribbling in his book and keeping a safe distance from Margaret Evans.

'Er, I wouldn't be so hasty, if I were you,' the Doctor warned, tapping Macready on the shoulder.

'Nonsense, man.' He continued to pull at the cord with the knife blade. 'Nearly through now.'

Tegan stood, arms folded, with the others, clustered round the doorway. Light strobed across the face of Macready as he hacked at the rope, and Tegan looked round puzzled trying to locate its source. The effect was regular, not like the flickering of the torchlight.

'Doctor,' she said. 'The light.' And then she saw the source, and pointed to the stylised eye glowing in the floor at her feet.

'The Eye of Horus,' Atkins breathed.

'Stop!' the Doctor shouted as Macready cut through the last strand of the cord and pulled open the doors.

The eye flashed brilliant red as the hurricane swept down the corridor. The Doctor had grabbed everyone he could as he dived for cover. Macready was holding on to the door handle, braced against the rushing force of the air as it was forced past him. Tegan grabbed Margaret as she was blown past, and pulled her down to the ground.

Simons, still scribbling in his notebook, had reacted more slowly than the others. He was caught full in the blast and hurled down the corridor, bouncing down the slope and crashing into the walls. His book burst apart in a frenzy of whirling paper, pencil clattering across the floor. He rebounded from the wall and slammed into the ground, head cracking open on a flagstone. A dark trail followed his body as it was tossed like a ragdoll along the passageway.

Tegan kept low, feeling the force of the wind tugging at her short hair, as it struggled to dislodge her. She felt her grip on Margaret slipping, and fought to keep hold. Out of the corner of her eye she could see the Doctor holding Atkins and Kenilworth back with one arm, and holding firmly to the doorpost with the other. Beyond him the doors to the tomb stood open.

From his vantage point, Sadan Rassul watched the door to the black pyramid blown open and the pages of Simons' book blasted into the heat of the day. And he smiled.

London
1986

Rejected Applications

10557/86 Structural alterations and renovation of grade two listed domestic residence. See full application for details and appendix 2B for reasons of rejection.

Henry Edwards swept his torch round the darkened room once more. The beam of light glanced off the polished floor and strayed over the tables of relics. It peered into corners, and licked round the feet of a sarcophagus standing against the far wall.

Edwards closed the door behind him, and for a moment the light from his torch continued to stray under the door. Then all was dark again.

A faint glow in the corner accompanied the crashing vibration of sound which echoed through the room. The glow resolved itself into a flashing light as a shadowy form solidified beneath it, then ground to a halt, and the TARDIS door opened tentatively.

The Doctor's head appeared round the door for a moment. Then it disappeared again. A few seconds later, the Doctor stepped into the room. He was holding a lantern. He made his way from table to table, letting the pale light pool around him as he examined and then discarded various vases and jars. He shook his head in annoyance and exhaled loudly. 'Should have paid for a catalogue,' he murmured.

He looked round for another display of relics, and set off towards the door. As he passed close to the sarcophagus, his foot caught something, sending it into a spin. Standing on the floor, close to the sarcophagus, was a canopic jar. The Doctor knelt down, catching the jar as it continued to wobble on its uneven base. He patted the top and stood up again.

Then he frowned, and bent down to examine the jar once more. The stopper was carved into the shape of a jackal's head. The Doctor lifted the jar and held the lantern close to it. He sniffed at it, shook it, then turned it over to see the base.

'That should do nicely,' he said quietly. 'An Osiran generator loop, rather the worse for wear, but it should do very well indeed.'

The Doctor stood up, hefted the canopic jar in his hand, and smiled at the jackal. Then he went back inside the TARDIS. A short while later, that too was gone.

CHAPTER
SIX

If Tegan had thought the excavating was boring, she was now
looking back on it as a time of excitement and intellectual
stimulation. Since solving the Osiran riddle and being half
torn apart by the hurricane of what the Doctor described as a
'psychic typhoon', the archaeologists had settled into a well-
rehearsed schedule.

The wind had died down after several minutes. They had
rushed to Simons' aid, but it was too late to help him. Tegan
had tried to comfort Margaret Evans while Atkins and the
Egyptian Nebka laid out Simons in one of the tents where
the supplies were stored. The dry desert air would preserve
the body for the time being – just as its preserving properties
had given the ancient Egyptians the first clues about the
possibilities of mummification.

Once the archaeology started in earnest, the Doctor was
in his element. He rushed from each archaeologist to the
next, checking their notes and reviewing their sketches and
catalogues. He helped with measurements and suggested
theories. He carried relics and copied down hieroglyphics.

Tegan, by contrast, was bored out of her brain. And she
wasted no opportunity to tell him this.

'Can't we just take Nyssa and leave?' she asked him as they
examined the tomb chamber yet again.

'Leave?'

It seemed as though the thought had not occurred to
him before. The Doctor continued to sketch a copy of the

hieroglyphics which covered a whole wall of the tomb into a notebook.

Tegan watched him for a while. She had initially tried to relieve her boredom by sketching scenes of the excavations. But her interest in expanses of sand, makeshift wooden scaffolding, and stone-floored rooms had foundered after a morning. 'Yes, leave,' she said eventually. 'As in push off and leave them to it.'

'But we didn't,' the Doctor pointed out. 'Did we?'

'You mean we can't?'

The Doctor closed the notebook, pushed his pencil down the gap between the binding and the spine, and stuck it in his jacket pocket. 'Probably not. But think about it, Tegan. We know one future set of events – or part of one, anyway – in which we stay with the expedition. And at the end of it, Nyssa is alive.'

'But if we leave now, we don't know what will happen.' Tegan turned away. 'I get the picture.'

The Doctor's hand clapped down on her shoulder. 'So why not enjoy it while you can.'

'You're joking. A load of crumbling brickwork?'

'It's stone, and it's not crumbling. Tegan –' the Doctor's voice betrayed a hint of exasperation – 'the pyramids are the oldest and the last surviving of the seven wonders of the ancient world. Each pyramid, including this one so far as I can tell, is exactly aligned along the points of the compass. The base of each is a perfect square. There is not enough space between the stone blocks in the Great Pyramid to insert a razor blade, but if you took those stone blocks and used them to build a wall a foot high and a foot wide, it would stretch two-thirds of the way round the equator.'

'So they're impressive.'

'Awesome.'

'Great. I'm impressed and overawed,' Tegan told him. 'And now I want to take Nyssa and leave.'

'So do I,' the Doctor said quietly. 'So do I.'

They waited in silence for a while, standing beside the casket that contained their sleeping friend. It was against one wall of the large room. The wall itself was adorned with row after row of hieroglyphics. Above the level of casket on its raised dais, a shelf ran the length of the wall. On it, labelled and ready to be packed for shipping with the other relics stood several items. There was a wide, heavy bracelet made of thick metal. The lower half was semi-circular, while the lot was flattened into less of a curve. Across the top was a carved beetle of brilliant blue stone.

Beside the bracelet, a ring with a large blue stone set in it rested on a small cushion of dusty, faded red velvet. Further along, a wooden cobra reared up from its coiled base, throwing a huge shadow of itself onto the wall behind.

Further still along the shelf was a statue of what looked like a black dog. It was about eight inches long, paws facing forwards as it sat upright. Its collar, eyes and tall pointed ears were picked out in gold. Its tail was curled back along its body.

'That's interesting,' the Doctor said as he looked along the shelf.

'What, the dog?'

'Dog? More like a jackal. That's Anubis, king of the dead. Watching over his own, no doubt.' The Doctor pointed at the other relics. 'No, I meant the spacing. The bracelet, ring and snake are evenly spaced. Then there's a gap of over twice the size before the statue of Anubis. Interesting.'

'Why?'

'The Egyptians, like their Osiran mentors, were into measurements in a big way. Exact measurements.'

'Like the pyramids.'

'Yes. The topography and geometry of the pyramids is phenomenal.' The Doctor was examining the shelf closely, peering at the gap between cobra and jackal. 'This chamber, for instance, like the King's Chamber in the Great Pyramid, is at a point in the structure where, if you extended the floor to the outside walls, then took the perfect pyramid rising above that plane, you would have one precisely half the size of the original.'

'Why? I mean, why did they bother?'

The Doctor was now examining a particular part of the shelf's surface. 'Oh it's all to do with power relays and receptor configuration. Boringly exact. Elegantly convoluted. Typical of Osiran technology. Take those shafts, for example.' He waved a hand vaguely at the sloping wall where Tegan had watched Macready, Kenilworth and Evans the previous day measuring a square hole.

'They're just ventilation shafts,' she said, repeating what Atkins had told her.

'So people will believe for the next hundred years or so. Strange how they're exactly aligned with different stars in the constellation of Orion, isn't it?'

Tegan considered this. 'Why hasn't anyone noticed?'

'Because the Earth wobbles slightly on her axis. I don't think the Osirans allowed for that, probably didn't notice.' He looked up from the shelf thoughtfully.

'So?'

'So, the relative position of the constellations varies over time. The alignment doesn't work now. But when they were built, it was exact. And it will be again in about twenty-one thousand years.'

'What happens then?'

'Hmm? Oh, I don't know. Street parties, perhaps. Tegan,

what can you think of that has a perfectly round base about three inches in diameter?'

Tegan closed her eyes for a second. 'I haven't a clue, Doctor. What?'

'I don't know,' he said in a hurt voice, and pointed to a barely discernible mark in the dust on the shelf, an area where the dust was slightly thinner. 'But whatever it is, it's been removed from its place between the cobra and the jackal.' He looked straight at Tegan. 'I wonder why,' he said.

Sadan Rassul stared into the falling sand and recited from the Scroll of Thoth. He had chosen a position from which he could direct his words, thoughts and power directly into the tent. The sand spiralled slowly down in a fine spray, building a perfect pyramid in the lower bowl of the hourglass.

As he finished speaking, Rassul set the hourglass down on the ground, and watched the tent, waiting to see movement from within. The hourglass balanced at an angle on the desert floor, but Rassul paid it no heed. He knew from experience that it did not matter whether it stood angled, toppled over, or was upended. The sands had been set in their courses, and whatever happened to the outside of the hourglass, they would continue their fall, would continue to pile perfectly on the foundations laid by previous grains, until all the sand had travelled from one bowl to the other. And then, then his work would be done. And the waiting would be over.

The tiny drops of sand continued to dribble in an almost imperceptible spray. The top bowl was almost empty, perhaps a fiftieth of the sand remaining. The pile of sand in the lower bowl continued to build its slow pyramid as Rassul lifted the hourglass and carried it back to his small encampment in the valley below.

Beside his footprints was a small impression in the sand,

an impression made by the base of the hourglass. It was a perfect circle, about three inches in diameter.

The evening sessions were getting gradually more enthusiastic. Kenilworth had a practice of gathering the members of his expedition together every evening after dinner to discuss the day's work and exchange views and information. The first few meetings had been rather subdued, overshadowed by the strange events in the passageway and the death of Simons.

The first evening had been mainly taken up with the Doctor giving assurances that they were over the worst problems and he did not anticipate any further *automata*, as Kenilworth described them, posing more fatal brain-teasers. Faced with the task of cataloguing the tomb and its contents, the others did not press the Doctor for more information. Tegan could see how relieved he was that they let the matter drop.

This evening was the first that Margaret Evans had felt up to joining them. Initially she had not ventured from her tent, having food and water sent in. The last two nights she had dined with the others, quiet and pale. Tonight she seemed to be making an effort to get back into things. Tegan made a point of sitting next to her at one of the trestle tables, and noticed that her father seemed hardly to have noticed her demeanour. She had overheard Evans telling Macready a few days previously that his daughter was suffering from fatigue brought on by loss of sleep. And then some, thought Tegan, who had no illusions about what she had really lost.

Perhaps because of Margaret Evans' reappearance, or perhaps because the Doctor opened the session by asking who had removed an uncatalogued object from the tomb, the proceedings were more lively than usual. Everyone vehemently denied removing anything, and Evans started again on his pet speech about scrupulous documentation. He moved from this directly into suggesting that the stone cladding of the tomb interior and the carved sections of the corridor be dismantled and stripped so they could be returned to England.

Tegan was surprised at the suggestion, and more surprised by the nods that it elicited round the tables. But she was amazed at the Doctor's reaction.

'You call yourself an archaeologist?' he said, standing up and leaning over the table at Evans. The small man leant away, obviously unsettled by the sudden outburst.

'Have you no idea of the damage done to the past by that sort of action?' the Doctor went on. 'I suppose you think that the wonders of ancient Egypt will be better displayed in the Victorian splendour of the British Museum than in their rightful place amongst the desert sands.'

'Well, actually, ahem—' coughed Evans.

But the Doctor cut him off. 'I don't know, when will you learn?' He looked towards the deep blue of the heavens, pinched the bridge of his nose, closed his eyes, and turned a full circle. 'I know,' he said more quietly, 'that it is common practice to return home with treasures and even the insides of the tombs that have been surveyed. But I have a theory that archaeology can be better appreciated *in situ*, and that, if we leave it as undisturbed as possible, then others can make their own assessments with as much evidence as possible.'

'I take your point, Doctor,' Macready agreed. 'But, given the finances that the British Museum has forwarded—'

'Money, is that what it comes down to?' The Doctor waved his hands in frustration. 'You'll destroy it, don't you see that.'

'It's preservation, surely,' Kenilworth interposed.

'What? How can you claim such a thing? Even Champollion himself cut the painted royal heads from the walls of the tomb of Amenhotep III so they could be hung in the Bibliothèque Nationale.' The Doctor paced up and down in front of the group as he spoke, his voice gathering speed until he was breathless in his hurry to finish what he was saying. 'Blank squares in the adorned walls of an ancient burial chamber, just so that the rich socialites of Europe can admire the works of civilisations the living descendants of whom they regard with contempt.'

Kenilworth blinked, but said nothing. Macready shifted uncomfortably on his bench, and Evans stared silently, mouth hanging open. Tegan and Margaret exchanged glances, each showing surprise and varying degrees of embarrassment.

'Preservation?' the Doctor finished, almost as a whisper, 'I don't think so.'

Kenilworth was the first to break the silence. 'Doctor,' he said, 'I don't think any of us here don't share your enthusiasm for the past and your desire to preserve it.' He looked round the others as if to gain their approval and confirmation. 'But it seems we may differ in our views about how to achieve this. Speaking for myself, I feel that whatever relics we can remove to the more civilised climes of Great Britain stand a better chance of long-term survival than those left in a country where every pyramid so far discovered has been robbed of its treasures. Every pyramid until this one.'

The Doctor nodded. 'I didn't mean to sound as if I doubted your honesty or your motives, and I apologise if that is how it sounded. But—'

Kenilworth held up his hand. 'But,' he finished for the Doctor, 'you do express some reservations, I think, about tampering with the structure of the find. Forgive me if I misinterpret your worries, Doctor, but it seems to me that your primary concern is for the integrity of the architecture.'

The Doctor did not answer immediately. He walked back

to his bench and sat down, staring at the top of the table for a while. 'I suppose that's true,' he said at last. 'The artefacts can be redistributed, though it's a shame to break up any collection, provided they are scrupulously catalogued and their whereabouts recorded. But I cannot sanction the removal of one block of stone or one chip of paint from the pyramid.'

'Is it because it's dangerous?' Tegan was wondering if the Doctor was concerned about the Osiran influences and science.

'No, Tegan.' The Doctor shook his head sadly. 'It's because it's criminal. We're talking about breaking things that don't belong to us, and which can never be replaced.'

'I am in charge of this expedition,' Kenilworth said loudly, standing up and looking it turn at each member of his party. 'But it is thanks to the Doctor that we are here at all. And probably that we are still alive.' He gave a short nod as if in thanks. 'So I think we should do as the Doctor asks, and disturb as little as possible. We shall remove relics we believe to be important, and we shall catalogue and document everything, including the minutiae of the structure. But the architecture remains intact. Any questions?'

There were none.

The session broke up soon after. Macready and Evans wandered off to compare some notes, Atkins and Kenilworth spoke quietly with the Doctor. Tegan found herself talking to Margaret Evans.

'Is your friend always so forceful?' Margaret asked.

'Only when he thinks it's important. Otherwise he varies from indecisive to aloof.' They spoke about the progress of the excavations and the catalogue as they made their way back towards their tents on the far side of the encampment.

The canvas of the low supply tents bowed and flapped in the quickening desert breeze.

'I wonder,' Margaret said as they passed another of the small tents, 'may I ask you a small favour?'

Tegan shrugged. 'Depends what it is. Ask away.'

'Would you wait here a moment?'

'Is that it?'

Margaret gestured to the nearest tent. 'This is where they put poor Nicholas's body. I look at him each day, just to check that he is…' She struggled for a word, and decided on 'peaceful.'

Tegan nodded. 'He meant a lot to you, didn't he?'

'He had been assistant to my father for a long time.' She looked down at the ground, making tiny circles in the sand with the toe of her leather boot. 'He was always so tense and jittery when I was near him. And now he seems so calm.'

Tegan crossed her fingers behind her back. 'I'm sure he valued your company enormously,' she said.

'Do you really think so?' Margaret's face lit up, catching the fading sunlight. In that moment she shed ten years.

Tegan smiled back. 'I'll wait here,' she said.

The scream came almost immediately. The flap of the tent's entrance had barely fallen back into place when Margaret re-emerged, her face white and her eyes wide and streaming.

'He's gone,' she said between deep rasping sobs. 'Nicholas has gone.'

A general search of the camp revealed nothing. Nebka, under Atkins's supervision, organised the reluctant Egyptian workers to check the tents and the surrounding area, but still they found nothing.

Tegan did her best to comfort the distraught Margaret. The Doctor seemed to be wandering aimlessly round the camp, his expression getting gradually darker as the evening drew in and faded into night.

'It's a mystery, and no mistake,' Kenilworth said as he called off the search due to bad light. 'What do you reckon, Doctor?'

'I reckon,' the Doctor said, 'that we should all get a good night's sleep and then do our best to finish here as soon as we can.'

'Well,' Atkins said to the Doctor as they parted company on the way to their tents, 'one thing's for sure, he didn't go for a little walk.'

In the darkening chill of the desert night, the Doctor's expression was unreadable and his muttered words were lost in the breeze.

The wind whistled through the canvas tents and swished across the sand dunes. It brought comfort to Kenilworth, who was used to the sound and felt almost at home when he could hear the desert. It annoyed Macready as it seemed to swell just as he was dropping off, jerking him wider awake each time. It was of no consequence to Atkins, who settled down neatly in his pyjamas and went immediately and efficiently to sleep, boots polished and clothes laid out for the next day. It irritated Evans as he was first concerned about his daughter's demeanour and wondered what could be the cause, and then worried about where he would find a personal secretary as trustworthy as Simons.

The wind blew Rassul's thin cotton clothes about him as he knelt beside the hourglass and watched the reflections of the stars of Orion wrapped about the glass. It wailed its complementary lamentation through Margaret's tent and punctuated her sobs with its moans.

It failed to register its existence with the Doctor as he sat cross-legged on the floor of his tent, deep in thought. And it drove Tegan to clasp a pillow over her head and think of her father's farm and the family she had lost.

Eventually she could stand it no longer, and Tegan threw off her covers. She grabbed the cloak she had not believed she would need, but had then discovered had been packed for her anyway. Then she fumbled with the oil lamp on the low table beside her camp bed until it flickered into life.

Tegan needed to talk to someone, and her choices were somewhat limited. She was not at all sure she was in the right mood to talk to Margaret; she was certain the Doctor was not in the right mood to talk to her. Kenilworth and Atkins would be asleep. And even if they were not, one of them would not understand the emotions she was feeling, while the other would not understand that she was feeling emotions at all.

Which left her just one choice. If you could have a single choice. Probably not, she decided as she realised that she had walked through the camp and was pushing through the canvas cover over the entrance to the pyramid even as she decided where she was going. No choice at all.

The corridor up to the burial chamber was steeper than she remembered. She leant forward and pulled her cloak tighter with one hand, holding her lamp in front of her with the other. The dim light threw a faint aura in front of her, and elongated the cuts of the engraved hieroglyphics. It lingered in the cold of her breath, and drew the painted pupils of the Shabti's eyes so the statues seemed to watch her as she passed.

When she reached the chamber, Tegan placed the lamp on the shelf at the head of the coffin. It fitted neatly over the circle the Doctor had noticed between the relics.

'Perhaps I should suggest it was an ancient Egyptian oil lamp,' Tegan said quietly to the carved figure on the coffin lid. Nyssa's painted, impassive features stared back without comment. 'Maybe they had oil lamps,' Tegan continued, sitting down with her back to the wall and drawing up her knees. She was looking along the length of the sarcophagus towards the doorway. Her head was probably on a level with Nyssa's within the casket.

'I hope you don't mind company, but I couldn't sleep. Could have gone to see the Doctor, I suppose. I doubt if he's asleep. But I don't think he'd understand.

'The wind sounds just like on the farm. Dad used to say it was there to keep us company, watching over us and keeping us safe. I believed him. I believed everything Dad told me. Well, almost everything. But it's different here. It sounds more spooky. Like it's out to get us, not to watch us.

'I can still hear Dad's voice, I can hear him saying "keeping us safe". Isn't that odd? Because I have to really think to remember what he looked like. And when I do remember, it doesn't matter where he is, he always looks like he does in the photo on the kitchen wall. Same expression, same position. Everything. Funny.

'I hope you don't mind me talking away. It's what I do best. Well, it's what I do most of, anyway. Get lots of friends that way. You never talked much. Probably keep lots of friends that way.

'The picture of you is quite good, by the way. Got the eyes, though the hair's not quite right. I keep thinking you will push off the lid, sit up and answer me. But I know you won't. I don't know if you can hear, and if you can I don't know if you'll remember. I'm sorry it's taking so long, but the Doctor says we have to do what Blinovitch says, or something. God, I'm bored – how must you feel.

'I miss you, Nyssa. I can talk to you. I mean to you, not at you.

'It was the same with Dad. It's not the sudden wrench or

loss – you get over that. It's the never-again. I can't remember how Dad looked when he was joking, though I could recognise it at once. And now I'll never know. I'll never feel his arms round me and his warmth as he hugged me home at the end of school. He was so warm, so safe. I can feel him now, holding me safe.

'He listened, always. I was always talking sense when I spoke to Dad; I was always interesting when I spoke to Dad; I was always right when I spoke to Dad, even if he then told me something that was even more right.

'But never again. It's not that we've lost him, it's worse. He's gone, and he's never coming back. Not ever.

'Oh God, Nyssa, talk to me. I'm sick of what I say and how I say it. I know how everyone else feels. The Doctor listens, but only so he can disagree. Though I suppose that's better than nothing.

'Nothing. Just me. Alone. Alone in the water trying to find the light.

'Please talk to me, Nyssa… Please…

'I've forgotten what your voice sounds like.'

Tegan sat alone in the flickering quiet for a while. Her arm lay across the top of the sarcophagus, her hand stoking gently at the face. Then she pushed herself up, knees braced so that her feet pushed against the floor and her back worked its way up the wall. When her shoulders felt the edge of the shelf behind her, she reached out her arm and pushed herself away from the wall as she stood upright. Her hand pushed against the centre of a hieroglyphic.

And she felt it give.

Tegan held the lamp up to inspect the damage. Her first thought was that she had pushed through a plaster covering, or damaged the paint. She could imagine the Doctor's comments if she had. The hieroglyph was a set of small pictures surrounded by an upright oval border. The top symbol was a jagged horizontal line, as if the stone had been cut with crimping shears. Below it was an outlined square with a section of the lower side missing, and below that a snake. The bottom symbol was a human figure lying on its back.

The incomplete square had pushed slightly inwards. Tegan could see the deeper recess between the outline cuts in the stone. She reached out, tentatively, and pushed slightly in the centre of the square.

Sure enough, it moved. She pushed harder, and it moved further inwards. And, with a deep grating sound, the whole of that section of the wall moved away with it. Tegan was looking at a huge hidden doorway. She could see nothing of the room beyond, shadows seemed to spill out of it. In panic she pushed at the square again, hoping to be able to prise her fingernails between the stone, and remembering what the Doctor had said about razor blades.

The square pushed back at her, and sprang forward. Tegan took a step backwards, and the heavy door swung shut again. She stared at the wall, holding the oil lamp close to the stonework. But it was impossible to see where the doorway was.

Tegan reached out again for the hieroglyph. Then, as her fingers touched it, she snatched her hand away, turned, and left the burial chamber.

'Well done, Tegan.' The Doctor was so enthusiastic that she thought for a second he was being sarcastic. 'I knew there had to be more to this than just Nyssa. It makes no sense otherwise.'

Tegan had not been surprised to find the Doctor sitting cross-legged on the floor of his tent staring at the canvas flap as it blew in the wind. But she had expected less interest in her discovery. At the very least she had thought he would make some comment about her wandering around the pyramid in the dead of night, but he hadn't even mentioned it. Perhaps from his perspective such things were perfectly normal behaviour.

Feeling rather more confident, Tegan demonstrated the hidden doorway with a degree of smugness which the Doctor seemed not to notice. In fact he peered closely at the hieroglyphics and seemed more interested in the symbols than in the area of blackness revealed behind them.

'All in good time, be patient, Tegan,' he murmured as she hopped from foot to foot.

'So what does it mean?'

'Hmm? Oh, I don't know. Have to think about it for a while. My ancient Egyptian isn't what it was four thousand years ago.'

'You mean you can't read it?'

The Doctor straightened up and whipped off his half-moon spectacles. 'Of course I can read it. But you asked me what it means.'

'Same difference.'

He shook his head. 'Context is key,' he said. 'Ask me again when we've looked inside the hidden room.'

'Why?'

The Doctor visibly braced himself and made a point of keeping calm. 'Egyptian hieroglyphs are not an exact language, Tegan. Their order is important to their meaning, yet the scribes would rearrange them so they looked good rather than meant what was intended. That set of hieroglyphs could be read from top to bottom or from bottom to top, and each way it means something different. It could be that the final symbol in the sequence – whichever that is – gives an overall impression of the word or phrase so as to reiterate and reinforce the thought. Or not. Depending on the exact age, the alphabet may have different inflections and meaning.'

'Not easy, then?'

'Not, as you say, easy.' He picked up the oil lamp which they had rested on the shelf beside the door.

Tegan nodded slowly. 'Why's it got a ring round it?' she asked.

The Doctor glared at her, pushed past, and disappeared into the darkness. 'It's a cartouche,' his voice floating out of the void.

The room was smaller than the chamber they had just left. It was almost completely bare. There was a central dais, and four large ornate sarcophagi stood upright, one in each of the corners of the room. The walls were covered in hieroglyphics, stretching up to the ceiling which arched above them. The only breaks were for ventilation shafts like the ones in the main burial chamber. There was one in each wall, dark openings about four inches square.

On the raised dais in the centre of the room was a casket. It was a sarcophagus similar to Nyssa's, but the outside was completely devoid of decoration. A matt-black oval of polished stone with a thin line of deeper black, which marked the point where the lid joined the base. The Doctor was already standing beside it, hands in pockets, examining the polished lid, as Tegan entered the room.

'So what's a cartouche?' she asked as she joined him.

'Hmm?' He looked up, eyes focusing at a point somewhere behind her head. 'Oh, French. Coined by Napoleon's team when they arrived in Egypt in 1798. They were the first real Egyptian archaeologists, and thought those oval shapes were like their cartridges. Cartouche is French for cartridge. And for carton.' A puzzled look swept over his face. 'Perhaps it was the cartons the cartridges came in they thought they looked like. Language again – needs a context.'

'Yes, but what is it, Doctor?'

The Doctor's face cleared as he answered. 'Oh, it's a royal name. The oval represents a loop of rope encircling the name. The loop represents eternity, and if you put your name inside it you'll live for ever.'

'Will you?'

'No, of course not,' the Doctor admonished. 'But they thought they would. And everything's about living for ever if you're a Pharaoh.' He returned his attention to the sarcophagus. 'Or an Osiran, come to that.'

Tegan folded her arms and shifted her weight to her right leg. 'You keep going on about these Osirans, Doctor,' she said. 'Who are they?'

'Who were they, rather,' the Doctor said. 'An odd sort from Phaester Osiris. Big on guile and cunning. Short on applied morals, though Horus got moving when his uncle started destroying everything for the hell of it. Here, help me lift this back, will you?' He gestured to the coffin lid, and took up position on one side of the casket.

Tegan stood opposite him as the Doctor counted to three. Then together they heaved the heavy lid back along the sarcophagus. The Doctor lifted the oil lamp which he had stood at the base of the dais, and they peered through the narrow opening.

'Oh, how boring,' the Doctor said as the contents were revealed. 'It's just another mummy.'

They pulled the heavy lid back over the coffin.

'What were you expecting?' Tegan asked.

The Doctor shrugged. 'Nephthys,' he said.

'Who?'

He exhaled loudly and spoke with exagerrated patience. 'The cartouche you found includes the symbol for a door, that square with a section missing. But being within an oval, it should be a name. If you read it from the top down and assume the horizontal figure is to give some context to the name, then it could read "Nephthys".'

'Was he an Osiran?'

'She,' the Doctor said, 'was the sister and wife of Sutekh. And sister of Isis and Osiris, though that's less worrying.'

Tegan did not reply.

The Doctor frowned at her lack of response. 'Nephthys was a goddess, and may not have actually existed. Sutekh, her brother according to legend, was an Osiran. He was cornered on Earth by Horus and seven hundred and forty of his fellow Osirans and imprisoned for all eternity beneath a pyramid.'

Tegan laughed. 'That's all right then.'

'Till he escapes in 1911, it is, yes.' The Doctor waved away her worried expression. 'But that's all sorted out now. All ancient Egyptian culture is based on the Osiran history. And I don't know much about an Osiran called Nephthys, but if the Egyptian myths are half true…' His voice tailed off into the darkness.

'Yes? If they're right?'

The Doctor turned and stepped down from the dais. 'If this time we have to deal with Nephthys, and the myths have a grain of truth in them—' He broke off again, considered, then went on: 'If Sutekh had escaped, no power in the universe could have stopped him from wreaking havoc and destruction. This time, it's worse.'

Tegan considered. The Doctor stood in the doorway and surveyed the room. After a moment he pulled out a notepad and a pencil and started to scribble frantically.

'What are you doing?'

He did not look up. 'I'm copying down the hieroglyphics. I'll make a stab at deciphering some of them later. But before that, I suggest we seal up this room, and tell nobody about it.'

'But why?'

'Oh, Tegan, haven't you been listening?'

Tegan joined the Doctor in the doorway and watched as he scrawled down line after line of symbol with uncanny speed and unerring accuracy. 'I thought you'd be getting into the thick of it all,' she said. 'I mean, it sounds like your sort of thing.' Tegan glanced at the nearest of the four huge sarcophagi where it stood upright in the corner by the door.

'I never get involved in stuff on this scale, if it is on this scale,' the Doctor said. Then he caught sight of Tegan's expression. 'Well, maybe occasionally,' he admitted. 'But what's the most important thing at the moment?'

Tegan had no doubts. 'To save Nyssa.'

'Exactly.' The Doctor turned away and she could not see his expression as he flipped shut his notepad and left the room. 'And I will not do anything to jeopardise that.'

Tegan caught up with the Doctor in the burial chamber. He was holding a larger notepad, which she recognised as belonging to Evans. She half remembered seeing it earlier resting on a low table in the chamber.

'What are you doing?'

The Doctor flipped the pad shut and replaced it on the table. 'Insurance,' he said. 'Come on.'

'What do you mean?'

'You were lucky to find the hidden door,' the Doctor said as they made their way down the corridor towards the desert night. 'But the clues are there in the hieroglyphs. We leave tomorrow, but there's always a danger someone will examine Evans' drawings and wonder what the symbols mean. And I don't think it's a good idea for people to poke about in the room we've just seen.'

'Even if it doesn't have a dead Osiran in it?'

'Yes, well the mummy was human enough. Female, *Homo sapiens*, circa five thousand BC. But even then…'

'So what have you done?'

The Doctor held aside the canvas doorway for Tegan. 'I've corrected Evans' drawing,' he said. 'So that the doorway and the name of Nephthys don't appear.'

Atkins ran the final day like a military operation. He had spent the previous evening mapping out an exact timetable for finishing the documentation and providing an inventory of relics to be removed and packed for transport back to Britain. It had been agreeably like planning the details of the servants' duties and listing the shopping requirements for the next day back at Kenilworth House. But without the helpful and agreeable company of Miss Warne.

He stood at the entrance to the pyramid, the early evening sun beating down on him, and ticked off the items on a clipboard as the Egyptians removed them. Nebka had agreed his men would enter the corridor, but they would not go so far as to enter the burial chamber itself. Macready, Evans and Kenilworth boxed up the relics, with help from the Doctor and Tegan. They worked from a hand-copied version of Atkins's list. Then Atkins checked the relics were taken to the packing tent. There, Margaret Evans seemed sufficiently recovered to supervise the loading of the boxes into larger packing cases. The packing cases were designed to fit into the panniers of the camels.

They were almost finished now, exactly to the schedule which Atkins had suggested. He was satisfied, but not surprised. The last few relics were carried out, and Atkins checked the details written on the box lid, then ticked them off.

'Jewelled ring on velvet cushion from shelf by sarcophagus in main chamber.' He scratched a tick against the same wording on his copy of the list. 'Snake statuette from shelf by sarcophagus in main chamber.' Another tick. 'Bracelet with scarab beetle motif from shelf by sarcophagus in main chamber.' Tick. 'Stone figure of Anubis from shelf by sarcophagus in main chamber.'

Atkins looked over his list during the pause before the next relic was brought out. There was only one thing left to be removed – the sarcophagus itself. The sarcophagus and the mummy inside, which only Atkins, the Doctor and Tegan knew was the entire reason for the expedition.

Atkins wondered vaguely what would happen after they sealed the pyramid that evening and made their way back to London, what would happen when they arrived back and Kenilworth House. And found he was still there.

Behind him, the Doctor, Kenilworth, Evans and Macready emerged slowly from the doorway. They carried the sarcophagus high on their shoulders. Tegan followed them, head down and face shrouded in shadow. They made their way slowly up the incline towards the packing tent, shuffling slowly through the soft sand like a funeral procession.

As they left the pyramid, Nebka and his men pulled shut the door.

The night was quiet and still. Two shadowy figures made their way past the snoring lookout and lurched down the shifting slope of sand into the pit where the entrance to the pyramid had been excavated. The door was tight shut, but the bearers had not yet buried it again in the desert.

Rassul reached out and pressed on the side of the door.

He knew the exact pressure point, remembered it clearly. Just as he remembered the low grating sound as the door swung slowly open. He glanced back towards the rim of the excavations, but nobody came running to investigate the noise. In a moment, the two figures had passed inside, and the door was an empty hole of blackness.

They made their way quickly up the corridor, pausing only for Rassul to light his lamp. In the flickering light, the two men surveyed the bare burial chamber, checked the shelf where the relics had stood beside the coffin. Rassul nodded slowly. He had known what he would find. He went over to the wall, scanned the hieroglyphs for a moment, then reached for the centre of the unfinished square in the cartouche of Nephthys's name.

Once inside the hidden chamber, Rassul moved to the nearest of the four sarcophagi and pulled aside the heavy lid. It hinged like a door, swinging slowly open in response to Rassul's efforts. He repeated the process with each of the other three.

His colleague stood silent and still in the doorway, watching unblinking as Rassul stepped into the centre of the room and raised his hands high above the raised coffin.

'Biesmey Nephthys,' he called out, 'um wallacha.'

In each of the open caskets, a figure stirred. As Rassul continued to recite the words of power, the four huge, bandaged figures stretched long-still limbs and stepped forward into the guttering light.

Each of the figures was seven feet tall. Heavy legs moving the body stiffly forward with a rolling motion that transferred the weight of the mummy from one leg to the other as the figure twisted its way forwards towards the central dais.

The linen-wrapped arms ended in large hands, fingers apparently wrapped together, thumb clamping against them.

The chest was a jutting slope of bandage beneath the enormous shoulders. The head seemed perfectly symmetrical under the bindings, flat surfaces pushing back from the middle as if the eyes beneath were huge ovals covering the cheeks.

The wind was picking up again outside, amplified and distorted by the corridor so that it sounded like organ music rising in pitch and volume as the mummies stopped in front of the dais and Rassul slowly lowered his arms.

From the doorway, the pale figure with dark sunken eyes, split skull and bloodstained clothes nodded slowly. 'As it was written,' the corpse of Nicholas Simons rasped.

His words sounded as though they were spoken through broken glass.

PHAESTER OSIRIS

The door slammed shut and the psi-projectors locked on maximum as soon as he was in the capsule. There was no meeting, no dissuasion, no concession. A trick to lure Osiris into the pyramid and then launch it into space.

Osiris looked round the bare interior of the capsule and felt the floor shudder under his feet. It was just an empty shell. There were no sensors, no projection dome, no psi-tronic particle-accelerators. It was a plain pyramid structure powered by a remote psi-projection.

The mind of Sutekh.

'A childish stratagem, my brother,' Osiris hissed, shaking his jackal-head. It was a mere thought to project himself back to Phaester Osiris.

His eyes glowed with the trivial effort. Then flared angrily as he felt another mind reach out like a hand and smother his thought in a fist of malevolent mental energy. It was unshaking, constant and solid. He was trapped.

The atmosphere was becoming noticeably thinner. For all his powers, Osiris needed to breathe. He gasped and clawed for air as he considered the options. It could not be happening. Sutekh's mental power was projecting the capsule. Great though his powers were, he could not project the capsule through space and cloud Osiris's mind at the same time. He had to have an accomplice – another Osiran was helping Sutekh.

But who would dare? Who would risk everything by

assisting Sutekh the Destroyer, the Lord of Death?

As he felt the faint chuckle of laughter in his mind's ear, Osiris knew. He fought to suppress the sound.

The walls of the capsule were blurring before his eyes as he struggled to breathe. Isis would come after him, of course. But by then it would be too late. All his sister-wife would find would be his body, the mind wrenched from it by death. Unless there was another receptacle close enough for him to project into. He could not break free of the grip enough to project his whole form, but perhaps his mind...

Osiris sank to his knees. And the laughter of his sister Nephthys rang unhindered in his head.

Chapter
Seven

Bakr was suddenly awake. He knew he had been sleeping with the clarity of thought and senses that only comes in the second of reawakening. Immediately he was on his feet, and looking round.

Something had disturbed his rest. Probably it was just a gust of wind, but it might be a jackal or some other potential danger. Since he was the lookout, he should be aware of whatever it was. If he failed to give the alarm in good time, he could forfeit some or all of his meagre wages. And that was all the money he and his family would have to live on for the next month at least.

All seemed in order. The breeze was getting up now after the calm earlier in the evening. Bakr completed a second tour of the camp without incident, and made his way finally towards the excavations. He paused on the ridge above the entrance to the pyramid, and peered down into the pit.

Again, all was quiet. But just as Bakr was about to move away, a faint glow caught his eye. It was coming from the doorway into the pyramid. A trick of the light surely, a star reflecting from the darkly polished stone. But he had better check. There was nothing else to do, after all.

Bakr stumbled his way down the steep side of the pit, his bare feet sinking into the soft ground and sending warm sand skidding down ahead of him. He was forced to increase speed as he made his way down, and almost pitched over when he arrived at the bottom.

Regaining his balance, Bakr saw that the door into the pyramid was standing ajar. The faint glow he had noticed earlier was growing steadily brighter, and the wind rolled around the bottom of the excavations, moaning and buffeting its trapped way round the hollow.

Bakr edged closer to the doorway, stepping lightly and feeling the fear rising in his stomach. He leant forward and peered round the edge of the door into the corridor beyond. With a sigh of relief that was lost in the sound of the wind, he saw that the glow came from an oil lamp held by the leading figure of a group of people heading down the corridor towards him.

Assuming that the party inside the pyramid consisted of Kenilworth and his colleagues, Bakr pushed the door fully open and raised a hand in greeting. He was keen to show that he had been keeping his vigil efficiently enough to know that they were there. But as the figure carrying the lamp reached the entrance, Bakr could see that it was not Kenilworth.

It was *Simons*. Simons with skin so pale it almost glowed in the lamp light. Simons with deep, dark sunken eyes which reflected nothing. Simons with sunken cheeks and dried blood down the side of his face and staining his jacket.

Simons who had been dead for days.

Bakr was still struggling to understand what was happening, when Simons gave a short nod to the figure behind him. It stepped forward, out of the pyramid and in front of the light so that all Bakr could see was the silhouette. The silhouette of a huge frame, arms outstretched as they reached towards him. The enormous bandaged hands closed like clamps round Bakr's neck, and he felt the edges of the linen wrappings as they bit into his throat.

His choked cry drifted away, lost in the sound of the wind.

*

Atkins was awakened by the noise. He glanced at his pocket-watch, laid out neatly on the chair beside his camp bed. It was early, too early for the camp to be rousing. But he could hear the Egyptians shouting to each other, though not clearly enough to make out what they were saying. He pulled on his clothes, checked his tie in a small shaving mirror resting beside a bowl of cold water, and set off towards the sound.

The Egyptian workers were all gathered round the supply tent. They seemed to be having a conference of some sort, huddled together and all talking at once. Kenilworth and Macready stood nearby, obviously having dressed hurriedly. Atkins guessed they too had been roused by the noise. They were conversing in low tones with the Doctor, whose attire seemed as casually immaculate as ever.

'I'm sorry, sir, I failed to appreciate that there was an incident until just now.'

Kenilworth nodded to Atkins and completed his words to the Doctor. 'We still have some blasting dynamite from the excavations. I could arrange to blow the sand down into the pit and cover the entrance completely.'

The Doctor shook his head. 'No point, really. I think whatever it was has already happened. The desert will close up the excavation site and seal up the pyramid again in a week or two anyway.'

'We shall be long gone by then,' Macready said. 'Too late for – what did you say his name was?'

'Bakr,' Kenilworth said.

Atkins listened to the exchange in puzzlement. Bakr was one of the workers, a second cousin of Nebka. He was lazy and slept when he should be on watch, but neither of those traits marked him out to Atkins as unusual.

'May I ask what has occurred?' Atkins asked when it became clear that nobody was going to enlighten him.

'One of the workers got himself killed last night,' Macready said.

'Murdered,' Kenilworth added.

As Kenilworth said the word, everything around them went quiet, giving it emphasis and volume. Atkins could remember once chiding one of the maids about her sloppy service at table just as there was a lull in the dinner conversation so that his reprimand carried clear and loud across the dining room. The effect now was the same.

'Sir?'

'Strangled,' the Doctor said. 'Though it's a moot point whether he asphyxiated first or died of a broken neck.'

'The Egyptians aren't pleased.' Macready wiped his glistening brow. 'They're having some sort of debate about it.'

Kenilworth was looking round, aware of the sudden silence. 'Good job we're leaving today. Wake the others, would you Atkins. Tell them to pack up so we can leave as soon as possible.'

'Of course, sir.' He turned to go, and almost collided with Tegan as she ran up to them. Behind her Atkins could see Nebka standing alone by the supply tent.

'Hey,' said Tegan, 'what's going on? I was nearly knocked down just now by a herd of Egyptians running into the desert.'

They all looked towards the supply tent, where Nebka was shaking his head, waving his hands up and down, and starting towards them. Atkins knew now why it had become so quiet, knew what enthusiastic debate had been so vocal to begin with.

The Egyptians had gone.

Despite the dryness of the air, Simons' body was starting to smell. Rassul assumed that the heat did not help, and tried to keep upwind of him. The huge, bandaged service robots lumbered onwards without discomfort, and when they paused it was for Rassul and the two Egyptians to rest.

Simons periodically stopped and stared at the sky, as if taking bearings. His cracked lips moved slightly as he spoke beneath what had been his breath.

On the third day following Kenilworth's expedition, Simons stumbled and almost fell. He gathered himself together immediately and continued. After the next time he paused to consult the heavens, he turned to Rassul.

'The power relay is not functioning at full capacity,' he said. 'Probably the sand that now buries so much of it is impeding its efficiency.'

'Is that why you are weakened?' Rassul asked. He had noticed Simons dragging his left foot slightly over the last few miles. Looking back, the marks Simons had left in the soft sand were skewed lines rather than imprints.

Simons nodded in reply. 'As the relics are taken from the tomb, so the power is dissipated.'

'What must we do?'

'The time is not yet,' Simons said, his bloodshot eyes drifting upwards again. 'When the time comes, as it must and will, you will collect the relics together with the mummy. But until then, to preserve the power, we must return at least some of them to the tomb to act as a focus for the psionic particle-accelerator.'

'When do we need to do this?'

'Tonight.' Simons turned, and Rassul followed his gaze. In the middle distance, the four mummies continued their ponderous march forwards. 'I shall take the servicers and recover the relics.'

'And the woman,' asked Rassul, 'the mummy?'

'Her destiny is already charted.'

*

They were one day out from Cairo and Margaret Evans could not sleep. She lay awake, knowing that she needed to sleep. But somehow that made it even more difficult to relax. The full moon outside shone in through the canvas of her tent, so that she could see the outline of the interior lit with a pale glow of diffuse light.

She stared at the low folding table on which her most precious belongings were laid out and tried to distinguish them in the gloom. Her mother's ring lay beside her day book. She could not see it, but she knew that sticking out slightly from the book, marking the current page, was the edge of a photograph. It was the only photograph she possessed and one of the few she had ever seen. It showed her father standing outside the Royal Society just before his acclaimed lecture on the discoveries at Saqqara in 1893. And beside him, on the steps, stood Nicholas Simons. Margaret Evans took the photograph everywhere. And those who knew, quietly admired her quiet dedication to, and love of, her father.

As she struggled to make out the strip of card, imagining its faded sepia tones and remembering the occasions she had cried herself to sleep clutching it, Margaret Evans felt the edges of sleep beginning to come over her. She relaxed slightly, trying not to be aware that she was drifting off, afraid that if she admitted to herself that she was falling asleep she would be instantly awake again. The pillow was soft under her head and her nightgown and the blankets held the warmth to her. She felt herself slipping away, sinking into the thin mattress. Her view of the dim interior of the tent softened and darkened, the effect of falling asleep emphasised by the dark shadow cast against the far wall of the tent.

Someone was walking past the tent, their shadow cast by the moon against the canvas. It was stretched and distorted by the irregular shape of the material as it lurched its way past.

Margaret watched the figure's progress, barely aware that she was wide awake again. She pushed back the covers and pushed herself off the bed. She had recognised the figure's shape.

She reached the front of the tent just as the figure passed and continued its slow progress through the small camp. She called out, called him by name, and the figure stopped, turned, and walked slowly back towards her.

'It is you, I was sure it was. Oh, I'm so relieved. What happened? Are you all right?'

The figure stopped in front of her. His face was illuminated by the light from the moon, and Margaret could see the sunken eyes and the pallor of the skin. She was vaguely aware of the smell, too, but did not associate the stench of rotting flesh with the man standing in front of her.

Simons said nothing. His expression did not alter.

Margaret sniffed, then shook her head to dispel the odour. Part of her mind was wondering how they could have been so wrong in their diagnosis of Simons' condition and wondered where he had been; most of it did not care. She shook her head, wiped her eye, and laughed in relief. 'I've missed you so much. So very much. We thought you were dead.' She reached out for him, but Simons took a step backwards.

'I'm sorry. You're nervous, I know. But you seemed so confident as you walked past just now, so assured. I thought you were looking for me. I thought that you knew – that you understood—' She broke off and looked closer at Simons' gaunt face. The smell was stronger now and she was finding it difficult to breath without coughing.

Simons blinked, once. The skin round his eyes seemed to tighten and his brow creased as if in concentration. Had the light been better, Margaret might have seen the skin of his forehead cracking and breaking as it furrowed. Had her concentration not been entirely focused on Simons' eyes, she might have smelled the colourless, viscous fluid which trickled down his cheek.

'Margaret,' he said. His voice was quiet and husky, and it sounded as if the word had been forced out of him. 'You are Margaret.'

'Of course,' she said. She stretched out her arms to him. 'Don't be nervous, don't avoid me. Not now.'

Simons moved forward, his hands reaching out. Margaret stepped back as he took her shoulders. She retreated into her tent, feeling the cold of his grasp through the material of her nightgown. She felt the camp bed against the backs of her knees and sat down on it.

Simons lifted his hands slowly to her neck, and she closed her eyes, lifting her head towards his. She tried not to flinch when the stench grew stronger as he leant forward, pushing her back onto the bed. Any moment she expected to feel his lips on hers, though she knew they would be pale and cold as death.

And when she opened her mouth, it was not to kiss, but to gasp desperately for breath.

The scream tore through the camp like a knife through tent canvas. Tegan was wide awake and out of bed by the time it finished. She pulled on her cloak and ran out of her tent.

The Doctor collided with her as she left the tent. He stared at her for a moment, and for a split second Tegan could see the relief in his eyes. Then he turned and started running in the opposite direction.

'Margaret?' Tegan asked.

'Margaret,' he agreed.

Kenilworth and Atkins were leaving their tents as the Doctor and Tegan ran past.

'What the devil's going on?' Kenilworth called as he struggled into his jacket.

The Doctor did not answer, but kept running. Tegan followed as fast as she could.

Margaret's tent was silent. The flap was pulled back, and the Doctor paused outside for a second, like a doubting disciple. Then he dived inside. Tegan arrived a few seconds after he had gone in, and made to follow. But the Doctor was backing out of the tent. He turned sharply as he bumped into Tegan, and opened his mouth. Then he shut it again, and shook his head.

Behind the Doctor, Tegan could see the figure sprawled across the bed, white nightgown stained at the shoulders as if charred. Margaret's head lolled back over the far side of the bed, and Tegan was thankful that the eyes were hidden. She knew they would be open and blank, the pupils dilated in the gloom.

Before either of them could comment, Atkins and Kenilworth arrived, out of breath and hurriedly dressed. Atkins for once was less than immaculate. But before any of them could speak, there was a shout from across the camp, and the sound of a shotgun.

The main focus of attention was the supply tent. Evans and Macready were backing slowly away from it. Macready had a shotgun raised and aimed to cover their retreat. Approaching them out of the darkness were three enormous shapes. They lumbered forwards, rolling from one leg to the other as if pulling their huge bulk forward by their own momentum.

Tegan, the Doctor, Atkins and Kenilworth arrived just as Macready discharged the second barrel of his gun. Tegan skidded to a halt and grabbed at the Doctor for support – both to prevent her falling as the sand gave under her feet, and for reassurance. Atkins stood open-mouthed, and Kenilworth swore.

The three figures were clearly visible in the moonlight. The shadows moved and stretched across their frames as they continued their slow but inexorable progress towards the group. The size of the bandaged bodies and the way the arms hung out from the massive shoulders made their legs seems slightly out of proportion as the huge mummies stepped through the desert night.

Macready's shot caught the leading mummy in the right shoulder. It slowed a little, the right side of its body pushed back by the impact, shreds of bandage flying from the tiny entry points of the lead pellets. But then it eased itself back into its rolling gait and continued without apparent discomfort towards them.

Macready broke open the gun and fumbled in his pocket for fresh cartridges.

'I wouldn't bother if I were you,' the Doctor said. 'They're Osiran service robots, a few bullets and a bit of buckshot won't worry them.'

'And what would you suggest?' Kenilworth asked.

'I'd suggest we run.'

'Admirable advice,' Evans said, turning on his heel.

The mummies continued their slow progress. One of them smashed its way through the edge of a tent standing in its path. Another kicked through a small mound of sand in front of it, the mound exploded into tiny particles and drifted away on the breeze. Behind them, the sound of splintering wood carried through the desert air. Silhouetted against the canvas of the supply tent, working by the light of the oil lamp which cast its shadows onto the tent wall, a huge shape ripped the top from one of the packing cases. Two smaller, thinner figures stood close by, watching.

The Doctor and his friends turned to follow Evans' example, just as the entrance to the tent nearest the leading mummy flapped open, and Nebka pushed his sleepy way into its path.

'Look out, man,' shouted Macready.

'Run,' Kenilworth and the Doctor both called together.

But Nebka was frozen to the spot, staring in horror and amazement at the mummy as it bore down on him. At last he shook himself free of the fear, and started to turn. But too late.

The mummy swiped, almost casually, at the Egyptian. Its arm caught him across the throat, sending him flying back at the tent he had just left. Nebka hit the doorway, his body colliding with the tent's main support and bringing it crashing down. A hand and forearm emerged from the mass of collapsed canvas. The hand clutched at the sand, grabbing and clenching, trying to gain a purchase on the shifting ground. Then it spasmed, stiffened, and the grains of sand fell from between the outstretched fingers and the hand flopped back onto the desert floor.

Kenilworth was already running forwards. Atkins tried to grab him, but missed. He started to follow, but the Doctor held him back and shook his head.

'Get the dynamite,' he said. 'I'll get Kenilworth.'

Atkins looked at the Doctor for a second, then he nodded and ran.

'Help him, Tegan.'

Tegan followed, Macready at her heel. Evans was already almost out of sight.

Kenilworth drew up short of the mummies. He could see that it was too late to help Nebka, but he was committed. Having challenged the mummies by running back at them, he was damned if he would turn and run away again.

A piece of broken wood from Nebka's tent post had landed almost at Kenilworth's feet. He picked it up, a pole about two inches in diameter and three feet long with a jagged and sharp end. He took up position like an enthusiastic cricketer out for a slog and waited for the first mummy to reach him.

Before it was within reach, though, he felt himself lifted from behind and dragged away. 'What the—' he spluttered, as the Doctor deposited him in the sand.

'Not a very sensible approach, your Lordship,' the Doctor said. 'You had even less chance of inflicting any serious damage than Macready's shotgun.'

'Maybe,' Kenilworth said grudgingly. 'But I'd have had a damn good try.'

'I admire your spirit. But I think we should keep out of their way.'

'We can't let them just ransack the place,' Kenilworth protested as he dragged himself to his feet, looked carefully at the length of wood he was holding and then dropped it to the ground.

The Doctor was backing away again, the mummies still lurching towards them. 'They're not. They're after something specific. Something in with the relics.'

'We've still got to stop them,' Kenilworth spluttered.

'Oh, I agree. That's why I've sent Atkins for the dynamite.' The Doctor's teeth gleamed in the moonlight as he smiled. Over his shoulder, Kenilworth saw the mummies slow to a halt. For a moment, their bodies swung to and fro as if they were surveying the land in front of them. Then they stood motionless. From the distance came the sound of another crate being ripped open.

*

Between them, Tegan and Atkins managed to carry the box of dynamite towards the supply tent. Tegan expected any moment to meet the Doctor and Kenilworth running back the other way. But they were almost where they had left them. The mummies stood a short way off, making no effort to move.

'They're stopping us from getting to the supplies and preventing whatever's happening there,' Kenilworth told them. 'The Doctor tried circling round, but they seemed to sense that, and one of them moved to cut him off.'

'So what did you do, Doctor?' Atkins asked.

'I decided discretion was the better part of valour,' the Doctor said. 'Now where's that dynamite?'

Atkins pulled the lid off the heavy wooden box to reveal several sticks of dynamite, fuses dangling like rats' tails from the ends. He produced a box of lucifers from his jacket pocket.

'Excellent,' the Doctor said, rubbing his hands together. 'Now which of you can manage a decent full toss, do you reckon?'

The first stick landed short of its target. The dynamite exploded noisily, throwing sand and pieces of Nebka's tent flying into the air. The mummy standing five yards from the blast did not so much as flinch.

But in the supply tent, Simons heard the report. He sent a mental signal to the servicer with him to continue searching through the packing crates. So far they had found the statue of Anubis, but none of the other relics had yet been recovered.

Simons picked up the small stone statue, its surface as cold as his hand, and went to investigate the noise. The image he was getting from the servicers outside was less than helpful, degraded and interrupted by the weakness of the power.

He emerged from the tent in time to see a figure step

forward into the moonlight and throw something towards the servicers. Simons sent the nearest mummy forward to counter-attack.

It walked right into the explosion.

The dynamite went off just as the mummy stepped over it. The blast ripped its left arm from the body and shredded the bandages which protected the robot's frame. The cloth still clinging to the robot's legs ignited, and after a second the whole body was ablaze.

The mummy kept going, following its orders, a lumbering torch of guttering fire. The metal frame charred in the heat, but it held together as the creature stumbled onwards.

But without the protection of its wrappings, the next explosion ripped the servicer apart. It punctured the tiny pyramid relay in the small of its back, and sent shards of heated metal into the air like shrapnel from a grenade.

The humans dived for cover. The other servicers stood immobile and silent. Simons weighed up the options, hefting the Anubis statue in his dead palm. One relic would suffice. He recalled the servicers, and made his way back to where Rassul and the Egyptians were waiting beyond the next sand dune.

Evans sat at the table in his daughter's tent, leafing slowly through her day book. He was not reading it, just turning the pages. In his hand he held the photograph that had marked her place.

Atkins stood into the tent behind him, watching. 'I thought I'd find you here, sir,' he said after a while. He tried to ignore the body sprawled across the bed.

'She loved me,' Evans said without looking up. 'So dedicated. So devoted.'

'Indeed.' Atkins clasped his hands tighter behind his back.

'His Lordship wonders if you would join us at the supply tent to go over the inventory again. He would welcome your expert opinion.'

'Look.' Evans held out the photograph from the book. 'She even kept my picture with her.'

Simons' young enthusiasm smiled back at Atkins from the cracked card.

'Indeed sir. I—' He broke off. He knew what he wanted to say, but not how to phrase it. 'She will be a great loss to us all, sir.' It felt inadequate.

But Evans nodded as he stood up. 'A great loss. Yes. Yes.'

Atkins held back the canvas flap for Evans as he pushed past. Then Atkins looked at the figure across the bed. He could feel an unaccustomed pressure behind his eyes, was aware of a tension in his stomach. He blinked quickly, and followed Evans out of the tent.

Isis left the navigation to the pilot. He sat within the projection dome, his mind entirely focused on keeping the craft on course, following the psi-trail left by the capsule.

With her mind, Isis reached out into the darkness, probing and searching for the thoughts of Osiris. At the very extreme edge of her consciousness she could sense a slight tremor. There was a chance, just a faint hope, that Osiris was not yet dead. But if they did not get close enough for him to break the mind lock and project out of the capsule soon, he would be lost.

Even as she struggled to lock on to the mind of her husband-brother, Isis felt it slip through her thoughts. Osiris was gone. And with nowhere to project to, he must be dead. No way to project his physical body into another place; no receptacle for his brilliant mind – he would imbue no psi-child now.

She brought her mind back to reality, to the interior of the pyramid. The pilot was standing in front of her. He had left the projection dome. And yet the craft was still travelling straight and true along the psi-trail. It took a phenomenal amount of energy to cope even with a slight mental lapse. Actually to leave the dome was impossible, no mind could summon the reserves of power necessary for that.

But as she stared into the glowing eyes of the pilot, Isis was aware of a deeper intelligence than she had perceived when they boarded the craft.

'Greetings, mother,' the pilot said. His voice was melodic, almost musical. She recognised it at once, and almost wept for joy. The words of the Osiran who had been the pilot resonated within the craft, seeming almost to be born out of the air itself: 'I am Horus, son of Osiris.'

Chapter
Eight

The *Golden Bough* docked early in the morning of Sunday 9 November 1896. Within minutes, the London dockers had secured her to the quay and gangplanks were lowered. Soon after that, the ship was a scurry of activity as packing cases and crates were hoisted ashore.

Atkins supervised the unloading, just as he had ensured that everything was properly stowed before setting out from Egypt seven weeks earlier. He stood on the dockside, notebook in hand, checking off each item as it was brought ashore. Then each was packed into one of the waiting carriages, depending on its destination.

'You seem to be having fun,' the Doctor said as he joined Atkins. His breath was smoky in the cold morning air. 'The change in weather is always a problem when travelling, I find.'

'Indeed, Doctor.' Atkins checked the stencilled letters on the side of a crate as it was carried past by two stevedores. He pointed the dockers to the nearest of the carriages.

'Mmm,' the Doctor continued as he watched the crate's bobbing progress towards the nearest carriage. 'And talking of problems…'

Part of the time on the journey back had been spent allocating the various relics to museums and members of the expedition. The British Museum took the lion's share, of course. Kenilworth kept several items, like the ring found on the shelf by the sarcophagus, for his private collection. He also kept, at the Doctor's insistence and to the evident disappointment of Evans, the mummy itself. They compromised by sending the lid of the casket to the museum.

Evans himself elected to keep only a few of the smaller pieces he was offered, including the scarab bracelet found in the burial chamber. The cobra statuette found with it went to Macready, together with several papyrus scrolls.

Atkins had repacked everything, with help from the others, principally Miss Tegan. He had found he grew to enjoy the time spent going through the inventory with her. Despite her attempts at small talk and her distracting manner, Miss Tegan was pleasant company and performed her allotted tasks with a speed and efficiency which belied her manner. Atkins found himself looking forward to the sessions in a similar way to his anticipation of the evening planning meeting with Miss Warne back at Kenilworth House.

And with this observation came the realisation that he was missing the meetings with Miss Warne. Indeed, he was missing her company generally.

So it was with a feeling of deep disappointment which he could not possibly voice or allow others to discern, that Atkins received the Doctor's words.

'I'm afraid I'll have to ask you to stay in the TARDIS for a day or two.' He slapped Atkins on the shoulder. 'You see, there are two of you here at the moment. Once your other self has left with us for ancient Egypt, then you can return to Kenilworth House and carry on as usual. But until then...'

The Doctor grinned as Atkins concentrated on his notes.

'It's all a bit complicated. I'm not sure that I actually understand it too well myself, now I come to think about it.'

Atkins said nothing for a while. The Doctor looked over his shoulder at the notebook, and frowned as he tried to decipher the handwriting.

'Is the TARDIS ashore yet, by the way?'

Atkins indicated a nearby warehouse with the end of his pencil. 'The harbour master says it can stay there till Wednesday free of charge.'

The Doctor nodded. 'More than generous,' he said. 'And more than long enough.' He patted Atkins on the shoulder again. 'I hope you don't mind, but it is rather important.'

Atkins did not look up. 'You know best, Doctor,' he said quietly.

Having installed Atkins in the TARDIS and provided him with an adequate pile of reading material (it turned out he was a devotee of Dickens), the Doctor and Tegan took their leave of the expedition members. Macready and Kenilworth were off to Kenilworth House, and the Doctor agreed that he and Tegan would meet them there that afternoon. Evans was keen to return to the British Museum and start right away on unpacking the relics returned from Egypt. He hoped to have some of them at least on display in the Egyptian Room by the evening. The only disappointment in his enthusiasm seemed to be that this time neither his daughter nor Simons would help him update the catalogues.

'So what do we do now?' Tegan asked the Doctor.

The Doctor consulted his watch, turned a full circle on his heel, and grinned. 'How about some shopping?' he suggested. 'It's nearly ten o'clock and Harrods has been open for forty-seven years. Should have stocked up on something other than groceries by now.'

'And Nyssa?'

The Doctor breathed out heavily, his breath hanging in the air amongst the other pollutants. 'Nyssa will be perfectly safe until tomorrow when we unwrap her. We managed to keep the casket level during the journey which was the main thing. Now I think we should let Kenilworth get back to his house and his wife and have some peace and quiet for a few hours. We'll see him this afternoon.'

The Doctor stepped out into the road and waved at an approaching cab. 'I think it might snow later,' he said as the cabby guided his horse to the kerb.

'You *know* it will,' Tegan said as she climbed in ahead of the Doctor.

They spent the morning at Harrods and looked in some of the other shops on the Brompton Road. Then they had a light lunch at Bond's Tea Shop before taking rooms at the Savoy. The Doctor signed the hotel register at three twenty-seven.

Kenilworth ordered afternoon tea for the drawing room.

'I thought we could discuss where the sarcophagus should be set up with the Doctor and Miss Tegan,' he told Atkins.

'Indeed, sir. And will the Doctor and Miss Tegan be taking tea also?'

Kenilworth laughed. 'When did you ever know the Doctor to refuse a cup of tea?'

'The Doctor, sir?' Atkins cocked his head slightly to one side. 'I'm not sure that I am aquainted with the gentleman.'

Kenilworth stared in amazement for a moment. 'Not sure that...' He looked from Atkins to his wife and back. 'Good grief, man. You'll be telling us you don't remember Miss Tegan either, next.' He smiled and gave a sharp nod to emphasise his point.

'Who, sir?' Atkins asked innocently.

Kenilworth opened his mouth, then closed it again. Perhaps Atkins was joking. Yet he seemed entirely sincere. 'Are you all right, Atkins?' Kenilworth asked. 'Come to think of it, you do look a bit pale.'

'I am in excellent health, thank you sir.'

Lady Kenilworth leant forward in her chair. 'That's all

right, Atkins. Just arrange the tea, would you?'

'Indeed, ma'am,' Atkins said with evident relief, taking his leave.

Kenilworth shook his head as Atkins left the room. 'I don't know,' he said.

'Leave him alone, dear,' Lady Kenilworth said quietly. 'He's been a perfect treasure while you've been away. As always.'

Kenilworth was not listening. 'Maybe it's the change in climate. He wasn't like this in Egypt.'

Lady Kenilworth smiled. 'But that was years ago,' she said. 'When you were both younger.'

'What? No, no. I mean this trip. The last few months.'

Lady Kenilworth frowned. 'I don't think I follow.'

'All I'm saying is that he was fine. His usual calm efficient self, and we had some dicey moments I don't mind telling you.'

Lady Kenilworth stood up and crossed to where her husband was sitting. She rested her hand on his shoulder. 'But he's been here,' she said, 'with me. Atkins never went to Egypt.'

In the distance, the doorbell rang. Kenilworth barely heard it. 'What are you talking about?' he asked his wife. 'I left him here with you, yes. But Atkins joined us in Cairo at the beginning of September. He must have left here four months ago.'

Lady Kenilworth did not reply immediately. She sat down again, and looked out of the window. The sound of several sets of footsteps drifted in from the hallway, getting steadily closer. 'Well,' she said at last, 'all I can say is that I had not noticed he was gone. And neither, I suspect, have any of the other servants.'

Kenilworth snorted and shook his head.

'Perhaps you should ask Miss Warne,' his wife suggested.

'I'm sure she will be able to tell you the whereabouts of Mr Atkins for the last year or more, let alone the past few weeks.'

Kenilworth was about to ask his wife what she meant, but at that moment the door opened and Atkins entered.

'The Doctor and Miss Tegan Jovanka,' he announced. Then he stepped aside to allow the Doctor and Tegan to enter.

'Ah Doctor, Miss Tegan.' Kenilworth was across the room and shaking hands enthusiastically before the Doctor and Tegan were properly through the door. He introduced them to his wife and waved them to chairs. Atkins watched the proceedings, then when he discerned that he was no longer needed left the room, quietly closing the door behind him.

'Perhaps you can help settle a small disagreement, Doctor,' Kenilworth said. Tea had been brought in and they were sitting with bone china cups and cucumber sandwiches.

'Ah,' the Doctor said awkwardly, replacing his cup on its saucer and looking carefully into it as if trying to decode the pattern of the tea leaves.

'It's about Atkins.'

The Doctor looked up. He did not look happy. 'Yes. I was rather afraid it might be.' He exchanged a pained glance with Tegan. 'Look, er, can I ask you a small favour?'

'Of course.'

'Please don't worry yourselves with where Atkins has been, or hasn't been. I'm sure he'll remember everything soon enough, and if you need an explanation then, he can probably provide it.' The Doctor gulped down the remains of his tea, draining the cup. Then he grimaced. 'I must be getting used to tea bags,' he said. 'Abominations.'

'I thought perhaps,' Kenilworth said as the tea things were cleared away, 'we should have the unwrapping in here.'

'Sounds good to me,' Tegan said.

'Excellent, capital.' The doorbell clanged in the distance, and Kenilworth consulted his pocket-watch. 'I've asked Professor Macready to join us this afternoon to help set up the sarcophagus. That'll be him now.'

The Doctor stood up and walked across the room, hands in trouser pockets. 'Were you intending to set up the casket about here?' he asked as he reached the far corner.

Kenilworth laughed. 'I told you,' he said to his wife. 'Never ceases to amaze. He even knows what I'm thinking now.'

The Doctor joined in the laughter. 'Hardly.'

'Good. Then you won't know that I've got some invitations printed up already. Should be delivered this evening. I'll drop one round to the Savoy for you so you can see it if you like.'

'Professor Macready,' Atkins announced, ushering in the small professor. Macready peered across the room at them, polishing his spectacles furiously on a handkerchief. When he was done, he popped his glasses back on his nose and beamed at Kenilworth. 'Good to see you again, old man.' He looked round the room, the light shining off his glasses as he tried to find the sarcophagus.

'It's in the dining room at the moment,' Lady Kenilworth told him. 'Which I must say is extremely inconvenient. Perhaps you gentlemen could ask Atkins to help you bring it in here instead?'

The sarcophagus was unwieldy rather than heavy. And with the added challenge of keeping it level, at the Doctor's insistence, it took the four of them several minutes to manoeuvre the coffin the short distance from the dining room to the drawing room. The effort seemed not to bother the Doctor, though Macready by contrast slumped into an armchair and dabbed at his forehead.

'Goodness me,' he said. 'So much exercise.' He stuffed his handkerchief back into his pocket and leapt to his feet again.

'Magnificent,' he said. 'Quite magnificent. Tell me, Doctor, have you yet formulated any opinions you are willing to share on the history or age of this piece?'

Tegan laughed. 'I'll say,' she started.

But the Doctor gestured for her to be quiet. 'I think we should reserve our opinions for the unwrapping, Professor.'

'Indeed, indeed.' Macready stroked his finger along the rim of the sarcophagus. 'I still find it quite astounding. This must be three thousand years old at least.'

The Doctor nodded. 'I'd put it a bit older than that,' he said. 'Another thousand years, perhaps.'

'Four thousand? Really?' Macready nodded slowly as he considered. 'We shall see,' he muttered, 'we shall see.'

The Doctor yawned and stretched. 'Well,' he said to Tegan, 'I think it's time we were making a move. A brisk walk followed by a bite to eat.'

'Don't let us keep you, Doctor.' Kenilworth shook their hands again. 'Macready and I have lots to talk about, and we'll see you for the unwrapping tomorrow.' He saw them to the door. 'I'll have Atkins drop round an invitation as soon as they arrive,' he said as they entered the hallway.

'Ah,' the Doctor said. 'Perhaps another small favour?'

Kenilworth laughed. 'What inscrutable request is it this time?'

'Could you perhaps ask Atkins to deliver the invitation to us outside the British Museum?'

'The British Museum,' Kenilworth echoed, as much as anything to check he had heard correctly.

'Er, yes. Outside the North door. At exactly midnight.'

'Midnight.'

The Doctor smiled broadly. 'You've got it.' He took Kenilworth's hand and shook it enthusiastically. 'Thank you so much,' he said. 'You've been very understanding.'

'Not at all, Doctor. Not at all.' Kenilworth opened the front door.

Tegan shook Kenilworth's hand as she followed the Doctor out. 'He's right,' she said. 'For a change. You've been great. Thanks.'

Kenilworth watched the two figures make their way down the drive. It was already dark, and a light sprinkling of snow was settling on the ground. It was strange, Lord Kenilworth reflected as closed the front door. The Doctor and Tegan had both behaved as if they were bidding him farewell for the last time. Yet they would see each other again tomorrow afternoon.

They arrived back at the Savoy at just after nine. The Doctor suggested he call for Tegan at ten for a late dinner. 'I've got a few things I want to think through,' he told her. 'An hour should be ample.'

Tegan was happy to have a few minutes to herself. Several parcels had been delivered from Harrods, the fruits of her shopping expedition that morning. Not noted for her patience, Tegan was keen to unpack them right away.

She waved to the Doctor as he unlocked the door to his room. But he seemed not to notice. She could see that he was already deep in thought. He pulled a battered notebook from his jacket pocket, and went into his room.

By half-past ten Tegan was fed up with waiting. She paused for the briefest of moments outside the door to the Doctor's room, then knocked. There was no answer, so she opened it and went in.

The Doctor was lying on the bed, hands clasped behind his head, staring at the ceiling. His notebook was still open, but laid face down on his chest.

'Ah, Tegan,' he said without moving, 'do come in.'

'You're late,' she said. 'And I'm hungry.'

'Dinner,' the Doctor heaved himself off the bed. 'Oh yes.' The notebook fell to the floor, and he picked it up.

'Any new clues?' Tegan asked as she followed the Doctor from the room.

'Mmmm,' he said. 'I'll tell you after we've eaten.'

'Don't want to spoil my appetite?' she joked.

The Doctor glared at her, then set off down the corridor without answering.

The dining room was almost empty. An old man sat on his own at a table near the door. A middle-aged couple occupied a booth in the far corner.

The old man eyed the Doctor and Tegan suspiciously as they waited to be seated. The Doctor smiled at him and Tegan frowned.

'Colonel Finklestone,' the man barked suddenly, wiping his mouth on his napkin. 'Don't have the salmon.' The waiter scowled at the man as he arrived to attend to the Doctor and Tegan.

'Er, thank you,' the Doctor replied. 'The Doctor, and Miss Tegan Jovanka.'

Colonel Finklestone snorted as if they had in some way insulted him, and returned his attention to his wine.

'Doctor, Miss Jovanka,' the waiter smiled widely and nodded to them, picking up on their names, 'dinner for two?'

'Please,' the Doctor replied. 'A table near the window, perhaps?'

'Of course, sir.' The waiter led them across the near-deserted room.

'Will this do?' he asked as they reached the table where they had eaten breakfast what seemed like several months previously.

'Admirably, thank you.' The Doctor seated himself and accepted a menu and wine list. The waiter pulled back Tegan's chair for her as she sat down.

'Oh no you don't,' Tegan said before he could push the chair in again, dragging it in closer to the table.

The waiter left them to look at the menu. Tegan flicked through, remembering the brief conversation they had exchanged before.

'I believe I'll have the oysters,' the Doctor said, laying his menu to one side and picking up the wine list. It was leather-bound, with a gold cord down the spine ending in a tassel.

'You know you will,' Tegan said.

'Yes, but you have to go through the motions.'

'Why?' Tegan dropped her menu heavily on the table by her plate. It clattered against the lead crystal and disturbed the double damask. 'You keep going on about how we can't change things, but you won't prove it.'

'I don't need to. I know.'

Tegan looked out of the window. The moon was shining through the murky night, its light diffused across the surface of the Thames outside. Snow was falling lazily through the smog, spiralling its way through the young trees which edged the Embankment.

'Doctor,' Tegan said quietly, 'in about an hour, we will arrive at the British Museum. What's to stop us – this us – going there and warning us – that us – to leave before anything happens to Nyssa?'

The Doctor said nothing for a while. He stared out of the window, or perhaps he was watching Tegan's reflection in the glass as she continued to watch the snow.

'You see those snowflakes,' he said at last.

Tegan nodded.

'As they twist and tumble their way down, they collide

with each other, get swept away in the breeze, melt in a warm updraft. Now, imagine you plotted the course of one of those snowflakes, and you found that it collided with another snowflake. And you found it collided with it not just once, but twice.'

'So?'

'And then you changed the course of one of the snowflakes so that the first collision never happened.'

'Yes. So what?'

'So, would the second collision happen?'

Tegan considered. 'Maybe. You can't tell.'

The Doctor nodded. 'That's right. As soon as you change any of the circumstances, all bets are off. The second collision may occur, or it may not. There may be a completely different collision, or the snowflake may melt on a gas lamp before it reached its rendezvous.'

'What's that got to do with Nyssa?'

The Doctor beckoned to the waiter who was standing on the far side of the room. 'Everything,' he said. 'If we change things, we have no idea what will happen as a result, what collisions we set up, what courses we alter. We might all end up mummified, and that would help nobody. Maybe we should try, but that's not the way Time works. You only get one chance.' He leant forward and looked deep into Tegan's eyes. 'We couldn't change a thing. We could go to the Museum, but we'd be delayed on the way, or miss ourselves somehow. Which is probably as well, given what would happen to the temporal differential if we actually did meet.'

'How do you know you can't change it? You won't try.' Tegan's frustration was cut short by the arrival of the waiter.

'Oysters,' the Doctor said immediately. 'And a bottle of the Morgon.'

Tegan had not decided, though she knew what she would

not be having. She grabbed back her menu as the waiter lifted it from the table, opened it, and went for the first thing she saw. 'Ham.'

The waiter was still startled. He blinked, then realised that Tegan had ordered. 'Very good,' he said, bowed, and left.

'Not having the cutlets?' the Doctor asked as soon as the waiter was out of earshot.

'Didn't fancy them.'

'And I thought you were making a point.' The Doctor turned his attention back to the snow outside. 'It's a shame you don't fancy the cutlets, though,' he said quietly, 'since you'll have to eat them.'

Tegan forced herself to keep relatively calm. 'How do you know?' she asked, on hand clenching on the edge of the tablecloth.

'Look, Tegan,' the Doctor cleared aside his cutlery and rested his hands on the table as he leant forward. 'You want to go and warn ourselves at the British Museum to leave at once.'

'Yes.'

'And what do you think will happen if we do that?'

'We'll leave,' Tegan said. 'We'll go back into the TARDIS and Nyssa will be all right.'

The Doctor nodded. 'And if we had done that, which we didn't, then who will warn us?'

'What?'

'Look,' the Doctor said, pressing his hands together and raising them so that his index fingers almost touched his lips. 'If we had left straight after we arrived, either through some warning or on a whim, we would not be here now. So we could not be having this discussion, coming to a conclusion, or rushing to warn ourselves. The fact that we are here now means that we didn't – will not – leave.'

Tegan frowned. 'So we can't change anything?'

'Well, I have seen it done. But never without immense initial cost, and always so that history returns to its original track as soon as it gets the chance.'

The Doctor leant back in his seat as the waiter approached again. 'You needn't take my word for it, though.'

The Doctor tasted the wine, swilling it noisily round his mouth and smacking his lips together appreciatively. He nodded his approval, and the waiter sloshed some wine into Tegan's glass, then carefully poured for the Doctor.

'Charming,' Tegan said as he left.

The Doctor smiled. 'An example of what we were just discussing, surely.'

'How so?'

'Why were you rude to him when we arrived just now?'

'Because he was so snotty last time.'

The Doctor nodded. 'But for him, last time hasn't happened yet. Though when it does, at breakfast tomorrow, he'll be snotty to you. And he'll be snotty to you because you were rude to him the night before.'

'Which for me won't have happened yet.'

'Exactly.' The Doctor sipped at his wine. 'This is rather good, you know. It's a sort of self-fulfilling prophecy.'

'I'll be nice to him, then,' Tegan said.

'Well, here's your chance.' The Doctor nodded to the waiter as he approached again, this time pushing a low trolley. 'Good luck.'

Tegan smiled sweetly at the waiter as he removed the silver lid from the platter he presented to the Doctor. He did his best to ignore her.

'Oysters, sir.'

Tegan continued to smile as he produced her dinner, trying to make meaningful eye contact as he set it before her.

'Cutlets, madam,' he said.

Tegan's smile froze. 'What?'

'Cutlets. You asked for lamb.'

'My compliments to the chef,' the Doctor slipped in quickly, 'these oysters are magnificent.'

Then Tegan exploded.

'We need to pack,' the Doctor said as they made their way up the stairs back to their rooms.

'Oh? Why?'

'Two reasons. First, the rooms will be needed later tonight.'

'By us, I remember.'

'And second, before dinner I managed to decipher some of the hieroglyphics I copied down from the tomb.'

They paused outside Tegan's room. 'And what does that mean?' she asked.

'I think it means that reviving Nyssa, starting irreversibly the hundred-year cycle to bring her back to life, was one of my less inspired actions.'

'I meant to ask you,' Tegan said after a moment's pause, 'why a hundred years? Apart from the fact it's a good round figure.'

'I've been asking myself that.'

'And?'

'And it just popped into my head. Which is at least part of the problem. And now the stars are set in their courses, and so…'

'And so?'

'And so we have to be there when she wakes. I'll see you in five minutes.'

As she gathered together her belongings, Tegan was in an ambivalent mood. The Doctor's comments had worried her, but they were off to a time which was rather closer to her own, and where she would be reunited with Nyssa.

She wondered what Atkins would make of the late twentieth century. She had understood enough to realise he would have to come with them until they could return him to the time after he had first left with them. Perhaps the Doctor was right after all about the way that Time crystallised like a snowflake around your actions and despite your intentions. Whether she tried to trick her way out of it, or to go with the flow, events seemed set in their preordained courses.

Before she left, Tegan carefully laid out the pale green dress she had bought in Harrods that morning.

EGYPT
JANUARY 1897

The three mummies stood forming a perfect triangle in front of the position where the sarcophagus had rested. They had remained there, static, for the last few months guarding the statue of Anubis while their masters had been to London and back. In front of them, Simons bowed to the jackal statue with reverence and respect.

'Will just the one relic remain sufficient?' Rassul asked.

Simons nodded. 'The energy you will need for the next century is not great. And when the time comes, the power will build as you need it. Orion will come into configuration and the signal strength will increase accordingly.'

Simons pressed the central square of the Nephthys cartouche and the heavy door to the inner chamber swung open. Rassul moved aside to let the mummies file through into the room beyond. As the third of the service robots passed through, the door swung shut behind it.

'They will return to their charge points until you need them.'

'Until *I* need them?' asked Rassul. 'Surely, you—'

But Simons was shaking his head. 'This body is already decaying, and the journey to the damper climate of England has not helped. The powers granted to you are more durable. You have waited this long, and now you begin the final stage of your journey. Another century is as nothing to you.' Simons turned back to the engraved symbol of Nephthys's name. 'For me…'

Simons' last words were a cracked gasp. Rassul was not sure if he had actually said 'for me' or 'free'. But before he could decide, Simons' slowly crumpled to his knees, the bones in his legs cracking as they splintered and fractured. He pitched forwards, face smashing into the wall of the tomb. His head cracked open, dry powder cascading out and falling to the floor like sand in an hourglass.

As Rassul watched, Simons' body slowly crumbled away until only a fine dust remained. A sudden, impossible breeze cleaned it from the stone floor, and sent it scurrying into the corners of the tomb.

Rassul waited for a while. Simons was right, he had waited a long time. And soon it would be over. Just a few short decades, and he too would be free.

The Valley of the Kings, Ancient Egypt
c.5000 BC

The rain was still falling heavily as the gods made their way into the pyramid. The rain cascaded down the smooth white slopes of the sides, and waterfalled over the entrance. A blast of lightning split the black sky, making the pyramid seem to glow. Rassul looked away as the glare hurt his eyes.

The gods made their ponderous way inside, their work complete. Horus and Anubis were last into the structure, Isis just ahead of them. Once across the threshold, Horus turned and looked back at the assembled priests. His face was just visible through the falling water as he nodded slowly in approval.

As Rassul watched, Horus raised his arms, made the sign of the Eye. Then he stepped back into the pyramid, out of sight in the darkness within. The next moment, without apparent change in the pyramid's form or shape, the water was no longer falling from the edge of the door frame, but continuing its cascade down the smooth unbroken side.

The lightning flashed again. And when Rassul blinked away the brightness and looked back, the pyramid was gone. The rain slowed, picking random holes in the dry square of sand.

CHAPTER
NINE

The first thing that Atkins noticed was the noise. The second was how clean and clear the air was. He walked along the Embankment in something of a daze. It was the world he knew, and yet it was not.

The trees had grown tall and strong; the buildings he recognised in the distance, like the Palace of Westminster, were gleaming clean as if encased in limestone. Only Cleopatra's Needle and its attendant sphinxes stood unchanged from the last time he had walked this route. They walked by the front of the Savoy, which the Doctor remarked was now the back, and they passed the warehouse which in 1896 had been the Necropolis Funeral Company. Atkins watched in amazement as boats sped past on the river, and gaped openly as horseless carriages noisily crossed the bridges over the Thames. The Doctor did his best to explain everything, and Tegan smiled and laughed.

When they reached Kenilworth House, the feeling of upheaval remained. He had hoped that the familiar architecture, set apart from the rest of the disjointed city would offer a still point of continuity in the turned world.

It did not.

They made their way round to the busy road at the front of the house, and found the driveway gates open. The jackals watched them with stony eyes, their upright ears chipped and their claws blunted by the elements. The wall bulged outwards where a tree was growing into it. The trunk was forcing its way through the brickwork in a way the architects and landscapers had neither intended nor anticipated. The house at the top of the drive, rising out of the ground like some huge ancient structure, was recognisable. Just.

The roof had been entirely replaced, the new one rising higher with a dormer window suggesting the addition of attic rooms. The ground floor had been extended outwards from the original house, the porch stretching the width of the frontage, and an annex added to the side. The upstairs bay windows had been replaced with something altogether more streamlined, looking like nothing he had ever seen before – so that, with the extensions at ground level, the whole house seemed to taper inwards from the base.

'That's the trouble with Time,' the Doctor said catching sight of Atkins's expression.

'What is, Doctor?'

'Things are never the same again.'

'Well, I think it's a definite improvement,' Tegan said. She led the way up the drive, feet crunching on the gravel.

Across the street from Kenilworth House, a blue Ford Mondeo stood shadowed by a beech tree. The car was in every way average, an unremarkable model in a standard colour scheme. The owner had selected the car for these very reasons.

He watched the Doctor, Tegan and Atkins make their way up the drive, then checked his timepiece.

'Right on time, Doctor. As always.'

He smiled, and returned the hourglass to his jacket pocket. The upper bowl was almost empty of sand. Then Sadan Rassul started the engine, checked his wing mirror and pulled out into the traffic.

*

Aubrey Prior was alone in the library when he heard the doorbell. He frowned, glanced at the wall clock, and put down the heavy leather-bound volume he had been reading. Reaching for his stick, he pulled himself to his feet. His palm closed easily around the familiar smoothness of the carved handle of his walking stick as he pushed aside his chair and headed off towards the door.

'I'll get it,' he called up the staircase as he crossed the hall. There was no answer from above; probably his daughter had not heard either the bell or his shout. Prior was not expecting visitors, so it was probably Norris calling for Vanessa anyway. He shook his head and opened the door.

Outside, clustered round the doorstep, were three people. None of them was dressed in what Prior would have described as 'normal' attire. The woman was small and slim with close-cut dark hair. She was probably in her mid-twenties, and she appeared to be wearing either her night clothes or her underwear. A short white linen jacket seemed to have been added as an afterthought in case she got cold.

The other two were men. One was tall and blond, his age difficult to estimate. His eyes focused on Prior with an inner intelligence. His hair was parted at the side and he was dressed like an Edwardian cricketer. The other man was tall with dark greased-back hair and a thin face. He seemed to be in his late thirties, and he was wearing evening dress, complete with wing-collared shirt and black bow tie.

'Ah, hello there,' said the cricketer extending a hand. Then he saw Prior's hand resting on his walking stick. He quickly pulled back his hand and offered the other one. 'I'm the Doctor,' he said. 'I wonder if we might have a word.'

'I wasn't aware that anyone was ill,' Prior told him, ignoring the offered hand.

The Doctor leant forward. 'You don't know who I am?'

'Certainly not. Should I?'

The stranger's mouth twisted up on one side, as if he was biting the inside of his lip. 'Maybe not,' he said after a moment. Then he broke into a grin. 'I know, perhaps this will help.' He reached into his jacket pocket, frowned, then tried the other pocket. He pulled out a piece of white card, tapped it proudly against his thumbnail, and offered it to Prior.

Prior took the card suspiciously. He did not let his eyes stray from the Doctor's face until he had the card held up in front of him. It was half of an invitation card, printed on plain white stock with a gilt edge. It had been torn across the middle.

'I think you had better come inside,' Prior said quietly.

'I'm terribly sorry,' the Doctor said as they were shown into the library, 'but I'm afraid we don't know your name.'

'Prior,' the man said. 'Aubrey Prior.' He limped his way across the room to a large oval reading table. Several chairs stood round the table, and the top was littered with papers and books.

'Thank you. Well, as I said, I'm the Doctor, and this is Tegan and Mr Atkins.'

Prior waved them to the chairs round the table. 'Please bear with me a moment, Doctor.' Prior was counting along the books in one of the shelves. He found the one he was after, and took it down. From inside the cover he took a faded brown envelope, which he brought back to the table.

Tegan watched Prior make his unsteady way back to the table. He seemed to be in his mid-fifties, grey and distinguished. A little overweight, perhaps, but he was evidently still fit, apart from his leg. He sat down heavily on the chair at the head of the table, and laid his walking stick down on the cluttered surface. Tegan caught one of the papers as it skidded out of the way, and replaced it. Prior smiled at her, a warm, genuine smile. Tegan smiled back, and looked away.

On the table in front of her, the handle of the walking stick was level with Tegan. The stick itself was light wood, highly polished. The handle was made from the same piece of wood, not added on to the main body. It was carved into the shape of a sphinx.

Prior opened the envelope carefully. The edges were worn with age. From within he drew a piece of card and laid it on the table. It was old and yellowed. Beside it he placed the card the Doctor had given him outside the front door. Then he gently teased the two halves together. They fitted perfectly. Except that, whereas Prior's card was discoloured and crumpled, the gilt faded and the printed letters chipped and worn, the Doctor's half was pristine.

'I've looked after it,' the Doctor offered as Prior stared down at the completed invitation.

'Evidently.' Prior looked up. 'I did not expect you would ever come. I didn't think – I didn't know what to think.' He shrugged, and picked up the two halves of card, holding them together and comparing them.

'Is she here?' Tegan leant across the table, eager to find out where Nyssa was.

'The mummy? Oh yes, she's here.' Prior lifted his stick from the table, gripping the sphinx as he pushed himself to his feet.

'Sir?' Atkins spoke quietly to Prior as he passed him.

'Yes, Mr Atkins?'

'May I ask a question?'

'Of course. I think there may be several questions.'

'I used to know this house extremely well, many years ago. It has changed.'

Prior nodded slowly. 'It must have been many years ago.

I've been here for nearly twenty-eight years, and it was my uncle's before that. It's been in the family since it was built by Lord Kenilworth in the last century.'

Atkins waited patiently, hands behind his back.

'There was a fire, several years back,' Prior explained. 'The house was gutted and needed extensive rebuilding. All finished now, I'm pleased to say.'

'A fire?' The Doctor was quickly at Prior's side. 'What about the mummy?'

'Oh don't worry, the basement was unaffected.' Prior nodded again, and looked round his three visitors. 'Come on, I'll show you.'

'Who is it, father?'

They were crossing the hall when the girl called down to Prior. She paused on the half landing, looking over the banisters. Her long dark hair fell forward so that her face was shadowed. She swept it back with a hand to reveal the immaculate features of her face, classical and slightly aquiline. Her green eyes were large and wide, the pupils slightly oval like a cat's.

Prior gestured for her to join them, introducing his guests as she made her way down the stairs.

As she reached the bottom, Prior took her hand. 'This is my daughter, Vanessa.'

'How do you do.' The Doctor dusted his hand on his lapel and offered it.

'Are you more Egyptian people?'

'Well, that rather depends on what you mean. We're not actually Egyptian by birth.'

'They're here for the mummy,' Prior said simply.

Vanessa looked at the Doctor, Tegan and Atkins. 'You're welcome to it,' she said. 'I think the whole thing's creepy.' She smiled, her face instantly alive with humour. 'Would you like some tea? I'm sure Dad didn't think to offer.'

'Er yes, thank you.' The Doctor looked round at his friends. 'That would be very nice.'

'I'll put the kettle on. Call me when you're back.' She turned sharply, her hair thrown outwards in a semi-circle of strands. As she reached the end of the hall, she looked back. 'You will stay for the party, won't you?' She did not wait for an answer.

Prior coughed. 'Tomorrow is her twenty-first birthday. We're having a bit of a bash tomorrow night. Mainly my friends, I'm afraid, though she has invited a couple of people from her old school. Along with James Norris of course, Vanessa's fiancé. It's something of a double celebration now they've finally made their minds up.'

Prior unlocked the door under the stairs, opened it and gestured for the Doctor to go first. 'Vanessa won't come down here now,' Prior said. 'Makes her feel funny seeing someone so dead, she says.'

'We may soon be able to allay her fears,' the Doctor said as he started down the stairs.

'Too right,' said Tegan as she followed him. 'She's not as dead as you think.'

Prior said nothing, but followed Atkins down the stairs.

The room was surprisingly large. It probably extended under a good part of the house above. The floor was flagged with stone, and the walls were covered with heavy velvet curtains. Angled spotlights set into the ceiling made the room seem stark and bare, despite the various low tables and shelves around it. On each stood several relics, so that the whole place looked like a small museum.

'I've moved things around a bit,' Prior said. 'After the fire, we put a proper staircase in when we restructured the house.

Easier than the old trap door that used to be there. I use this as a sort of relic room now for my collection.'

At the far end of the room, on a raised dais, stood the sarcophagus. It was darkened with age and exposure to the moist English air, but was recognisably the same coffin. Tegan ran across to it.

'Are these genuine?' the Doctor asked, pausing by a display case. It contained an alabaster goblet, hieroglyphics on the rim picked out in blue pigment. The light inside the case shone through the cup making it seem to glow. Two handles projected from opposite sides, shaped like lotus flowers growing up and out from the base of the goblet. Beside it lay a dagger together with its embossed gold sheath. The blade was silver, the handle an intricate lacing of cloisonné.

Prior joined the Doctor. 'Magnificent, aren't they? And yes, they are genuine. The lotus wishing-cup, and Queen Ahhotpe's dagger.'

'Why is it called a wishing-cup?' asked Atkins.

'I imagine because of the inscription.' The Doctor indicated the coloured rim. 'The hieroglyphs probably wish for long life and happiness, or some such thing.'

Prior nodded. '"May the Ka live, and mayest thou spend millions of years, thou who lovest Thebes, sitting with thy face to the north wind, thy two eyes beholding happiness,"' he quoted. 'Or so Tobias St John translated it.'

The Doctor nodded. 'Not at all bad, actually.'

'Doctor,' called Tegan impatiently from the coffin.

'All right, Tegan, all right. She's waited for a long time, a couple more minutes won't make much difference.'

'They will to me.'

The Doctor ignored her and examined the relics again. 'You obviously know and love the subject,' he told Prior.

'That's your fault.'

'Oh?'

'Oh yes. Well, indirectly. I knew nothing about Egypt, even where it was, until my uncle showed me the mummy soon before he died. It fascinated me. When he passed away, I could afford to devote more time to the hobby. Now it's an obsession.' He smiled. 'Or so Vanessa tells me. She has little interest in the past. The future holds everything for the young. Like your impatient friend here.'

They made their way slowly to the sarcophagus, where Tegan was almost hopping with anticipation. 'What does your wife think to it all?' she asked Prior as the Doctor leant over the coffin and started examining the bandaged body within.

'My wife is dead.'

'I'm sorry.' Tegan looked away.

'You weren't to know. It was a long time ago. She died giving birth to Vanessa.'

The Doctor straightened up. 'Well, everything seems to be going swimmingly,' he said with a smile. 'In a few days she'll be back to normal.'

'A few days?'

'Tegan.' The Doctor raised a finger to stop her outburst.

Prior looked into the sarcophagus. Where the Doctor had pulled at the bandages there was an exposed area through which the bare flesh of an arm was showing. 'I realise that I have inherited an obligation of some sort to you people,' he said quietly. 'But I do think, Doctor, that you owe me some sort of explanation.'

They were in the drawing room. The layout and decor had changed surprisingly little over the last hundred years, although a large organ stood incongruously in one corner of the room. 'My late wife used to play,' Prior had commented when Tegan asked him pointedly why he possessed such a baroque piece of equipment.

The Doctor gave a brief and simplified explanation of events over tea. He glossed over the problems of timing and dates, suggesting but never actually stating that he and his friends were under a similar obligation to some unspecified ancestor to be there when Nyssa awoke. Explaining how she came to be sleeping inside the wrappings of an Egyptian mummy was rather less simple.

'I am aware of the notion of suspended animation,' Prior said huffily at one point as the Doctor tried to explain. 'I did some reading up on cryogenics a long time back, in a previous career. So while I don't understand what's happened, I can begin to believe it.'

'It all sounds complete nonsense to me,' Vanessa said, offering round a plate of shortbread. 'But I failed science.'

'Snap,' said Tegan.

'You mean the nonsense or the science?'

Tegan laughed. 'Both. But you get used to believing nonsense when you're with the Doctor.'

Atkins leant forward. 'I have found, Mr Prior, that even though I understand little of what the Doctor says or does, or what happens around him, he is able to make perfect sense of it all.'

Prior drained his cup. 'Well, that's good enough for now, anyway. So, you say it will be several days before this Nyssa person wakes up?'

The Doctor nodded. 'I need to examine her in more detail to be sure, but yes. Three, maybe four days. I wanted to arrive a few days ahead just to check everything's all right.'

'Then you'll stay for the party,' Vanessa said, tidying up the tea things. 'We insist, don't we, Dad? We've plenty of room, and you'll be right here to look after the lady downstairs.'

'Thank you,' the Doctor said. 'That would be ideal.'

Tegan was in a better mood after dinner. She had been rather down for most of the afternoon, disappointed that they still had to wait several days before they would know for certain that Nyssa was all right. But as dinner progressed, she became philosophical. The Doctor was right after all, a few more days after waiting so long was nothing really. And Prior and his daughter seemed so pleasant and hospitable that she was actually beginning to welcome the opportunity for a short holiday.

The Priors seemed to live alone in the huge house, though Vanessa mentioned that someone came in to clean twice a week, and they had a part-time gardener for the grounds.

'No cook, though,' Tegan said, and they all laughed.

Vanessa had rung for an Indian take-away, which, contrary to its description had been delivered. Tegan loved Indian food, and the Doctor expressed his appreciation as well. Atkins confessed that he had never been to India or tried their cuisine. But he tucked in with as much enthusiasm as he ever showed, and before long was wiping his glistening brow with a crisp white handkerchief.

After dinner, the Doctor had suggested they get a good night's sleep. They had had a long day, and tomorrow promised to be a late night with Vanessa's birthday party in the evening.

Vanessa had already sorted out rooms for them all, expressing no apparent surprise at their lack of luggage, and offering to lend Tegan whatever she needed. Prior and his daughter bade their guests goodnight, and left them to find their own way upstairs.

Now Tegan, Atkins and the Doctor were sitting in the large room allocated to the Doctor. He had asked them if they could spare a minute for a quick conference before turning in. And already Tegan was beginning to worry that her few days of quiet might not be as relaxing as she had hoped.

'I've been working on deciphering the hieroglyphics from the secret room behind Nyssa's tomb over the last few days,' the Doctor explained. 'And I've made a fair bit of progress, though there's still a lot to work through.'

'Good news?' asked Tegan.

'No,' said the Doctor. 'Not really.'

Tegan and Atkins exchanged glances.

'Terrific,' said Tegan.

'I think you had better divulge whatever information you deem of significance, Doctor,' Atkins told him.

'Yes,' said the Doctor. 'Right.' He coughed, stood up, walked round the room, then sat down again. 'The second mummy, the one you found in the hidden chamber, Tegan, is Nephthys. Or at least, given it seemed human and Nephthys was an Osiran, it represents Nephthys. Whatever that means.'

'Is he making sense to you?' Tegan asked Atkins.

'Not at all. I was not even aware that there was a second room or mummy.'

The Doctor ignored them and continued: 'The inscriptions tell the story of Nephthys and how she secretly helped her husband Seth, also known as Sutekh, to kill Osiris. His son, Horus, imprisoned Sutekh for ever beneath a great pyramid. The inscriptions say that he also imprisoned Nephthys, though they're a bit vague on where and how.'

'That is hardly a revelation, Doctor,' Atkins said. 'The legend is well known, although the exact part, if any, played by Nephthys has been a matter for some speculation.'

'Oh, I agree. But these inscriptions are quite specific on certain points. And they tend to be the areas of Osiran influence. They don't just retell the myth, they document the actual events.'

Atkins shook his head. 'Actual events?'

Tegan said: 'It's all to do with these Osiran things the Doctor keeps going on about.'

The Doctor took a deep breath. 'As I think I told you, the Osirans came from Phaester Osiris. They mastered the power of pure thought and used psi-power to project themselves through space in capsules driven by the power of the mind. All their power was based on mathematical exactness, in the same way that the pyramids are exactly proportioned and aligned. That's how they focused their powers. They drew power from the alignment and geometry of certain star systems, which they then tempered with their minds and harnessed.'

'The pyramids?'

'Yes, the pyramids were built to the plans and instructions left by the Osirans after they visited Earth.'

Atkins considered. 'It would explain some of the history of ancient Egypt,' he said. 'The country changed far more rapidly than anyone really believes is possible. They moved from a culture based round villages with chieftains to countries with kings in about two hundred years.'

The Doctor nodded. 'You'll also find that there is evidence that those kings were significantly taller and with much larger heads than their subjects. The Osirans not only left their mark in the style of architecture, they used their powers to project mental energy into their chosen rulers so that they and their descendants would follow through on the grand plan. Probably the pyramids had to be built exactly as they are for some great reason. Like keeping Sutekh and Nephthys restrained.'

'So who were Sutekh and Nephthys?'

'Sutekh was an evil Osiran of almost unparalleled mental power. The weight of it drove him mad, and he sought to destroy all life that was not his equal. He destroyed planet after planet and left a trail of havoc and devastation across half the cosmos before his brother Osiris caught up with him. Then, so far as I can tell, he and Nephthys killed Osiris, destroyed their planet, and fled to Earth.'

'Egypt?'

'Exactly. Horus and his fellow surviving Osirans cornered Sutekh and Nephthys in ancient Egypt. They overpowered them and imprisoned them.'

'So that's all right,' Tegan said. 'Isn't it?'

'Well, no, actually, it isn't. You have to understand the Osiran mentality. They were a cunning lot. Devious and enigmatic just for the sheer fun of it. They wouldn't execute Sutekh or Nephthys as that would mean stooping to their level. But they didn't think just locking them up was good enough either.'

'So?'

'So they left the means for their escape just out of reach. Sutekh knew that in the next chamber to where he was kept paralysed was all the equipment he would need to build a pyramid-powered missile to destroy the power source that kept him captive. And he knew that there was an infinitesimally small chance that he would ever get to activate the Osiran service robots that would build and operate the missile.'

'Robots?' asked Tegan. She was beginning to feel apprehensive.

The Doctor nodded. 'Yes. Wrapped in protective bandages impregnated with chemicals to protect them from corrosion and decay.'

'So, the creatures that attacked the camp—' Atkins began.

'Were service robots working for Nephthys. Yes.'

Tegan considered. 'So, you say you know what happened to Sutekh. But where is Nephthys actually imprisoned, and what was *her* infinitesimally small chance of escape?'

The Doctor looked her in the eyes. 'I haven't a clue,' he said. 'But I have a horrible suspicion that what we are doing may be exactly what she needs and intends. The Osirans live for a terrifically long time, so Nephthys can afford to be patient. To her, a thousand years is like an inconvenient wait for the next train. That's how she managed to take Nyssa back in time.'

'How do you mean?'

'Osirans can somehow absorb the time spillage. The time expended has to go somewhere. Whether you travel backwards or forwards, there's an equal amount of time that has to be accounted for, a bit like conservation of energy. Nephthys can absorb that temporal differential into herself and just get older by the same amount as the journey through time.'

They were silent for a while. Eventually Tegan said: 'You're really worried about this, aren't you, Doctor?'

He nodded. 'Remember I said the figure of exactly a hundred years just popped into my head?'

Tegan nodded. Then realised the implication. 'Mental powers!'

'Exactly,' said the Doctor. His face was set. 'And it's too late now to reverse the process. In a few days Nyssa will wake up.'

'And when she does?' asked Atkins.

'I'm not really sure. But I have a feeling that when Nyssa is revived, Nephthys will also live again.'

SOTHEBY'S AUCTION HOUSE
1978

'Lot number fifty-eight: a bracelet of early dynastic origin, with a scarab beetle motif as described in the catalogue.'

Sir John Mapleton flicked through to the right page and briefly skimmed the description. He remembered the piece, unremarkable to look at, but it had a certain charm. He had stood for several minutes at the preview staring at it. The workmanship was really quite good. Probably worth a shout.

The auctioneer seemed surprised at the interest, his eyebrows raising higher with each bid.

Mapleton mentally set himself an upper limit, and continued his bidding by habit as much as discretion. When he approached his limit he would assess the other contenders and decide on a strategy, whether to bid them up or try to slow the rise. So sad that poor old Arthur Evans had come to the point where he had to sell off even his most precious collection. But it really was an excellent piece.

With a start, Mapleton realised he had just bid over his limit. He really should pay attention. But he was trying to remember, wasn't the bracelet the one that Evans said some relative had brought back himself from Egypt? He raised his hand, and the price, while he thought about it.

He ended up bidding far more than the bracelet was really worth, but what was the point if you couldn't indulge yourself now and again. And it would keep Evans happy to know it had gone to a good home.

'An excellent purchase, Sir John,' a voice said quietly as he left the hall. 'I know you will look after it well.'

He swung round. 'Thank you.' He was not sure he knew the man. Surely he would remember someone so striking? The man was completely bald, not tall, but built like a wrestler. His accent and bronzed skin suggested he could be Egyptian. A faint tracery of lines, possibly scars, ran across the surface of his face so that it looked cracked like an old oil painting. And he was smiling in a way that set Sir John's teeth on edge.

Chapter
Ten

The party soon split into two main groups. Vanessa took Tegan to meet her school and college friends, who by and large occupied the old servants' quarters, in particular the kitchen area. Atkins, despite his natural affinity for the servants' area, stayed with the Doctor and Prior in the drawing room. Here Prior's friends and associates gathered to drink sherry and whisky and to try to ignore the vibrant beat of loud music emanating from the opposite end of the house.

Atkins stuck close to the Doctor, who seemed to have no trouble integrating himself into the proceedings, introducing them to complete strangers and striking up interesting conversations where none had previously existed.

Atkins felt out of place at two levels. First, he did not feel he had much in common with any of the people present, almost all of whom were contemporaries of Prior and therefore rather older than himself. At least, in terms of actual age if not date of birth. Second, given that he was there, he felt he should be offering round a tray of drinks. To make matters worse, he understood very little of what was said.

'You're a bit young for this room, aren't you?' the Doctor asked a tall man in his late twenties, out of the blue.

He was wearing a smart suit, and had a small moustache that was slightly more ginger than his brown hair. 'So, I think, are you,' the man replied.

'I'm older than I look, though.'

The man nodded. 'Neat costumes, by the way,' he said to

the Doctor and Atkins with a straight face. 'I didn't realise it was fancy dress.'

'Is it?' The Doctor looked round. 'I must have misread the invitation.'

The man laughed. 'You'd probably fit in with Nessa's crowd better than I do. Not really my scene. But so long as she's happy.'

The Doctor snapped his fingers. 'James Norris, of course. Aubrey Prior mentioned you.'

Norris smiled. 'The same. And you are?'

The Doctor introduced them both.

'Oh yes,' Norris said. 'Aubrey mentioned you. Says you knew the house before we got at it, is that right?'

'I spent some time here a while ago,' Atkins offered.

'And what do you think?' He leant closer, in mock conspiracy. 'I should warn you that I was the architect, before you comment.'

'I think it's terrific,' the Doctor said quickly.

'Thank you. But I don't.'

'No?'

'No. Competent. But Aubrey had some strange ideas about what he wanted. And I was young enough to go along with them rather than say they were silly. I suppose I was flattered he asked me, being so inexperienced. A bit more experience and I'd have made a better job of it.'

The Doctor smiled. 'Keeping it in the family?

'God, no. I hardly knew Nessa when we started. Got to know Prior as I had an interest in Egyptology, inherited a few worthless relics from an aunt years ago. Aubrey valued them for me. He's a real fanatic. Lives for it, though he came to it rather late, I suppose.' He finished his wine and toyed with the glass, twisting his fingers round the slender stem. 'Got to know Nessa while we were having the work done. She was still at school. After we finished, I hung around. Got to know her rather better.'

'And now you're engaged.'

'Yes.' His face lit up. 'Still can't quite believe it. Look, can I get you another drink or something, I'm having another glass.'

'Thank you,' the Doctor said. 'Perhaps an orange juice or lemonade?'

'And you?'

'Is there any single malt?' Atkins asked. He rather thought he might need it.

Norris returned with their drinks a few minutes later. By then the Doctor was deep in conversation with an old school friend of Prior's, Leonard Cranwell. Norris waited long enough to be polite, then murmured his farewells and moved on to talk with someone else.

Cranwell turned out to be a retired major. He was gruff but pleasant, and exuded common sense. Atkins was pleased to note that the military type seemed much the same as it had a century earlier.

'Dunno why we kept in touch, really,' Cranwell said. 'Used to write when I was posted abroad. Knew Prior's uncle a bit. Good chap, terrible tragedy, Cancer of some sort. Aubrey was very cut up about it. Then of course his wife and all that.'

'Yes, of course.'

'Vanessa's a lovely thing, though. Does him proud. Found a good lad in Norris too, though he never saw service. Bit of an arty sort, but he'll muddle through, I dare say.'

'What was her mother like?' the Doctor asked when he got a chance.

Cranwell frowned. 'Never met her. Don't think many of us did. They were married and having Vanessa before we knew about it. I didn't even know he'd met anyone until I heard about her death. Tragic.' He grabbed a passing woman by the arm and guided her into their group. She struggled to keep her drink in the glass as she changed course.

'Did you ever meet Aubrey's wife, Margaret?'

'His wife's name was Margaret?' asked the Doctor.

'No,' the woman smiled. 'My name's Margaret. I don't know what her name was. It was all very quick, a lightning romance and a swift wedding. No, I never met her.' The woman looked away into the distance. 'She died in childbirth poor thing. It must be terrible for Vanessa to know that. I didn't think it happened any more.'

Tegan had enjoyed the evening enormously, meeting people of about her age and talking to them about everyday normal things like jobs, boyfriends, and the weather. She was just wishing Vanessa a happy birthday when the Doctor and Atkins arrived.

'We weren't sure we really fitted into the other group,' the Doctor said. 'So we thought we'd try this one.'

'Well, you're more than welcome. Help yourselves to drinks.' Vanessa waved to the kitchen table which was covered in bottles and cans. Some of them still had liquid in.

'I like your ring,' the Doctor said. 'I didn't notice it earlier, was it a present?'

Vanessa smiled. 'Yes, isn't it lovely? Dad gave it me this morning.'

'Congratulations, by the way,' the Doctor said, looking closer at Vanessa's hand. 'May I see?'

'Of course.' She held her left hand out so that he could examine the large ring better. 'I don't usually like Dad's Egyptian stuff. But this is different. It feels so old and full of wisdom, you know?'

'Thank you,' the Doctor stepped back, motioning for Tegan to take a look at the ring.

It was made of heavy gold, inset with a large pale blue stone. As she peered into it, Tegan could see tiny flaws in the ancient gem, seven tiny dots or imperfection forming a pattern that seemed vaguely familiar. 'It's—' she began in surprise.

'Beautiful,' the Doctor finished for her.

Tegan looked at Atkins, and he gave a slight nod. He had recognised the stone too. When Tegan had first seen it, the ring had lain on a small red velvet cushion. In the tomb, beside Nyssa's sarcophagus.

'Is it important?' Atkins asked as they trooped up towards their rooms as the party drew to a muddled close some time later.

'Probably not,' the Doctor said. 'It's a nice present for a beautiful young woman, that's all.' He pointed up the stairway to the ceiling of the floor above. There was a small skylight set against the outside wall of the house. 'Remind me to ask Norris what that's for,' the Doctor said. 'Seems like an odd addition. What do you think, Tegan?'

Tegan did not answer. She thought she had drunk too much. And it didn't help that the outer wall she was leaning against as she went upstairs seemed to be sloping at an odd angle. But then that was nothing to the Mexican wave the ceiling was doing...

'That thing's sharp,' complained Norris, not for the first time. He pushed Nessa's hand away. 'I know it was a present, but can't you take it off for a bit? At least while we're in bed?'

'I like it,' she said. It was what she had said on each of the previous occasions that he had asked her to remove the ring.

'Well, I don't.' Immediately he was sorry. He could see he had upset her. It was her birthday, and he should let her have her way today of all days. 'I mean, I do like it. But I don't like it digging into me like that. It could do someone some serious damage.'

'Rubbish.'

'Fine. Well, I'll sleep somewhere else then. I won't get any rest knowing you've got your knuckle-duster on.'

He expected her to laugh, and then to give in and take off the ring. They had each made their point, they had each won. And then they would curl up together and each feel the warmth of the other's close body as they drifted off to sleep.

Instead, she turned over, away from him, and said: 'Fine. See you tomorrow.'

Norris considered for a moment. 'I thought I'd go down to the cottage tomorrow,' he said. 'Got some work to finish up before the weekend.'

No response.

'Look,' he said, 'I'm sorry I was rude about the ring. It's great. I like it a lot and it's a wonderful present. But it hurt me, OK? Just take it off for a while, hmm?'

She turned towards him, her eyes flaring. 'No!' she shouted, and pushed him away.

Norris rolled back, surprised. He edged his way out of bed, and looked back at Vanessa. She was still glaring at him, her body curled up like a cat ready to spring.

'Fine,' he said. 'I can't cope when you're in a mood like this. I might as well go now.'

She said nothing as he got dressed. He paused in the doorway. 'I'll call you tomorrow,' he said. 'I love you.'

The sound of the car woke Tegan from her feverish sleep. Her mouth was dry, and she was sober enough to know she needed a drink of water or she would have a hangover the next day. She tugged on a T-shirt Vanessa had lent her, and creaked down the stairs hoping she could remember the way to the kitchens. It was not until she had taken her third wrong turning that it occurred to her she could have got a glass of water from the bathroom.

The corridor looked exactly like the way to the kitchen. It also looked exactly like the previous corridor. And the one before that. Neither of them had taken Tegan where she wanted or expected. This one was no exception. She exhaled loudly, and in desperation flung open a door she knew was not going to take her where she wanted to go.

She was right. But as she stepped into the dark room to pull the door shut again, the pale light from the passageway fell across a bookcase just inside the room. Tegan stood poised on the threshold, and as her eyes adjusted to the dark, she could see more bookcases and cabinets arranged around the walls. And the room smelled. It was a dry, musty smell. The smell of a place not dusted for years, and unoccupied for longer.

Intrigued, Tegan felt round the wall inside the door until she found the light switch. The light seemed filtered through the specks of dust that hung in the air and Tegan's fingers were coated with a sheen of grimy black from the switch. The dust was catching in her dry throat now, and she was even more desperate for some water.

She did not venture further into the room. As she had seen, bookcases lined the walls. The uncurtained windows were smeared with dirt and grime, reflecting an imperfect darkened image of the room back at Tegan. A murky image of herself stood poised in the doorway. The centre of the room was dominated by a large reading table like the one in the library. The rest of the floor space was almost covered with boxes and piles of magazines, journals and books. Everything was layered with dust.

Tegan glanced along the nearest bookcase, reaching out and wiping the labels on the shelves. One had been attached with sticky tape that was now so yellow and brittle that it flaked away as Tegan's hand touched it. The label fluttered to the floor. But Tegan's attention was on the other labels and the titles of the books. One shelf was labelled 'Jackson Laboratory (from 1929)'. One of the larger volumes on the shelf was titled *The Lane List of Named Mutations & Alleles of Polymorphic Loci of the Mouse*. Most of the others were too dusty to read the spines.

Tegan looked down at the piles of papers and magazines. Here was a set of the *Journal of the Reticuloendothelial Society*. There was a pile topped by volume ten of the *Revista Brasileira de Genetica*. She shook her head and turned to leave.

Her hand was on the light switch when she saw the rows of specimen jars. She was already in the process of turning out the light as she began to realise what the shapes floating inside the discoloured fluids might be.

She was trying to think of an excuse not to switch the light back on again when a car went by on the road outside. The headlights flashed across the ceiling of the room, and Tegan pulled the door shut behind her.

She concentrated on finding the kitchen, tried to dispel the memory of what she had just seen as the after-effects of the party. In the reassuring light of day, that would probably be how she would remember it.

After a few minutes she had managed to retrace her steps to the stairs. Starting again, from there she found the kitchen almost at once. Relieved, she downed three tumblers of water straight off. It made her throat feel better, cool and moist. But she could feel the water sloshing around in her stomach, and that made her feel a bit queasy again. You can't win, she decided, as she refilled the tumbler to take back to bed.

As she turned the tap off, Tegan heard movement outside in the corridor. 'Hello,' she called, catching sight of a figure as it passed.

There was no answer.

By the time Tegan got to the door, the figure had reached the end of the corridor. It was Vanessa, dressed only in a plain, white, ankle-length nightgown. She turned the corner and disappeared from sight without looking back.

Tegan shrugged. Probably in the same state as she was.

Vanessa's eyes were wide and blank as she unlocked the back door. Her movements were slow and measured, as if she were under water. She drew back the bolt and slowly opened the door.

'Thank you, my child.' Sadan Rassul stepped into the house. Vanessa did not react, her eyes remained set and unseeing. 'And now you will take me to the basement room.'

Vanessa nodded slowly, then turned and set off down the corridor. Rassul followed close behind. In his hand he carried a small stone statuette. It was about eight inches long, the features picked out in gold against the black of the stone. It was a likeness of the jackal Anubis, God of the Dead.

Sir John Mapleton did his final round of the antiquities room before locking up. His collection was vast, one of the largest in Europe. He could remember where and when he had acquired every single piece, and usually how much he had paid for it. Someone had been round the previous week suggesting he catalogue it all on computer, but Mapleton didn't need a computer. He had a complete catalogue in his mind.

He flicked a speck of dust from the top of one of the display cases, and turned off the main lights. Moonlight streamed in through the windows down one side of the room, throwing strange shadows across the floor. Somewhere behind him, a door banged. But Mapleton ignored it. He was staring across the room.

In the centre of the room, a single display case still glowed. He must have forgotten to turn off the lamp. Inside, the heavy bracelet he had paid too much for at Sotheby's many years previously rested propped up at an angle on a perspex stand. The scarab beetle on the top glowed blue in the faint light.

He made his way carefully over to the case, picking his way through the shadows which seemed to twist and turn as he approached. He was halfway across the room when the moon went behind a cloud and he realised that when he switched out the light in the case he would be in utter darkness. He cursed quietly and turned to make his way back to the main switches.

But then he stopped, and looked back at the case. He was sure he had turned the lamp off. In fact, now he came to look, it seemed as though the illumination emanated from the bracelet itself rather than the spotlight in the base of the cabinet. He frowned, took a step forward, and collided with something solid.

In the faint blue glow of the bracelet he could just make out the edges of the huge shape beside him. Odd, there was no cabinet here. Mapleton reached out to feel what it was, and his hand closed on what felt like coarse linen.

He shook his head, and rubbed at the material. There were no mummies in the room, they were all at the other end of the wing. This room was strictly for smaller relics, jewellery and household artefacts.

He was still puzzling over the problem as he felt the shape

move under his hand. At the same moment the moon came out from behind the cloud, sending rays of pale light dancing across the room.

The mummy was turning towards Mapleton. It was massive, towering over him as he pulled away. Its arms reached down for him as he staggered back, his hand pressed to his mouth. Then the rough bandaged hands closed on his throat, pressing down, pushing him to the floor.

The bracelet glowed more brightly as the mummy turned towards it. It stepped over the figure sprawled across the floor, and lumbered over to the display case, its arm raised. As it reached the case, it smashed its heavy arm downwards, shattering the glass of the display cabinet. Shards and splinters tore at the bandages as the mummy reached into the case and took hold of the bracelet. A strand of cloth ripped away from the hand as it pulled it out.

The mummy left the same way as it had come in, through the smashed remains of a side door. It crunched heavily across the gravel of the drive way to where a Ford Transit van waited, the back door open.

Sadan Rassul took the bracelet carefully from the service robot. The servicer bowed, and climbed into the back of the van, bending almost double to fit inside.

Rassul carried the bracelet with both hands to the open driver's door. On the seat was an open wooden box, the inside lined with satin. He placed the bracelet inside, then closed and locked the lid.

A few moments later, the van drove off into the moonlight.

EGYPT
1798

Captain Jean Tombier led the general deep into the building. He had led him first to the pyramid itself, and then inside the maze of passageways found and cleared by the archaeologists.

The general had carefully avoided the rubble which still littered the floor, and had seemed unperturbed when a swarm of bats swept past them, squealing in rage. He followed Tombier in near silence towards the heart of the pyramid, blazing torch held high so that he could see the magnificence of the edifice, could marvel at the colour and intricacy of the graphics on the walls.

Now they stood at last outside the King's Chamber, the centre of the pyramid. 'We are here, sir.' Tombier made to enter the chamber, but he felt the general's hand on his shoulder, pulling him back.

'I think not, Jean,' the general said. 'This I must see alone.' He smiled in the gloom, and patted Jean's shoulder. Then he turned, and was gone.

Tombier waited for what seemed like hours. At first he could hear the general's boots ringing on the stone floor of the chamber. But after a while the sound stopped, and he was alone with his breathing and his thoughts.

His torch was burning low. If they did not start back soon, they would not have enough light to find their way to the entrance. Tombier bit at his lower lip and weighed up the unpleasant alternatives: risk having to grope out of the pyramid in darkness, past the fallen rubble and the bats, round the sudden holes in the floor that dropped away for ever; or brave the general's wrath if he disturbed him without good cause.

He was reaching the point where he thought he had good cause, when there was a sudden blaze of light from inside the chamber. Brilliant whiteness blazed out into the corridor and imprinted a negative image of the doorway on Tombier's retina.

'Sir,' he shouted. 'General!' And he stumbled towards the doorway. He collided first with the wall, and then, just as his eyes fought to readjust, with the general as he left the chamber.

'What was it, sir? What happened, what did you see?'

Even in the dim light, his sight washed out by the sudden flash, Tombier could see that the general was pale as death. His hand shook as he pushed his hair out of the way. He seemed to notice, and pushed it inside the front of his jacket. 'Nothing,' he said eventually. 'I saw nothing.'

'Nothing? But the light – I saw—'

'I tell you, there was nothing. Nothing happened here. If anyone asks, I went into the chamber, stayed a few moments, then left.'

Tombier stared at him. He would not question the orders of his general, but clearly something was wrong.

The general clapped him on the back and tried to smile. Instead his mouth stretched into a grimace. 'One day, perhaps, I will tell you about it. One day I may be able to discuss it with you over a cognac while armies burn behind us. One day, perhaps. But not today.' He turned and looked back towards the entrance to the chamber. 'No,' he said softly, 'not today.'

Tombier led the way out of the Great Pyramid in silence. It was the only time that he saw Napoleon Bonaparte afraid.

Chapter
Eleven

The next morning Tegan was not at her best. She survived the cotton-wool cloud that was breakfast, feeling revived by copious quantities of orange juice washed down with strong coffee. By the middle of the morning she was feeling decidedly better, and eagerly agreed to accompany the Doctor when he suggested he was going to examine Nyssa again.

Atkins was waiting for them in the hall. Probably, Tegan thought, he was a bit bored and lost. But of course he did not show it, any more than he showed any real emotion.

Within a few minutes, it was Tegan who was feeling bored and lost. The Doctor was listening for Nyssa's heartbeat with an ear trumpet pressed to her chest. 'Best not to disturb anything at this late stage,' he said when Tegan asked if they could remove some of the bandages. She desperately wanted to see Nyssa's face again, to check that she at least looked well and peaceful.

Disappointed, she wandered despondently round the room, glancing at the various relics on their shelves and tables. Atkins was examining some of them in detail, apparently fascinated by the pieces. Tegan gave each a cursory glance, then moved on. Only one of the exhibits she looked at did she find at all interesting. It was a bound collection of the notes and drawings from Kenilworth's expedition. She flicked through it, noticing odd torn pages from Simons' notebook which had been glued onto larger sheets and then bound in with the other notes and sketches.

'Hey, Doctor, look at this,' she called at one point, but he merely grunted and continued his examination of the inert body.

'Please yourself,' Tegan grumbled, looking round to see if Atkins was interested. But he seemed engrossed in a display of necklaces. Tegan looked again at her sketch of the excavations outside the pyramid entrance, then she closed the book and moved on.

She turned to watch the Doctor as he leant over the coffin. He was now wearing a stethoscope and seemed to be listening to Nyssa's arm. He nodded with satisfaction, coiled up the stethoscope, and stuffed it into his pocket. Then he dashed round to the other side of the sarcophagus and started tapping on the edge. Tegan could see she was in for a long wait, and leant back against the red velvet of the curtain behind her. She could feel the wall straight and hard behind the curtain. And she felt it give way under her weight.

Atkins grabbed Tegan's elbow as she slipped in surprise. 'What is it?' he asked.

'I don't know. The wall wobbled.'

Atkins pushed experimentally at the curtain close to where Tegan had been standing. 'You're right. There's some give in it certainly.'

The Doctor was frowning across at them. He had stopped his tapping on the coffin and seemed to be paying attention.

Atkins went to the corner of the room, and hunted around for the edge of the curtain where it met the one covering the next wall. The curtains were all fitted to tracks set into the ceiling just in from the wall. Atkins pulled at the edge of curtain, and drew it back a few feet, revealing the wall behind. Tegan stared in amazement, and even Atkins seemed surprised.

The Doctor stepped down from the dais and crossed to

join them. 'Interesting,' he said quietly. 'Very interesting.'

The wall beneath the curtain was actually a plasterboard partition, probably erected as a skin for the real wall behind and several inches away from it. The board was relatively thin, and wobbled if any force was applied to it. It was covered in painted hieroglyphics.

'You know what this is?' the Doctor asked after they had spent a few minutes examining the paintings.

'Yes,' said Tegan. 'It's weird.'

The Doctor shook his head. 'A little eccentric perhaps, but not really weird. Atkins?'

'It's a copy of the tomb,' Atkins said simply.

'Exactly.' The Doctor stepped back and waved an arm round the room, gesturing at the other walls. 'They've painted a copy of the interior of the tomb. Probably from Kenilworth's expedition's notes.'

'The notes are over there.' Tegan pointed to the book she had been looking at. 'But why bother? And who did it?'

'Oh, just a bit of fun, probably. Or perhaps an attempt at some context and authenticity for the mummy. Either Prior did it, then changed his mind about the ambience and put up the curtains, or one of his predecessors had the paintings done, and someone later didn't think much of it.'

'So someone, if I understand you correctly, Doctor,' Atkins said, 'for whatever reason, created an exact replica of the original tomb?'

The Doctor nodded. 'Or rather, they think they did.' He pulled back the curtain from a section of the adjacent wall. 'But we know one thing they'll have got wrong, don't we, Tegan?' He grinned widely and pointed to a cartouche halfway up the wall. Then his smile froze. 'I don't like that,' he said.

'What's wrong, Doctor?'

'Nothing, that's the problem. This name is exactly as it is in the actual tomb.'

Atkins nodded. 'That does seem reasonable, Doctor.'

The Doctor shook his head. 'Not when Tegan and I altered the only sketch made by the expedition so that it was inaccurate.'

Atkins gaped. 'But why, Doctor?'

'Because it is the name of Nephthys, and it conceals the mechanism that opens the door to the secret inner chamber we told you about.' He reached out, hesitantly, and pressed in the middle of the open square in the centre of the cartouche. As soon as he pushed, he whipped his hand away as if burned.

They watched and waited in silence for several seconds. But nothing happened.

The Doctor exhaled heavily. 'Well, thank goodness for that,' he said.

The murder of Sir John Mapleton and the theft of a single bracelet from his collection made the local early evening news. Tegan and Atkins had spent the afternoon in town, each finding that they enjoyed the other's company. Atkins was secretly impressed with Tegan's openness and her forthright nature. Tegan admired Atkins's control and reserve.

The Doctor had warned Tegan before they set off that she was not to explain too much to Atkins. But in fact Atkins did not seem interested in explanations. He took everything in his stride, nodding politely at Tegan's inadequate descriptions of cinemas, aeroplanes, and the one-way system.

They arrived back just after six-thirty, and found the Doctor, Prior and Vanessa sitting in the lounge watching the television. 'Don't even ask,' Tegan told Atkins, and he shrugged and settled into an armchair.

'Good grief,' Prior said as the article finished. They had all listened in silence, the Doctor, Tegan and Atkins exchanging worried glances when a picture of the bracelet was shown. Vanessa sat silent and still, her eyes fixed on the television.

'I knew Mapleton,' Prior said. 'Only slightly. Did some business with him. You remember?' he asked his daughter.

She nodded, but still said nothing.

'What sort of business?'

'Oh, bought a couple of pieces he was bored with. Vanessa fancied that bracelet, strangely enough. But he wouldn't part with it. I think we went for a necklace instead.'

'Why the bracelet?' Tegan asked.

'Oh, I don't know.' Vanessa seemed to switch back on. 'Just liked the look of it. It was years ago. I probably thought it would impress some boy at school.'

'It probably would,' the Doctor agreed. 'Certainly somebody wanted it very badly.

Vanessa had been feeling strange all day. She was tired and felt as if she was floating just above reality. At first she put it down to the excesses of the previous night's party, but by the evening she was wondering if perhaps you felt like this all the time after you turned twenty-one. It would explain the behaviour of many of the adult population, after all.

The news about Mapleton left her with an odd mixture of emotions. She was at once saddened by the loss of an acquaintance of her father's, and at the same time she experienced a bizarre feeling of excitement. And now she wanted to – to, well she was not sure what. But something had to be done soon.

She sat alone in the lounge, staring at the blank screen of the television, and listened to her mixed thoughts and emotions. It was almost as if they were in some way no longer her own.

'Could I ask you something?' The Doctor's voice jolted her out of her reverie.

'Of course, Doctor. How can I help?'

He sat in the armchair next to her, perched on the edge of the leather, hand clasped in front of him and elbows resting on his knees. 'Your great-great several times uncle, Lord Kenilworth, brought back various relics from one of his expeditions.'

Vanessa nodded. 'Like your mummy, you mean.'

'Er, yes. Yes. Well, those relics included several which were all together inside the tomb, and which have some significance we don't yet really understand.'

'How do you know?' Vanessa asked. But in the back of her mind she felt sure she already had the answer.

'Oh, well, it's probably all in Kenilworth's notes, which are down in the basement. Anyway, there are four relics I'm interested in. One is a statue of a jackal. That was stolen many years ago, while the expedition was on its way home.'

'Anubis,' muttered Vanessa. 'He who is in the Place of Death.'

'Yes, absolutely,' the Doctor said slowly. 'I thought you weren't interested in Egyptology.'

'I'm not. But you pick things up.' Vanessa shrugged. Where had she heard the phrase before? Never mind, it wasn't important.

'Well, interested or not, the second relic is the ring your father gave you last night.'

Vanessa's hand immediately closed over the ring, and she pulled away, sinking deep into her armchair.

'It's all right,' the Doctor said quietly. 'I just want to be sure it stays safe. Because the third relic is the bracelet stolen from Mapleton last night.'

'You think someone is after them?'

'What do you think?' the Doctor asked quietly. When she

did not answer, he went on: 'The last of the relics is a carved statue of a snake. A cobra. You wouldn't happen to know where it is, would you?'

His eyes were deep and blue. Penetrating, searching, pleading. Did she know where the snake was? 'No,' she told him. 'I don't.'

The Doctor nodded as if this was the answer he had expected. 'Well, just a thought.' He stood up.

'I'm sorry. You could try the family records, Kenilworth's account of his expedition might say what happened to it.'

'Thank you,' said the Doctor from the doorway. 'It might indeed.'

Vanessa watched the door close behind him. She would feel better after a good night's sleep. She wished James had not had to go away. She'd have done anything to keep him here, with her.

The Doctor did not sleep that night. This was not unusual. Instead he waited until the house was quiet, then went to Prior's library. He hunted out every volume he could find about the various dialects and styles of early Egyptian hieroglyphics. Then he looked for any documentation of the myths about Seth, Nephthys, Osiris and Isis.

He read every word of each of the books at lightning speed. But it still took him almost until dawn. With his new and deeper insight into the legends and the writing, he hoped to be able to decipher more of the inscriptions he had copied down from the tomb. He was not sure when he would next get a chance to spend a useful amount of time on his studies, but even from what he remembered of the inscriptions, he did not feel that all was well.

In fact, he had several very nasty suspicions.

*

It did not take the Doctor long the next morning to convince Tegan and Atkins of the importance of finding the cobra. He also gave then a brief description of his conversation with Vanessa the previous night, and mentioned in passing that he was still hoping to decipher more of the inscriptions.

'It seems a sensible suggestion,' Atkins volunteered. 'Although we already know where the cobra went.'

The Doctor nodded. 'Yes. To Macready. Still, given Vanessa's contact with the ring and the bracelet, I thought she might have heard what happened to the cobra.'

'Prior would be more likely to know,' Tegan pointed out. 'He's the expert in this stuff, after all.'

'Good thought, Tegan. Let's go and ask him. At least he might be able to point us to some sort of inventory of snake relics in the collections of the world.'

They found Prior in the library. He limped over to them, leaning heavily on his sphinx-handled stick, and listened patiently to the Doctor's request.

'Did Vanessa ever tell you how she and James Norris met?' he asked as they sat round the library table.

'I thought he was the architect for the alterations you did to this house,' Tegan said.

Prior nodded. 'Indeed he was. But Vanessa and I knew him before that. He practically begged me for the work, in fact. He was young and enthusiastic.' Prior laughed. 'He still is, I suppose. Anyway, I had him draw up the plans and supervise the work. Did a damned fine job too, as it turned out. But I could see that Vanessa valued his company, even then. And I must confess I like the lad myself.'

Atkins coughed quietly, and everyone turned towards him. 'He did mention, Mr Norris that is, that he originally came to you when he inherited some relics of Egyptian origin.'

Prior nodded. 'Indeed he did. He had no idea of their value, but he had read an article I wrote for *Newsweek* about how tourism and neglect are eroding the great sites of ancient Egypt and they should be preserved. Shocking.' He leant across the table. 'Do you realise that—' He broke off. 'Never mind, hobby horse of mine. Sorry.'

'Not at all,' the Doctor said. 'There's a long way to go before people understand the importance and delicacy of their own past.'

'Indeed so,' Prior nodded. 'Indeed so. Anyway, you were asking me about the cobra from Kenilworth's expedition.'

'And you were telling us about James Norris,' Tegan said.

'Well, naturally,' Prior replied. 'After all, he's got it.'

'What?' The Doctor looked round at his friends. 'Does Vanessa know that?' he asked quietly.

'Oh yes,' Prior said. 'It was one of the relics he brought to me for valuation. Pure coincidence, he had no idea that it was almost a family heirloom.' Prior gave another short bark of laughter. 'Wouldn't part with it, though. Vanessa tells me he's got it out on his mantelpiece in that cottage of his in Cornwall. I've told him a thousand times, anyone could just walk in and—' He stopped short again, mouth open and brow creased as if a terrible thought had just occurred to him. 'My God,' he said quietly.

'What?' The Doctor was leaning across the table, his hands reaching out towards Prior.

Prior turned to him gravely. 'I hope he's got it insured,' he said.

'Where is Vanessa?' Tegan asked. 'I haven't seen her all day.'

'Oh, she went to have a lie down for a bit. She's been a bit under the weather last couple of days. Probably missing James. He's down in Cornwall.'

'At this cottage of his?'

'Yes, Doctor.'

The Doctor considered. 'Two of the four relics are missing already,' he said to Prior. 'Of the others, Vanessa has one and James Norris has the other.'

'You think they might be in danger?'

The Doctor nodded. 'It's possible,' he said. 'If you keep an eye on your daughter, perhaps you can lend Tegan a car and tell her how to find Norris's cottage.'

Prior nodded. 'I can lend you a map,' he told Tegan. 'But it's about a four-hour drive from here. Might even be five.'

'And why am I going to see Norris?'

'To warn him he might be in danger.'

'You could phone him,' Prior offered.

The Doctor shook his head. 'I'd rather Tegan saw him in person. He's more likely to take things seriously then. But perhaps you could call and make sure he's there when she arrives.'

'Of course.'

'But why am I driving? And why aren't you coming?' hissed Tegan. 'There are quicker ways to get to Cornwall, you know.' She glanced across at Prior, but he had pulled himself out of his chair and was hunting through a pile of books, presumably for a road atlas.

The Doctor nodded. 'I know. But Atkins and I have an appointment somewhat further afield, and I rather fancy we have a greater need for the quicker means of transport you have in mind. I don't think there's a great need for haste, and it will give you something to do while we're busy.'

Tegan sat back in her chair. 'Terrific,' she said. 'I get the second rate assignment again.'

'Not at all, Tegan. We're on a short quest for knowledge, but you could be saving lives.'

'All right, Doctor.'

The Doctor rubbed his hands together. 'Splendid.' He stood up and started towards the door. As he passed Tegan, he said quietly: 'Oh, there is just one other thing.'

'What's that?'

'We really have no idea if Norris can be trusted.'

'I have no idea if anyone can be trusted,' Tegan told him. 'Why did Vanessa lie about the cobra?'

'I don't know. Perhaps she's got a rotten memory, or perhaps she didn't want to implicate her fiancé.'

Tegan nodded. 'Maybe.'

'You like her, don't you?'

Tegan nodded. 'She's OK. She reminds me of someone. To look at, I mean. But I can't think who it is. Maybe someone I was at school with.'

'Yes,' said Atkins, 'there is a certain familiarity in her features.'

The Doctor grinned. 'Perhaps she's just got that sort of face,' he said.

Vanessa felt no better than the previous evening. Her head was still swimming, and she could hear disjointed and distant voices echoing in the back of her mind. She had tried to call James, but all she got was the answerphone. Either he was out, or he was working and did not want to be disturbed.

She had also tried to sleep, but even when she managed to doze off for a few minutes she had nightmares. They were gone when she awoke, just the memory of a distant terror lingering on the edges of sleep.

After she woke the third time in a cold sweat, she decided to have a shower, and then to read or watch television in the hope of taking her mind off things. She let the cool water splash across her body and run down her skin towards the drain, washing over tiles that had been parched for a thousand years.

A thousand years? Where had she got that idea? She shook her head, her long wet hair swinging round and sending droplets of water skidding against the glass walls of the shower cubicle.

Prior seemed happy for Tegan to take his car. He could, he pointed out, always borrow Vanessa's should he need to get out. And since they were actually in the middle of London anyway, he could choose between taxi, bus and tube for any local journeys.

So, soon after lunch, Tegan found herself sitting behind the wheel of a Jaguar, wondering where the windscreen wipers were operated from should she need them, and wishing the seat were a couple of inches higher. Another of the shocks she got from being over ten years behind in automotive technology and not used to the state of the art even in her own time was the power steering. She had gone almost a complete circle in the driveway before she managed to crunch to a halt on the gravel and learn about the latest anti-lock braking systems.

Prior tapped on the driver's window, and after a short pause as Tegan discovered electric windows, handed her a road atlas.

'A bit easier on the steering,' he said as he showed where he had marked the relevant page with a sticky yellow notelet. Then he showed her the pencilled circle in the middle of what appeared to be a trackless swamp where Norris had his cottage. 'There is a track. I've drawn it on the map for you, so far as Vanessa could remember where it is. Had to drag her out of the shower to show me.'

'Is she still not feeling well?'

Prior shook his head. 'Not a hundred per cent. I thought she'd ask why I wanted to know, but she just pointed and went back into her room. I can't fathom what's up with her, but I hope she's better soon.'

Tegan agreed, and studied the map. 'Doesn't look as easy as it might be. I could end up in a ditch.'

'Well, the car's insured,' Prior laughed.

Tegan laughed too. 'I'm not sure I am, though.' She thanked him, almost caught his nose in the window, and swung the car round carefully so that it faced back down the drive.

As she turned past the front of the house, she caught sight of movement at an upper window. As the car stopped, Tegan adjusted the rear-view mirror so she could see what the movement was. Vanessa was standing at her bedroom window, the curtain pulled back.

Tegan turned and studied the figure in the mirror for a moment. The window was almost full length, and she could see Vanessa framed against the dark interior of her room. She was strikingly beautiful, tall and slim. Her dark hair was still folded up on to her head in a towel after her shower. Her features were aquiline, and her eyes large and cat-like with huge pupils. She was dressed in a simple white nightgown which reached to her knees.

And in that moment, Tegan realised who Vanessa reminded her of. With her long hair tied up, she was the image of the Shabti figures in the entrance corridor of Nyssa's tomb.

Vanessa watched the car set off down the drive. Then she pulled the towel from her long hair, and shook it free. She sat in front of her dressing table, head slightly to one side as she dried and brushed her hair. In the mirror, Vanessa could see the door to her room. She had almost finished when she saw the reflected handle begin slowly to turn.

She swung round on her seat, putting down the hairdrier and comb, one knee pulled up to her chin. As the door swung open, she stood up, backing away from the figure which filled the doorway.

The mummy stepped into the room, the floor shaking slightly beneath its heavy feet as it swung towards Vanessa. She stood, back to the far wall, staring at the huge shape as it lumbered towards her.

Behind the mummy, Sadan Rassul appeared in the doorway. His broad squat shape was silhouetted against the wall of the corridor outside. 'Do not be afraid, my child,' he said gently as the mummy reached out for Vanessa.

An unholy roaring sound broke the stillness of the desert air. One moment, nothing but sand and the breeze; the next, the TARDIS melted into existence on a dune overlooking a deep crater. After a pause, the TARDIS doors opened and Doctor and Atkins emerged.

'What we really need,' the Doctor said, 'is to contact someone who was on the expedition. If there was an expedition. But someone must have been here, to know about the Nephthys hieroglyphic.' He handed Atkins a heavy torch, and showed him how to switch it on.

Atkins considered. 'So we see if we can find clues as to how long ago the pyramid was re-excavated, then use the TARDIS again to try to trace someone who can divulge information to us about the expedition.'

'Exactly,' the Doctor smiled. 'Now then…' He twisted round trying to get his bearings, licking his index finger and holding it up. Then he stared out across the desert sands in the opposite direction to the crater. 'That way, I think.'

'Actually, Doctor, if I may?'

The Doctor nodded.

'I'd suggest this way.' Atkins pointed down into the crater. The far side was a more regular shape than the other ragged edges. In places a gleaming blackness glistened beneath the sand. It was the side of the pyramid.

They stared at it for a moment. Then the Doctor said: 'Can I ask what methodology you used for that inspired geographical deduction?'

It took them several minutes to stumble and trip down the steep side of the crater. As they approached, they could see the door of the pyramid standing open, a deep pile of sand covered the floor and prevented the door from closing again. It had been open for a long time.

'Do you think they survived the traps?'

The Doctor nodded. 'Oh, I should think the traps were deactivated when we removed Nyssa's body. Pretty much served their purpose by then.' He clambered up the shifting pile of sand and through into the main passageway. Light came in through the open doorway, but they still needed their torches to see where they were going.

There was gradually less sand as they made their way up the corridor. The Shabti figures were gone from their alcoves, and the sound of the echoing footsteps seemed deadened and dull. At last they reached the burial chamber. The doors were pulled shut, but not fastened. The Doctor and Atkins looked at each other. Then the Doctor nodded, and they each opened one of the heavy double doors, and together they stepped into the chamber.

It was empty.

They walked to the centre of what had been the burial chamber, stopped and slowly turned round. Their torchbeams played over the floor, ceiling and walls as they took in the enormity of the change.

'You know,' Atkins said, 'I can understand the removal of

relics and even furniture. But why take the walls?'

The Doctor nodded. The stone had been hacked away, leaving a scarred mess of stonework where once there had been carved hieroglyphics. 'They certainly did a thorough job.'

'I don't remember this.' Atkins crossed to an open archway on the far side of the rough cave that had been the chamber. 'What was it?'

The Doctor joined him. Beyond the archway, illuminated by their torches, was another smaller cavern. Like the main chamber it had been stripped bare, the walls hacked down.

'This,' said the Doctor, 'was the hidden chamber I described where the second mummy was incarcerated.'

'Not hidden any more,' commented Atkins.

'No,' agreed the Doctor grimly. 'And, as we should have realised, the mummy, like everything else, has gone.'

ST HELENA
1821

Napoleon had managed to struggle into a position where he was half sitting, propped up by the pillows. He had sent the nurse from the room, and was alone now with Tombier. They looked at each other for a while, saying nothing in the way that only friends can. From outside, came the cry of seagulls, and the faint sound of the waves lapping on the shore as the tide went out.

'Not long now, my friend,' Napoleon whispered hoarsely. 'I am losing my final battle, I fear.'

Tombier said nothing. He grasped his general's – his emperor's – hand tightly.

Napoleon laughed, a half cough of humour. 'A good habit, Tombier, to say nothing when there is nothing to say.' He reached over and patted his friend's hand as it held his. 'Yet I am always so open with you.'

Tombier smiled, though the smile did not reach his eyes. 'Yes, sir.' He stood, and walked to the window. 'Except once.' He hoped that Napoleon had missed the way his voice caught, and that he had turned quickly enough to hide the tears welling up in his eyes.

'Ah, yes,' Napoleon said from behind him. 'The Great Pyramid.' He was silent for a while. Then he said: 'I have spoken to no one about that. Ever.'

'Nor I,' said Tombier softly. But he knew that even if Napoleon had heard he would have expected no less.

'Even when the Prussians linked up with the British at

Waterloo, I was less afraid than I was in that chamber.'

Tombier turned from the window. 'What happened? I have never asked before, not since that day. But I have always wondered what could engender such fear. Even now you seem calm by comparison.'

Napoleon shook his head weakly. 'Death holds no terror for me. After that day in the pyramid, I could face anything with a strong heart.' His body was wracked with a sudden fit of coughing. Tombier went back to the bed and eased him up so that he was sitting almost upright.

Eventually his coughing subsided, and Napoleon sat wheezing in the bed. 'I will tell you, Tombier, you who have been my friend even in the darkest adversity. I will tell you what I saw that day.' His head rested into the pillows, he was breathing deeply and erratically.

Tombier leant forward. 'Yes, my general? What did you see?'

Napoleon stared at Tombier, his eyes misted over as if he was looking into the past. Then his eyelids fluttered, and Tombier knew that he was drifting back into sleep. He beckoned weakly for Tombier to lean closer, turned his head slightly so his mouth was close to his friend's ear.

For a moment, all Tombier could hear was Napoleon's shallow breathing. Then the former emperor gave a sigh. 'What's the point, Jean?' he murmured. 'No one would ever believe me.' And he sank back into dreamless sleep.

Chapter
Twelve

The Doctor was examining one of the walls of the inner chamber. He peered through a magnifying glass held close in front of his half-moon spectacles while Atkins held both the torches.

'Judging by the amount of weathering and discoloration of these marks,' the Doctor said as he pocketed the magnifying glass, 'I'd say that the work here was done quite recently.' He turned to Atkins and whipped off his spectacles. 'Maybe as little as twenty years ago.'

'Twenty-three, actually.'

Atkins swung round, waving the torches in a low arc. The beams of light passed over a bundle of rags in the far corner of the chamber, then stopped and swung back. The rags were untangling themselves and sitting up. A grubby, weathered face lifted towards them, eyes gleaming in the light. Blackened teeth cracked into a broken smile, and the figure slowly stood up.

The track Tegan was driving along finished at a gate. She skidded to a halt, and slammed her palms against the steering wheel in frustration. A cow watched her from the field beyond the gate. Its lower jaw moved rhythmically as it ground up a mouthful of grass.

'I hope you choke,' Tegan said, reaching yet again for the map.

She peered at it in the fading light and wondered how

many single-track lanes there were left in the area that she had not yet tried.

The Egyptian was about five feet tall, aged perhaps in his late forties, dirty, unshaven, and introduced himself as Kamose. 'I am on my way to Cairo,' he told the Doctor and Atkins. 'I often shelter in here during the heat of the day if I am passing. My feet are not as young as they once were, and it is good to rest in the cool shade. Especially in a place that nobody else knows about.' He glared suspiciously at the Doctor and Atkins. 'Or so I thought.'

'Ah, well, I'm sorry about that,' the Doctor said. 'We were on an archaeological expedition here some time ago, that's how we came to know about it. I'd be interested to hear your story.'

'You want to know about the excavations.' It was not a question. 'You were not on the expedition, I would remember you. Englishmen, I would remember.'

'Ah,' Atkins said. 'So were there other English people involved?'

Kamose shook his head. 'You are too eager for information. You should wait, draw out of me what I do not know you think is important.' He wagged a finger. 'How do you propose to pay for my information?'

The Doctor stuck his hands in his trouser pockets and leant down towards the short Egyptian. 'How about the offer of transport to Cairo?' he asked. 'Spare those old feet of yours.'

Kamose's eyes sparkled in the torchlight. 'You have a camel?'

The Doctor laughed. 'Now who's betraying his eagerness? I can get you to Cairo far quicker than a camel.'

Kamose narrowed his eyes. 'A car could not get here, there are no roads. Not even a Land Rover crosses the desert in these parts.'

'Well, of course, if you're happy walking.' The Doctor gestured to Atkins and they headed towards the main door out of the chamber.

Kamose caught up with them before they reached the corridor. 'I have decided to offer you my help,' he said.

James Norris had converted the second bedroom of his small cottage into a study. It had not taken much work, mainly a case of putting up shelves and ensuring there were enough electrical sockets and a phone line.

He was working on a set of plans for a barn conversion when there was a knock at the door. Norris lifted his head from the drawing board, and stared out of the pool of angle-poised light which was the sole illumination. He frowned, checked his watch, and went to the window.

The outside light was on, and in its glow he could see a figure standing outside the front door. He could not see her face, but he could see it was a young woman. The stairs creaked as he hurried down them. The staircase emerged into the corner of the main downstairs room. He crossed to the front door, drew back the bolt and opened it.

He started as the woman turned towards him. 'Vanessa?'

She pushed past him into the room, barely acknowledging his presence. Her eyes scanned the surroundings, head moving to and fro as if she were searching for something.

'What the hell's happened to you?' Norris asked. Vanessa Prior was in her nightgown. The hem was grubby and torn, and her feet were bare and muddy. Her toes curled on the carpet as she looked round.

Norris stepped towards her and reached out, intending to embrace her. But before he got close enough, she stepped away, her arm flying out. He ducked, but the gesture was not a blow. She was pointing to the mantel-shelf above the fireplace. And as she walked slowly, stiffly, like a sleepwalker towards it, Norris stared at the blue ring on her wedding finger, and the thick gold scarab bracelet hanging heavy on her wrist.

She stopped in front of the fireplace, silent and still for a moment. Norris crossed towards her, hesitant, worried.

'Look, if something's happened... Can I help?' Another thought occurred to him. 'Is anyone with you?' he asked. 'How did you get here? I mean—' He pointed to her nightgown.

But she ignored him, her eyes focused on the cobra poised to strike at the end of the shelf. She reached out for it.

And he caught her hand. 'Look, tell me what's wrong.' Her hand inched forwards, closer to the statue. 'Vanessa!' And she turned and glared at him. Just for a second. Then she lashed out with her other arm, caught him across the cheek, sent him reeling across the room in surprise.

Norris lay on the floor, rubbing his jaw in painful disbelief. 'What do you think you're doing?' he shouted.

Vanessa picked up the heavy statue, winding her hand inside the snake's coils to get a better grip. She turned from the mantelpiece, and advanced on Norris. He watched her incredulously as she lifted the cobra above her head, poised to crash it down on his skull. He could feel a pulse ticking in the corner of his eye, flinched as the arm started to descend, tried to push himself back and out of the way, shook his head and tried to speak.

The snake slashed down at him, gathering speed. Between its coils, Norris could see Vanessa's eyes gleaming bright and wide like a cat launching finally at an injured mouse. He squeezed his eyes shut, knowing he could not avoid the blow.

He heard the statue connect, the wrenching tearing smashing sound of it crashing into something solid. And he opened his eyes again.

The statue had smashed into a small coffee table. Norris recognised it and vaguely wondered what had happened to the half-empty coffee mug that had been resting on it a few moments earlier. He did not recognise the young woman who held the table, who was now struggling to prevent Vanessa from shoving her aside.

Norris hauled himself to his feet, and went to help the stranger. Together they managed to push Vanessa back towards the fireplace. Norris grabbed Vanessa by the shoulders, unsure whether to keep her at arm's length or hug her to him.

'What is it? What's wrong?' he asked as he struggled to hold her still.

The young woman who had saved his life was still trying to pull the cobra statue from Vanessa's grasp, but without success. She did seem to be managing to stop her from using it as a weapon, though. 'It's no good,' the woman said. 'She's not listening, or she can't hear you.'

Norris ignored her. 'Vanessa, look – it's me, James.' The fire in Vanessa's eyes did not diminish. She still struggled to escape, to smash the snake across his face. 'Vanessa,' he was close to tears, holding her still by the shoulders, shaking her with no effect. 'I love you.'

He let go of her, and she fell towards him. Norris clasped Vanessa to him, and pressed his mouth to hers. For a moment she was unresponsive, like a statue. Then she twisted, pulled away, her face suddenly creasing in bewilderment, tears welling in her eyes.

'James?' Her voice was scarcely a murmur. She looked round, as if surprised, as if waking up disoriented. Then her eyelids fluttered, and she crumpled to the floor.

Norris and the woman stood over her, breathing deeply

and watching to see what would happen. But Vanessa seemed to be unconscious.

The woman bent down and tried to prise the cobra from Vanessa's grip. After a while pulling at the long slender fingers, she gave up. 'It's no good, she won't let it go.'

'We should lie her down,' Norris said quietly.

'The sofa?'

Norris nodded. As they lifted Vanessa's limp body onto the couch, he asked: 'Do you come from New Zealand?'

'Australia.' The woman straightened Vanessa's legs, then stepped back and dusted her hands against each other. 'But not today.' She turned to Norris. She was quite small, with straight dark hair cut short. 'I'm Tegan.'

Norris knelt down beside his fiancée and took her hand. The large ring made it awkward to hold, but did not move when he gave a gentle tug to try to remove it. 'Will she be all right?'

'Yes,' Tegan said after the briefest pause. 'Yes, of course she will.'

Rassul's eyes snapped open. 'Something has happened,' he muttered. 'The link is broken.'

He stared across the moonlit moors in the direction of Norris's cottage. A faint mist was rising from the area of swamp. He had driven as close as the van would get to the back of the house. A frontal approach was too risky: he could not afford to be seen, did not want to reveal his hand too early. And using Vanessa had seemed a simple and efficient solution.

But now something had gone wrong. So he must play another card. Rassul turned to the huge bandaged figures beside him, and gave a curt nod. The nearest mummy lurched forward and started its laborious progress towards the house. The full moon glinted off the murky surface of the swampy water. The mummy started to wade through, leaning forward as it pushed its way forward. The surface scum receded in large ripples as the enormous figure broke the surface tension and pressed its way through the swamp.

Kamose took in the TARDIS without comment. If he was impressed, he did not show it. He grunted in a non-committal way and sat down cross-legged on the floor of the console room.

Atkins stood beside Kamose as the Doctor set about adjusting controls on the console. 'How do you know about the excavations at the tomb?' he asked. 'You say the work was done twenty-three years ago.'

Kamose nodded. 'I was there,' he said simply. 'They were looking for workers, and I had a mother and a family to feed. Then.' He rearranged the rags he was wearing and patted his canvas bag to check it was still there.

'You were a part of the expedition?' Atkins asked.

Kamose nodded. 'It was well-paid work. Three weeks we spent, working in shifts all day and all night. Each piece of stone was numbered and coded before we could remove it. Then it was packed away and labelled again.'

'Why?'

Kamose looked up. 'So that they could reconstruct the tomb exactly.'

The Doctor had joined them, the central column of the console rising and falling slowly behind him. 'So that who could reconstruct it?' he asked.

Kamose looked from the Doctor to Atkins, as if unable to believe they did not know.

'You are from England, no?' Atkins nodded.

'And you have not seen the tomb? The reconstruction?'

'Seen it?' the Doctor asked. 'Seen it where?'

'They told us it was to be rebuilt. In the British Museum.'

Norris and Tegan sat on the floor beside the couch sipping brandy. Vanessa was still unconscious, the snake statue gripped firmly in her hand. Tegan was unusually quiet, while Norris was uncharacteristically garrulous.

He was keen to talk about Vanessa, about how they met at Prior's, about the party the previous night. Tegan told him a little about the Doctor, but Norris took this as an opening to talk about the party again. Yes, he had met the Doctor and Atkins, but he did not remember Tegan.

Tegan was doing her best to draw the conversation back to the subject of Vanessa and what might be wrong with her. 'I saw her last night,' she said, 'outside the kitchen. She seemed a bit distant. Like a sleepwalker.'

'We had an argument,' Norris said. He leant over and stroked Vanessa's hair. 'Nothing important. It never is.' He half smiled sadly. 'My fault, of course. I forget how young she is. How sensitive.'

Tegan opened her mouth to reply. But before she could speak, they both heard the sound of heavy footsteps dragging on the gravel outside.

'Are you expecting anyone else?'

Norris climbed to his feet. 'I wasn't expecting anyone at all.' He walked quickly to the front door and slid home the bolt. Then he went over to a tall wooden cabinet beside the door to the kitchen, scrabbled around on the top and pulled down a key. 'You never know,' he said quietly as he unlocked the cabinet. Inside was a bag of golf clubs, a fishing rod, and a double-barrelled shotgun. He pulled out the shotgun and hunted through a pile of junk at the bottom of the cabinet for a box of cartridges.

The footsteps were louder now, shuffling towards the front door. Tegan stood against the far wall, listening for a knock, hoping that it was as simple as someone lost on the moors. Beside her Norris broke open the shotgun, pushed in two cartridges, and snapped it shut again.

The silence seemed to last for ever as they stood together, facing the front door of the cottage. Then the handle moved, turned, and they could hear the rattle as the door was pushed against the bolt. The rattling stopped, and Tegan crossed her fingers behind her back, hoping whoever was at the door would give up and move on.

The sound was amplified in the confines of the cottage, echoing off the stone walls. With a wrenching noise like a scream of tortured agony, the door hinges were ripped from the frame. The door splintered, exploding inwards. Pieces of wood flew across the room, scattering over the carpet. The screws holding the bolt tore from their sockets, and the shattered remains of the heavy door crashed to the floor.

The figure in the doorway was thrown into silhouette by the bright moonlight outside. It paused for a moment on the threshold, then stepped inside, bandaged feet smashing through the panels of the door lying in front of it.

Tegan screamed. She recognised the mummy as identical to the creatures that had attacked the camp in Egypt. The lower half of its body was soaking wet, discoloured with grime and mud.

Norris gaped at the mummy in amazement. Then he raised the shotgun to his shoulder, and fired. One of the barrels spat flame, and the mummy lurched back under the impact. The bandages on the upper body tore and smoked as the lead shot ripped through. The creature steadied itself, and started across the room towards them.

'Run!' Tegan shouted, pulling at Norris's sleeve. 'You can't stop that thing.'

But Norris stood his ground as the mummy lurched towards them. Then it halted. And Tegan realised with horror what it had actually come for. It had stopped in front of the sofa, and as they watched, it bent slowly forwards, reaching out for the unconscious body of Vanessa.

'No,' shouted Norris, dropping the gun and hurling himself across the room at the mummy. He dived over the back of the couch and collided with the creature's chest, sending it reeling backwards. He landed in a winded heap on the carpet. The mummy recovered immediately and started back towards Vanessa. Norris grabbed at its foot, hugged it to him in a tight embrace, and grunted in pain as the mummy wrenched it free from his grasp.

Tegan grabbed the gun from the floor, and leapt between the mummy and Vanessa. 'I don't know if you understand this,' she said, 'but stop right there, Boris.'

The mummy took no notice, reaching out to brush aside the weapon just as Tegan closed her eyes and fired. The shot ripped up the mummy's outstretched arm and tore into its shoulder. It staggered back, cloth smouldering and torn across its chest. Then it smashed Tegan aside and continued inexorably across the room. It bent down in front of the couch, reaching out for Vanessa. Then, surprisingly gently, it scooped her limp body into its arms and lifted her up.

Tegan and Norris lay together in a crumpled heap on the floor. They watched helplessly as the mummy carried Vanessa through the broken remains of the door and out into the night.

Tegan struggled to her feet and ran to see where it was going. Norris was close behind her, choking back a sob. The mummy was almost out of sight round the corner of the house. They ran to catch up, and watched in silence as it strode through the back garden and started across the swamp.

It was dusk, and the last tourists had left. There was nobody to hear the echoing grind and wheeze of the TARDIS as it faded into existence in the King's Chamber of the Great Pyramid. The door swung open, and the Doctor stepped out. He stopped dead, frowned, and then stepped aside to let Atkins and Kamose join him.

'Not quite as planned, I'm afraid,' the Doctor said. 'But fairly close.'

'The Great Pyramid,' Atkins breathed.

'Yes.' The Doctor swung round, hands in pockets. The lights were still lit for the day's visitors, throwing their shadows distorted and lengthened on to the walls. 'Pyramid power, I should have realised.'

'What's that, Doctor?'

'What? Oh, yes of course.' The Doctor set off across the chamber. 'Let's get Kamose pointing towards Cairo, we can talk on the way.' He noticed Atkins's worried glance at the TARDIS. 'Don't worry. Like the sarcophagus there,' he gestured to the huge open coffin hewn from a single solid block of stone, 'the TARDIS is too big to fit through the door.'

Atkins nodded. 'We know that the pyramid was built around the casket, Doctor.'

'Was it?' The Doctor grinned. 'And will the same archaeologists who are so sure of that maintain that it was also built around the TARDIS?'

Kamose and Atkins stared at the Doctor. Kamose was the first to speak: 'Are you saying—' he started, but the Doctor waved him to silence.

'They're probably right. Though of course it isn't a sarcophagus. No body was ever found buried inside a pyramid. You will recall that this chamber was empty save for the casket when it was found.'

'Is that to do with pyramid power?' Atkins asked as they left the chamber and started down the corridor outside.

'In a way. The shape of the pyramid is perfect. It's designed to focus power beamed from Osiris and from a relay station on Mars. It's that focusing ability which drew the TARDIS here when I tried to land nearby. She operates on a similar sort of energy.'

They reached a junction in the corridor, and the Doctor waved a finger tentatively at one of the passages. 'This way, I think,' he said, setting off down the other one. 'The power to operate the servicers – the mummies – the time-travel sarcophagus at the museum, all the Osiran technology in fact, goes through this relay chain.'

'Chain?'

'Yes, the pyramids which are built in the shape of the constellation of Orion.' The Doctor stopped and turned to Atkins, who almost cannoned into him. 'Where did you think the power came from?' he asked abruptly.

Atkins shook his head. 'Can't we shut it off somehow?' he asked. 'Would that help?'

'I don't know what it would do,' the Doctor admitted as he set off again. 'But since that would involve destroying Osiris, which Sutekh has already done, the entire constellation of Orion, which nobody would thank us for, Mars, which would throw the solar system off balance in a rather big way, or most of Egypt, I don't think we're about to find out. Do you?'

The full moon shone across the dark rippling water of the swamp. Trees overhung the edges in the distance, framing the scene. Rassul watched the mummy wading through the water towards him, its bandages tattered, muddied, and riddled with pellet holes.

It was carrying the woman across its outstretched arms. The water was up above the mummy's knees, but it continued walking towards Rassul, seemingly unworried how deep the swamp might be.

The woman flopped like a doll, her long, straight dark hair cascading down from her lolling head and dripping into the water. Her features were classical, slightly aquiline. She was slumped as if unconscious, although her eyes were open. Cat's eyes with large pupils.

She was wearing a white nightgown, legs dangling from its white hem. In one hand, she held a carved statuette of a cobra, gripping it tight. On her wedding finger was a ring inset with a blue stone shaped into a scarab beetle; round her wrist an ornate Egyptian bracelet of gold.

Rassul waited as the mummy slowly approached. His attention was focused on the woman. He did not see Vanessa, but another woman. A figure from across the millennia.

'But why Mars, Doctor?'

They were in a walkway close to the outer edge of the pyramid. As Atkins spoke, they reached a low window looking out over the desert. It was little more than a small square hole in the side of the structure, allowing the dying sunlight to creep in and wash across the stone floor.

'It's the one planet in the solar system without a magnetic pole. No disruption, so they could gather the energy from a fairly diffuse beam over such a distance. Osiran technology depends on magnetic monopoles, which only work outside the influence of a bipolar magnetic field. Some power keeps the Martian end of things running, like the Eye of Horus and the force-field generators. The rest they refocus, and relay to Earth.'

'Which does have magnetic poles?'

The Doctor nodded. He stopped and looked out of the window. 'The pyramids collect the energy beam, then pass the power on to the dispersal point. That gathers it all up again, boosts it like a transformer, and sends it out to power the mummies, the sarcophagus, and whatever else there is that the Osirans want to keep running.'

Kamose seemed to be following even less of the conversation than Atkins. 'What is this dispersal point?' he asked.

'Another pyramid?' Atkins hazarded.

The Doctor shook his head, and nodded at the window. Atkins and Kamose both crowded closer to see out. The sun was setting slowly, its flames licking round the head of the Sphinx as it fell. They both turned and looked back at the Doctor.

He nodded. 'The line the sun takes as it sinks traces perfectly round the head of the sphinx when viewed from here. What perfect geometry.' He shook his head in admiration, and set off down the corridor once more.

'The Sphinx?' Atkins hastened to catch up.

'It's older than most people think. When it was carved out of the living rock, and I mean living, between eight and ten thousand years ago, the sun would have risen exactly between the Sphinx's feet.'

'But that's older than the pyramids.'

'Of course. The dispersal unit was built and charged up by the Osirans. Then, when they departed, they left strict instructions on how to build the pyramids to supply a constant stream of power. On Mars they either did the building themselves, or found another religiously fanatical

258

people to do it for them. I can think of a couple of candidates.'

'I have heard it said,' Kamose spoke quietly, and they slowed to let him catch up so they could hear, 'that there is a Sphinx on Mars.'

Atkins guffawed loudly. Then stopped suddenly. 'Is that true?'

'Oh yes,' Kamose said seriously. 'But it was an American, from Oregon. I do not know if they can be trusted any more or less than other Americans.'

Atkins frowned. 'I meant, is it true that there is a Sphinx on Mars.'

'Of course,' the Doctor was off again, lengthening his stride. 'That's how the refocused power gets beamed onto Earth. And both Sphinxes have had their heads reshaped, as it were, to resemble a great local ruler. The original face of the Sphinx was the face of Horus.' He paused at a junction, then continued along the passage they were in. 'There's an identical set of pyramids too, though they look like a range of mountains from space.'

'A great undertaking,' Kamose offered.

'Yes. Ingenious. But not without its problems.'

'Such as?' asked Atkins.

'Well, as the angle of the Earth slowly alters, the alignment moves off. So the power is dissipated over time. Constellations shift, alignments change, sunrise is in a slightly different position. The sunset is a less perfect match to the Sphinx's shape as the Earth moves and the Sphinx erodes. Also, the Sphinx periodically gets buried, and that fogs the focus, so to speak.'

'So it's best to keep it clear of sand?' Atkins asked. 'I see it has been dug out since I last saw it.'

Kamose looked sideways at Atkins, but said nothing.

The Doctor nodded. 'There's something of a failsafe for

that, though, I fancy. Remember the story of Thutmose, who was told by the Sphinx in a dream to dig it out. More than likely that was a pulse of Osiran mental energy focused on someone with the power to make it happen while he was in a particularly receptive position relative to the pyramids and the Sphinx.'

Atkins recalled the legend. 'He was sleeping by the head of the Sphinx, which was buried up to its neck. He rested in its shadow during the heat of the day.'

The Doctor stopped again, and this time Atkins did walk into him. The Doctor spun round, but seemed not to have noticed the collision. 'Of course,' he said, 'I should have realised.'

'What?'

'Napoleon had the Sphinx dug out as well. And just before he gave the orders, he visited this pyramid. According to contemporary reports, he insisted on taking just one trusted captain inside as a guide, and he left him outside the great chamber when he went in. When he came out of the pyramid he was white and shaking with fear.'

Atkins struggled to fit this into the facts they already had. 'You think he saw some manifestation of the Sphinx's power?'

The Doctor bit at his lower lip. 'It would be an enormous coincidence if he didn't.'

They had reached a corner in the corridor. The Doctor rounded it first. 'Ah,' he said loudly, and they hurried to catch up. The corridor opened out slightly ahead of them, and in the distance, they could see the opening. An iron gate barred the end of the passage, the darkening desert visible beyond.

'Now then,' said the Doctor as they reached the gate, 'we'll just let our good friend here through, then we'll see if we can't find some record of who was behind the expedition.' He pulled a piece of wire from his top pocket, and set to work on the lock. After a few moments, it clicked free, and the gate swung open. The Doctor gestured for Kamose to go first. 'Thank you for all your help,' he said. 'If anything else happens to occur to you, perhaps you could leave a message with whoever mans this gate tomorrow?'

Kamose stood for a moment in the gateway, looking out across the desert as the sun set behind the Sphinx. 'Is the shape of the Sphinx significant in itself, Doctor?' he asked.

The Doctor and Atkins followed his gaze. The Sphinx was back-lit by a glorious crimson glow. 'I don't know,' the Doctor admitted. 'Probably it's geometrically primed to accept and hold the energy, but it's more complex than the pyramid designs.'

'I remember little of detail about the excavations,' Kamose said quietly, 'except what I have already told you. There was great care taken in the cataloguing and packing, but an unhealthy speed to the excavation work itself. There were accidents, of course. One in particular I remember.'

He turned towards the Doctor and Atkins. They were listening carefully, and Kamose went on: 'The man in charge, the man I think you seek, got careless. He climbed a pile of stones that had been cut from the tomb, I think to see how the work was progressing beyond them. The stones shifted, moved, and he fell.'

'Was he killed?' asked Atkins.

'Oh no. But his leg was trapped and broken in the fall. He refused to take time to have it set, insisted on remaining at the site and continuing to oversee the work. The physician did his best, but he said the Englishman would never fully recover.'

'Englishman?'

'Oh yes, he was English. I told you – the excavations were for the British Museum.'

'And did he recover?'

Kamose shook his head. 'I was reminded of the incident just now. The Englishman bought himself a walking stick from one of the expedition who had worked on it in the evenings, between the shifts. The handle was carved into the shape of the Sphinx.'

LONDON
1991

The smell of petrol was everywhere. He had to hold the handkerchief tight to his face to keep the fumes out, and still he was coughing. He held the can away from his body, careful not to get the clear viscous liquid on his clothes. He was backing down the stairs, shaking the can as he went, spilling an intermittent stream of fluid over the carpet.

When he reached the bottom, he continued to back round the staircase. He came level with the door, and set down the jerry can. He had checked the floor twice already, but he ducked through the door into the area under the stairs once more. The cupboard was dark, but the light from the hallway illuminated the floor. And the fresh cement which concealed and protected the trapdoor beneath.

Satisfied, Aubrey Prior closed the door behind him. They could chip out the cement afterwards, could dig their way back into the cellar. To the mummy.

He paused in the doorway, looked round the hall for the last time. Then he struck a match, heard the zip of the match-head along the strip of sandpaper, watched the flare of ignition, and tossed the tiny flame into the house. He jumped back, slamming the door before the hall erupted into a mass of flames.

From his car across the road, Sadan Rassul watched as Prior ran from the house. Then he lifted the hourglass from the dashboard, and held it up to the light of the fire as it took hold in the main hallway of Kenilworth House. The sand trickled almost imperceptibly from the upper bowl of glass. But Rassul smiled and nodded. So soon now and it would be finished.

So soon.

The flames licked up the staircase and swirled along the hall, driven by the draft from the open windows. In the cellar, the mummy lay calm and still, oblivious to the inferno raging above her.

Chapter
Thirteen

They picked their way over the broken splinters of the front door, and looked round the debris-strewn lounge. Norris immediately slumped into an armchair and sank his head into his hands. Tegan stood over him, hands on hips as she watched Norris rubbing his eyes with the palms of his hands.

After a while, he looked up, his face sagging and his eyes sunken, perhaps from rubbing them, perhaps from the strain of holding back his tears. 'I should have known,' he said quietly. 'It was all too good to last. When I found out about her, I should have known something would happen.'

Tegan looked at the ceiling for a while. She could see that there was no easy way to shake Norris out of his mood, and she appreciated something of what he must be feeling. But she had to persuade him to help himself. 'Look,' she said after consideration, 'the Doctor will be back soon. He'll know what to do.'

Norris leant back in his chair and exhaled loudly. 'I don't see he'll be able to do much good.'

'Why not?' Tegan was getting exasperated. Then she remembered something else Norris had just said. 'And what did you mean, you found out about her? What did you find out?'

Norris did not react to Tegan's frustration or rising voice. He continued to stare at the carpet. Then abruptly, he looked up and his eyes met hers. And Tegan could see the depth of distress and the very real emotion lurking inside him.

'I found out,' he murmured quietly, 'that Vanessa Prior does not exist.'

Atkins was not bored. He had sat and watched Lord Kenilworth studying manuscripts and volumes for hours, just as now he sat watching the Doctor go over his notes yet again.

They were in the TARDIS library, sitting on opposite sides of a reading table in a small bay between the infinite lines of bookcases. The Doctor's main focus was the notebook in which he had copied down the inscriptions from the hidden chamber of Nyssa's tomb. But round this lay concentric semi-circles of books and papers, scribbled notes and rolls of papyrus. As he went through the notebook, the Doctor would reach out, usually without looking, and pull some ancillary document towards him. Then he would peer through his half-moon spectacles, frown, make a hurried annotation in the margin, and push the document away again. Occasionally, the Doctor referred to the illuminated screen set into the tabletop, pressing areas of the glass with his finger and staring at the streams of text and pictures which flowed across the surface like lilies across a pond. But most of the time he stared at the copied inscriptions, shaking his head.

Atkins watched. He enjoyed watching academic work in progress, experienced a vicarious excitement from research. It had been years before it had occurred to him that he could join in, could learn things for himself in the same way. But he still enjoyed simply watching the process of discovery. And in the current circumstances, he was sure that any help he offered would merely impede the Doctor's progress. As it was, the Doctor seemed grateful for his presence. He would look up, say something completely incomprehensible, then smile as if he had scored a major point and continue working.

'Of course,' he said on one such occasion, smacking his palm to his forehead. 'They actually convinced Scaroth that building the pyramids would help hasten human evolution in the way he needed. So he oversaw the construction work for them.' The Doctor shook his head in disbelief. 'Staggering.' Atkins nodded in agreement, and the Doctor returned his attention to his notes.

As he watched, Atkins reflected on the way the last few days had turned out. Certainly he had not expected to be caught up in the Doctor's life to any extent when he had left to deliver the invitation. But he was beginning to gain an appreciation for the tricks Time could play, and could start to believe some of the things the Doctor had been saying about the inviolable nature of past events. 'Whatever will be, has been,' he had told Atkins at one point, and this seemed to be ratified by the way in which Kenilworth's accusations and assertions concerning Atkins's part in the expedition had subsequently been borne out. He had been there. And at the same time (or was it actually earlier?) he had been in London helping Miss Warne to keep house.

Miss Warne. Atkins had thought a lot about the housekeeper while he had been away. He had thought about how he was finding that he missed her. He had thought about how she was still poised with soup over the stove waiting for his return from the British Museum. He had thought about whether she was missing him, although at the same time he knew that she probably did not know he was away. It all depended on when he returned. If he returned. And until he did, he would not know when it would have been. Whatever has been, will be.

He thought about Tegan too. She and the Doctor were a strangely well-matched pair. They seemed forever to be arguing, yet they also seemed so much in accord. There was a synergy between them, in the way the Doctor was calm and measured while Tegan was rash and impulsive. Yet the Doctor's calm was often hurried and noisy, while his measured manner gave an impression of improvisation. And Tegan's rashness smacked of common sense, while her impulsiveness was often justified as if she had thought through her actions to a degree which belied the manner of their execution.

But it was the fact that Tegan showed her emotions so clearly, and that she brought out extremes of emotion in others which impressed Atkins the most. He had read and heard of the value of expressing one's emotions. But Tegan was the first case study which bore out the theory. Watching her, being with her, hearing her tell people like the shop assistant who was too busy to help a potential customer just what she felt, he could begin to appreciate the value of being emotionally honest and sincere. For the first time he was realising that he did actually have emotions which were valuable and useful rather than a waste both of energy and of time.

It was a subject, Atkins thought, as he watched the Doctor reach for a book just out of range, that he might raise with Miss Warne at one of their evening discussions. He passed the book to the Doctor, placing it into his outstretched fumbling hand. The Doctor took it, looked up, and smiled. And Atkins felt himself return the smile.

'Careful,' said the Doctor as he returned his attention to the book, 'you'll be enjoying yourself before you know it.'

Atkins continued to smile. He *was* enjoying himself. He knew things were bad, that there was real danger. But he was exhilarated by the experiences he was having, enthralled at seeing the future, amazed at the things he had witnessed in

Egypt. And above all, he was excited at what the future held in store.

The lounge was not large, and the splintered remains of the front door lay spread across most of the area not taken up with furniture. The TARDIS chose about the only remaining free space in which to materialise, the pile of the carpet flattening as the blue box faded into existence.

Norris stared open-mouthed as the door swung open and the Doctor and Atkins emerged.

'Am I glad to see you,' Tegan said almost before they were out of the door.

'Ah, Tegan. Likewise.' The Doctor waved his rolled Panama hat distractedly. 'I'm glad you got here all right.' He nodded politely at Norris, who was sitting stiffly in his chair and blinking. 'Now whatever happens,' the Doctor said seriously to Tegan, 'they mustn't get the cobra.' He looked round the room. 'Where is it, by the way?' His voice trailed off as he surveyed the damage. His gaze came full circle and met Tegan's.

She flinched, and looked away. 'Doctor,' she said, 'they got the cobra.'

'Oh Tegan.' With an obvious effort he pulled himself to his full height, jammed his hat on his head, and started a quick tour of the room. 'Well, I suppose it's not too disastrous,' he admitted. 'Just so long as they don't get Vanessa.'

Tegan said nothing. Norris stared at the Doctor.

The Doctor closed his eyes. 'Oh no,' he said quietly. 'I can't leave you for a moment, can I?'

'Maybe it doesn't matter,' Tegan said. She did not sound convinced.

The Doctor sat down on the sofa and thrust his legs out. 'Doesn't matter?'

'Does it matter?' Atkins asked.

The Doctor shook his head. 'I don't know,' he admitted. 'But I think it probably does. I'm not sure how she fits in yet, but she's important to what's going on.'

Tegan gulped. 'But Vanessa doesn't exist,' she said.

The Doctor and Atkins exchanged glances.

'You mean, she's dead?' asked Atkins.

'No.' Norris leant forward in his chair. 'I was telling Tegan, Vanessa literally does not exist. I wanted to get her a passport, so we could go away for a holiday – maybe a honeymoon. But her father wouldn't let me borrow her birth certificate.'

The Doctor frowned. 'What did Vanessa say?'

'She was upset at first, then she seemed to decide she didn't need or want a passport.'

'Well, I suppose there's nothing too suspicious in that.'

'No. But I decided she was being hassled by her father and I'd apply for one anyway. So I looked into getting a duplicate certificate. Even went to Somerset House to look up the records.'

'So?' asked Atkins.

'So, Prior's story is that he married Vanessa's mother and almost immediately Vanessa was conceived. Then his wife died in childbirth. But I can't find anyone who's met Vanessa's mother apart from Prior. I can't get Prior to tell me the same story twice about his wife, or his wedding. And I can't find any record in St Catherine's House of the marriage. Or of Vanessa's birth. I even went to the hospital where she said she was born.'

'No records there either?'

'No, Doctor. Nothing at all.' Norris looked round at them. 'Neither Vanessa's mother, nor Vanessa have ever officially existed.'

The Doctor nodded gravely. 'I think it's time we got back

to Kenilworth House. Probably long past time,' he said, unlocking the TARDIS door. 'And on the way, I'll tell you what I've discovered from the inscriptions in the hidden burial chamber.'

Fragments of Inscription from
THE TOMB OF NEPHTHYS

First Fragment (from earliest inscriptions)

After the great battle, Horus had Sutekh and his sister-wife Nephthys brought before him. And, despite the entreaties of his colleagues, he would not have them put to the mind-sword as that would have made him no better then they.

Instead, he imprisoned Sutekh, bound him for ever in the Eye of Horus such that he could neither move nor project his mind beyond the walls of the chamber which held him. And to increase his suffering, Horus provided the equipment Sutekh would need to effect his escape: to implant his mind in another from a distance and to destroy the Pyramid of Mars. But Horus ensured that it was outside of Sutekh's reach. He had the means, but lacked the access. He knew the infinitely remote possibility of escape, and that in turn increased his despair and his punishment.

But Nephthys, Horus treated differently. He knew that she was the greater evil, the greater cunning, the greater danger. So he imprisoned her too within a great pyramid. But before she was imprisoned, he had her mind removed to another body, a frail human, and the human was mummified alive to entrap the mind of Nephthys and bind it to the failing flesh.

Then, as the human woman was entombed, Horus ripped her mind into two fragments, even as it struggled to escape. The instinct, the intuition, Horus left within the dying woman. But the reasoning, deliberate, calculating evil he removed to another vessel. He placed it within a canopic jar, sealed with an inner force which bound the half-mind within it for ever. And Horus knew that the evil of Nephthys was diluted and destroyed and her terror would never again awaken.

Second Fragment (from later inscriptions)

But when the robbers stole into the tomb, despite the traps and puzzles left by Horus, greatest of the ancient Osirans, the canopic jar which contained the essence and strength of Nephthys's evil was cracked. Fearing that her mind might yet escape, the high priests followed the wisdom of Horus as laid down for them in the writings of Isis and passed through the years.

The gods arranged another receptacle. And this was another human. She appeared in the appointed place at the time foretold. And she was without sin or blemish. Her spotless mind was a perfect container for the evil of Nephthys. She was imbued with the spirit of the Queen of Evil, and it was bound into her by the power of the stars. Then the newborn Child of Orion was laid to rest in the outer chamber, beyond the firstborn of Orion's earthly children. And she slept the sleep of the damned.

(Translated by the Doctor, from his own transcriptions)

Chapter
FOURTEEN

Tegan, Atkins and Norris listened in silence as the Doctor finished the recitation from his notes.

Tegan and Atkins had filled Norris in on the background on the way to the TARDIS library. He had taken a little convincing that the Doctor, Tegan and Atkins had travelled in time, but the apparently impossible inner dimensions of the TARDIS and the events he had already witnessed that night left him little room for scepticism.

Now they sat round the reading table, the Doctor's notes and papers strewn over its surface, and looked at each other. Nobody seemed to want to be the first to venture an opinion.

Eventually Tegan spoke. 'Why Nyssa, Doctor?' Her voice was uncharacteristically quiet. 'And how did they know where to find her?'

The Doctor shook his head. 'I don't really know. There's obviously a temporal paradox, probably caused by the interference of the lodestone sarcophagus with the TARDIS's relative dimensional stabiliser.' His voice gathered an enthusiasm which belied the gravity of the subject matter. 'My guess would be that it plucked us out of the vortex, and somehow signalled the mind of Nephthys, the intelligent, reasoning side of her mind. She in turn influenced the unpleasant Egyptian gentleman we met at the British Museum, and he sent Nyssa back in time to the point where they were expecting her.'

'But why Nyssa? Why not you or me? Or anyone?'

The Doctor flicked through his notebook. 'It mentions how the receptacle had to be without blemish. I suspect they were trying to recreate the exact state of the canopic jar, which probably excluded external influence and energy rather like the Zero Room here in the TARDIS did. Nyssa would have been ideal.' He set down the notebook and leant forward across the table, chin resting on his hands, and eyes alive with thought. 'Think of it, Tegan; Nyssa is from the Traken Union. For all her life the Keeper and the Source ruled such that there was no concept even of evil. What more pure mind could one hope to find anywhere in the universe? Nyssa must have been ideal for their purposes.'

Atkins coughed politely. 'Er, Doctor, I wonder if you could clarify one small point for us?'

'Just the one?' asked Norris quietly.

The Doctor nodded. 'If I can.'

'You said that Horus created the receptacle, the original canopic jar, in order to imprison the mind of Nephthys.'

'Part of the mind, yes.'

'But then you said, just now, that it was Nephthys that brought the TARDIS to Victorian London, and who in effect found Nyssa in order to replace the jar.'

Tegan could see what Atkins was asking. 'That's a point,' she said. 'Why would Nephthys provide another prison?'

The Doctor looked at them across the table. 'Horus was long gone, him and the rest of the Osirans,' he said. 'The jar was cracked, and I think just a tiny fragment of Nephthys's mind was able to leak out. Enough to take control of a servant or agent, probably someone already with plans in line with her own objectives. Also, enough to detect the TARDIS and draw it to the British Museum.'

'But why bother?' Norris asked. 'Why go out and find your own new prison?'

The Doctor steepled his fingers. 'Say you were in the same position.'

'God forbid.'

'No, just consider for a moment. The high priests know the jar is cracked, and they will certainly find a replacement of some sort. Yes?'

Norris agreed.

'Wouldn't you rather, if you could manage it,' the Doctor asked quietly, 'find that replacement for them?'

Norris gave a short laugh. 'Not much of a choice, though, is it? Unless—' He stopped short, the smile freezing on his face.

'Unless?' prompted the Doctor.

But it was Atkins who answered. 'Unless you provide a prison you know you can escape from,' he said.

'Exactly.'

'But, how?' Tegan asked.

The Doctor shrugged. 'I wish I knew. The Egyptians and Prior are acting on impulses seeded thousands of years ago and passed on. The power seems to be focused through the relics, which our Egyptian chum is now collecting. Somehow they seem imbued with some of the instinctive power of Nephthys. I can only assume that she is working on some incredibly long-term masterplan.' He leant back in the chair, swivelling it slightly to and fro. 'But I do know one thing.'

'What's that?'

The Doctor's face was grim, his voice equally grave. 'Somehow we've been caught up in the plan. Or perhaps we were always part of it. When Nyssa awakens, which will be very soon now, Nephthys, the most dangerous and evil of the Osirans, will be born again.'

For a long while, nobody spoke.

Then the Doctor stood up. 'Come along,' he said, grinning

widely. 'We're nearly there.' And he started towards the library door.

Norris caught up with him ahead of the others. 'Doctor,' he said, 'I don't think I follow everything you've said.'

The Doctor smiled. 'I don't think any of us do,' he said as he held the door and waved them through into the corridor outside.

'But,' Norris went on, 'how does Vanessa Prior fit into all this?'

'Ah.' The Doctor stuck his hands in his pockets and looked down at the floor as he walked. 'I really don't know,' he confessed. 'You call her Nessa. Nessa; Nyssa; Nephthys. You can be sure she fits in somewhere.' From the distance came the melodic chime of the TARDIS landing. 'We're here,' the Doctor said, increasing his pace along the corridor. 'Perhaps her father can enlighten us as to Miss Prior's role in all this.'

When they reached the console room, the Doctor immediately opened the scanner. It showed the basement tomb room of Kenilworth House. The sarcophagus containing Nyssa's body was in the foreground, the staircase behind.

'It's funny,' said Tegan, 'just an hour ago I was desperate for Nyssa to wake up. And now I almost hope she never does.'

The Doctor clapped her on the shoulder. 'Brave heart, Tegan,' he said. 'We'll think of something.' He closed the scanner again and reached for the door lever. 'If only we knew where the local power was being channelled from.'

'Local power?' Atkins asked. 'Couldn't it just be sent from Egypt?'

'Oh indeed it could. And undoubtedly is.' The doors swung heavily open. 'But there has to be a reception point. Even the mummies have a tiny pyramid on each of their lower backs to collect and focus the power they need.' The Doctor stuck his hat on his head and made for the door.

'Pyramid power,' Norris said, his eyes wide. 'So that's what he was doing.'

The Doctor stopped in mid-stride. 'Is there something you feel you want to share with us?' he asked politely, leaning forward and pushing his hat back on his head.

Norris looked at him, his face blank. 'I was the architect for the rebuilding of this house,' he said.

'We know,' Tegan reminded him.

'I drew up the plans and supervised the work. But the plans were pretty much dictated by the owner. They reflected what Prior wanted; I just drew up the design, however bizarre.'

Tegan frowned. 'Bizarre?'

Norris nodded. 'I thought so then. Now I'm not so sure. The whole of the top section of this house – you must have noticed the slope of the upper walls, the heightened elevation of the roof?'

The Doctor said nothing. Tegan and Atkins looked from Norris to each other, and back again.

'I thought I was drunk,' Tegan murmured.

'Doctor,' Norris said, 'the whole of the upper part of this house, the internal structure, is a perfect pyramid.'

The Doctor walked slowly back to the console. He rested his hand on the door lever for a moment, staring down at the control. Then he looked up. 'I think I'd better make a couple of extra stops before I speak to Mr Prior again,' he said.

'Where are we off to now?'

The Doctor shook his head. 'Not we, Tegan. Just me. I'd like you, Atkins and Norris to find Prior. He probably doesn't realise we're on to him. Try to find out all you can about what's happening here.'

'And what will you be doing?' Atkins asked.

'Don't worry about me. I'll be back here before the fun starts.'

'You think this will be fun?' Tegan asked.

'Oh yes,' the Doctor said as he ushered them out of the TARDIS and into the basement. 'I'm just not sure who for, that's all.'

Prior was in the drawing room. He was sitting alone by the empty grate, a facsimile of the notes from one of Carter's expeditions open on the coffee table beside him. He was leaning forward, chin resting on the sphinx handle of his walking stick. He was staring into the fireplace, as if transfixed by the dancing yellow of the fire that was not there. Perhaps he was daydreaming, or perhaps he was watching the flames raging through his house as the fire took hold.

Tegan, Atkins and Norris stood just inside the door, watching him. He seemed unaware of their presence, even when Atkins coughed quietly and asked if they might join him. As they exchanged worried looks and sidled into the room, Prior turned slightly, his watery eyes staring past them.

Then his eyes seemed to focus, and he coughed suddenly and shook his head. 'I'm sorry,' he said quietly as he looked from Norris to Tegan. 'Really I am.'

'Sorry?' Norris stood directly in front of Prior and bent forward so that he was looking directly into Prior's face. 'What do you mean, Aubrey? What's happening? What's going on here?'

Prior did not react. The answer, instead, came from the other side of the room:

'That, Mr Norris, I think we shall all discover before too long.' Sadan Rassul stepped forward. He had been standing by the window, looking out into the night. Now he faced them across the drawing room, a semi-automatic pistol in his hand. 'You are back from Cornwall rather earlier than I had anticipated,' he said as they backed away from the gun. 'No doubt the Doctor gave you a lift. Where is he?' He addressed the question to Tegan.

'I don't know. And I wouldn't tell you if I did.'

Rassul raised an eyebrow. 'In that case, I won't bother to ask you again. But your tacit confirmation that he brought you here is sufficient for the present.' He laughed. 'The *present*. What a strange term to those of us who exist outside Time,' he said. 'Though I confess the Doctor's particular relationship with Time does give him several advantages. For example, I had to drive back from Cornwall like the very devil.' His round, hairless face cracked into a broken smile. 'But perhaps that is my prerogative.'

Atkins pushed his way in front of Tegan and Norris. 'May I ask what you intend, sir?'

'Indeed you may. Though I am sorry to have to decline to answer. For the moment.' He nodded to Prior, who stood and walked stiffly towards the door. 'In the meantime, however, I would invite you to join me in the basement for what will be the culmination of my long life's work. And of Mr Prior's rather shorter existence.' He waved the pistol to encourage them on their way. 'I would suggest that you all accept my kind invitation without too much fuss.'

Nobody moved. Prior stood stiffly at the door, his eyes again glazed over. Tegan, Norris and Atkins held their ground. Rassul smiled, his face cracked across with satisfaction as from behind him a loud swell of discordant music rose from the organ and echoed round the room.

'I have had so long,' Rassul said quietly as the organ music faded, 'so very long to form an appreciation of the motivations and eccentricities of human nature.'

'Oh yes?' said Tegan. 'And what's it taught you?'

'That a short sharp shock, to coin a rather modern phrase, is an especially effective incentive. Now, you are all expendable to a greater or lesser degree, and I do not intend you to disobey me again.'

He raised the pistol, and sighted along it. The report was like a fist slammed into an open palm. It echoed and ricocheted round the room like the organ chord before it. Norris stood for a second, open-mouthed in amazement. Then his eyes rolled upwards, as if trying to see the hole in his forehead from which the blood poured down his face. The viscous liquid dripped off his chin and splashed to the wooden floor. Norris tottered, seemed almost to slip on the sticky mess at his feet, and collapsed.

They descended to the basement in silence. When they reached the bottom of the stairs, Tegan went over to the sarcophagus. Atkins joined her at the dais, looking down at the body of Nyssa. It was completely wrapped in the bandages, silent and still. But Tegan knew that before long her lungs would heave in a great breath of air and she would begin to waken. As Tegan watched, she was almost sure that there was a slight movement, a rise and fall in the chest. Almost.

'The Doctor, I see, has returned.' Rassul was between the dais and the door. Prior stood quietly beside him as Rassul levelled the pistol at the group by the coffin.

Tegan looked round, and saw in the corner of the room the solid shape of the TARDIS.

'Indeed I have.' The Doctor stepped out from the behind one of the heavy curtains and advanced on Rassul, who swung round slightly to cover him too with his gun.

'I've been having a bit of a poke round,' the Doctor said, undeterred. 'And I think you should stop this nonsense right now.'

Rassul gave a short laugh. 'Oh Doctor,' he said, 'ever the optimist.'

'I try my best.' The Doctor looked round at the others. 'Where's Norris?' he asked quietly.

'Mr Norris will not be joining us, I fear,' Rassul replied.

Immediately the Doctor's face darkened and his eyes narrowed. 'Rassul, I promise you I'll prevent—'

Rassul's short laugh cut him off. 'I have watched from afar your pathetic attempts to prevent the inevitable, Doctor. Nyssa told me that you would interfere.'

'Did she indeed?'

'But I had no idea that your interference would be quite so entertaining.' He motioned for the Doctor to join the others on the dais. 'So kind of you to provide one of your own companions as a receptacle. So kind of you to have the entrance to the black pyramid excavated so I could recover the relics of power. So kind of you to return now to witness the final becoming.'

The Doctor stood his ground. 'And you are?' he asked levelly.

'I am Sadan Rassul. I am the high priest of the tomb of Nephthys and guardian of the sacred spirit.' He gave a short bow, keeping his eyes on the Doctor the whole time. The gun did not falter in his firm grasp.

The Doctor nodded thoughtfully, and wandered slowly towards the dais. He paused on the way to tap his finger on the top of a specimen table, and to examine the necklaces laid out on it. A small spotlight set into the ceiling cast a brilliant glow across the polished wooden surface.

'High priest and guardian,' he said quietly. 'I imagine that you were charged with protecting and preserving the prison of Nephthys.' He looked up suddenly, blue eyes piercingly bright in the spotlight. 'Since you seem to be working to ensure that Nephthys is resurrected, I would suggest you have betrayed the trust and duty of your post. Wouldn't you agree?'

Rassul shook his head slowly. 'How little you understand, Doctor.'

'I understand this,' the Doctor said grimly, 'if Nephthys is born again, there is not a power in the universe which could stand against her. Her brother told me that all life would perish under his rule. That where he trod he left only dust and darkness. Nephthys is worse. What has happened to your loyalty to your task? What has happened to your loyalty to your fellow humans, to all forms of life?'

'You know me even less than you know what is happening here,' Rassul told him. 'My loyalty is to one person only. I betrayed her once, but now I will see that justice is done, that the wrong is righted.' The gun shook slightly in his hand as if his grip were too tight, too tense. 'One person, Doctor, is worth everything.'

The Doctor shook his head sadly. 'No, Rassul. You don't know what you're doing. One person, whoever it is, is very insignificant. When all life is at stake, what is the life of one person? Make the choice, Rassul,' he begged. 'Give up the notion that you can effect a rebirth. It just won't work.'

Rassul laughed again, his eyes gleaming. 'So you would sacrifice a single life to prevent the rebirth of Nephthys, Doctor, is that what you are saying?'

The Doctor nodded.

'Tell that to Nyssa,' Rassul said quietly. 'That is the choice you had a hundred years ago. And you chose the life of your friend.'

The Doctor looked up at the dais. Tegan caught his eyes for a second, then he looked away. 'No,' he said. 'No, that's different. I didn't know what I was doing.'

'And you say I do not?' Rassul's lip curled. 'You are right about one thing, though, Doctor. As I said before, you don't know. You will never understand.'

Tegan could hear the Doctor breathing deeply as he looked down at the floor, hands in pockets. Then suddenly he darted across the room to the nearest wall.

Rassul's pistol tracked his movements. Rassul's smile remained fixed, as if he were amused by the Doctor's antics.

'I understand this,' the Doctor said, and grabbed a handful of the heavy velvet curtain. He heaved, face creased up with the strain, and the curtain collapsed, bringing the ceiling rail with it as it came away from the fixings and crashed to the floor. Behind it, the painted facsimile of the wall of the tomb wobbled slightly.

The Doctor walked quickly round the other walls, pulling down the curtains as he passed until they were all piled on the floor. The room seemed brighter without the dark curtains, and the sound echoed slightly where before it had been dulled and quiet.

'A copy of the outer tomb of Nephthys,' the Doctor said as he dusted his hands on his sweater. 'A perfect copy, I grant you. But still a copy.'

Rassul nodded. 'And a copy will never allow the psionic energy we need to be focused and controlled as the original would. Is that your conceit, Doctor?'

'That was what I thought at first,' the Doctor conceded. 'But now I know better.'

'Then enlighten us, please.'

The Doctor seemed to consider. Then, unexpectedly, he grinned. 'If you'll let Mr Atkins lend me a hand, I will.'

Rassul nodded to the group on the dais. Tegan waited by the casket while Atkins joined the Doctor by the wall.

'What do you require us to do, Doctor?' asked Atkins.

The Doctor tapped the plasterboard wall behind him. 'Help me break this down, would you?'

The sound of the shot echoed round the room for what

seemed like minutes. Tegan instinctively ducked. She had seen Rassul raise the gun, sight along it, and then fire directly at the Doctor – a slow-motion replay of the way he had shot Norris. But although it seemed to take forever to happen, she had no time to call a warning. The bullet ripped into the wall, punching a fist-sized hole beside the Doctor's head. Chips of plaster lodged in the Doctor's hair and peppered his clothing.

Rassul lowered the pistol. 'Just to get you started,' he said quietly. 'Since we don't have very much time.'

'Thank you.' The Doctor sounded calm, but Tegan guessed his hearts were beating a little faster.

It took only a few minutes to rip down the thin wall. Atkins managed to get his hand through the hole made by Rassul's bullet and pulled out handfuls of plasterboard. Before long the hole was large enough for the two of them to tear out pieces, and when the first board was gone, they were able to get behind and push down the other plasterboards which formed the skin wall of the room.

'Help them clear the rest of the walls,' Rassul said to Tegan. She joined the Doctor and helped him pull down the last next sections. Prior was already working on one of the other walls, while Atkins completed the last.

When they had finished, the basement was full of dust. It settled slowly, drifting like mist and catching at the back of Tegan's throat. Through the dust, Tegan could see the actual basement walls which had been concealed by the plasterboard. She looked round, and could tell from Atkins's expression that he was as puzzled as she was.

He was peering at the closest wall. 'What is it?' he asked. 'Some sort of inscription?'

'In a way,' the Doctor said. 'We are standing inside the tomb of Nephthys. Brought stone by stone from Egypt over twenty years ago, and reconstructed here.'

'How right you are, Doctor,' Rassul said. 'And your next logical deduction must therefore be?'

The Doctor stared at Rassul for a moment. Then he nodded, and crossed to another wall, opposite the main entrance. Most of the dust had settled, though the Doctor's feet kicked up new showers and clouds as he walked. Tegan watched as he approached a familiar symbol within the inscription. The cartouche, the name of Nephthys.

He paused for a moment, then pressed the centre of the open square. And the wall swung back to reveal the secret chamber behind.

'Shall we?' Rassul walked up behind the Doctor and pushed him lightly in the small of the back with his gun. The Doctor stepped through the open wall, and Rassul waited for everyone else to follow.

The room was exactly as Tegan remembered it. Except that the two Shabti figures from the corridor were standing either side of the door as they entered, as if on guard. She stared into the face of one as she passed. It was the image of Vanessa.

Rassul entered the room behind them, standing just inside the doorway. One hand was in his jacket pocket, the other held the gun steady.

The Doctor had crossed immediately to the mummy. 'An impressive set-up,' he said. 'Why not release Prior's mind so he can tell us about it?'

'Really Doctor,' Rassul sounded disappointed. 'Prior's mind has not been his own for many years. And I'm afraid all vestiges of self-control are now extinguished.'

The Doctor shook his head sadly. 'You won't succeed. Even with all this, it won't work.'

'Oh?'

'You obviously realise that the configuration of the tomb is key. The psionic focus must be exact if you're to harness the raw power of the stars of Orion. So, you've altered the structure of this house to construct a pyramid, and you've rebuilt this whole area of the tomb in the basement. You may even have got the measurements exactly right and have the top of the pyramid the right height above the floor of this chamber.'

'Oh, we have, Doctor. Trust me.'

'I do, I do. But have you considered the alignment of the ventilation shafts within the pyramid? They're actually transport corridors for the power before it is focused by the Sphinx. The position of the Sphinx is, I grant you, not so important. But you have to have the power here to focus in the first place.' He grinned and leant on the edge of the sarcophagus.

'Do you think I am totally naive?' Rassul's voice was a snarl of contempt. 'The skylights are exactly positioned to allow the energy to pass down the shafts and focus.'

'And the stars?' Tegan said. 'The Doctor says the constellations shift over time, and anyway we're not in Egypt.'

Rassul threw back his head and laughed. 'To miss something so elementary,' he said. 'Incredible.'

'Ah!' The Doctor pointed a victorious finger at Rassul. 'So you have missed something.'

Rassul shook his head. 'No, Doctor. You have. If the constellations move, or rather the Earth's position relative to them, then so must we.'

The Doctor's eyes narrowed and Tegan could almost hear the calculations going on inside his head. 'We're talking over twenty thousand years until the alignment is back to the original position. By now the off-set must be thousands of miles. At a rough guess—' He broke off and his eyes widened.

'What is it Doctor?' Atkins asked.

'The Doctor has just worked out, at last,' Rassul said, 'that the alignment of Orion's Belt relative to the Egypt of the Osirans exactly matches that over London today.' He smiled. 'Or rather, tonight.'

'But you still need a receptacle.' The Doctor punched the air with his fist, a sharp jabbing motion to punctuate his point. 'You need a living form for Nephthys to inhabit. This one's dead,' he gestured at the mummy he was standing beside. The bandages were stained and crumpled. The form sagged, barely resembling a human form any more than a rag doll.

'I know,' Rassul said, his voice suddenly low and forced between clenched teeth. 'Believe me, Doctor, I know.'

The Doctor frowned. 'And you need the life force already to have taken hold. You need it to be somehow intrinsic to the recipient.'

Tegan felt her stomach tighten and she realised what he was saying. 'Doctor, what about Nyssa?'

'It's all right, Tegan. The reason she was ideal as a constraining container for the reasoning, calculating evil of Nephthys is exactly the reason she can never become Nephthys. Every atom and dendrite of her would rebel against the evil that is so alien to her as soon as it gained any sort of consciousness. It would never work.'

Rassul said nothing.

'So where does that leave us?' Atkins asked.

'Well, it leaves us with this sad unfortunate.' The Doctor drew his hand along the mummified form in the coffin. He shook his head and patted the bandaged arm.

A strip of cloth fell free as he touched it. It slipped over the edge of the arm, revealing a dusty grey area beneath. The Doctor stared at it for a second. Then suddenly whipped out his spectacles, and leant closer.

'Someone's been taking tissue samples,' he said. His voice

was a mixture of anxiety and disbelief. 'Who on earth would want to do that?' He looked over the tops of his glasses at Rassul.

But the answer came from Tegan as the facts clicked into place in her brain. 'Prior,' she said quietly. And Rassul smiled in confirmation.

'Prior?' Atkins asked. 'But why?'

'Norris told us that Prior wasn't always an archaeologist. I found a room, the other night... Before he got this bee in his bonnet about Egyptology, I think he was into genetics.'

'Oh no,' the Doctor said quietly. Then he sat down cross-legged on the floor.

'The study of Egyptian genetics is fascinating,' Rassul said. 'As is the application of computerised axial tomography to mummified remains.'

'Of course.' The Doctor slapped the floor between his legs. 'I should have realised. A CAT scanner. He scanned the Nephthys mummy.'

Tegan looked from the Doctor to Rassul and back again. 'A cat-what?' she asked.

The Doctor looked up at her. His face was slack and resigned. 'CAT scanning is quite simple really,' he said. 'You X-ray the mummy from all angles along the central axis, and the computer builds a three-dimensional picture from the X-rays. People have been doing it since the 1970s. You can see all sorts of interesting things – bones, jewellery, even internal organs, wherever they now happen to be packaged. And all without unwrapping the mummy.' He looked over at Rassul. 'You can also unleash an awful lot of trapped psionic power. Like the mind of Nephthys.'

'Nephthys is already free?' Tegan was horrified.

'No. Horus would have planned for that. Some power would leak into the immediate area. That's probably how

Rassul here got control of Prior. The rest would be stored in some sort of back-up container.'

'Like Nyssa?'

'Same principle. It means this mummy is worthless, though.'

'You are very astute, Doctor.' Rassul stepped towards them. 'The back-up containers, for there are in fact four of them, now house the instinctive side of Nephthys's mind. But the mummy in here has other uses.'

'Of course, the relics. They acted as focus points for the power anyway, so they were ideal to pick up the released evil and loathing.'

Rassul nodded. 'They must be present when the sleeper awakes, then her mind will be whole and she will live again.'

'Aren't you forgetting something?' Atkins asked. 'The Doctor said that Nyssa could not become Nephthys. You still need a host for her mind.'

'Doctor?' Rassul asked. 'Do you understand yet?'

The Doctor's voice was scarcely audible. 'The skin samples.'

'Exactly. Prior took the samples twenty-two years ago. Using his expertise in genetics he rehydrated the tissue.'

'Twenty-two years?' Tegan said. 'That would be a year before Vanessa was born.'

Rassul nodded. 'Yes,' his voice was a hiss of triumph. 'That is what Prior used the reconstituted tissue for. Vanessa Prior is a clone of Nephthys.' He raised his arms above his head, as if in supplication to the gods.

And Atkins launched himself across the room, cannoning into Rassul's heavy frame and sending him flying through the open doorway.

The Doctor was on his feet in a flash, and ran to the connecting room. Tegan raced after him, but it was already over. Rassul was shaking his head and picking himself up from the stone floor. Atkins stood in front of him, holding Rassul's pistol.

'Well done, Atkins.' The Doctor strode across to join him. Atkins offered him the gun, but the Doctor shook his head. 'No, no. You keep it. Now, I suggest we continue our discussions somewhere a little more comfortable. There's still a couple of things to clear up, I think.'

Atkins and the Doctor crossed to the main door, Rassul following them warily. Prior remained standing motionless in the other chamber, so Tegan brought up the rear.

Atkins stopped at the bottom of the staircase. 'After you,' he said to Rassul.

Rassul smiled. 'I think not,' he said calmly.

The heavy bandaged hand of the Osiran service robot lashed out from the shadows of the lower staircase. It caught Atkins full on the chest, hurling him across the room. He crashed into a display case, sending it smashing to the ground. The headress within cracked on the stone floor, beads and precious stones ricocheting along the room.

The massive mummy descended the last few steps into the chamber, and started to lumber towards Atkins. Behind it, another mummy stepped down into the basement.

Atkins recovered himself quickly, rolling onto his back and climbing to his feet. The mummy lurched towards him, seeming to increase its speed as it approached. Atkins raised the pistol and fired in one movement. The crack of the shot echoed off the walls and the bullet tore into the mummy's extended chest.

It did not even slow down. The slight trail of smoke rising lazily from a tiny hole was the only sign that the robot had been hit. Atkins aimed the gun again, but the mummy was already upon him. It smashed his arm aside, sending the gun skidding across the floor. The mummy raised its right arm high above its head, read to crash it down on Atkins's skull.

'No.' The voice rang across the chamber like a chord from a giant organ. Vanessa stood in the doorway at the foot of the stairs, a mummy standing either side of her. She was still wearing her nightgown, together with the ring and the bracelet. Beside her, one mummy held the cobra, the other the statue of Anubis.

Rassul had already recovered his gun before any of the others realised what was happening. 'You see,' he said, his eyes gleaming and his voice full of eager anticipation, 'already the instinct and impulse of Nephthys is taking hold. She knows not to kill him yet, although she has not thought through the reasoning that he may be useful. Perhaps as a hostage to ensure the Doctor's cooperation.' He bowed to his goddess. 'Soon you will be whole again. Soon you will be as you were before Horus ripped your mind apart. And in there too, somewhere, will be the woman you were before Nephthys joined her mind with yours.'

The two mummies beside Vanessa lumbered forward and positioned the relics on the low shelf behind the dais on which the sarcophagus rested. Then they swung round and lurched their way back to Vanessa.

As Rassul watched them, Atkins eased his way round the motionless mummy that had attacked him. It was still standing with its arm raised ready to strike. As he passed it, the huge figure seemed to relax, its arm lowered, and it turned to face Vanessa. Atkins joined the Doctor, and Tegan in the middle of the room. 'Sorry, Doctor,' he said.

'So what happens now?' Tegan asked the Doctor. Her voice was trembling. 'Is Vanessa already gone?'

'Not quite. At least, I don't think so.'

Rassul had heard the exchange. 'The presence of the relics and of Nyssa when she wakes will complete the cycle.

Nephthys will be reborn, complete and anew. The relics without Nyssa are already enough to possess the clone with the spirit of Nephthys. Her instinct and intuition are keyed to the DNA pattern of the original... host.' He paused before the final word, as if trying to think of an alternative.

'And that's what you're after, isn't it?' The Doctor stepped forward, and stared Rassul straight in the face. 'It's not Nephthys that really interests you. It's the woman she was before Horus forced Nephthys's mind into her body.'

Rassul said nothing. He returned the Doctor's stare impassively.

The Doctor continued: 'And you'll destroy another human being for that. Clone or not, Vanessa is a living human with her own personality.'

'You should use the past tense when you speak of Vanessa,' Rassul said in a low voice.

'Doesn't that mean anything to you?' Tegan shouted at him. 'What about Vanessa and the people who love her?' She stepped forward, but the Doctor placed a hand on her shoulder to hold her back. 'What about her life? What about Norris, didn't he have a right to live? What about her father?'

'Her father—' Rassul stabbed the pistol towards Tegan. Then he stopped mid-sentence, stepped back, and regained control of himself. 'Ah yes,' he said. 'I think we can now dispense with the services of her *father*.' He almost spat the final word with contempt. Then he turned to Vanessa. 'Don't you agree?'

Tegan heard the scuffing footsteps from the other room before she saw Prior shuffle into the main chamber. His eyes were still glassy and unseeing as he approached them. Then he blinked, and immediately they focused and he looked round himself in surprise.

'Vanessa?' He seemed to latch on to the person he knew

best. 'Oh, thank goodness you're safe.' He went over to her, looking in bewilderment at the mummies standing beside her.

Vanessa reached out, the back of her hand stroking down his cheek. To his neck. Then she gripped him tightly with both hands, squeezing his windpipe, choking off the coughed gasps that might have been words. Prior sank to his knees, smoke rising from his daughter's hands as she throttled him. A sickly sweet smell drifted across the room, and Prior collapsed to the floor. His eyes were glassy and unfocused again.

There was silence for a while. In the doorway, Vanessa stood flanked by the two mummies. Prior's smoking corpse lay in front of them. Rassul stood beside the other mummy, pistol in hand. The Doctor stared open-mouthed at Rassul. Atkins and Tegan looked in horrified fascination at Prior's body.

'It's time to make the final moves,' the Doctor said suddenly in a loud voice.

Everyone looked at him, including Vanessa.

He shrugged. 'Someone had to say something.'

From behind them came a faint rustling sound, almost like a breeze through the trees in a forest. The Doctor ran to the dais, Tegan close behind. Rassul joined them as they looked down at the bandaged form inside the casket. It was moving slightly, the chest rising and falling, the wrappings on the lower arms creasing and uncreasing as if the hands were clenching into fists. A faint sigh came from beneath the strips of cloth covering the face.

'Oh no,' Tegan said huskily. 'She's waking up.'

Ancient Egypt
c.5000 BC

She was still alive, but Rassul did nothing.

He watched as they dragged the girl's sagging body towards the tomb. He followed, taking his designated place as the last of the relics were carried after her. The ring of Bastet, borne on a velvet cushion; the snake statue of Netjerankh; the scarab bracelet; the figure of Anubis, god of the rituals of death. Rassul followed, holding the hourglass before him like the talisman it was. And at his back he could hear the Devourer of the Dead snapping in frustration as she was cheated of her victim.

The girl was still alive as they removed the dress. She could stand alone now, unmoving apart from her eyes. She was still alive as Anubis directed the priests to smear her naked body with bitumen.

She was still alive as they started to smother the bandages round her. And Rassul did nothing.

As the wrappings reached her face she screamed again, head back and mouth wide, as if to remind them she still had her tongue. A single word, screamed in terror, anger and accusation. A single word hurled at Rassul as he stood before her. And did nothing. The next twist of cloth cut off her voice, bit deep into her mouth and gagged her.

She was still alive as the bandages covered her forehead, leaving a thin slot through which Rassul could see her eyes widen. She was watching him, locked on to him. And he could see her pupils dilate, could almost feel her terror.

The opening of the mouth. Her scream had been like a pouring in of energy. His muscles tightened and his whole body tensed. She screamed a single word.

'Father!'

Chapter
FIFTEEN

They were all standing round the casket now. The Doctor, Tegan and Rassul had been joined by Atkins. As they watched the bandaged figure's movements become gradually more pronounced and emphatic, Vanessa stepped up onto the dais. The mummies grouped behind her and, as she raised her arms high above her head, they mirrored her movements. The chamber seemed to fill with discordant music, perhaps from the organ in the drawing room above, as the wide sleeves of Vanessa's nightgown slipped down to her shoulders, exposing her bronzed arms.

The figure in the casket was struggling to sit up now, the arms still bound to her sides, but working to loosen the wrappings.

'Now it happens,' Rassul said, his voice barely audible above the rising noise of the organ. 'Now she becomes whole. Now the goddess Nephthys lives again.'

'And what good does that do you?' Tegan shouted across the coffin.

'My daughter will live again too. When the mind of Nephthys is complete, so too is the remains of my daughter's. Some part of her, however small, will be restored.' The sweat glistened on his forehead as he raised his arms above the coffin. 'That is worth everything. Nephthys is the instrument of my daughter's rebirth.'

The Doctor shook his head emphatically. 'You think you're using Nephthys,' he shouted. 'But in fact she's using you. She's been using you ever since Horus chose your daughter.'

'No Doctor, you are wrong.'

'Am I? That blind faith that drives you to try to save some vestige of your daughter is how Osiran mental control works, don't you see that?'

'What do you mean?' Atkins asked

'It's not just the complete take-over of the mind that the Osirans use. It's the passion for discovering all you can about a mummy in your basement, it's the devotion of a high priest, the impulsive selection of a good round number like a hundred years. It's the love of a daughter.'

Rassul was shaking his head now. 'No, Doctor, you still don't understand.'

As he spoke, two of the mummies stepped onto the dais. They took up positions either side of the casket, forcing Atkins to move aside. They reached into the coffin and took the writhing, bandaged figure, raising it to its feet with a gentleness that belied their massive strength.

'When Nyssa's eyes open from the long sleep, and she sees the goddess, Vanessa and Nyssa will be joined and Nephthys will be whole again.' The triumph was evident in Rassul's voice.

Vanessa reached out, working her slender fingers between the bandages round the head. 'Let the universe tremble,' she said, her voice blending into the rhythmic swell of music. 'Let the darkness start here.' Then she tore the bandages from the face of the figure standing in the sarcophagus.

Tegan screamed, and the organ music stopped. Tegan stepped back, hands to her mouth, and almost fell down the step. Vanessa froze, her eyes meeting the gaze returned from beneath the torn remains of the bandages. Atkins looked puzzled, and Rassul stood open-mouthed in horror and amazement. The Doctor nodded slowly, his face set in grim satisfaction.

The figure standing in the coffin, held either side by an Osiran mummy, her head now almost free of bandages, was recognisably Nyssa. The grey hair hung in ringlets about her neck, the round face was creased and wrinkled round the bright intelligent eyes. The pale lips were pursed slightly as if in defiance.

When Tegan had seen the Doctor unwrap Nyssa's head in 1896, it had been to reveal the young woman she remembered from the previous day. Now she looked nearer ninety than twenty.

'What is this?' Rassul screamed. His voice echoed round the chamber. 'What has happened?'

He looked to Vanessa for an answer, but she remained frozen in position, staring at Nyssa.

'I think we're a little late,' the Doctor said. His voice was quiet, but everyone turned to him. Even Vanessa swung her head slightly. 'I'm afraid your calculations were slightly off. As you can see, Nyssa has actually been awake for quite some time. Or at least, in a sort of waking sleep. Just enough to continue the ageing process while she dozed.'

'No,' breathed Vanessa, her voice an exhalation of disbelief.

'You know it's true,' the Doctor told her. 'You just scanned her mind, looking for the reasoning, calculating, intelligent part of your own self.'

'It is not there.' Vanessa's voice was low, despondent.

'So, even at the instinctive level on which you're operating you can tell that the rest of the mind of Nephthys no longer exists. It was freed when Nyssa awoke, and you weren't here. Now it's lost for ever.'

'How long ago did she wake?' Atkins asked.

'She woke up in 1926.'

'Seventy years,' Atkins murmured.

The Doctor nodded. 'I like good round numbers,' he said.

'Doctor.' Tegan's voice was accusing, shaking with emotion. Her face was set and she was glaring at him.

'I'm sorry, Tegan. If there had been any other way.'

'How could you?' She was in tears now. 'How could you do this to Nyssa, after – after everything?'

The Doctor smiled sadly. 'Rassul knows. He asked if I could sacrifice a friend to save the universe, if I could make that choice.'

Tegan turned away. 'He didn't believe you could,' she said through her sobs. 'And neither did I.'

Rassul too was shaking with anger. 'Doctor, I shall kill you for this.'

The Doctor returned his stare. 'I don't care,' he said levelly. 'The universe is safe now. All you have is a woman who hardly knows who she is and can't make a decision beyond the next instinctive moment. She can respond to circumstances, make impassioned speeches from the heart of the evil goddess she once was, but longer term than that she can never make up her mind.' He grinned suddenly. 'I hope you'll excuse the choice of phrase.'

'She will be whole,' Rassul insisted. 'We shall find a way.'

Vanessa stood watching them, listening to the exchange but taking no part. Her face was impassive.

'Not without going back to 1926, you won't.' The Doctor frowned, as if surprised at his own words, and bit his lip. He turned away, went to comfort Tegan.

Rassul's brow creased in concentration. '1926, of course. Nephthys must be there when your friend wakes. Must have been waiting for her first moments of this waking sleep. Then, her mind will meld and be one.'

He looked across at Vanessa, and she in turn reacted,

nodding to the nearest mummy. The mummy let go of Nyssa, who sagged, still held by a second mummy. She had been paying careful attention to what was happening, but said nothing.

The mummy lurched towards the Doctor, grabbing him by the shoulder and spinning him round. Then it pushed him towards Rassul.

'You will take us, Doctor,' Rassul said. 'You will take us back to 1926.' He pointed the gun at the Doctor's head to emphasise the demand.

But the Doctor shook his head. 'Oh no. No, I won't. And threatening my friends here will make no difference, either,' he said as Rassul moved the gun to point at Tegan. 'By now you must realise that I value even their lives below the imperative of keeping Nephthys subdued. The past is over and done with, dead and buried in a box. And you can't change it.'

Rassul considered for a moment, then suddenly he smiled and lowered the gun. 'But we can,' he said. 'Thank you for the suggestion, Doctor. We shall use the sarcophagus. It can open a vortex tunnel to 1926 as easily as it transported Nyssa to ancient Egypt.'

The Doctor's jaw dropped, and for a second he was speechless. 'No!' he cried, his arm flung out in appeal to Rassul, an almost theatrical gesture.

But Vanessa was already turning to the mummies. 'Go,' she said, and her voice was like the cracking of hell.

The mummy still holding Nyssa's arm released it, and she fell back into the casket. Atkins and Tegan went to help her out, as two of the mummies turned and lumbered towards the staircase. The third stood beside Vanessa, a silent bodyguard. Rassul moved to join his goddess.

'Where are they going?' Tegan asked the Doctor.

'To fetch the sarcophagus, I imagine. If they bring it here, then Vanessa or Nephthys or whoever she now is can use it to travel back to 1926 and be in this room when Nyssa's consciousness returns.'

'And Nephthys will live again, complete,' Vanessa said, her eyes now alive with menace.

'Where is the sarcophagus?' Atkins asked.

Nyssa sat down on the edge of the dais, and the Doctor rested his hand on her shoulder. It was a strange gesture, comforting yet distant. 'I imagine it's still in the British Museum. It's a bit of a walk, but who's going to argue with those two at four o'clock in the morning?'

It was the quietest time of the night in a city which is never completely silent. Aldwych was deserted, and Drury Lane had already shed its last theatregoers. The two mummies kept to the darkest shadows as they lumbered across London. The instinctive force of Nephthys which guided them knew intuitively that avoiding confrontation would make for the quickest journey.

Even so, several meetings were unavoidable. A drunk stirred in the gutter as one of the massive figures stepped over him. He stared in fuzzy horror at the shape moving above him, then dragged himself to his feet and fled noisily in the opposite direction.

As they neared the end of Drury Lane, a police patrol car drew alongside. 'Good party?' the driver called at them, but the robots ignored him. The patrol shadowed for a while before receiving a call about a hit and run in Bloomsbury. It wailed off into the night and the mummies continued their ponderous progress towards the north entrance to the British Museum.

*

Henry Edwards was making his routine tour of the ground floor when he heard the crash. It sounded as if the north door was being smashed open. The penetrating scream of the burglar alarm echoed round the museum. Henry reached for his radio as he ran down the corridor.

What was left of the door was hanging from a bent hinge, swinging slowly in the night breeze. Henry stared at it, fumbling the buttons on the radio. He had it almost to his mouth when a huge shape resolved out of the shadows and stepped towards him.

His first thought was that one of the exhibits from the Egyptian Rooms on the floor above had somehow come to life. But then he realised that it must just be a student prank. He was still thinking of a witty put-down when the huge bandaged hand lifted him by the neck and flung him down the corridor. His head hit the wall with a thud, leaving a sticky trail behind it as his body slid slowly to the floor.

The mummy continued on its way, hardly slowed by the encounter. It followed its fellow to the north staircase, and up to Room 66, which was just at the top of the first flight.

The Osiran sarcophagus stood in the corner of the room. It glowed with an eerie internal light as the service robots approached. They lifted it easily between them, and started on their return journey. They were just leaving by the north door as the first police cars screeched to a strobing blue halt outside the main entrance on the opposite side of the building.

The Doctor, Tegan and Atkins were sitting on the floor. The Doctor was cross-legged, staring at the ground.

Tegan was sitting with her back against the wall and her knees drawn up under her chin. She looked round at the others, avoiding catching Nyssa's attention, and thought back to the last time she had sat in a similar position on the same piece of floor. It had been a hundred years ago and thousands of miles away. But the real shift was in her perspective. Then she had been desperate for Nyssa's long sleep to end. But now that Nyssa had finally awoken, Tegan was depressed and confused.

Nyssa sat close to Tegan. Her frail old body seemed shrunken and bereft of energy. She stared at the Doctor, as if for reassurance. Occasionally the Doctor looked up and smiled faintly at her, and Nyssa visibly relaxed a little. But Tegan was unable to decode the communication between them, if there was any. Soon after the mummies had left, Tegan had tried to talk to Nyssa, but she had been unresponsive, answering in monosyllables or nods of the head. 'Are you OK?' Nod. 'How do you feel?' Shrug. 'Do you want to talk about it?' 'No.'

Rassul was pacing nervously up and down beside the raised dais. Vanessa stood motionless, her eyes flicking back and forth as if she were seeing events played out somewhere else. Beside her, the Osiran mummy stood massive and silent. Its upper body swayed slightly as it kept watch over both the group sitting on the floor and Rassul.

Despite their bulk, the mummies moved almost silently. It surprised Tegan when the Doctor suddenly leapt to his feet and dusted himself down. A moment later, the two mummies entered the chamber, carrying the sarcophagus between them. They positioned it on the dais at the head of the casket in which Nyssa had slept, bowed slightly to Vanessa, and stepped back. The third mummy joined them, and together they raised their arms. From the house above, the organ roared into strident life and a cacophony of powerful noise swelled through the basement.

The Doctor helped Nyssa to her feet and led her by the elbow towards the dais. Tegan followed, and heard the Doctor whisper to Nyssa. 'Just here, where you will have a clear view of the sarcophagus.' He glanced round as Nyssa stood where he had indicated.

'Typical, Doctor,' Tegan called across at him. 'All hell is about to break loose, and all you're worried about is getting a front row seat.'

The Doctor caught Tegan's eye, then looked quickly away again as Atkins joined them.

Rassul was already beside the sarcophagus as its inner glow seemed to swell with the organ music. 'That's right,' he said to the Doctor and his friends. 'Watch the final apocalyptic becoming of the goddess.' He raised his arms high in the air, mirroring the mummies. 'Nephthys shall live once more.'

'She's using you, Rassul,' the Doctor said. 'Can't you see that yet?'

But Rassul ignored him as Vanessa went up the steps towards the glowing casket. As she approached, the carved front of the sarcophagus seemed to melt away in a blaze of light. Then the light turned in on itself and was sucked back into the casket. The sarcophagus's shape blackened so that it looked like a child's outline of a human being, a hieroglyph. Light seemed to pour in from outside, spinning and spiralling inwards and tumbling towards the vanishing point.

'What's happening?' Atkins asked the Doctor.

'She's established a time tunnel back to 1926,' he replied quietly. 'Her power is greatest here, so it's the best place to start the tunnel.'

'So she can do it,' Tegan said. 'She can travel back to Nyssa's waking moment and become complete. She can become Nephthys reborn.'

'To destroy the world,' Atkins murmured.

Vanessa turned to them, as if she had heard Atkins's words. She was standing directly in front of the time tunnel so that the power and energy seemed to flow past and around her into its depths. Her eyes were holes of tumbling light and her voice had taken on an echoing melodic resonance. 'So, Horus, your naive stratagems have failed as I always knew they would. Now I reclaim my birthright of evil. Now I begin the reign of dust and darkness. Now all life shall wither and perish under the reign of Nephthys.'

She raised her arm, the bracelet and the ring glowing with the same intensity as the time tunnel. Out of the corner of her eye, Tegan was aware that the cobra and the jackal were also strobing and glowing like alabaster lit from within.

'Abase yourselves,' she ordered. 'You are as nothing before the power of Nephthys.'

Tegan felt her knees give way, and collapsed painfully to the stone floor. Beside her Atkins was also kneeling. The Doctor remained upright for a second longer, then he too collapsed to the ground. Nyssa seemed unaffected, standing between them and Vanessa now, watching as Vanessa stepped backwards into the tunnel. As she sank back into the darkness, her hair and white dress blew around her as if, like Eurydice, she were falling through the heavy air back into Hades itself.

There was a faint noise in the darkened basement, like the sound of a massive church organ playing in the distance. Slowly it grew in volume, and as it did the chamber was lit with a throbbing blue light. And in the centre of the light, at the head of the open coffin on the dais, a figure faded into existence.

Nephthys reached into the sarcophagus, lifting and cradling the bandaged head of Nyssa. The head that contained the reasoning, calculating side of herself. Slowly, carefully, reverently, she looked though the bandages, and stared into the closed mind of the sleeping woman. And reached gently into her thoughts.

For a moment she was still. Then she threw back her head and screamed. The mind of Nephthys was there, buried inside the woman Nyssa. She could detect it, could sense its presence. But it was still too submerged in the sleeping woman to be of use.

She could also tell that Nyssa would not wake for another seventy years.

In the house above, old Lord Kenilworth stirred in his sleep, and reached out for the warmth of his wife.

While in the basement Nephthys, acting on the instinct and impulse which was all her mind could draw on, faded back into the vortex of the time tunnel.

'Any second now, I should think,' the Doctor said.

Tegan stared at him. He was actually smiling. But before she could say anything, the sarcophagus glowed back into life in front of them.

'Prepare to meet your doom,' Rassul said in triumph as he bowed low before the blazing gateway.

A tiny dot appeared in the distance, growing slowly as it seemed to fly towards them. Nephthys was returning.

The figure that still resembled Vanessa hovered right at the edge of the time tunnel, staring out at the group kneeling in front of her. And then at Nyssa. With a sudden scream of inhuman agony, Nephthys tumbled away from view…

… To reappear in the empty basement of 1926 at the moment she had arrived before. Nyssa lay before her in the casket. Her face was still covered with the bandages, but Nephthys knew immediately that she still slept. With no deductive or reasoning powers to help her, she again acted on impulse.

Nephthys could tell from the depth of Nyssa's coma when she would wake, and stepped back into the time tunnel to return to 1996…

… And found Nyssa awake, all vestiges of the mind of Nephthys gone from her brain. Even before she reached the end of the tunnel, she knew the age of the woman. She could tell when she must have woken, and returned to 1926.

'What's happening?' Tegan watched as Nephthys faded back into the tunnel for the third time. The mummies stood impassive and still, but Rassul was on his feet now, shaking his head and murmuring beneath his breath.

The Doctor got slowly to his feet. 'That's better,' he said. 'She's weakening already. I knew there had to be a local focus, now it's working for us.' He frowned and scratched his ear. 'I wonder where it is.' He reached out and patted Nyssa on the shoulder. 'You're doing an excellent job there.' Then he turned to Tegan. 'When someone travels down an Osiran time tunnel, the effects of time aren't cancelled out. You travel a distance, doesn't matter whether it's forward or back, but you age that amount. Now Osirans can take that time onto themselves. So when Nyssa was sent back to ancient Egypt, Nephthys got older to the tune of several thousand years. Not a clever thing for Nyssa to do, but Osirans are extremely long-lived.'

'I think I understand what you're saying, Doctor,' Atkins said as he rose to his feet. 'A sort of conservation of energy or something. But how does that help us?'

The Doctor turned to watched Nephthys arrive on the threshold of the tunnel again, then fade back into the distance. 'Well, she's got nobody to pass the process on to, so she has to accommodate the time differential herself,' he said. 'Which means she's ageing by a hundred and forty years on each round trip. So this could take some time.' He turned back to the tunnel.

They could begin to see a difference in Nephthys now. Her face was sagging, bags under the eyes and a slackness of the jaw. On each successive appearance the difference grew more pronounced. Her body was thinning and becoming frail, her hair fading to grey, and her face concaving to show the line of the cheekbones jutting through. Her skin was cracked and lined by the time her hair started to thin. Her scalp was scarred and wrinkled with age, and the shape of her jaw changed as her teeth began to rot. The flesh was pulled back from the bloodshot eyes so that the bone of the sockets was clearly visible beneath the stretched skin.

Then with a drawn-out wail of pain and exasperation, Nephthys collapsed. A single out-flung arm trailed over the edge of the time tunnel and into the real world. It was barely more than a strip of faded bone. As they watched, it crumbled and powdered to dust, leaving a faint shadow of itself in its place. The bracelet and ring it had been wearing survived a fraction of a second longer, then they too exploded in a puff of ashes.

Across the room, the rearing cobra collapsed back into its coils as it crumbled away, and the statue of Anubis sank lower on its haunches before its back broke under its own weight. The snarling head sat for a moment on the broken paws, then the jaw fractured and the stone deteriorated into a pile of sand.

Rassul stared across the room at the powdered relics. Then his gun clattered to the floor as he fumbled desperately in his jacket pocket. He pulled out an hourglass, held it up to the light as if in supplication.

It exploded in a crash of organ music, showering him with

sand and glass, and Rassul collapsed to his knees. He knelt in front of the Doctor and his friends, reaching out towards them. Tegan thought he was begging for help but, as she watched, he curled his fingers like claws, turned them, and ripped into his own face. The flesh and tissue disintegrated as he tore at it, pulling his head to pieces. He gouged a trail down his cheek, and dust fell from the rotting bone beneath. He was still tearing at the dry stump of his shattered neck when he toppled forward. His body rolled off the dais and crashed to pieces on the floor below.

The Osiran mummies smashed and crumbled to the floor beside him, their arms still raised in supplication to their goddess Nephthys.

LONDON
1880

The needle stretched up above the buildings behind it, a sharp point into the sky. George Vulliamy's gaze was fixed on its growing silhouette as he approached along the Embankment. As he got closer, he could see the imperfections of the stone edges against the clouds. Closer still, and he could begin to discern the carved hieroglyphs which covered the obelisk.

But Vulliamy's mind was elsewhere. It was a miracle, he thought, that Cleopatra's Needle was there at all. It had been lost on the turbulent voyage from Alexandria – along with the lives of six sailors. Then incredibly, one might almost say miraculously, it had been recovered, the wooden casket reappearing in the expanses of the ocean, and towed to London in January 1878. Where nobody had decided what to do with it.

And it was almost by chance that, after eight months of deliberation, it should be erected on the Embankment. Vulliamy could see again in his mind the great stone pillar being rotated on a wooden construction more like a child's overgrown treehouse than scaffolding. He had watched, fascinated, as it was lowered into place on the plinth. To Vulliamy, it was close to a miracle that he had been asked to be a part of it all.

He had supervised the steps down to the river, and planned the geometric perfections of the plinths either side of the needle. He had drawn up his plans and had the full-size plaster models positioned on the plinths to judge the effect. And everyone had proclaimed his Sphinxes to be the final aesthetic touch which completed the perfect Egyptian tableau.

Almost there now. If only his wife had not been taken ill, if only he had not waited for the doctor to arrive, he would have been present for the final act. But as it was, he had almost certainly missed it. The bronze Sphinxes he had designed would by now have replaced their plaster twins torn down the previous day. Perfection was now complete.

But something was not quite right. He peered forward squinting into the distance. The sun glimpsed out from behind a cloud and Vulliamy could see the rays of light reflecting off the bronze hide of one of his creations. Bronze, not painted plaster, so the Sphinxes had already been hoisted into position. He knew every contour of the beasts, every curve of their metal flesh and every engraving of the hieroglyphics on their chests. He had specified every sinew of the arms and every coil of the snake on each Sphinx's headdress.

So he knew that it was impossible for the sunlight to be reflected in quite that way, at quite that angle, from the Sphinx nearest to him. The light, however, continued to shine in his eyes as he approached, so he was almost there when he saw what had happened.

He was running, running like a schoolboy. He raced along the pavement, shouting to the workmen packing away their tools and nodding to each other at the end of a job well done.

Well done. He swore.

The nearest of the workmen turned to him as he pounded up. Surprise gave way to recognition. 'Mr Vulliamy, sir. A damed good job, I must say.'

'Must you?' he spat between gut-wrenching rasps.

'Indeed. Very elegant. Works of art and no mistake.'

'No mistake?' Vulliamy grabbed the man's lapels, shaking

him so hard that he dropped the canvas bag he was holding. A hammer and several chisels clattered across the paving slabs. 'No mistake? Look at them. Look!'

Vulliamy spun the man round. The other workmen mirrored their fellow as they swung round to look at the Sphinxes guarding the obelisk.

'Look what you've done.' He knew from the finality of his own words that it was too late to change it. He let go of the man's jacket, and sat down heavily on the ground shaking his head in disbelief. After so much, after so many minor miracles, after it had seemed that his design was somehow *meant*, to find this crass error.

The workmen continued to stare at the Sphinxes, apparently unable to see the problem. The beasts themselves continued to stare inwards at Cleopatra's Needle, oblivious to the consternation and confusion around them.

Vulliamy breathed deeply, his chest still aching from running. He pulled himself back to his feet, forcing himself to stay measured and relatively calm. 'How could you make such a mistake? Quite apart from the aesthetics, didn't you remember that the Sphinxes you tore down only yesterday were facing *outwards?*'

The man Vulliamy had grabbed shook his head, his mouth working soundlessly.

'How could you do it?' Vulliamy's voice cracked, close to tears as he turned away.

'I don't know, sir. I really don't. An impulse, perhaps. Somehow it just seemed right at the time.'

Chapter
Sixteen

The Doctor picked his way through the carnage. The mummies lay across each other, crumpled and limp, their power suddenly gone. Discoloured areas of dust marked the positions where Rassul, the relics, and Nephthys's arm had disintegrated. The time tunnel was strobing a reassuring green, the light diminishing as they watched.

The Doctor reached round the back of the sarcophagus for a moment, then straightened up, dusted the palms of his hands against each other, and beamed across at Tegan and the others.

'There, that should do it. Don't want the thermal balance to equalise just yet, do we? There'll be quite a fire in this enclosed space, and I'd rather it was a few hours from now. The house should be safe, but it will destroy the incriminating evidence down here.' He looked at the fallen mummies and the stained stonework. 'The sands of time wash us all clean,' he said quietly. Then he brightened. 'Still, all's well that ends well, eh?' And with that he strode back across the room and slapped Tegan on the shoulder.

She pulled away. 'Is that it?' she asked. Her voice was vibrant with suppressed emotion.

The Doctor seemed not to notice. 'Yes, I think so. A pretty good result considering. All over—'

'Doctor!' Tegan screamed at him, her whole body tense with anger.

'—bar the shouting.' The Doctor frowned, his eyebrows

knitting together as he leant towards her. 'Yes?' he asked irritably.

Tegan turned away, arms folded.

'What is it?' The Doctor asked the group collectively. 'What's wrong with her now?'

'I think she might be worried about Nyssa,' Atkins suggested quietly.

'Nyssa? Oh yes, I nearly forgot.' The Doctor fumbled in his pocket and drew out the TARDIS key. 'Well, let's go and wake her up then.'

The old woman who had woken in the sarcophagus followed the Doctor to the TARDIS. It was only after he had unlocked the door and ushered her in ahead of him that he seemed to realise that nobody else was following. They were standing open-mouthed, watching him from the other side of the dais.

'Well, are you coming or not?' he demanded.

Tegan and Atkins looked at each other in silence.

'May I be permitted to ask what's going on?' Atkins had followed Tegan into Nyssa's room only to be confronted with yet another puzzle.

The old woman he had been told was Nyssa was sitting in a chair beside the bed. She patted the hand of the young woman who lay on the bed. A young woman who might have been her granddaughter, except that even across the years between them the resemblance between the two was uncanny.

A small piece of machinery that looked like it was cobbled together out of wires, small boxes and ceiling wax sat humming quietly to itself on the floor beside the bed. The Doctor was just disconnecting it from the young woman on the bed as they entered. As he switched off the machine, the hum died away. And the young woman yawned and stretched.

318

'That's the delta wave augmentor, isn't it Doctor?' Tegan asked.

He nodded, without taking his attention from the sleeping woman. 'Yes. Though I had to rig up another delta source to replace the sonic screwdriver, of course.'

Atkins coughed politely. 'Doctor, I take it that this young woman is your friend Nyssa. But perhaps you could introduce us all?'

The Doctor stepped back from the bed, apparently satisfied with Nyssa's progress. 'Of course,' he said. He turned to the old woman. 'Do forgive me, but things have been a little hectic for formal introductions.'

'Not at all, Doctor. I quite understand.' She let go of Nyssa's hand and stood up. 'Tegan, of course, I know already. But your other friend?'

'Mr Atkins.'

Atkins inclined his head slightly. 'Delighted, er...'

Tegan was frowning. 'Do I know you?'

'Of course, my dear. And you haven't changed a bit.' The woman smiled, and the way her face suddenly brightened made her look younger. 'Though I must confess, I have.'

Tegan shook her head slowly. Then her mouth dropped open. 'Ann?'

The woman nodded. 'I'm Lady Cranleigh now. Have been for a very long time. The Doctor came to the wedding, you know.' She smiled at him, and he beamed back.

'When?' Tegan asked.

'In 1926,' Lady Cranleigh said.

'About three hours ago,' said the Doctor.

Atkins coughed politely.

'Ah, yes. An explanation.' The Doctor shuffled his feet uncomfortably. 'Well, this is Lady Cranleigh, née Ann Talbot, an old friend.' He paused, apparently embarrassed by his choice of words. 'Forgive me,' he said to Lady Cranleigh.

'Of course. But you're right.'

The Doctor continued. 'Ann was the image of Nyssa when we first met. Even I couldn't tell them apart. So I asked Lady Cranleigh if she would do me a small favour and stand in for Nyssa.'

'So she was in fact merely feigning sleep?' Atkins asked.

Lady Cranleigh laughed. 'I had to lie very still and wait for a password from the Doctor. All terribly exciting.'

'Yes, I do apologise for the melodramatics. And for not telling you all what was going on. Especially you, Tegan. But I had to make sure that Nephthys was convinced that this was Nyssa, and that she had been semi-awake, just enough to age, for seventy years. Rassul would never have believed I could do it if your reactions weren't genuine.'

Tegan said, 'So when Nephthys looked in Ann's head for the other half of her own mind...'

'It wasn't there, of course.'

'And she thought it had sort of evaporated in 1926 and went back to look for it?' Atkins asked.

'Exactly.' The Doctor punctuated the word with a stab of his index finger.

'And when she found Nyssa was still asleep, she sort of bounced back?'

The Doctor nodded. 'She was able to tell when Nyssa would wake, so she came forward to that point. But because she could only act on instinct and impulse...' He left the thought unfinished for them.

'She kept going back and forth in time till she aged to death.' Tegan laughed. 'Simple.'

'Sometimes, Tegan,' the Doctor said, 'you take my breath away.'

'And what, Doctor, happens now?' asked Atkins.

The Doctor picked up a canopic jar from the floor under Nyssa's bed.

'Well, if you'll excuse me just a moment, I think Nyssa is about ready to wake up. And there's something in her mind I would like to remove.' The top was shaped into the head of a jackal, and he gave it a sharp twist to unscrew it. 'Osiran technology, complete with generator loop.'

'With what?'

'A sort of force field,' he explained. 'I picked it up at the British Museum on the way to collect Lady Cranleigh. Wouldn't have worked for Rassul and his friends, though. But now that I've built in a few modifications and refinements it should be up to the task.'

'Rassul? I thought he was the bad guy.'

'Oh, indeed.' The Doctor held the jar up and inspected it as if he had never seen it before. 'But initially he was the "guy", as you say, that Horus left to guard the tomb. When Nephthys's energy leaked out, she used his suppressed guilt at sacrificing his daughter to turn him against Horus and into her servant. Quite handy from her point of view, since Horus was already expending the energy to keep him alive.'

The Doctor held the open jar close in front of Nyssa's face. A wire from the cat's cradle contraption he had been fiddling with earlier was connected to the base of the canopic jar. Suddenly, the Doctor snapped his fingers. The noise was like a pistol shot, and Nyssa's eyes snapped open.

For a moment they burned with a brightness and intelligence which almost radiated with intensity. Then they dulled slightly, and she blinked. The Doctor jammed the stopper on the jar, and twisted it shut. Then he pulled away the wire and gave a loud exhalation of relief.

'Doctor?' Nyssa lifted her head slightly from the pillows. She looked up at all the people crowding round her bed.

'What's happening?' Her eyes flickered, and she yawned. 'I've had the strangest dream,' she said.

The Doctor smiled. 'Don't worry about it, Nyssa. Everything's fine now.'

Nyssa seemed to have drifted back into sleep, and the Doctor waved everyone from the room. 'I know it seems odd,' he said as he led them back to the console room, 'but she'll be quite tired, I think. She might sleep for a little while.'

Tegan looked sharply at him.

'I mean, maybe an hour or two.'

It seemed as if, despite his frequent protestations, the TARDIS was becoming a taxi service. The Doctor had taken Lady Cranleigh back to Oxfordshire. Atkins had bid a sincere farewell, actually with tears in his eyes, before leaving them outside the back entrance to Kenilworth House a century earlier.

Nyssa was feeling rather weak and drained, so Tegan explained what had been going on. Nyssa seemed to be taking the news with characteristic composure.

The Doctor welcomed the few moments he had to himself. He looked back at the TARDIS, shimmering in the intense dry heat, then continued on his way. He half ran, half slid down the sand, remembering his similar descent with Atkins earlier.

The empty shell of the pyramid afforded some relief from the efforts of the sun, but the air was still close and hot. When he reached the area that had been the main burial chamber, he calculated the position of the point on the floor he was looking for. He couldn't be sure, of course, but the Osirans put a lot of store in geometric patterns and exact points in space. Horus must, he reflected as he started to dig into the sandy remains of the floor with his hands, have chosen this place for a reason.

When the hole was big enough, the Doctor carefully placed the canopic jar inside. Then he covered it over with the sand he had scooped out. He stood, bowed slightly, and made the Sign of the Eye.

As he left the main door of the pyramid, it swung slowly shut behind him. When the Doctor reached the TARDIS, he turned and looked back into the crater in the sand. He nodded in quiet satisfaction, and opened the TARDIS door.

The TARDIS shimmered in the heat of the day, and faded from existence. A moment later, a trickle of sand started running down the crater sides. Perhaps the Doctor had dislodged it, perhaps the TARDIS had shaken the ground slightly as it left, perhaps there was a sudden inexplicable breeze skitting across the desert. But whatever the cause, the trickle grew into a river of sand flowing down into the crater. Before long it was an avalanche, filling the bottom of the hollow. By the time Orion rose in the night sky, all signs of the black pyramid of Nephthys were buried deep beneath the shifting desert sands.

'Did you find him all right?'

It took Atkins a few moments to realise what Lord Kenilworth was asking him. It was a long while since he had departed to deliver an invitation to the Doctor outside the British Museum. He smiled. 'Indeed, sir. And I must say I'm very glad I did.'

Kenilworth grunted. 'Didn't take you long; didn't think you'd be back till after I'd turned in.'

Atkins smiled and watched his employer start up the stairs. Then he continued on his way to the kitchens. He felt a nervous excitement above and beyond anything he had experienced during his time with the Doctor and Tegan, and his throat felt as dry as if he were still in the desert.

Miss Warne was standing by the stove. She was stirring a saucepan of soup.

Atkins watched her from the doorway for a while. Her mind was obviously not on the task in hand. She was staring off into space and humming quietly. Atkins shook his head – such a lack of proper decorum and deplorable laxity of attitude.

'Miss Warne,' he called across the room.

She flinched, and turned. She had stopped humming at once, and her stance was somehow more upright and proper. But in her eyes he saw a flicker of emotion, a moment of suppressed happiness.

'I didn't realise before,' Atkins said as he crossed the room, 'just how long you must have been prepared to stand here and stir soup on the off-chance that I should remember your kind offer and avail myself of it.'

'I don't mind waiting up.' If she was surprised at his comment, she hid it well. Her head was tilted slightly to one side so that the dark hair fell away slightly. Atkins could see the edge of her ear beneath. He did not remember ever having seen her ear before, and he was struck by how round and perfect it looked. Pale skin beneath dark hair.

'If I didn't know better,' Atkins said, leaning over her shoulder to inspect the soup, 'I might think that you enjoyed waiting for me.'

'If you didn't know better.'

Without changing position, Atkins looked up from the saucepan. His face was close to hers, and he could see that her pale skin was now slightly more pink than a few moments previously. He looked deep into her large, dark eyes.

Miss Warne turned away.

'Forgive me,' Atkins said, 'but may I address you as Susan for a moment?'

She looked back at him, puzzled. 'Mr Atkins, why?'

He smiled. 'It makes a proposal to have dinner together seem so much less formal, that's all.'

Kenilworth was not sure quite what the change in Atkins was. But certainly he had changed. He seemed more like he had been on the recent expedition than the sudden reversion to type after they had returned. But there was more to it than that.

Kenilworth waited for Atkins to show in his dinner guest, and reflected again on the events of the past few months, trying to put his finger on what was going on. His wife had mentioned that the housekeeper too seemed strangely distracted.

Atkins held the door open and stood to one side to let the guest enter. He was a tall, lean young man, with a hooked nose and dark hair that was already starting to recede. Kenilworth rose to greet the newest member of the Royal Society.

'Professor Marcus Scarman,' Atkins announced.